THE DESPERADOES OF GALLOWS GULCH

SILVER VEIN CHRONICLES
BOOK 3

CLAY HOUSTON SHIVERS

For Mom and Bill and all of the Sharvernaudskis.

A FEW WORDS ON THE ACCOUNT
THAT FOLLOWS

As I sit here and write these words, with my bony skeletal wrinkly old hands, Sally and I are cozy in our cabin as a blue norther blows through. Not through the cabin, mind you, but outside. A lot has changed in the world since I was born, especially here in West Texas, but one thing that hasn't changed is the weather—which is as ornery and unpredictable as ever. I can hear the wind attacking the windows and door jambs, trying to break inside and freeze us to death.

Without tooting my own horn too much, I feel I need to set the stage for how things were when this story opens. At this point in my career as a lawman, I was one of a handful of names people associated with the frontier. Dozens of delusional and false tall tales had been written about me. And these books had traveled (unlike me) all over the world. There are a little more than a handful of men from the frontier who are household names. But there are three that stand above all the rest, and do to this very day: Kit Carson, Wild Bill Hickok, and myself, Curly Barnes. The frenzy of dime novels created a false world for people who lived in cities back East. They would get notions in their heads about the frontier, and then, based upon fiction and false advertisements by greedy merchants and governments, pack up all their worldly possessions and make their way west, all to live in a place that didn't really exist. Instead of a land of bounty and rich soil, the majority of the people who made their way west found heartache and violence. Some of those who made their way west would find themselves in Silver Vein, and, more often than not, almost immediately, regret it.

Wild Bill Hickok was a good friend of mine, but as you will see, he was a much more complicated person than his myth would have you believe. Some people will balk at seeing Bill in anything other than a hero's light. In which case, I can recommend dozens of dime novels that do just that.

This here is the unvarnished truth, or my name isn't Curly Barnes.

—Curly Barnes
Winter, 1927
Amarillo, Texas

PROLOGUE

1

I was on my way to the Milton jail to save a young man's life. He'd been accused of having his way with the daughter of Sam Milton, the man who'd discovered the coal deposits under the ground, and the man who'd named the town after himself. But I had a sworn testimonial from Boffroy Hackett, who declared that the young man in question, Taylor Stephens, couldn't have done what he was accused of, because on the night in question he'd been staying with his uncle in Amarillo, and Boffroy said he and the boy's uncle took him to dinner and that he'd never been out of their sight.

Taylor was due to hang. Old Sam Milton ran the town, and it was said that the law did whatever he told it to. It was my hope that the sheriff of Milton, a man named Bool Marlowe, once he saw the testimonial, would see that he had no choice but to let the boy go. To not do so would be too much even for a corrupt sheriff.

Milton didn't even exist a year ago, I thought, as I made my way along it's still-being-built Main Street. When the coal had been discovered, the town had sprung up seemingly overnight to feed the ever-hungry railroad interests. It wasn't completely true to say the town didn't exist a year ago, so much as it seemed that way to me because I'd never been to the town and had only heard of it from people who were passing through Silver Vein. The last time I'd been in these parts it was nothing but dirt.

The town was a cacophony of hammers hitting nails and fresh timber being sawed, and building facades being hoisted up into the sky. I made my way through the growing town and reined Horse up and dismounted and hitched him up outside the jail.

"Wait here," I told Horse. He would have waited anyway, but I liked to let him know my thoughts. Horse was very well-trained, and clearly loved me. I didn't really need to hitch him up, but I did it anyway because I didn't want other people to feel bad about how untrained their horses were in comparison.

I walked into the brand-new jail and saw Marlowe sitting at a brand-new desk with his boots up, snoring away in mid-nap. I didn't know the man, but I thought I'd have a go at him anyway. I took the jail door and slammed it as hard as I could.

Marlowe woke up, reared back in his chair and fell over backwards in alarm. He thrashed about, got his legs under him, pushed himself off the floor, and then saw me standing in the doorway laughing at him.

"Sorry," I said.

He looked like he was thinking about whomping me, but then he saw the badge on my waistcoat that said I was a Deputy U.S. Marshal.

"I reckon I must have—"

"Relax, sheriff," I said. "I'm sorry. I couldn't help myself. I've had the very same thing happen to me on a number of occasions."

Marlowe's shoulders lowered and he relaxed.

"On slow days, ain't much to do to kill time but take a snooze."

"That is the truth of it," I agreed.

"Especially when it's hot out," Marlowe added.

"Also true."

"Well, Marshal..." Marlowe asked, realizing at last my appearance in his town was not the norm.

"Curly Barnes," I said. This had the effect I was hoping for.

"Sheriff Curly Barnes? From Silver Vein?"

"The very one. But I'm not here on behalf of Silver Vein."

"Well, this here is an honor! I know all about you, I bet!" Marlowe opened a drawer in his desk and pulled out a book with some hideous illustration of me that some fella back East thought I might look like on the cover. The illustration was such a ridiculous likeness that I was immediately insulted.

"Don't think I've seen this one," I said, and then I tossed the stupid book back in the drawer. I was already me. I didn't need to read a bunch of made-up bull chips about myself. If anyone was going to make up a bunch of stuff about me, I was going to be the one doing it.

"I expect you might just be the most famous person to ever set foot in Milton! I would love to spot you a bourbon in the Milton Saloon if you'll allow it."

"I'll allow it, of course. But you might not want to spot me anything when you find out why I'm here." I reached into my waistcoat and came out with the Boffroy testimonial and handed it over. He read through it carefully, and then, not meeting my eyes, handed it back.

"I'm afraid it's too late," he said.

"He's been hanged?" I asked.

Marlowe shook his head. "He'll be hanged tomorrow morning. Do you know anything about this town, Marshal?"

"No," I said. "Other than it's a coal mining town. And Sam Milton runs it."

"Care to walk with me? I find it's getting awful hot in here."

The sheriff walked over and collected his hat from the hat rack and opened the door and I followed him outside.

"Sam Milton runs this town, all right," he said. "And he dotes on his daughter Katie. His wife, Ellie, died of fever some years back. It's just the two of them now. And he's a very protective father. If I were a boy, I would never even consider having anything to do with the daughter of a man the likes of Sam Milton."

"The boy might have been thinking with his nether parts. When I was becoming a man, just about all I cared about was making my nether parts happy. But the boy is innocent," I said. "You read the letter." The man who preceded me as sheriff of Silver Vein, Jim Shepland, was the most honest man I would ever meet. His presence was still very much alive in me, and I would often ask myself what old Jim would do in this or that situation. And he would have never allowed a boy to die based on what might be a false accusation. But I knew that Jim Shepland was the white buffalo of sheriffs. All too many sheriffs were perfectly willing to do whatever someone told him so long as that person was willing to pay.

Marlowe was looking down at his boots now, but then he finally nodded.

"Here, whether you're guilty or innocent depends on the decision of one man."

I was afraid of this. Marlowe wasn't loyal to justice. He was loyal to Sam Milton. Or he was afraid of him. Either way, I could see he wasn't going to be much help.

"Look sheriff, I under—"

"The only reason I'm sheriff is because Milton told me I was. There was no election or anything of that sort. Just his *choosing* me for the job. And all I have to do is whatever he tells me, and I make more money being the sheriff of this town than in any of my previous occupations. One thing you can say about Sam Milton, he will pay a fella good money."

Walking down the street, I noticed a doctor's office and a bank and a restaurant and general store. All brand-new and doing good business. Five years ago, it would have been crazy to start a town this far south. But the Comanches and Kiowas and the bandits coming up from Mexico had all been pushed back, and now it was safe for people.

The saloon was brand new and smelled like fresh lumber, but there was nothing to it but a small wooden bar in a tent with but a few bottles behind the bar. As a saloonkeeper, who knew about such things, it was hard for me to take seriously. But I needed to try and get Marlowe on my side when it came to the Stephens boy, so I couldn't let my true thoughts out on the matter.

"Nice place," I lied.

"Now, we won't be able to talk in here," Marlowe said. "Johnson, a bottle." The skinny kid behind the bar looked at me and asked, "Mister, are you Curly Barnes?"

I nodded. "And what's your name?"

"Cooper Johnson, sir." He scurried behind a tent flap and disappeared.

"Told you. Famous!" Marlowe cried, smacking me on the back.

I could only shrug. "I expect I've got a recognizable face." And this was true. My red hair and thick mustache made me stand out. And with Silver Vein not that far to the north, and with the badge on my waistcoat, it wouldn't have been all that difficult to figure out who I was.

Cooper came back with a nice bottle of bourbon I recognized and set out three glasses. Marlowe said, "There's just the two of us."

"Sheriff, I can't *not* have a drink with Curly Barnes! It wouldn't be right! This here, Curly, is reserved for special occasions. And I'd say that's you!"

"Aw, it's okay, Sheriff," I said. I could tell he was a little put off by the bartender. "This *is* a quality bourbon," I said. "If you're ever in Silver Vein I'll return the favor."

Cooper smiled and poured out three toots of bourbon and the three of us slurped them down.

"A toot with Curly Barnes. My word," Marlowe said, shaking his head. Then he took the bottle and the two of us walked outside and sat down at a small wooden table.

"I'm in a pickle," Marlowe said. "If I do the right thing, for all I know Milton might just up and arrest me and lock me up in my own jail."

"If you show him the letter—"

"It won't matter. He's blind with rage over this thing. Katie is pregnant, you see. And the boy, Taylor, the more he insists on his innocence, the angrier Milton gets. Why do you think he's set to hang? It ain't like he shot some fella in cold blood. It's because he had the dumb gumption to go and get sweet on the only daughter of Sam Milton."

"Sheriff, I understand your situation. But I can't let you do Milton's bidding. Not in this case. I know the truth. And the magistrate in Amarillo, Judge Baines Murphy, knows the truth, as does the editor of the *Amarillo Times*. Hanging that boy would be an outrage."

Marlowe poured himself a stiff measure of bourbon and took a slug.

I felt sorry for Marlowe, but I wasn't about to ride out of town knowing that boy was set to hang for something he didn't do.

"I don't know what to tell you, Marshal. There's nothing I can do. Whatever the truth is, Sam Milton is set on this. The way he sees it, Katie's reputation, as well as his, is at stake."

"There's one thing you can do," I said.

"And what's that?" he said, giving me a sincere look.

"Take me to see Sam Milton."

———

Sam Milton's house sat on a rise, perching over the east end of town. The biggest building in town, it had an iron arch with the initials SM on it, and there was a long wagon road that led up to the sprawling two-story mansion. It was the house of someone who wanted to show off. It was a house big enough for fifty.

"Nice place," I said.

"They say he's worth a hundred thousand dollars, maybe more," Marlowe said. We were sitting on our horses under the arch, not moving. "I reckon that house is his way of reminding everyone that the town belongs to him. Yep. I bet that's the way of it. Of course—"

"We're not moving, you know," I said. We *had* been moving, but then, under the arch, Marlowe just up and stopped his horse. But he was acting like we were still moving. It was almost as if he was thinking he could just *pretend* to be walking on his horse. We'd been not moving for so long it had started to feel awkward.

"I have to get ready. Sam Milton isn't the easiest man to get along with. I'm sure to catch some abuse. He's so angry about this thing, raging and cursing is just about all he's doing."

"I'll let him know this was all my doing," I said. "If you want, I can pull out my gun and point it at you and I'll tell him I forced you to take me to him. Would that help?"

Marlowe gave a look. "No, I don't think that will be necessary."

And so, Marlowe finally kicked his horse into a trot, and I did too. Horse wasn't normally one to go in for trotting. He preferred a walk or a lope, the same as me. Trotting, as everyone knows, is rough on the nether parts. Before we'd gotten half-way up the wagon trail to the house, a man with a scattergun walked out of the house and started walking towards us.

"That's far enough!" the man yelled, bringing the scattergun to his shoulder. "What's your business!"

"It's me, Sheriff Marlowe."

"Sheriff Marlowe?"

"Yes, the sheriff of Milton!"

"Oh! Well, what are you doing here? Sam ain't exactly in the mood for guests. Excepting the judge, of course. If I go in there and tell him he has guests, I'm like to catch a heap of abuse."

"I'm sorry," Marlowe said. "But this is important. I need to see him."

"Well now, who is that you got with you?" the man asked.

"Deputy U.S. Marshal Curly Barnes!" Marlowe yelled.

The man dropped the scattergun to his side, so it faced the ground and said, "Well then, you go on around to the back and hitch them horses up. I'll go and let him know you're here." And then the man turned around and walked up and back to the house. He got to the back door, took a deep breath, paused, looked back at us, and then shrugged and disappeared inside.

"That's Mulvaney," Marlowe said. "He's the leader of what you could call Milton's own private army."

"What does Milton need a private army for?" I asked.

"Power, I reckon," Marlowe said, spitting off the side of his horse. "He likes to scare people. You'll see."

"I know the type," I said.

We rode our horses around to the back of the house and hitched them up and dismounted—and there was Mulvaney waiting for us.

"He's in the library," Mulvaney said. "He's got Judge Dempsey in there with him. That judge seems to be the only person Sam can stand to be around. He don't ever ask me to play cards with him anymore. Of course, as grumpy as he is these days, I reckon that's a good thing. I expect you can find your way?"

"I know where it is," Marlowe said.

"Good. I'm going to just go and hide somewhere for a couple of hours," Mulvaney said.

We were walking up the back steps to go into the house when I heard a noise above me and looked up just in time to see a woman's head disappear from a window. I looked at Marlowe and he shook his head in warning, and we walked inside. If the outside was finished, I could see that the inside was a work-in-progress. Technically we were in the kitchen, but there was no kitchen table, or even any chairs. Just a stove that didn't look to get much use. It was, in my opinion, for a house of its size, a complete and utter waste of a kitchen.

"He moved in about six months ago," Marlowe said.

"No excuse for not having a kitchen table," I said.

"I don't think he even thinks about it."

We walked through the empty kitchen and then through an office, passing by a dining room with no dining table, and then on towards the front of the house. It seemed like he only had the furniture for a much smaller house, and the stuff was spread so thin in this uselessly large house that it seemed every room I saw was under-furnished. But, if it was as Marlowe said, and the house was a way to remind the town who it worked for, maybe he'd only been focused on the size of the house and not what all furniture he would need to put inside it.

"He should have let us go through the front door," I said. "Less walking." I was not much for walking, and never had been, and walking through one empty room after another was worse than walking through a room with furniture.

"This house annoys the shit out of me," I announced.

Marlowe didn't say anything to that.

We walked into a large front room with a fire in the fireplace in the middle of the summer and two men were looking at each other in silence, sitting in big leather chairs facing each other across a small table. Both men were smoking cigars. One of the two men, the one who wasn't enormously fat, stood up and walked over, with his hand leading the way.

"Sam Milton! Welcome to the growing town of Milton! You must be Curly Barnes!"

I offered my hand and said, "That's me." He didn't look me in the eye, but rather down the hall.

"Where's Mulvaney?" he asked.

I looked at Marlowe. He shrugged. So, I said, "He's hiding from you. Said it would be a couple of hours before you would be able to find him."

"That disloyal scamp! He's fired! And I'll tell him that as soon as I find him!" he yelled into the big empty house.

"I'd offer you a chair, but we only have the two, and we're using them."

I looked around the library. It was a big circle of a room with plenty of space for more chairs.

"I'm guessing the chairs are on order," I said.

"What?"

"Nothing. I'm not here to sit down anyway. I had to sit on a horse to get here, after all."

"Great! Hadn't thought of it that way! Are you here for the hanging? It's the first real entertainment this young town has had. I was just talking to Judge Dempsey here about how the town needed some sort of yearly event or attraction to draw people to the town. I believe Silver Vein has a Meteor Hole, does it not?"

I nodded. I didn't want to get to talking about the Meteor Hole. In truth, it was just a hole in the ground left over when an old paranoid coot named Dixter Pip accidentally set off one of his own booby traps and blew himself to pieces. But old Ely Turner, who is as sly as he is beneath contempt, marketed it as a hole made by a meteor, and it drew the curious and the gullible to Silver Vein from as far away as Europe and even South America. Even now, all these years later, when I think about old Ely Turner, I want to air out my insides. But he was certainly crafty when it came to making money.

"Not here to talk about the Silver Vein Meteor Hole. And I'm not here for any hanging. But I *am* here to talk about Taylor Stephens," I said.

Sam Milton's face hardened, and I got the sense I was about to take some abuse.

"What about him?" he asked. "What's this all about, Marlowe?"

I reached into my waistcoat and pulled out the testimonial. "This is from the magistrate in Amarillo. I have been given orders to escort Taylor to the Amarillo jail where he is to be detained until he stands trial."

"He's done stood trial!" the fat judge, Dempsey, said. "Guilty verdict! He hangs tomorrow!"

"I'm afraid new evidence has come to light," I said. I didn't like the judge. He had angry black eyes, and corruption oozed out of him like a farting horse.

Milton read through the testimonial from Boffroy Hackett, and then said, "This doesn't mean anything. I don't even know who this fella even is!"

"The magistrate in Amarillo finds him honest," I said.

"So?"

"So, it means Taylor was out of town at the time he has been accused of being with your daughter," I said.

"You keep her out of this!"

"I don't—"

"You come into my town, and then come into my house, demanding something impossible, and then you insult me by bringing up my daughter? Why, I'd be within my rights to shoot you dead, and you know it!"

"That would be murder, and then you would be the one in jail. I don't want to insult anybody. But this is an alleged crime against your daughter, and so she's involved whether you want her to be or not. I didn't have to come up here. I could have demanded Marlowe give Taylor over to me without your consent, or that fat judge there's consent—sorry, but it's true, you are a remarkably fat individual—and then I could have been on my way, and, believe me, I would have been happy to have skipped walking through all your empty rooms with not enough furniture in them. I don't know if it's by choice or not, but I believe you need a *lot* more furniture for a house of this size. I only came up here because I wanted to do the right thing."

"Well," Milton said, tearing the testimonial into tiny pieces and dropping the pieces of paper into the fireplace, "you've done the polite thing—"

"The hell he has!" Judge Dempsey cried, and then tried and failed to come to his feet. "Dang. I reckon I'm stuck."

"I don't pay you to get stuck in chairs, Dempsey! And you! You can go on and get on out of here! And you, Marlowe, your wages for the month are going to be docked for bringing this useless—"

"Finish that sentence and you'll get whomped," I said.

"Both of you get out of here! That boy isn't going anywhere! He's gonna hang tomorrow and that's that!"

"You do it your way, it will be murder," I said.

"He raped my daughter! She's upstairs pregnant with that bastard's baby! No man of substance will ever want anything to do with her! Her life is a ruin!"

That was probably true, but I was doing all I could not to whomp the man senseless and wasn't in any mood to feel sorry for him.

"Thanks for your time," I said. Then I turned to the judge stuck in his chair. "Fatso," I said, and I put my hat back on and headed out of the house.

"Tell that judge in Amarillo what I said!" Milton yelled to my back.

"And Marlowe, get that dumb look off your face and you get on out of here too! And don't ever bring anyone to my house ever again without my permission! I made you Marlowe! Don't you forget I can also break you!"

"What was I to do? He's a Federal Marshal." Marlowe was fooling himself if he thought Milton was in any state to listen to reason.

"Out here he's nothing! Nothing! I run this town!"

I walked out the back door, looked up, and saw Katie Milton in the window. This time she didn't disappear.

This time she waved.

2

"You were right, Baxter," I said. We'd made camp outside of Milton, off the trail in a stand of cottonwood trees, on a rise that offered a view of the town. If anyone were heading our way, we would see them. I'd left my deputies Baxter and Merle in camp when I'd gone into Milton so that I wouldn't come across as threatening—since I had decided to start with the reasonable approach. Now the reasonable approach was done with. Sam Milton chose a different path. Boy, was he an asshole.

"Told you," Baxter said, with a big grin on his face, casually lying on his bedroll and flipping a deadly knife up in the air and catching it without looking.

"Does that mean we can blow the town up?" Merle asked.

"No, it does *not* mean that. But what it *does* mean is that we're going to have to go with Plan B. We tried the reasonable way. And now we're just going to have to up and break that boy out of jail."

"Oh good!" Merle said.

The town of Milton was pretty much empty at night, since all the buildings were still being built, and weren't ready for occupation. Even the saloon, what little there was of one, was closed. The only people living in the town were still living in tents out by where the coal mines were.

There was a light coming from inside the jail though.

"Shame about Marlowe," I said. "But there's nothing for it." We rode our horses around behind the jail. There was a window back there with bars on it.

"Baxter, see who's in there."

Baxter hopped off his incredibly old horse, Colonel, and handed the reins to Merle and looked in the jail window.

"You Taylor?" He whispered.

Then he walked over and nodded at me. "He's in there, all right. Should we pull the window out?"

I thought about it. And I thought about Marlowe. He seemed like a good enough fella. He was going to be in enough trouble with Milton once we'd made off with Taylor. I figured we should at least make things as easy on him as possible.

"I got a better idea," I said. "But go ahead and put the ropes on in case my idea doesn't pan out. Merle, follow me." I dismounted, and Merle dismounted. We'd brought a spare mount, and so we hitched up all the horses to one of the bars on the jail window.

We walked around to the front of the jail. I tried the knob, but it was locked.

"Hope this works," I said, and knocked on the door.

"Hey!" Marlowe cried, "who is it?"

"Curly Barnes," I said. "Open up."

He opened the door and said, "What—" and I whomped him on the head. He fell into Merle's arms, and we went inside and closed the door behind us.

"Truss him up to his chair," I said. Being a sheriff, I knew my way when it came to jails. So, I opened the drawer of his desk, and, sure enough, there were some jail cell keys and some hand irons. I took the hand irons, not because I was going to use them, but because a sheriff can always do with an extra set, and I took the keys.

There were four keys on there, and they all looked the same. I found the key I was looking for on the third try and used it to open the door to the cells.

There were three cells.

Only one had a person in it.

Taylor Stephens.

He was short and skinny. He had a terrible brown beard of fuzz, and his hair was a mess and he smelled to the moon and back. Not at all what I was expecting. For a girl the likes of Katie Milton to be sweet on, I was expecting someone a girl would actually want to look at. Not this pitiful creature.

"How long since you've bathed?" I asked.

"Bathed?" Taylor asked. "Not since they locked me up in here, and that was, that was, a long danged time ago. They— what's going on here?"

"I'm taking you to Amarillo," I said. "It's either that or you get your neck stretched in the morning."

"I'll come with you," Taylor said, getting up off the jail cell floor. He wasn't dumb. Not totally dumb anyway.

"Good choice. Don't say a word unless I ask you something, don't make any noise, and do whatever my deputies ask. You don't you'll get whomped."

Taylor nodded.

"You can talk now if you want. I meant once we got outside for the silence to start."

"No. I'm pretty good at being quiet. Have to be, stuck in a cell by myself all the time."

I nodded. I put the key in the lock and opened the cell door.

"Hey!" Marlowe cried from the other room.

I nodded at Merle, and he went and gave Marlowe another

whomp. It was a good one. I didn't think Marlowe would wake up any time soon. Hopefully, his brain wouldn't turn to mush, something I'd once seen happen to a killer named London Tom, who had turned into a drooling vegetable after a good whomp. One day he was a killer, the next day he just stared at nothing all day, drooling up a storm.

I opened the cell and Taylor walked out and we walked back into the office, and I shut the door to the cells and broke the key off in the lock.

Marlowe's head was on his chest. I walked over to make sure he was still breathing. "You got him a good one," I said.

"I didn't want him to wake back up."

"I always like to whomp the back of the head," I said. "You didn't have to whomp him right above the eye."

"He didn't know who I was. He was about to shout."

'Dang," I said. "I hadn't thought of that." Baxter and Merle are intimidating if you didn't know them the way I did. They were both tall and eager for a scrap, which is why they had so many scars, which only made them scarier to look at.

"He was nice to me, the sheriff." Taylor said. "He was the only one that wasn't an arsehole."

"When we open the door, go around to the back of the jail. Boffroy Hackett loaned us his horse. He said you would recognize it."

Taylor nodded.

"My other deputy, Baxter, is back there waiting for you. You ready?"

Taylor nodded. He was taking this silence thing very seriously.

I opened the door and looked around and all was still dark and quiet.

"Let's go," I said. Taylor was a little too eager, because he kept bonking into me as we walked around the corner.

"Sorry," he said.

We got to the back of the jail and Taylor walked right up to Boffroy's horse and hopped on. I got on Horse and the four of us took the short way out of town at a lope.

———

"Okay, you can talk," I said.

"What about them other two?" Taylor asked. "Ain't they with us?"

"They've got an errand to run," I said. "We'll meet up with them soon."

"Why are you helping me?" Taylor asked. "Did my uncle send you?"

"Boffroy Hackett swore in front Judge Murphy that you were in Amarillo on the night you have been accused of being in Milton."

"That was Katie's doing, I expect," Taylor said.

I didn't know what he meant by that, and I didn't even think to ask. I was too intent on getting us safely away from Milton. I didn't know how long Marlowe would be out, and I expected someone to raise the alarm at any moment. If a fella knew what they were doing when it came to cutting sign, our tracks would be easy to follow, especially if they had torches.

"Milton ain't going to let this go," Taylor said.

"I know it," I said.

"He would come to the jail sometimes and sit in a chair outside my cell and tell me how I was going to die, and what would happen to my body when the rope…"

"He's not the nicest person I've ever met," I said. "And he has a dumb house."

"I don't know how someone as sweet as Katie could have a father like that."

"If she's so sweet," I said, "how come she accused you of rape?"

"I could see how you could think that," Taylor said. "But she didn't accuse me of rape."

I kicked Horse into a faster lope, and we made our way back to our camp outside of town where I was supposed to meet back up with Baxter and Merle. I found the stand of cottonwoods and dismounted, and we hid our horses among them. It wasn't much cover, but I hoped it would be enough.

"Whatever posse comes after me, you should know they're likely to shoot first. Milton won't think nothing of killing you and your deputies. And don't think he'll pay any attention to that badge. He's surrounded himself with killers that do his bidding."

I nodded. "Figured as much," I said.

"Whoo! But I'd sure love to see the look on that man's face when he sees that cell empty!"

"You're not out of the woods yet, Taylor. You still have to stand trial."

"I ain't worried at all about that."

I looked at him and he seemed totally sincere.

"We've got some time, if you want to tell me why that is," I said, looking down at the still-sleeping town of Milton.

"I didn't rape anybody, especially not Katie," Taylor said. "Milton made it all up. He hated me the minute Katie told him we were sweet on each other."

I didn't want to jump ahead in his story, but I think I was starting to figure some stuff out. My first thought when I first saw Taylor was how below average he looked. He just didn't look like the kind of person the likes of Katie Milton would spend any time with at all. But hearing him talk, I could totally understand a protective psychotic father lashing out at a short fuzzy-bearded skinny boy his only daughter had fallen in love with.

"How did he find out?" I asked.

"Katie told him. She was happy. You have to understand

that Katie begged me to do what we did. I know I ain't much to look at. Known it my whole life. But Katie was always nice to me, always would smile at me. She would look out her window and I'd see her up there and she would smile and wave."

"You worked on the Milton property?" I asked. "Or did you hide in the brush and peep up there all the time?"

"I was in charge of the horses," Taylor said. "I would come up to the house and clean out the stalls every couple of days."

"Oh boy," I said. I could see where this was going. "Tell me about Katie."

"One day she opened the window and said hello, and we got to talking, and then that guy with the shotgun would show up, either he'd walk out the back door or come around the side of the house. He wouldn't let her out of the house if Sam didn't want her to. She didn't have any friends. The truth is she was so sheltered and lonely she didn't know she shouldn't be interested in someone like me. It was a long time before we even did anything. We would mostly just talk about life. She even talked about wanting to start a family with me. And she would ask me about the town and the people in it and she told me she wasn't allowed out of her room, and that everywhere she went she was followed by someone wearing guns. Well, everywhere but the horse stalls."

"She accused you of rape," I said, mostly to remind myself of the facts.

"She accused me of rape on the one day she knew I could prove I was out of town. Her daddy made her accuse me of rape once he found out she was pregnant. But she was smart, don't you see? If she'd said it was some other day, any other day just about, you wouldn't have come to save me."

I thought it over and could see that it made sense. Of course, Katie was pregnant. There was no getting around that. But if she'd purposely accused him of rape on a day she knew he had an alibi, it would go a long way of convincing a judge that wasn't as corrupt as Dempsey.

I'd gotten the whole thing wrong, of course. Katie hadn't accused him out of spite or regret. She'd only done it because she was forced to. I could tell just by the way Taylor was talking that he was still in love with her.

"She waved at me," I said. "Looked at me out that same window." I thought back to earlier today, at Milton's stupid house—and seeing her face in the window was altogether different now. She was now a prisoner, in a big house run by a tyrant. I'd seen the guy with the shotgun. Mulvaney. And who knew what the hell the judge, Dempsey, was talking about when me and Marlowe had showed up? What had they been plotting?

"What do you know about Judge Dempsey?" I asked.

"He does whatever Milton tells him to. He's on the payroll just like everyone else. I never had a chance in his court. The jury was made up of all the gunfighters and killers on Milton's payroll. My lawyer was also on the Milton payroll."

"Dang," I said.

"The whole town is on his payroll."

"Everybody?"

"Not directly. But the name of the town is Milton. If it weren't for Sam Milton, there wouldn't even *be* a town."

"Good point," I said. "Here they come."

Baxter and Merle pulled up and got off their horses.

"All set," Baxter said.

"Now comes the hard part," Merle said. "Waiting."

"It could be nobody will come after us," I said. But I didn't believe it.

"Shouldn't we keep going?" Taylor asked.

"Yes," I said. "As soon as any lights come on," I said. "No use blowing the horses or risking a broken leg unless we have to."

"You sound like Frank Kilhoe," Baxter said. "He's always talking about horses breaking legs."

"That's true. I reckon all his talking about horses breaking legs must have gone into my brain from him saying it all the time. It's good advice though. Horses aren't much good on three legs," I said.

The lights in Sam Milton's house came on.

———

"Won't be long now," Merle said.

"If they get to that tree just outside town yonder, we'll know." The tree looked to be about two hundred yards from the north side of town.

"They'll wait for sunup," I said. "Won't be long."

We watched as the dawn began, and, sure enough, it wasn't much long after that we saw what looked to be ten men race out from under the arch of the Milton house road and straight on through town.

Just as the first rider made it past the tree, there was a huge explosion, and the tree fell across the trail blocking the way.

"Dang," I said. Baxter had come a long way when it came to blowing things up.

"That was amazing," Merle breathed, in awe.

"Down to three," Baxter said, pulling his Winchester out of the scabbard on his horse.

Merle and I also took out our Winchesters.

"What are we shooting at?" I asked.

"The base of that tree up in front of them three," Baxter said, shooting. I aimed and shot, and Merle aimed and shot, and the three of us kept on shooting—and then one of us got lucky and the tree exploded and crashed and fell across the trail. Only one of the three riders made it past the second tree. I took a quick glance through my glass and saw that it was Sam

Milton himself. He looked behind him and his horse slowed and then stopped altogether. He looked our way, but I couldn't tell whether he saw us or not.

The two horses that had made it past the first tree but not the second, now turned their horses back towards town and headed back the way they'd come. They were stuck on the trail between two trees—and I could tell the fight had gone out of them.

I looked over and saw Baxter aim his rifle at Milton.

"Don't—"

Baxter fired and I heard a horse scream.

"Missed," Baxter said.

"Dang," Merle said.

Sam Milton was stuck under his horse, which was struggling to stand up. The horse struggled back to its feet leaving Sam Milton in the dust holding his leg. He got up and limped back down the trail, yelling a ton of colorful curses at his hired guns.

"And now, zero," I said. "That's the problem with paid killers. They're not going to risk their life chasing after some kid they don't even know. They'll go back to Milton's house and then ask for more money, and then they'll eventually move on to some other town, and some other guy willing to pay them."

I walked over and mounted up on Horse.

"To Amarillo," I said.

BOOK I: HENDRIX

1

MAJOR HASTINGS

"You see what I see?"

"I do," Major Hastings said, raking a hand through his thick black beard.

"That's a white woman and a white girl in a camp with all them savages. What do you think?"

The two soldiers were up on a ridge looking down at the Comanche camp. The major was an old hand in the Indian Wars; but Corporal Grimes, the one who'd discovered the camp, was green and, it seemed to the major, overly naive, and too consumed with morality. Hastings knew better. Morality had no place on the frontier. Morality, Hastings knew, could get you kilt.

"I think they're hostages," the major said. "And I think they've probably been ruined. Comanche treat their women worse than dogs."

"What do you think we should do? The colonel said not to take any actions." Colonel MacKenzie had sent the scouting party ahead to take note of any encampments they came across, take note of the locations, and report back. Nothing more.

"You can't think of those Comanches down there as people.

You have to think of them as a supply chain. They cook the food the warriors take with them, and they make the arrows the warriors use to kill innocent homesteaders when they raid our land and savage our people."

"So, what, you want us to kill them?" Grimes asked, a blush rising in his face.

"All except for the white woman and the girl," Major Hastings said. The answer was obvious, yet Grimes seemed not to know that.

"I don't know. I ain't never kilt nobody but warriors. Them down there is nothing but old people and little ones." Hastings was pretty sure Grimes had never kilt anything bigger than rabbits and squirrels. But there was a first time for everything.

"Then you best start thinking of those down there as warriors. Take that old man with the white hair. He may look harmless but he ain't. Ain't a Comanche alive that's harmless. You go easy on them, before you know it, you'll end up tortured and kilt. You haven't been out here as long as I have. You haven't seen the things I've seen. Ain't a thing we can do to these Comanches they haven't done to us and worse."

Hastings patted the corporal on the shoulder and gave him a grim smile. "You can do this, Corporal. You can't think of them down there as people."

The two soldiers reverse-crawled down from the top of the ridge and made their way to the rest of the group, which consisted of four men hand-picked by Hastings himself to take part in the scouting expedition. The men were all hardened Indian War veterans and fighters, and they worshipped the major like a hero. Grimes had been assigned by MacKenzie due to his scouting and tracking ability—he was the only soldier new to the group.

"All right men," Hastings said. "We'll descend on the camp at first light tomorrow morning, when they're all asleep and warm in their *tipis*."

"If you don't mind, Major," Grimes said, clearing his throat, "the colonel just said to report back. He didn't say nothing about taking any action. He actually said not to, as I recall."

"Corporal Grimes, I outrank you, number one, and that means you take orders from me. And number two, once we go back to the colonel and tell him what we found, he's just gonna send us right back here to do what we're about to do. If we go and report back, and do it the way you suggest, they might have moved on, and then it will be too late to find them. Also, not that there is any further reason for discussion, there's number three: there's a white woman and a white girl being held as slaves down there who would probably like to be reunited with their family and their own kind—away from this desert and these savages."

"They got them some white slaves?" Captain Shelby asked, spitting into the dirt. "I got a sister, and if some savage did something to her, you can bet I'd want some sort of revenge."

"I agree," the major said.

"I think it's a mistake," Grimes said. He had a sister too, two of them in fact, and they would hate it if he killed old men and innocent women and children, whether they were Comanches or not. "I don't think Colonel MacKenzie would want us killing children."

"I see," Hastings said. Then he nodded at Captain Shelby, and the captain took out a knife from the scabbard on his belt and ran it across the corporal's throat. Grimes's eyes went wide, and blood cascaded down the front of his shirt and he fell over into the dust.

"I don't think he's got any qualms now," Shelby said, nudging the body with his boot and wiping blood from his knife. "You two, put this'n here into the dirt."

Sergeant Pulaski and Sergeant Sykes grabbed the now-dead Grimes by the arms and legs and dragged him off to find a hole to dump him in.

Captain Shelby and Corporal Horvath mounted their horses. "See you back at camp, Major," Shelby said.

"First light, gentlemen," Major Hastings said—and then he walked off far enough away to light his pipe and strategize.

"This is gonna be fun!" Corporal Horvath said.

"This'll probably get us a promotion," Captain Shelby said. "We rescue those hostages, I reckon they'll write songs about us."

"Shame about Grimes though," Horvath said.

"He wouldn't have lasted. An arrow or wild animal or bullet would have gotten him sooner or later," Shelby said. "I reckon it's better him dying the way he did than him going and getting us all kilt doing something stupid."

Then the two soldiers and old friends walked their horses further away from the canyon, and, once they were sure they were out of even remotest earshot, gave them the spurs.

2

I was back in Silver Vein, behind the bar of my saloon, wiping the big mirror down from who knows what all manner of unsavory body fluids the various failed miners and complaining ranchers and rude cow-boys had managed to get on there from the previous night's drinking. I didn't like to think about the various splotches and spit drippings. Such things were best not thought about.

It was a quiet and hot summer evening in Silver Vein, and there were only a few people in the saloon—my best customers and the town's most dedicated drunks. It wasn't that much cooler than it was outside. The two fans I had installed on the ceiling were moving so slowly that they seemed only there to be annoying. Baxter and Merle were there, of course, because they mostly weren't allowed indoors anywhere else. Micah was at the piano, sporadically poking notes while turning and looking at me every few minutes to check and see if I was still in the saloon. I knew as soon as he looked over and didn't see me, he would rush over and sneak a few toots of the good stuff. Micah was a hopeless drunk who pretended he only rarely indulged in drink. Micah lied as often as most fellas drew breath. He was what you would be right to call a scoundrel—but Silver Vein wasn't exactly overrun with quality help.

On the other side of the billiard table, in the back, was Jeffers. He was in charge of cooking up chow for the miners and ranchers and soldiers that got hungry while they were thirsty. Currently he was cooking some sort of stew that smelled delicious. Jeffers was small and jumpy, as he'd previously been held prisoner by a savage gang of Comancheros, who had been led by an insane former colonel who had never stopped fighting the war—even though it had ended some years ago. He would kill people and then take their boots, because he felt the confederacy would have won the war if not for a lack of boots.

I made Jeffers wear a big hat—he'd had his hair lifted by those Comancheros before they realized he was a cook—because his scarred-up head terrified the mostly peaceful drunks and prospectors and miners and homesteaders of Silver Vein who made up the majority of the saloon's clientele.

There was also a guy I didn't know hunched over the bar, protectively nursing a bottle of bourbon whisky, hugging the bottle like it was his last meal. He had a few days of scraggly beard whiskers, and hair down to his shoulders which he kept under control with a big unusual floppy brown hat. He smelled to the moon and back. Like something a buzzard might eat and puke up. Worse than Taylor Stephens had smelled when I broke him out of jail. The saloon was clearly this stinky man's first stop off the trail. He didn't talk much. But I could tell that he wasn't a miner because his clothes were more like the kind that a buffalo skinner might wear. There was dry splotchy blood all over it, which is something you didn't see with prospectors. They were mostly covered up in dirt.

"I'll take another, please," the man said, pushing the empty bourbon bottle my way. He might have smelled bad, but at least he was polite.

"Where did it go?" I asked.

"Not far enough," the man said, looking up and making brief eye contact before staring back down at the bar again. I'm a saloonkeeper, and I can't really be all that picky when it comes to giving people drinks. And this fella looked like he could handle his business and wouldn't air out his insides onto the bar—something that happened more often than you would think—so I felt no worry in supplying the man with a second bottle.

"This here cue ball is going to hit that there ball," Baxter said to Merle, "and that ball is going to bounce off of this here and then head right on over and hit that there ball yonder, which is going to then hit that other ball, which will go into that there corner pocket."

"Okay," Merle said, and then he turned and walked away from the billiard table and up to the bar to get another beer without a backward glance.

"Dang," Baxter said, watching his shot play out in a way completely inconsistent with his elaborate plan.

"I didn't hear any balls dropping," Merle called out, turning back to the game. "It don't look like *any* of those balls did *any* of the things you said was going to happen. Which is completely normal for you."

"You can shut that hole in your face right up, unless you want to eat one of these balls," Baxter said.

"You're just mad because you've been practicing this game for years and you're still terrible at it."

"I'm mad because of how ugly you are," Baxter said. "Your face is so ugly it effects the way the balls travel on the table."

"We're twins, fool. We have the same face!"

"The hell we do!" Baxter shouted, waving the billiard cue like he was thinking about whomping Merle with it.

Such behavior was perfectly normal for Baxter and Merle. They had come up to me one day when I first became sheriff and told me they were going to be my deputies and needed me to deputize them. They had more or less deputized themselves, leaving me with no say in the matter. I believe they were worried that without them being around to protect me, I would do something dumb and get myself kilt, and then—were that to come to pass—they would then have nowhere to drink. I can't say they were wrong. Baxter and Merle were both tall and rangy, with matching black mustaches and matching Tennessee accents. When they weren't beating people at cards, or helping me keep the peace, they mostly blew stuff up or set things on fire or argued with and whomped on each other.

I got a new bottle of bourbon out from under the bar and opened it and was setting it in front of the smelly guy in the ratty coat when a voice from outside the saloon doors suddenly called out:

"I know you're in there! And I'm calling you out!"

The smelly guy suddenly sat up straight, wheeled his head towards the door, and shouted, "Who's out there? Show yourself!"

I looked at the saloon doors, and then I looked back at the guy, but now he had shrugged out of his stinky old coat, and he had a pearl-handled Colt in each hand. In short order, the man on the outside of the doors started to push his way inside, and four gunshots rang out from the guy at the bar and the guy outside screamed and crashed through the flapping saloon doors headfirst.

The smelly guy had done some pretty nifty shooting, I had to admit. He could have aimed higher and killed his unseen attacker, but he'd aimed low, which was risky on account of how unreliable a bullet coming out of a gun was—especially if the shooter had an entire bottle of bourbon in his belly.

The ratty guy got up from his stool and walked over to the man on the floor, who now had blood splashing out of both of his kneecaps and was screaming to wake the moon. He stood over the man, both pistols still aimed and leaned down over him until their heads were almost touching.

"Do I even know you?" the man with the pistols asked.

"I didn't know you were so fast," the man said. Then he started screaming again, and thrashing about, so the smelly man whomped him with the butt of one of his pearl-handled Colts.

"Hell, son," the man said, putting his pistols back into the red sash around his waist, "the *whole world* knows how fast I am. And that's the goddamn problem!" He pulled a coin out of one of his pockets and dropped it on the guy's chest. "For the doctor," the man said, and then he stood up, and he no longer looked like some smelly buffalo skinner. With his long hair and mustache and red sash, I had a pretty good idea who he was.

I heard a billiard cue drop to the floor, and I looked over to see Baxter and Merle standing and staring at the man with their jaws open wide enough for a bird to build a nest in.

I walked out from behind the bar and looked at the man on the ground. He was out and snoring. He would survive, but probably not with working legs. Better than being buried in the dirt I suppose.

"It was a clean shoot," I said. "And I thank you for sparing my saloon doors from bullet holes. Baxter, you mind bringing Doc Watson over here?"

"He's not like to be awake this time of day, on account of the fact that the sun is out," Baxter said.

This was true. The doctor, Spack Watson, tended to dose himself throughout the day with his own drugs. On most days he was a terrible doctor, but when a situation called for real serious doctoring, old Spack could sometimes on occasion rally and reveal the good doctor hidden away behind the drunken old sot he'd become.

Baxter walked by the smelly man who could only be none

other than Wild Bill Hickok himself, staring at him in a way that had to be awkward for the both of them.

"Wild Bill," Baxter said, tipping his hat as he walked by, a strange grin on his face. He was spending so much time gawking, he almost stepped right on top of the passed-out fella bleeding all over the floor.

"The hell with it!" Wild Bill said, throwing his hands up in the air in disgust. Baxter shook his head and walked out the door and headed off to fetch the doctor.

"The hell with what?" I asked.

"I was trying to be incognito. This is supposed to be a vacation! Oh well. James Butler Hickok!" he said, offering up a hand for me to shake, "though most people call me either Bill or Wild Bill, as you obviously already know."

We shook hands.

"Curly Barnes," I said. "Most people call me Curly."

3

———

"I've heard of you, of course," Wild Bill said. "Thought you were the sheriff. If I'd known it was you back there behind the bar, I would have introduced myself sooner. I read about the goings on at Pitchfork Pass. Read about it after finding it in a bookshop in New York City. You're about as famous as I am, I expect."

"Pitchfork Pass doesn't exist, not as an actual place on a map anyway, but the fame certainly does," I said, having a hard time believing I was having a regular old conversation with the most famous shootist in the West. "I am the sheriff," I said, "and I also own this saloon."

"The fact is, Curly, the reason I'm here, the reason I'm back in godforsaken Texas, which is next to Mississippi hands down the worst state in this newly stitched-up Union, is because I wanted to meet you."

"You wanted to meet *me*?" I asked. "What the hell for?"

"Yes, *of course* I wanted to meet you."

"Why?"

"Well now, the way I see it, there's only a few people I can complain to. There's you, and then there's that unholy bastard Wyatt Earp, and I expect I've talked to that fella all I ever care to in one lifetime. Him and his whole asshole clan."

"I've never met the man," I said.

"Don't."

"Who was that guy you just shot in the legs?"

"No idea," Wild Bill sighed. "A fan, probably."

"A *fan*?"

"A fan who also wanted to see if the stories were true, to see if I was as fast as was claimed. Hoping to get famous himself most likely. It happens a couple of times a month. Though I didn't expect it would happen here, especially not while wearing this smelly coat. And certainly not while on holiday."

I nodded. "You might not have fooled him, but your outfit certainly fooled me. I didn't even think to ask if you were armed."

"I reckon I might have lost a step when it comes to being incognito. I was a spy during the war, you know. I used to impersonate Texans if you can believe it. And nobody ever thought twice. And now here I've up and been made a fool of by some kid ain't yet got chin whiskers!"

"You impersonated Texans?" I asked.

"Sure. It ain't all that hard. All you have to do is talk about yourself in a very loud voice as if you're the greatest human being that ever lived. Texans, each and every one of them, and I'm guessing that means you Curly, think they are the greatest people that ever drew breath—and that's a known fact."

"You do realize you are *in* Texas?"

"Why do you think I'm drinking so much?" Wild Bill took another healthy slug of bourbon. "But enough about me. How do *you* handle it?" he asked.

"Handle what?" I asked, sipping on some of the good bourbon whisky I kept for myself for special occasions. Like meeting a fellow famous lawman.

"People showing up randomly trying to shoot you dead."

I gave that some thought. "It *doesn't* happen to me. Most people that are drawn here to meet me mostly just want to share a toot of whisky so they can say they drank with the great Curly Barnes," I said, blushing obscenely. My ancestry is so Irish, I can blush with the best of them. Half the town took advantage of my blushing tendency by finding all sorts of ways to see me turn the color of a beet. Which, I shouldn't have to note, is embarrassing for a sheriff.

"Not one person," Wild Bill asked, leaning over the bar, and lifting an eyebrow, "ever thought to get the drop on the great lawman Curly Barnes?"

"I think it's on account of the fact that I'm not known to be any good with a pistol," I said, shrugging. "I'm mostly known as a whomper."

Wild Bill sat back down on his stool with a loud exasperated sigh. "I never set out to—" he leaned his head back and slugged down two bits worth of bourbon and slammed the empty glass on the bar and grew quiet.

Then the saloon doors flapped open and there was Doc Watson. He walked in, with Baxter behind him, blinking furiously, and cautiously approached the bar. Wild Bill watched the doctor intensely. The doctor, even as doped up on his own opium as he was, seemed to sense this, because he looked up and smiled and said: "Bill, how are ya?"

"Doc," Wild Bill said, nodding. "That man over there on the floor sawing logs is my affair. I gave him a coin for any work needs doing. It's on his shirt there on top of all the blood."

"You two know each other?" I asked. For some reason— maybe because Spack Watson was usually so out of it there was no way to have any sort of conversation with him—it never occurred to me that the doctor might have had a life before he showed up in Silver Vein. The Doc had his priorities, and so he ignored the man bleeding on the floor and walked up to the bar.

"Drink," he said. I gave him a measure of rye and he slurped it down.

"Drink," he said again. So, I gave him some more rye, and he slurped that down too. This seemed to sober him up.

"Doc was a surgeon in the war. That's when I met him, anyway," Wild Bill said.

"We don't talk about the war," Spack said, wiping his mouth. "Baxter, help me get this poor fool down to my office." Baxter and the doctor wrestled the unconscious man onto a door that the doctor used to tote unconscious people around on. I'd seen at least a dozen men carted off on that door. They lifted the door and the body and then backed their grunting way through the saloon doors and down the Main Street board-walk, leaving two trails of leaking kneecap blood behind them.

As the doors stopped flapping back and forth, Wild Bill turned his attention back to the bar and grunted to himself.

"Let me ask you something, Curly. Is there a place around here a fella can get a bath? I've got two days of trail dust I've got to get rid of, and I like to stay clean when possible. More than the normal fella anyway."

"Well, if you go to the hotel, you can get a bath ordered up. But I must warn you, and I mean this sincerely, the Ely Turner Hotel is possibly the worst hotel in the entirety of the world. I have it on good authority that the bedsheets are cleaned only during lunar eclipses."

"I guess I'll have to take my chances. I've stayed in some real dumps. I was just in New York City with Bill Cody, basically acting as a crazier version of myself, and I had to stay in places you wouldn't store a hog. To live in that city, you have to have a great capacity for filth."

"Buffalo Bill?" Merle asked. He was now standing

awkwardly by himself, staring at Wild Bill so intently I was worried he might up and shoot Merle just to keep from getting gawked at.

Wild Bill turned and took Merle in, giving him the once over. "The very one," Wild Bill said. "Acting is an unholy occupation, but I have to admit that Bill Cody is a genius when it comes to putting on a show. And he's got a good head for numbers. I expect one day he'll wake up and find himself a millionaire."

"A millionaire," Merle repeated, for no reason.

"I enjoyed my time in New York. In the beginning, anyway," Wild Bill said, nodding his head. "I was what the newspapers there called a sensation. They used that very word. Cody had me dress in fancy beaded buckskins. I would say some dumb line or another, and then shoot my pistol at things, and the crowd would eat it up."

"You got paid to shoot your gun?" Merle asked. "Dang. That sounds easy."

"The problem is, the womenfolk, while eager for my company, treated me like an exotic wild animal—like a mink purse or a buffalo topcoat. I made good money—all of which has since been completely lost—but I couldn't take the acting every night. I felt like an animal in a zoo. And the buildings were too tall, which made me feel hemmed in. People will absolutely ruin whatever they set their mind on improving."

Wild Bill had been telling the truth. He really had come to Silver Vein to complain. Somehow, I couldn't stomach the idea of the great scout and frontier lawman Wild Bill Hickok spending the night at the Ely Turner Hotel. He seemed much too good for the place, which is how I found myself saying, "Well, if you go over there, and find that you don't care for the hotel none, I have a spare bedroom upstairs. My wife and dog are up there, but they don't take up much room."

"I appreciate the offer, Curly, but I'm much too independent to take up space in another fella's home. If the hotel is not to my liking, I reckon I can just find a place to unwind my bedroll. Maybe I could sleep in the livery with my horse if that strange hacking fella will allow it."

"Suit yourself," I said.

4

Wild Bill eventually got off his stool and ambled out of the saloon, off to the Ely Turner Hotel, and a guaranteed night of misery. I got a bucket and mopped up the kneecap blood. People in Silver Vein, even when drunk, didn't care for the sight of blood.

Wild Bill was back inside of ten minutes.

"Dang, Curly."

"I know it."

"That hotel smells like the plague and a whole decade's worth of farts."

"The offer still stands," I said.

"Then Curly, I will await your leave. I hesitate to go upstairs into your home without your escort. In the meantime it couldn't hurt to sit back down on a stool. I find walking to be effortful at the moment."

"It's called being drunk," I said, nodding.

Wild Bill shook his head. "I don't get drunk, Curly. I should know because I have spent a good part of my life trying. I have always been an avid fan of whisky, but never, not one time, have I at any moment resembled your piano player yonder."

I looked over to see Micah with his head on top of the piano snoring up a storm. I looked around the saloon and it was at that time when all the decent and broke people had gone home, but before the cow-boys showed up. On this evening, and at this time of year, I didn't think that any cow-boys would show up, so I set about cleaning up and getting ready to close for the night. I figured closing up early was the least I could do for a celebrity who had come all the way to Silver Vein to meet me—even if it was to complain.

I knocked on the door to my own home to let Sally know I was bringing a guest with me. Hap Morgan—the famous Texas Ranger and a good friend—was the only other person I'd ever given use of the guest bedroom, so me knocking on the door was a rare thing. It was a signal Sally and I had developed, letting her know she shouldn't be walking around in anything frilly that could set a fella to ogling. Some of the miners in town would give away their worthless silver claims just for a glimpse of one of Sally's ankles.

"It's me," I said to the door. That's when my dog Bart went crazy. Any time anyone knocked on anything, that little fluffy fool lost his wits. I opened the door, and he was squeaking and hopping around in circles, greeting me by putting his fluffy paws up on my leg. Then he looked over at Wild Bill and went over and greeted him by putting his paws up on his leg too. Wild Bill must have had a soft spot for dogs, because he had no problem squatting down and reverting to dog talk.

Bart, being nobody's fool, and knowing what that tone of voice meant, flopped over on his back so Wild Bill could scratch his belly. Sally came out of our room wearing a frock coat over her nightgown.

"Curly, who is your friend?" Sally asked. She had a look on her face letting me know she hadn't decided whether she was about to be mad at me or not.

"This here is—"

"James Hickok, Ma'am. You've got a great little dog here."

That was the right thing to say because Sally let loose with one of her best smiles. Her eyes lit up, and I knew Wild Bill's charm was already working.

"His name is Bart," Sally said, "on account of Curly thinks he looks like a bandit."

"It's his beard," I said. "Looks like he's wearing a bandanna."

Wild Bill lifted an eyebrow and gave Bart a good looking over, tilting the dog's head in different directions, and basically taking the matter under way too much consideration. "I reckon it could be," Wild Bill finally said, though not with much conviction.

"James just got off the trail from Amarillo. I believe he is in need of a bath."

"I'll heat up some water," Sally said.

"You don't have to go out of your way," Wild Bill said. He took off his big floppy brown hat and put it next to mine on the hat rack by the back door.

I showed Wild Bill to his room. It was just a straw mattress and a dresser and a chest with a lamp sitting on it.

"It ain't much," I said.

"A damn sight better than that hotel, Curly. Your hospitality is much appreciated." I walked into the kitchen and then lugged the wash basin into Wild Bill's room. "You hungry?" I asked. "We keep weird hours, so we don't eat until the saloon closes for the night."

"I reckon I could eat. Though, to tell you the truth Curly, I mostly just drink my food."

Sally brought a pail of hot water and dumped it in the basin. Wild Bill took the pail. "Now you tell me where the water is, and I can heat it myself. It's the least I can do ma'am." Wild Bill bowed to Sally like an actor at the end of a stage play, which made her blush and giggle.

She handed him a bar of lye soap.

"Thank you," Wild Bill said, "but when it comes to soap, I bring my own." He reached into his saddle bag and pulled out a small canvas bag, which he opened up and reached in and pulled out a few different bars of soap, along with a wide variety of different hairbrushes.

"That's a lot of hairbrushes," I announced, before I could stop myself.

"Each one has its purpose, Curly," Wild Bill growled. "Having long hair is a commitment, you know." I didn't know, and I think he knew that I didn't know, but I said, "I'm not familiar with long hair upkeep," to calm him down, as I could see he was defensive about his hairbrushes. It probably wasn't the first time the subject had come up.

"James, maybe when we sup, we can explain to Curly the upkeep that goes into having long hair," Sally said.

Wild Bill shook his long hair out and smiled.

———

We left Wild Bill to his bath, and I hovered over Sally while she went about cooking up some stew, which smelled a lot like the stew Jeffers had been cooking earlier. I knew the two of them often were of the same mind when it came to cooking and went food shopping together and so they often ended up cooking the same things. Which was fine with me.

"That's Wild Bill Hickok, you know," I said. "I know he said James, but that's just because he's on vacation."

"Wild Bill Hickok? That stinky man? I figured him for a buffalo skinner."

"So did I. It's that jacket he's wearing. I believe he was trying to disguise himself. Probably because people are always taking shots at him. We already had a fella call him out, and he ain't even been in town a day yet."

"He seems nice enough," Sally said. "Bart likes him." Anyone the dog liked was okay with Sally.

"I can hear him in there singing," I said. "Maybe we better head off over to the kitchen table. I don't want him to think we're spying on him. He's apt to have a gun in the tub with him. People are always trying to challenge him, so I expect he's quite jumpy, even singing in a tub full of water." I would like to say that Wild Bill had a lovely singing voice, but this was not the case. His singing sounded like someone dragging a fork across a dinner plate. But people do weird things when they're soaping up their nether parts, and that's a known fact.

When Wild Bill emerged from his room, Sally and I were sitting at the kitchen table having a staring contest. It was something that started when I first started up as sheriff and was working on a mean glare—one that I would use to scare people into not getting out of line. The key to a good mean glare is you can't blink at all. You have to look at someone as if you are a lizard. Like something in your brain is out of sorts, or even broken. I would come to realize that you can't just pretend to have a mean glare, you have to have the attitude that comes with it. And the truth was, even as sheriff, I couldn't bring myself to stare at a fella too long without breaking out laughing. Wild Bill had it, though, when he looked down at the man whose kneecaps he shot holes into. He looked down at the guy like he wouldn't think twice about shooting a couple more holes into the man. Like he wouldn't lose a wink of sleep over it.

"Am I interrupting anything?" Wild Bill asked.

I broke eye contact first and looked up at Wild Bill. He'd smacked all the trail dust off his clothes and had hacked off the whiskers that had grown out on the trail, keeping only the mustache, and his hair looked clean and didn't have any burrs or twigs sticking out of it.

"You clean up well," Sally said.

"I know it sounds odd," Wild Bill said, "but I like to keep

myself clean when I can. I am a frequent bather and can't understand a fella that don't believe in using soap. Many people don't, you know. Especially buffalo skinners. Of course, if I'm telling the truth, what with all the guts and blood, ain't much point in using soap if'n you're a buffalo skinner."

"I am also a fan of the bath," I said, blushing because my very skin likes to humiliate me. Sally tried not to laugh at me, which made me blush all the more. "Sally don't like it when I smell like a pig trough."

"More like sour beer and tobacco smoke," Sally said. "Bart doesn't like it neither."

"The dog's opinion is all important," I said, giving Bart a nod.

"So, Wild Bill—" Sally started, then caught herself and slapped a hand over her mouth.

Wild Bill turned and gave me a look. I'd forgotten he'd introduced himself as James. I shrugged.

"Aw hell, looking like this, being incognito was never going to last," Wild Bill said, pulling out a chair and sitting down with a dramatic sigh. "My main problem, I suppose, is that I'm me." I could see that he was still trying to get the acting out of him, because some of his gestures might have looked good from far away, but up close were somewhat silly.

"There's no point in being incognito now," I said. "For one thing, you already shot up some fella's kneecaps."

"Which I paid for," Wild Bill said, smiling at Sally. "I ain't one to hold grudges."

"...But once you threw that stinky buffalo skinner coat, and everyone got a look at that red sash, incognito was done with. By now the entire town of Silver Vein knows you're here. Why, Pap Kickins is probably at the hotel knocking on doors looking for you this very minute. Pap puts out the town newspaper. And knowing him as I do, he won't rest until he snags an interview. He's relentless in such matters."

"I'm through with giving interviews, Curly. I reckon giving that nobody journalist an interview was the biggest mistake of my life. Outside of drunken gun battles, of course."

I thought about Pap Kickins, and his imagination. He'd made me a household name without me having to do all that much if you want to know the truth of it. If you were to shoot a fella, by the time Pap wrote it up in the paper, it would be an entire outlaw gang.

"It is weird, I have to admit, to be about to sup with someone I've read about in books," I said.

"It's all hooey, as I think you know. Hank Stanley, I think his name was. It's his fault I'm in this predicament. I got half the West chasing after me because of him. Well, him and all the made-up stories I told him."

"Curly wouldn't know anything about giving a reporter a tall tale," Sally said, laughing.

Wild Bill looked at me.

"I'm a saloonkeeper," I said, "I can't help but talk."

Wild Bill nodded. "The way I see it, I need some new adventures. And then what I'm going to do is write a book of my own. In fact, I've already started it. Almost finished with it actually. Since those reporters done already taken my best stories, I reckon I have to come up with some new ones. It was Bill Cody who got me thinking about how much money a fella could make telling his own story."

"I'd love to read it," Sally said.

"Aw, it ain't written yet. Not all of it, though most of it is, though I don't think I'm ready to show it to anyone just yet, on account of how it's still in rough form."

"I understand," Sally said, which is more than I could say, because it sounded to me like he'd said a whole platter of stuff.

Then Sally said, "Oh!" and ran to the stove.

"Hope you like stew!" Sally yelled out from the kitchen.

"Nothing better," Wild Bill said. Which is what I was going

to say. In fact, it's usually what I *did* say. I probably didn't need to be jealous, but I told myself I should keep an eye out, especially now that Wild Bill no longer smelled or looked like a goat.

"That's what Curly says," Sally said, giggling.

I fell in love with Wild Bill when he got that bowl of stew in front of him. Because he turned from a dignified man into a wild beast. He stopped talking and set to packing away that stew with an earnestness that was hard to fake. He had worse eating manners than Bart, which is really saying something, because the dog didn't have anything but his face to eat with. I don't know why I found Wild Bill's entirely graceless eating style endearing, but I did. I also knew it would make Sally want to air out her insides—which took care of the whole jealousy problem. Sally didn't go in for bad table manners.

"That was good," Wild Bill said, wiping the now empty bowl with a finger, as Sally and I were only just taking our first bites. He then licked the bowl with his tongue, just like Bart did.

"You *did* like it," Sally said, a little shaken by his violent slurping.

"I did indeed," Wild Bill said. His mustache was dripping with stew liquid, but he gave no sign of noticing.

"Well, I reckon I better turn in," Wild Bill said. "Got a long day tomorrow."

"Oh?" I said.

"Well, now that you put it that way, I don't believe I have anything to do tomorrow. Or the day after that, and so on. In fact, everything on the other side of right now is one big blank at the moment. Though I suppose I'll have to make my way to Deadwood over in Dakota Territory at some point."

"What's there?"

"They say gold," Wild Bill said, finally wiping the stew juice off his mustache with a sleeve.

"Well, good luck," I said. "This place was supposed to have silver, so much so that they even put it in the town's name, but ain't but one person ever found a lick of silver here."

"No silver at all?"

"Never."

"Well, I'll be. Hope can be quite the bastard."

5

The entirety of the town was abuzz with the news that the legendary shootist and lawman Wild Bill Hickok was in town. The man who had single-handedly tamed the rowdy town of Abilene, Kansas. I could almost hear it from my home. I waited for Wild Bill to wake up, but as I was to learn, he almost never slept. "Too many bad dreams," he would say, whenever I suggested he get some sleep. He was awake and sitting up in bed brushing his hair with such intense purpose it was almost off-putting. I figured, for Wild Bill, considering all the upkeep involved, instead of having a dog he just had long hair. Or maybe it was like having a plant on your head that you had to always be watering, so it didn't die.

"I need to warn you, Wild Bill, Silver Vein is nothing but a collection of some of the worst gossips you can imagine. If we go outside and the whole town isn't out there gawking, I'll be very surprised."

"Aw, I appreciate the concern, but I'm used to getting gawked at. In New York City, I was basically paid to get gawked at. You could say getting gawked at was my job. And that's why I like to dress well. You don't want to be gawked at for being a slob in my opinion. That's the responsibility that comes with being celebrated."

"I suppose you're right. I thought maybe we could walk down the boardwalk to the restaurant. Kate will take good care of us."

"Breakfast is my favorite meal; in many cases, it's my only meal. I would be happy to."

"I can also show you the jail," I said, unable to brag a little bit. "It's new, on account of the old one got destroyed."

"If the jail is one of Silver Vein's highlights, and the town doesn't have any silver, then I fear for its future. But then again, this is Texas, and people think different down here, when they think at all."

"Okay," I said. That's what I said whenever I didn't have a good answer to something. I liked Silver Vein, but that was because I was the second most successful person in town. Whether a person was riding high, or living in a horse trough, no matter which was the way of it, they liked to drink. What it was is that me and old Ely Turner made out like bandits supplying everyone else's broken dreams.

Sally and I and Wild Bill set off down the boardwalk.

"That's the courthouse," I said, because I could see Wild Bill looking at it.

"It's a ruin," Wild Bill said.

"The judge that used to run the court," I told him, "choked on a biscuit and died one day, and we haven't had a court case or a judge since. So, no need for a courthouse."

"Why not put something else in there? It don't have to be a courthouse."

"Hmmm," I said, because nobody in town had ever even considered such a thing; and now, suddenly, it made complete and total sense.

"That's a good idea," Sally said.

"That there..." I said, changing the subject, "...is Ely Turner

Mercantile, where everything is at least thrice as expensive as it needs to be. I bought a winter coat in there one time—that's what it was called—Winter Coat—and I regret it even now. When it gets cold at night, that coat encourages the chill to come inside without putting up any sort of fight at all."

"And this is Doc Watson's office, I gather," Wild Bill said. I nodded. There were groups of people standing about on the street for no special purpose at all. Each of the groups were staring at Wild Bill as he made his way down the boardwalk. I tried to wave them off, but they just waved back like we were in a parade. "And here on the left is Kate's Restaurant." I walked up and opened the door and let Sally through and then tried to hold the door for Wild Bill, but he was having none of it, and took the door from me, and then he stood there in the doorway for a lot longer than necessary. He might not have liked being an actor in New York, but he certainly had no fear of attention.

When I'd opened the door, the restaurant had been filled with jibber and jabber, as is expected at breakfast time, but now it was as silent as a tomb, because everyone was looking at Wild Bill standing in the doorway. After he'd sucked up enough attention he joined us at my table towards the back, which had once been the old sheriff's table.

We sat down, and Kate came over and hugged on Sally, and asked who Wild Bill was, and so Sally told her, and Kate nodded as if he was just a normal regular person. Then she walked off to get us some coffee.

As we were talking, a little head and some little eyeballs appeared at the end of the table. It was little Jimmy Shepland, and he had jumped up and pulled himself up, so his head was now at table height.

I looked down and saw his feet dangling about two feet off the ground. "Dang," I said, "but you're strong."

Wild Bill had a look, and said, "Dang, I thought he was standing on something."

"He's like his dad," I said. "His dad was strong. He was the sheriff before me."

"What happened to him?"

"He was kilt by Silas Bondcant," I said.

"The runt of the litter, and angry for it" Wild Bill said, nodding his head. "I had my own run-in with the Bondcant brothers."

"Well, not anymore you won't. They're all dead now."

"It was the only way it was going to end for them. Some of those Confederate guerrillas have gone and turned themselves into gangs and are begging to get their necks stretched."

I nodded. Then I looked over at Sally, so she didn't feel overlooked. She didn't have much patience for law talk. She fell in love with a saloonkeeper, and then that saloonkeeper had gone and up and become sheriff. So, I tried to keep talk about bad guys and arresting wrongdoers to as little as possible.

Jimmy Shepland might have been strong for a toddler, but he also had plenty of endurance, because he just stayed in place with his head over the top of the table for an impressive amount of time. It wasn't until Kate came back with our coffee and gave him a playful swat that he let go of the table and ran off.

"He is a strong one," I told Kate.

"You don't know the half of it," Kate said. "The other day he broke a table glass just squeezing it between his tiny hands."

"Jim Shepland was a strong man," I said. "I reckon Jimmy got more than a healthy dose of that strength."

Wild Bill's head jerked up at that. "I knew a Jim Shepland in the war," he said.

"Jim fought for the Union in the war," I said, nodding.

"If it's the man I'm thinking about, he was a natural leader and fair. The soldiers under him would charge into a fusillade of cannon fire just because he said it. He wasn't some West Point dandy preening about. He was well respected."

"He was a very fair sheriff," I said, looking at Kate to make sure she was okay, as I knew the old sheriff's passing was still raw with her. The sheriff used to spend many hours at the table where we now sat, talking with Kate, and drinking coffee. Kate didn't know she was pregnant until Jim Shepland was already dead.

"He was a good man. And I thank you for those kind words," Kate said, then she turned and walked off.

"Jim Shepland's death rankles still," I said. "When he got here, after the sheriff before him, Sheriff Langtry, got kilt while he was taking a piss outside the livery, the town was wild. He tamed it, then he handed it over to me when he was dying in my arms." I looked down at the table. The memory was still fresh, and thinking about it often got my eyes to leaking. Sally, under the table, gave me a pat on the leg and left her hand there. It was warm, and it felt good. Sally's gift was her ability to comfort and thinking about her caring nature threatened to turn me into a bawling mess, so I shook free of my thoughts.

"Sorry," I said.

"No need to apologize," Wild Bill said. "I've had many a fella die in my arms, and that is something you flat out never get used to."

I was about to reply when Sally squeezed my leg, and I looked up—and here came Orville Benson. He worked with Steve Pool, the undertaker, and lately had specialized in the building of caskets. He wore his hair greased back just like his boss and had a long messy gray beard—often full of lumber shavings and paint chips. Right now, he had a weird look on his face, and he kept stopping and turning around and then turning back around, and doing all of it over again, before he finally managed to get to our table.

"Sheriff," Orville said, nodding.

I nodded back. "Anything I can do for you?" I asked, knowing he had no interest in me whatsoever.

"Well, Curly, I actually came over to say hello to Wild Bill."

"He's on vacation," I said. Which made Orville's mouth fall open in confusion. He didn't know what to make of that.

"Well," Orville said, "I won't trouble you too much Wild Bill. I just wanted to say hello."

"Do I know you?" Wild Bill asked, turning his head slightly, like Bart sometimes does when a human does that doesn't make sense.

"Well, I used to live in Abilene, and I would sometimes see you playing cards from time to time, though I never had excuse to introduce myself."

"I'm afraid I lost that job," Wild Bill said. "I reckon the problem was I was too good at it. Once the town was settled, my salary was too much of a burden for the town."

"It's my understanding that you spent too much time drinking and playing cards with the people you were supposed to be arresting."

I didn't know Orville that well, but any normal person should have known that was probably not something you should say to a man that had two ivory-handled pistols on his person. Especially not someone like Wild Bill, whose right eye was now twitching.

"I'm sorry," Wild Bill said, his voice like a knife through an unprotected kidney, "now what did you say your name was again?"

Orville must have realized he had just poked a grizzly bear, and he no longer seemed to have the ability to speak at all, much less recall his own name.

"Orville spends too much time with dead people," I said. "He don't really know how to talk to people that are yet living."

"I reckon that was the way of it," Wild Bill said, letting out an enormous sigh. "I figured the best way to keep an eye on the ruffian element was keeping them across the table from me at the card table and winning all of their money while doing it. As it would turn out, I was the only one in Abilene with that particular philosophy—which, as it so happens, is a philosophy I still believe in."

Orville relaxed, seeing he was no longer courting death, and turned and looked to the other side of the restaurant where his wife was. He nodded his head and turned back to Wild Bill and said, "Could I maybe trouble you for a lock of your hair?"

Wild Bill looked at Orville. "My hair has been with me for many years, and I aim to keep it that way."

"Okay. My wife—it don't matter. It was nice meeting you." Orville turned and walked off.

"Nobody's ever asked me for a lock of hair," I said. "Hair seems like a weird keepsake, especially if it ain't belonging to a loved one," I said. "I reckon Orville to be a weirdo."

"I expect it was his wife that sent him over here," Sally said.

"He ain't the first person to ask for some part of me as a keepsake, though never before has it happened at breakfast. Sally can have a lock of my hair if she wants one."

"She doesn't," I said, answering for her, which got me a strong squeeze on my leg.

"That's why I would give her one. I am always suspicious of those that ask. The truth is most people expect me to die any day. If I were to get shot to death in a gun battle, I reckon a lock of my hair might be worth a few bits—though it seems an odd keepsake."

"This is some conversation," Sally said, letting us know we needed to move on from collectible hair locks.

"I recommend the steak and eggs," I said.

6

When we emerged from Kate's restaurant, a herd of people stood around the town in clumps, ogling the famous shootist.

"That one over there with the paper in his hand and the ear trumpet is Pap Kickins," I said. He puts out *The Daily Silver Vein*, which comes out only when something actually happens in this town. In this case, I'm guessing that's you."

"I'm done with reporters, Curly," Wild Bill said. He stepped off the boardwalk into the road and people backed up and turned around, all trying to pretend that they had some purpose to their being in town. I was famous, but not in the town of Silver Vein. In Silver Vein, most people just ignored me, except for kids trying to make me blush; and seeing how people reacted to Wild Bill—staring at him like he was some sort of exotic plant—I was thankful they paid me no mind. But, as I would learn later, when it came to being left alone, Silver Vein was the exception. I never did learn to put up with all the attention I would get with the same good grace of Wild Bill.

"Oh! Wild Bill! Would you care to comment about the

gunfight yesterday?" Pap asked, his voice at a volume that could drop birds from the sky.

"I would not," Wild Bill said.

"It is my understanding the four men are all dead?"

"It was but one man, and he ain't dead!" Wild Bill said, throwing his hands up in exasperation.

"Four is better than one," Pap said, writing feverishly, "and dead is better than not. Trust me on this."

"Scat!" I said into Pap's ear trumpet. He turned on his heel and walked back to his office, looking back over his shoulder at me.

"You're a terrible journalist!" I yelled at his retreating back.

"I believe I'll scope out the Mercantile," Wild Bill said. "I'm tired of my current duds."

"I don't recommend it," I said.

"I was in New York City, Curly. An entire city of price gougers, hucksters, schemers, and con artists from all over the world. The very best ones. The ones who work hard and make their way to the very top of the price gouging profession. I reckon I can contend with your little mercantile here."

"Okay," I said. I could see he was set on the matter, so I ate my words, and followed him to the other side of the street and into Ely Turner's Mercantile. Sally and I busied ourselves looking at the outrageous prices Ely charged for dinner plates.

"Dang," I said, showing Sally a two-dollar dinner plate with a ten-dollar price tag.

"Dang," Sally said, holding up a two-bit fork that Ely was charging five dollars for. Every single thing in the store was priced to outrage.

I kept my eye on Wild Bill, waiting for him to react.

"You sir!" Ely said, coming out from behind the counter, "I'm going to have to ask you not to paw the clothing."

Wild Bill turned around and gave old Ely what I would come to think of as the full Wild Bill. He pulled back his coat, revealing the sash and his pearl-handled Colts, and stood up straight and said, "I believe you must be talking to someone else." There was nobody else, other than me and Sally. I know because I checked.

The words stopped Ely just as surely as a slammed door. He stopped walking, saw who he was talking to, and then said, "Yes, I was not referring to you at all. It was some other scalawag. Must have raced out just now. Wild Bill Hickok, is it?"

"That's the name people know me by," Wild Bill said, nodding.

"Are you in the market for a waistcoat then?" Ely stammered.

"I just might be. And a new shirt. And pants. Maybe a coat."

"Ah! The works! For you, Wild Bill, I will—Not you, Curly—provide a discount. I would be honored for you to be wearing clothes purchased in my fine store! Probably the best selection of clothing for gentlemen west of the Mississippi. Finer, even, then that of San Francisco!"

I could see Ely Turner doing the math in his head, trying to figure out just how much he could gouge the famous gunfighter without incurring his wrath.

Ely walked off and rummaged around and came back with a huge pile of clothes. It looked like he was going to try and sell Wild Bill every piece of clothing in the store.

I couldn't bear to watch. I didn't want to know what Wild Bill was willing to hand over to the greasy little thief. Sally and I stopped pretending to shop, and we left Wild Bill with that little weasel and headed back home.

———

"I didn't get my first nether part hair until I was already in the war," Wild Bill said.

My sheriff duties done for the day—nothing of consequence happened—me and Wild Bill spent the afternoon killing time, telling tall tales, and getting to know one another —all while drinking ourselves silly. Every once in a while, some miner would sidle up and try to horn in on our jabbering, but they soon got dissuaded when Wild Bill would give them a look and kept to themselves—though I expect they did some eaves-dropping. The saloon was a lot more crowded than usual. One man, who called himself Lord Nelson, because he had only one arm, was a teetotaler; but he was in the saloon anyway sipping on bourbon. Every sip he took, he made a face and cursed under his breath. Wild Bill's presence was making everyone in town behave like asses.

"I remember the first time I saw mine," I said. "It was like this little pioneer, just sticking out by itself, with no other nether part hairs for company. I didn't even understand what it was at first."

"Like a lone prairie dog in an empty desert," Wild Bill said, nodding. "But it don't take long before the reinforcements show up."

"After that first one, I had a red forest of hairs in no time," I said. These were not high-quality conversations we were having.

"I got one now that's gray," Wild Bill said, looking down at his lap. "I reckon it's a pioneer of a different kind."

"I reckon," I said, not knowing what I was about, "when they dig us up, we'll be nothing but bones and nether part hairs."

"Is that the way of it? Listen here, Curly, and I want you to know this, because I already love you like a brother. In a hundred years, nobody will know we ever were. You'll see."

"I hope not," I said. "In a hundred years, was I to still be alive, I reckon I'd be shriveled up like a raisin, just drooling away in some chair."

"I didn't mean we'd still be on this earth in a hundred years.

What foolishness. I mean, as famous and celebrated as we are today, one day we'll just be a box full of sand that everyone has gone and forgotten about."

"You got one more thing in common with Frank Kilhoe. He's always saying that exact very thing to me."

"What thing is that?"

"He's always saying, 'What foolishness!'"

"I reckon me and a Texan can have one thing in common. But any more and I would have to just call myself out, up and shoot my own self, and be done with it."

"What would happen," I said, hoping I wouldn't be kilt, "if you died and in your obituary they said you were a Texan?"

"I would have to come back to life and strangle some fella."

I saw a large blurry object in my left eye and turned my head to see it was just that old white mouse, confidently dithering with itself on the billiard table. It looked enormous, but I knew that mouse, and it was a small old mouse, and not big at all—and so I knew I was drunk, maybe drunker than I'd been in a long time; but Wild Bill, he seemed like he could go right on jabbering away until morning, and, as much as I didn't want to disappoint him, being as how I considered him a hero, I needed to get upstairs and fall dead asleep on my straw mattress.

"That mouse," I said, for no reason. Not that Wild Bill was listening to anything I had to say right then anyway.

"Well," Wild Bill sighed, "I reckon now is as good a time as any."

"As good a—"

Wild Bill, who had, despite my warnings, gone and spent a heap of money at Ely Turner's Mercantile, buying a whole new outfit, fished a wadded-up piece of paper out of a pocket.

"What's that?" I asked.

"It's my autobiography. I got most all of it in there. Go on and read it and let me know what you think."

I was in no shape to do any sort of reading, or much of anything else, but I could tell by looking in Wild Bill's eyes that it was important.

So I read:

CHAPTER ONE OF THE OFFICIAL AND ONLY AUTOBIOGRAPHY OF WILD BILL HICKOK AND ALL THEM OTHERS ARE LYING

This here is the real story of me, Wild Bill Hickok. The real Wild Bill Hickok, unlike what unscrupulous journalists might have written to try to sell papers, is a half-blind drunk all broken down by life at no more than not even middle age. Here I am, a staggering 32 years old—-no Hickok has ever lived so long on this here earth as of yet. So it theretofore I guess makes sense that I can't see all that well these days. I reckon I spent too long astride a horse loping through the prairie sun while the dang sun bored little holes into my future vision ability. I used to be able to shoot a hole through a quarter with either hand from fifty yards! Not no more!

I went to New York to be an actor and I got some venereal disease from some whore from Boston. I think her name was—well now, I suppose there's no need to bring her into this. In the fact that I was drunk at the time, I most probably was.

The honest truth is and was that I am almost never sober. Some of those gunfights were accidents and verbal confusions and misunderstandings brought on by all manner of digested and smoked substances. Strange stuff people would sell you right off the ships in port! There's a plant from Africa that will...well, anyway.

New York City smells like the inside of a desiccated

camel penis. And there's too many daggum buildings, a person can't see nowheres.

Give me a horse and some town to tame or place to go, and give me a fair tankard of whisky, and give me several good brushes for my hair, and give me a wide variety of quality soaps...but most of all give me my old eyes back, at least for a few more years yet, so I can get out of this mope.

This here is the second chapter of --

_____

Well, it was a terrible thing, having to read that. It was even worse to read it in front of the man who wrote it. I don't consider myself some sort of Shakespeare, but I can certainly wield a quill better than that! Wild Bill was looking at me intensely, making his eyebrows lunge together in a way that made my bowels jumpy.

"It has a suspenseful ending," I ventured, like a fella standing in the middle of a melting pond. I thought it was one of the worst things I'd ever read, even as short is it was.

"Um-hum," Wild Bill said.

"I would say to keep trying," I finally said, on account of I had to say something.

"What for? I got everything in there!"

"Wait," I was confused, "are you saying this is the *whole* autobiography?"

"It's certainly got all the highlights."

I read it again, and it made less sense the second time.

"There's not much really in here," I said, blushing like a tomato. "And it's sort of depressing. People don't want to read about a broken-down mopey hero." I finally figured there was no way for Bill to shoot a hole in me with Sally upstairs. He would look bad in her eyes were he to up and kill me. Here

Wild Bill had been going on and on and on about the autobiography he was writing, and it was nothing but a ratty piece of paper full of gripings that didn't even make no sense!

This is the part they don't talk about in the dime novels like the one in Sheriff Marlowe's desk drawer. The part where the hero drinks too much and falls apart and humiliates himself in front of strangers. It made me happy to have Sally in my life. If I didn't have her and Bart, and if I didn't feel the need to keep Baxter and Merle in line, I might end up all mopey like Wild Bill. I could see he was at some sort of crossroads. He was a man at war with himself inside his own head. And, if you want to know the truth, I'm rather glad I met Bill at this particular time in his life. Being laid low had clearly humbled the man. I don't know if I would have had any stomach for him if he'd showed up all cocksure and self-promoting.

"I think," I said, unable to meet the man's eyes, "it needs more action."

Wild Bill thought for a minute, took a toot of bourbon, and slammed down the glass on the bar and said, "My thinking exactly!" I took a toot of bourbon myself, and turned my head so he wouldn't see me wipe my sweaty forehead with a rag.

"What is the card action like?" Wild Bill asked, changing the subject. "If I don't play a game of cards every day, I get mopey." He was already mopey, but I didn't tell him that. I was perfectly happy to move on.

"See that dirty fella sitting about half-way down the bar? The one purposely wearing a top hat with a hole in it?"

"Yes."

"That's Tad Bowltree. He used to work at the old bank, not the Ely Turner Bank, but the one before it. It got destroyed when some of Torp Mayfair's gang robbed it. Anyway, he might not look like much, but he is an absolutely terrible card player who never seems to run out of money."

"You're telling me that filthy tramp has money?"

I nodded. "A seemingly endless supply. I know. It makes no sense at all. Now, if you want to challenge yourself, and play with good card players, you want Baxter and Merle. Though, since they're hero-struck by you, they might just up and give you their money."

"What about that fella at the end of the bar in that ridiculous dandy outfit with all the lace?"

I looked at the end of the bar and there indeed was some dandy looking fella I'd never seen before. And I would have known if I had. I had a good memory for faces, and this one was a doozy. The man had done something to his mustache that, even from all the way down at my end of the bar, looked like two black horns jutting out about six inches off each side of his upper lip. I watched as he methodically lifted up his enormous belly and placed it to rest on the top of the bar.

"I don't know," I said.

I walked down to the other end of the bar and introduced myself to the man I would come to know as Sherwood Floop.

"Can I get you a drink, friend?"

"Well, my good man, first and foremost, you could do me a capital favor and relieve me of my pistol and dagger. I always like to obey the rules, you see."

Most people I have to badger to get them to give me their pistols, or I have to whomp them on the head and take them, so the fact that the man had the manners to hand them over without having to even be asked made me think very highly of him—despite his ample belly resting on the bar like a sleeping house cat.

"I believe you just earned yourself a drink on the house," I said, taking the pistol and dagger. The pistol had an engraving on it, which read: "To Sherwood, one of my sons." The dagger had emeralds on its scabbard.

"Interesting knife," I said.

"I was given it by a Moghul princess after servicing her to

her satisfaction. Beautiful woman. She smelled of heaven and saffron!"

I didn't know what to say to that. "What can I get you to drink?"

"Call me Sherwood. I imagine I will be spending the bulk of my time in here. And you *are* Curly Barnes, yes?"

"That's me," I said. "And this is my saloon."

"Capital! Yes, I have it on good authority that you are *the man* I need to see. I like your saloon. It's just how I pictured it. So rustic and smelling of sweat! Curly, I appreciate your offer and I accept it. I'll have a horned blueberry."

"Is that a drink? I don't believe I have that. What I do have—"

"Excelsior Street Spritz?"

I shook my head. "I've got—"

"A Bombay Oyster?"

"No."

"Philadelphia Mary?"

"No."

"London Mulch?"

"No."

"Chocolate Malta!"

"I—"

"Well, I had no idea saloons could be so barren of choice. What exactly *do* you have?"

"I've been trying to tell you," I said.

"Go on! This I will want to hear!"

"Bourbon whisky. Irish whisky. Rye whisky. Rotgut whisky. Gunpowder moonshine. And beer."

"That's it?"

I nodded. And added: "I'm the only saloon in town."

Sherwood gave this some serious thought. He finally asked, "Do you recommend the rotgut then?"

"No. I recommend top shelf bourbon or Irish whisky."

"Ah, but I hate the bloody Irish. I'll try the top shelf Bourbon then."

"Fine." I walked down to the other end of the bar and got a bottle of good bourbon, the best I had—this guy looked like he had plenty of money even though he was clearly a little bit off —and poured a belt into a shot glass and walked over and pushed it around his dormant belly so he could reach it.

He put his head back and upended the glass over his mouth.

"It burns!" Sherwood cried, and then set off on a serious coughing fit. "Ooh! But I like it! So harsh and primitive! So authentic! Well, Curly, it looks like I'm a bourbon man!"

"You said someone told you to see me about something?" I asked.

"Capital! Right to the point I see. Yes! Just so! Well, Curly, the reason I am enjoying the squalid frontier hospitality of Silver Vein is I happen to be in the market for silver. Lots of it."

Before I could tell him the town had no silver, he plowed on.

"You see—have you heard of New York City?"

"Yes."

"Excellent! Capital! Well, as it so happens that is where I lived when I was forced to flee London. Have you heard of the panic?"

I shook my head.

"Well, lucky you. You see. They've taken silver and have decided to no longer recognize it as standard, leaving gold as the only remaining monetary standard. And, you see, the price of silver has therefore suffered a grievous blow! Nobody wants the stuff."

"I wouldn't go spreading that around," I said, looking around to see if any miners might be listening. "Not in this town."

"But Curly, it will soon be made plain that the bankers in

New York have made an awful mistake! Silver, which I intend to buy as much of as a human can while it's all but worthless, will once more be made standard. And when it is—there is but one man, myself, Sherwood Floop the Fourth, who you happen to be conversing with—and I'm talking about myself Curly—it is I who will be the only one who will have had the foresight and the gallstones to see silver's prominent future. I will then be made the richest of men, and on that day I will march back into New York City to great awe and acclaim. And then, listen up Curly, I will be made the first king of New York City. And I mean that literally! My first act, of course, will be to rename the place Floop Town. Or Sherwood City. I go back and forth on that one. My God! This bourbon seems so angry when you swallow it!"

"So what is it you want me to do?" I asked. I had not been able to follow one word he had said.

"Tell any man interested that I will, sight unseen, purchase any silver claim a person is willing to sell, and I will buy at a fair price, and, Curly, be sure to mention this, as I believe the miners—that fellow over there perhaps? He looks the sort, certainly dirty enough—will see this as a good selling point, so make sure you tell them this: I will *hire* any man on that sells me a claim, and at good wages, and *share* with them any silver we find. I have no intention of digging in the dirt myself, you see. I am not a man for toil!"

"I will pass this along," I assured him. There were many miners that owed me money for drinks extended to them on the slow days when I got desperate and starved for someone to listen to me jabber. They would be the first people I would tell. But, this being Silver Vein, the word would soon be out.

———

Sherwood had been right about the fella sitting at the bar. His name was Idaho O'Malley. And he did look the sort, all covered in dirt like he was.

"You owe me thirty-six dollars," I told him.

Idaho looked at me and said: "Now?"

"See that guy at the end of the bar?"

"The one with the belly?" Idaho asked. "Kind of hard to miss. What the bloody hell is wrong with him?"

"He's an odd one," I agreed. "He says he wants to buy your silver claim."

O'Malley looked at the end of the bar. "Why?" he asked.

"Something to do with...the truth of it is I never did understand what he said. But he did say he would be willing to hire you on for wages, and that he would split any silver you found."

"It's too good to be true!"

"I know," I said. It made no sense to me at all. "If I were you, I would go and talk to him before he changes his mind."

O'Malley didn't have to be told twice. He got up and walked to the end of the bar. I saw Floop slap O'Malley on the back, let out a triumphant bark of a laugh, and then reach into one of his pockets and pull out a piece of paper and hand it to O'Malley. And O'Malley walked back over and handed me the fifty-dollar bill he'd been given, and said, "You got change for a fifty?"

"I think I can scramble up fourteen dollars."

"Actually, can you just let me know when that there is used up? You weren't wrong. He offered me five hundred dollars before I even got the opportunity to offer to sell my claim to him for two hundred. Now I can afford to move on out of here and head over to Milton and strike it rich digging up coal."

I'd done my job. The fuse had been lit.

———

The next morning, as I was making my way to jail, I walked down the back stairs to find Wild Bill squatting carefully in the dirt trying to teach Bart to shake hands. A fool's errand if ever there was one. Bart only cared about food and hugs. He wasn't about to lift a paw unless there was something in it for him.

"Good luck with that," I said.

"Watch this!" Wild Bill said. And dang if Bart didn't up and offer up his paw. Sally and I had been talking about teaching Bart something like that, but then always gave up before any of our teaching made its way into his dog brain.

"Smart dog," Wild Bill said, scratching on Bart's ears.

"Maybe," I allowed.

I left Wild Bill to his dog training and made my way to the jail. When I got there, there were three miners I'd never met before demanding to know how to get in touch with the man looking to buy silver claims.

"I don't know where he is. His name is Sherwood Floop. If you see him, you'll know it. Look for a man with a big belly and a mustache that looks like horns."

"*That* guy?"

I nodded.

"He was in Kate's restaurant making a spectacle of himself."

"His very presence is a spectacle," I said.

"Well, where can we find him now? We need to do this before he comes to his senses, the dumb bastard."

"Come to the saloon tonight. He said he'd be spending a lot of time there."

I left the miners and walked into the empty jail and sat down at my desk and immediately fell asleep. Sally never knew it, but a lot of time when I was sitting in jail, I was taking involuntary naps. There wasn't anything to do—and so that's what I did. Marlowe hadn't been wrong about how easy it is to fall asleep when it's hot out.

I don't know how long I was asleep. When I woke up,

nothing had changed except for Tiny standing in the doorway. His shadow was so big he blocked out almost all the light. He just stood there, blinking and not saying anything. Such was the way with Tiny.

"I don't need you today, Tiny," I said. "No one's in jail at the moment."

"Miners," Tiny said.

That's all I was getting from Tiny, so I got up from my chair and pushed Tiny out of the way, and there was Potter Ding, preparing to knock on the door.

"Sheriff! It's the miners! There's more than thirty of them, all hanging outside the saloon!"

The miners could sometimes get grumpy, so I took one of my shiny Winchester '73s off the wall, and sent Tiny on his way, and locked the jail behind me. I didn't really need the rifle, but I just liked holding it. It was one of my favorite possessions. The very apex of rifle design, and easy on the eyes too!

I walked into the middle of Main Street and looked over, and, sure enough, the miners were all grouped up outside my saloon—which didn't open until after noon. If they were to all make a clammer at once, demanding to have Sherwood buy up their silver claims all at the same time, he might flee the town and give up on his scheme. Which, to be fair, I didn't want to happen—because I'd seen for myself how much one flush miner could drink, and I wanted more.

"Okay, Potter, here's what I want you to do. Go down there and write all of their names on a piece of paper. Bring the paper back to me, and I will have Sherwood work his way through the list."

"What if they don't know their own names?" Potter asked.

I hadn't thought of that because that was a ridiculous notion. Potter Ding mostly just wandered around town. I'd never seen him do anything other than deal Faro from time to time in the saloon. I was thinking maybe he might just be a fool.

"Potter, I appreciate the question. But let's hold off on worrying about that possibility unless it comes to pass."

"Okay," Potter said, and he wandered off towards the saloon.

———

Later that afternoon, I walked down the stairs from my home into the saloon and walked to the front and opened the door to find Sherwood standing there. His head was tilted down, and he seemed to be asleep on his feet like a horse.

Then his head popped up and he said, "At last! Capital!" He patted me on the back and let out his bark of a laugh and walked into the saloon. Wild Bill was already sipping on a bourbon. He had easy access to the saloon since he was staying upstairs with me. I had heard him earlier playing a game of billiards with himself, taking advantage of having the entire saloon to himself.

"Sherwood, I've gone ahead and made a list of a few miners who have expressed interest in your offer."

I handed Sherwood the piece of paper. "Ah! Quite a long list indeed! Might I ask you how many miners have claims here in Silver Vein?"

"More than that," I lied. That list had just about every single miner on it—and all of them were desperate for Sherwood's money. O'Malley had clearly done a good job of spreading the word.

"I see. Good then. Capital! You see, I'm not looking to buy the town! If I did that, why, I'd be the only person in the saloon!"

"It's happened before," I said. "Not here in Silver Vein, but over in Hutton. Some rancher, Coop Purtle, bought up everything in the town, and since nobody liked him, because he'd bought everything, nobody wanted to pay him rent."

"What a sallyprattle!" Sherwood exclaimed. "What happened?"

"One morning the whole town up and left, leaving him in a town all by himself. He tried to trick people into moving into the town, but it didn't work, because nobody wanted to move to a town that didn't have any people in it. Now the town is falling into ruin except for old Coop's house, where he lives to this day by himself."

"Why Curly, what a story that is! Well, you can rest easy! I have no intention of buying this town. If I were going to buy a town, it would be New York City. Or Boston. Not some—well, anyway, let's just say this town would need *a lot* of refinements before I would even consider it worthy of purchase. No, I'm only interested in silver. It is silver that's going to allow me to become New York City's first king."

"Now that is a foolishness," Wild Bill said. "I've been to New York City, and the people of that town would thumb their nose at any king. They're the rudest people on this here earth! Totally full of themselves!"

"On this, Mister—"

"Hickok."

"Very good. Capital! A most wonderful name! Your opinion of New York City is exactly in accord with my own. When I triumph and return to New York covered in laurels and acclaim, my first order of business, you will be happy to learn, will be to kick every New Yorker out of the city and start anew with a better class of people!"

"I'll drink to that," Wild Bill said; though, in fairness, he said that to just about everything. His bourbon consumption was something to behold.

"Yes, let us have a drink, Mr. Hickok! It has been a long

wait!" Sherwood walked past me and slapped his hand on the bar, looking around.

"I see," he said. "Curly, I believe you need more bartenders."

"There's only three people in here, and I'm one of them," I said, walking behind the bar.

"There's the man I'm looking for," Wild Bill said. "You got me yesterday. Today's gonna be a different story." I looked over and saw Tad Bowltree walking in. He was sporting a new top-hat.

"Do you know, Wild Bill—"

"Wild Bill Hickok!" Sherwood cried. "Why, do you know, I almost saw that circus you were in! And I bought a book that you were on the cover of! Unfortunately, I'm not a fan of animals—well, except for my horse, Juniper—so I never saw you in person, but I took a sporting lady to dinner, and she knew someone who knew some lady that saw it and she said there was a lot of mud and dirt involved. Can't remember her name at the moment, but she smelled like syrup."

"I don't think you would have liked the circus," Wild Bill said. "I didn't enjoy it—and I was in it!"

"I see, Mr. Hickok, that you can already tell I'm not a trivial man. Curly, I will have one of your bourbons. I've grown to like the stuff since I have no choice."

Tad sat down at the back table with Wild Bill and the two started to play cards. Every once in a while, I would hear Wild Bill curse or Tad Bowltree cry out in triumph. Once Wild Bill even stood up and threatened to hack one of Tad's ears off.

Wyatt Gilmore came in, all covered up in trail dust. He and Tack Randle, his business partner, had a large spread almost a day's ride southeast of town. He was a big friendly guy who looked like he wanted nothing more than to shoot you dead. The reason he looked so scary was he had a scar that crawled down his face from the tip of his scalp to the bottom of his chin.

"Afternoon, Curly."

"Wyatt, how're things?"

"Could sure use some rain."

That's what Wyatt always said. All the boys and home-steaders lived the entirety of their lives wondering whether it was going to rain or not. The way I saw it, you couldn't move into a desert and complain that there was no rain. Silver Vein was a town plopped down in the middle of what was one big desert. And deserts were known almost entirely for their lack of rain.

"You'll have to settle for whisky," I said.

"My God, man! What has happened to your face!" Sherwood cried.

Wyatt turned and took Sherwood in. The big belly resting on the bar. The outlandish mustache. The extremely tall top-hat. The jodhpurs and hosiery and high-heel boots. The red powder on his cheeks...

"Horse kicked me some years ago," Wyatt said.

"Which is precisely why I'm not a cow-boy," Sherwood said, patting his belly like a pet. "But I *am* curious about your sort. As you can well see, I'm rather established here at the end of the bar. Why don't you come down here and talk? I'll stand you to as many drinks as will be required to loosen you up. You seem rather tightly wound to say the very least!"

"Well," Wyatt said, "free drinks sounds pretty good." He took his glass of bourbon and went and sat down a cautious couple of stools away from Sherwood.

"Damn your damned eyes goddamnit! You didn't have anything at all?"

"I just like to see the money on the table go up," Tad said.

"You called and raised with, let's see here...a pair of twos and three other cards that go together in no way at all!"

"I guess so."

"And I folded with three nines!"

"This is so," Tad said.

"You are a rotten bastard. Are you toying with me?"

"I don't believe so. I'm a loser at cards. Have been my whole life."

"Deal!" Wild Bill barked.

The saloon doors flapped and Baxter and Merle walked in already arguing. Soon they would set to whomping each other.

"It was mine! You had no right to it!" Baxter said.

"How was I to know?"

"You should know!"

"I had no idea it was your dead squirrel."

"You find a dead squirrel and you just throw it away? Who does that?"

"Everybody but you," Merle said.

"I could have—"

"What? What could you have done with a smelly squirrel carcass?"

"Well, we'll never know now, will we? Because that option no longer exists!"

Baxter leaned over the billiard table and hit the cue ball with such force it jumped off the table and rolled into the wall.

"It ain't the white ball's fault," Merle said.

Baxter took a deep breath, and his shoulders drooped. "It's just a disappointment is all. Next time let me know what dead critters you come across."

"To be honest, I didn't even think about it," Merle admitted, lining up his shot.

"Thinking, Merle, is all I'm asking you to do," Baxter said.

———

The afternoon proceeded normally. Other than Tad actually beating someone at cards, and Sherwood heedlessly insulting one person after another, and Frank Yonder the town minister telling Wild Bill he was going to hell if he didn't give up his guns and start going to his church, nothing of note happened.

But one of the things about being a sheriff is, just when you relax and let down your guard and get drunk, something happens that requires your attention.

Such was the case now as Pap Kickins came screaming into the saloon like someone had set fire to his pants. "Sheriff!" he wailed, looking in every direction except behind the bar, which is where I always was when I wasn't napping the afternoon away at the jail. He even ran over to the piano and screamed at it.

"It's Sheriff Langtry! He needs help!" He was waving a telegram around.

"I'm right here, Pap," I yelled. But he was all but deaf, and so went right on wailing. So I walked from behind the bar and took the telegram from his hand.

Well, Curly, looks like I've done it again. Reckon this could be it for me if you don't come save my bacon. I'm up and held hostage in my own jail.

   -Ike Langtry

"Not this time," I said, shaking my head.

"But he's the last one!" Pap said. Which was true. At one point, not really all that long ago, there had been at least four of them. Four different Sheriff Langtry's, all in different frontier towns. One of them had even been Sheriff of Silver Vein. Right up until he got kilt taking a piss outside the livery one night. Another Sheriff Langtry died in a gunfight, a gunfight in which he forgot to even draw his gun, which, at any rate, didn't have any bullets in it. Yet another one had been bushwhacked—by his own deputy—while chasing after bandits on the border.

Which left us with only one Sheriff Langtry left. They were not and had never been—it was agreed by one and all—good lawmen. Ike Langtry had survived longer than his brothers, but not because he was any good at his job. Mostly, it was because he was the sheriff of Hendrix, which had no more than a hundred people living in it. As a town, there wasn't much to it. If you'd been on the trail sleeping in the dirt for days, and you made your way to Hendrix, you would probably just want to turn around and go back out into the dirt.

A couple of years ago, then sheriff Jim Shepland had to go to Hendrix to free Ike Langtry from a smokehouse a homesteading family from Sweden had locked him into. He might be the only one of the Sheriff Langtrys still above ground—but that didn't mean he wasn't unlucky.

"Reckon we gotta go save him?" Baxter asked. He was now playing a game of billiards with Deedee Yonder. And he was, as usual, letting her win. He'd beaten her one time a while back, and she got mad and took a swipe at him with the long knife she kept lashed to her hip, and half his eyebrow went missing.

Merle was always trying to get Baxter in trouble, and he was doing it now. "Why Deedee, can't you tell that Baxter isn't even trying?"

"Now Merle, let's not—"

"Don't you take it easy on me," Deedee growled.

Baxter put his pool cue down. "I reckon we'll never know. We have to go save the Sheriff!" He walked away from the table fast enough to avoid anything she might try behind his back.

Baxter and Merle walked over to the bar. Frank Yonder, who had been napping at one of the tables, woke up when Deedee smacked him in the head with the billiard cue. "Wake up! You have to play me in billiards!"

Frank, rubbing his face, which had a rather pronounced crease on it where the table had been serving as a pillow, said, "Aw, Deedee, do I?" But he knew the answer to that question, and so he grumbled his way to his feet and made his way to the billiard table like a fella about to get his neck stretched.

"You gonna save him?" Pap screamed, three feet away from me.

"Will you pipe down, Pap, goddamnit. I'm right in front of you for the sake of Adam. I suppose I *have* to save him," I said. "He's the last one, after all."

———

About ten minutes later, before I'd really put too much thought in exactly *how* I was going to save Sheriff Langtry, Wild Bill finally got drunk enough to be in a good mood. He stood up to show off his new outfit to Tad Bowltree—a man with no interest at all in fashion judging by his choice of clothing.

"You were absolutely right, Curly," Wild Bill said, turning in a circle, "Ely Turner is a money-grubbing skunk. But I don't feel right unless I look good. At this point, it would be disappointing for people to see me looking rumpled. Since I am no longer incognito, I have no choice, you see, but to be the most Wild Bill I can."

"Okay," I said.

"You like the waistcoat? I think it's quite serviceable."

"It is a nice waistcoat," Baxter gushed.

"You don't even like waistcoats," Merle said.

"Of course I do. I always have!"

"You're just kissing up to Wild Bill so he'll help you with your quickdraw."

"What?" Baxter asked, quite loudly, looking around the mostly empty saloon. "Why that is a ridiculous thing to say! If Wild Bill wants to help me with my quickdraw, I reckon that's his business. And I would certainly not object if he were to do so."

Wild Bill ignored Baxter, and turned back to me, an eager light in his eyes, and said, "Tell me about this Sheriff Langtry."

"Baxter, you tell him. I ain't got the wind," I said. So Baxter, with Merle adding a detail and an insult here and there, got out the whole story of all the different Sheriff Langtry's, and all the various ways they had all ended up kilt.

"It's like the Earp Brothers, only they're all idiots," Wild Bill said, nodding. "Which means they are probably Texans. What is the difference between a longhorn and a Texan?"

"One's a cow and one ain't," Merle said.

"Nope. Anyone else want to take a guess?"

Nobody did.

"Well, there *ain't* no difference. They both have the same amount of brain in their head, and not either one of them ever uses it."

"This *is* Texas," I pointed out uselessly. I was starting to learn that once Wild Bill got wound up, there wasn't much point in getting him pointed any other way than the way he wanted to go.

"Well, I'd say this would be a good thing for my book, Curly, as there is bound to be action, so I will go along with you fellas if you don't mind. I don't reckon there's much point in being in Silver Vein, Curly, if you're gonna be off somewhere else. This town has the personality of a rug!"

We sat around talking about going to Hendrix, and at the same time we were talking about it, we were still drinking whisky, so we never did make all that much progress. At one point, I forgot about saving Sheriff Langtry in the entirety, which is not a proud thing to say coming from a sheriff.

Then Sally came down into the saloon, which she only usually did when it was just me and Jeffers in there. It wasn't that she wasn't allowed to—she wasn't confined to her room like Katie Milton, she was allowed to freely roam wherever she wanted. She chose not to go into the saloon, because the miners and cow-boys couldn't help but ogle her like a beef-steak, the lusty fools. Sally was far and away the most beautiful woman in Silver Vein. But that didn't mean she took to getting gawked at by perverts.

"Curly, I got something I need you to see. Well, I guess you all can see it too if you want. Curly, you're going to want to see this, as much as you've been talking about it."

We all looked at her, except for Micah, who was asleep, and that set her to blushing, and her blushing, for reasons that go beyond anything that makes any sense at all, got me to blushing too.

Instead of going back upstairs, she went to the back door of the saloon and opened it. "Come on Curly! Come see what Horse can do!"

This had me intrigued. Horse was an exceptional horse, even if I never did get around to giving him a proper name. He was the former sheriff's horse, and the sheriff had bought him off some soldier who had done all the training. He was a warhorse and wasn't afraid of anything. He had once dragged me through a burning house, giving me no say in the matter. He was a tall, black, prancy horse, with a handsome white blaze on his forehead, and his two front legs had what looked like fresh white stockings on them. I'd never loved any horse as much as I loved Horse.

I stumbled out from behind the bar and followed Sally out the backdoor of the saloon to where the corral was. There was Horse, who I think I have already gushed about enough, and, also in the corral was a horse on the completely other side of the spectrum. Molly had once been a stout quarter horse who liked to run, but now she'd grown fat and lazy, and didn't really care to be a horse at all. She'd up and turned herself into a hog basically. She was fat as an outhouse, and twice as lazy.

"I was down here having a conversation with Horse—"

"Did the horse keep up his side of it?" Wild Bill asked, "or did you do all the talking?"

"Horse doesn't talk, but he's a great listener," Sally said, taking him seriously. "Anyway I was rubbing horse's face and then I went and was rubbing on his right ear like this, and I said, "There now, and—"

As she said that, and touched Horse's ear, he immediately flopped to the ground.

"It can't be," I said, looking at Horse in awe and wonder. I had been trying to teach him to flop to the ground ever since I got him. It was something I'd seen Frank Kilhoe, the former Texas Ranger and famous bounty hunter, do with his horse— and I'd been trying to get Horse to flop to the ground ever since.

And all along he knew how!

"Let me try it!" I said. We told Horse to stand up again, and he obliged. I reached up and rubbed on Horse's left ear, and said, "There, now,"—and nothing at all happened.

"Wrong ear," Sally said.

Very specific. Okay. So I reached over to the right ear and said, "There now..." And once again Horse flopped to the ground, and then I went and laid down on top of him. "Horse," I whispered in his furry velvety ear, "I love you. You are the greatest horse that ever lived."

"That ain't all that much of a trick," Wild Bill said, "but I'll concede that it's useful on the flat plains. My horse, which I got in New York, can walk backwards just by me telling it to. Penn can also hold an umbrella with his teeth, which is something of no use at all outside of a circus."

"Dang," Baxter said, "why would any horse ever need to hold an umbrella?"

"It would if it was raining. Ain't that right, Wild Bill?" Merle asked.

"No, it wouldn't. And that's one of the reasons I quit the

circus. Not much of anything in a circus makes any sense anywhere else."

"I don't plan to ever see a circus," Merle said.

"Me neither Wild Bill. Not if it's as you say," Baxter added, mostly so Merle wouldn't get the last word.

After seeing Horse's new trick, we all tromped back into the saloon. I was off in my own world, thinking of all the ways I could get the drop on outlaws now that I knew Horse could flop to the ground. We went back to plotting how we were going to save Sheriff Langtry, with Wild Bill not saying a word the entire time, until he finally said: "I reckon I've got it figured out."

And his plan is the one we went with.

7

That night, the whole town found their way into the saloon to eavesdrop and make fools of themselves—all trying to get a Wild Bill story to tell. Tad Bowltree, the disgraced banker, was sitting at the back table, sporting a new white shirt with no food on it and new pants, in addition to the new top-hat—and still confounding Wild Bill at cards. I must have watched him win twenty straight hands. Something I would have said was impossible.

Tad had fallen on hard times some time ago. When he'd run the bank in town, he'd dressed the part. But that was a long time ago. Now, he no longer bothered much with his appearance, and he bathed infrequently to say the least. And yet now he had fresh new clothes and most of Wild Bill's money.

Next to him was Ely Turner, who never came to the saloon, as he was cheap, which meant he must have seen Wild Bill as someone to sell more stuff to. He would occasionally laugh, sometimes even if nothing funny was happening, and I felt sorry for his relatives—if he had any.

Baxter and Merle were trying to play Faro, but Potter Ding was too distracted listening to Wild Bill tell stories that he kept forgetting to do his job. He would lean out of his chair and hold his head to the side, and then either shake his head in confusion or laugh and nod his head.

"That is a handsome waistcoat," Ely Turner said, nodding at Wild Bill.

"It does suit me," Wild Bill said, "but I think you would admit you charged more than was probably required. I expect you made a tidy profit."

"Making money is not a crime. And Silver Vein isn't exactly New York City. Merchandise takes a hard road to get here."

"I don't take exception to you charging more than a fella is prone to expect, but I do *not* appreciate you trying to drum up business while I'm trying to play poker. The poker table is a sacred place."

"It's church that's sacred!" Frank Yonder cried out from the billiard table, wild eyed—for which he got no response at all.

Ely Turner, not paying any heed to the obvious fact that he was getting on Wild Bill's nerves, shook his head and laughed at Wild Bill as if he'd just heard a funny story instead of Bill warning him off.

"Well told, my good friend! Well told indeed!" Ely chortled.

Wild Bill responded by placing a knife on the table. "I have too much respect for Curly to poke a hole in you with my pistol, so if you laugh again, I'll just have to reach over there and stab you in the ribs."

Ely Turner shot up from the table and walked quickly out of the saloon, forgetting all about owing me money for his drink. One of Ely Turner's great gifts was being almost completely disagreeable. I bet he owed me for dozens of drinks over the years, and every time I thought about bringing it up, I would remember that it would require engaging him in conversation, and thus give up on the effort. And I bet I wasn't alone. I was surprised how long it took Wild Bill to get tired of the man.

"I'll take five cards," Tad said.

"You might just want to fold," Wild Bill said. "When you get to the point where not a single card is worth having, it's best to just fold. I've told you that a dozen times already." He nevertheless dealt Tad five new cards.

"Ooh!" Tad said, "I will call you and then raise you."

"If you think I'm falling for that, old man, you got another thing coming. I will raise your raise and then raise again!" Wild Bill said.

"And I believe I will accept your raise and raise that raise even more."

"Damn your ever-confounding eyes, on this hand I will not yield. I'm on to you! Call!" Wild Bill barked, looking sadly at his remaining pile of coins, and taking a long slug of bourbon.

"I have four of the seven cards," Tad said. "Two red ones and two black ones. That, and an Ace."

"Four sevens and an ace. You mean to tell me you turned in all five of your cards and that's what you got back?"

"Indeed," Tad said, raking all of the coins, most of which started out as his, back into the same pockets from which they came.

"Again?" Tad asked, raising an eyebrow.

"Sure thing," Wild Bill said, spending the next twenty minutes meticulously shuffling the cards and grumbling to himself.

8

The only problem with Wild Bill's plan was it required more people. Silver Vein was filled up mostly with people who had either fled from danger or were hoping to avoid it altogether. It was a peaceful town where people kept their heads down and avoided conflict. Nobody in Silver Vein would even consider helping us. So I was hoping I could wrangle a few volunteers from the T Bar ranch as it was out of town to the north, on the way over to Hendrix.

It was early in the morning when I got up and walked to Bill's room and found him using a variety of brushes on his hair. There were five of them, more brushes than I had owned in my entire life, all sitting next to one another on the bed. They came in different shapes and sizes. I didn't say anything, because the efforts he was going to, and the way he was going about it, seemed too intimate for another person to witness. I would have rather barged in on him naked than seen him playing with his hair the way he was going about it. My hair was too thick for a hairbrush to navigate. And if I had let it grow, I reckon it would have probably grown straight out like a bright red bush.

I left Wild Bill with his brushes and went out the back door and down the stairs to the corral. The town was asleep, and it was quite nippy at that early morning hour. I had on the winter coat I'd broken down and bought from Ely Turner during a momentary bout of gullibility; but, just like when I bought it, it didn't seem prepared for winter at all. But it was better than nothing, and my buffalo robe was working double duty as a blanket on the bed—and, as such, was currently being used by Sally and the dog.

Molly, my old horse—the one we both were happy that I was now neglecting—was asleep standing up with her tongue hanging out. Either that or she was pretending. Either way, I wasn't about to turn my back on her or she'd take a chunk out of my rear end. She was by now more wide than tall. In fact, if she were to lay on her side, a fella could be excused for thinking she'd grown a foot taller.

Horse, by contrast, was not only awake, but looking right at me. He had a questioning look in his eyes, which meant he was trying to figure out if I was bringing him an apple or a carrot. I walked around the corral until Molly was out of my line of sight, because, while she was fat as an outhouse, she loved an apple just as much as the next horse. But I only had the one apple, and it was for Horse.

I walked up and started whispering in his ear and scratching his muzzle. I wanted to flop him to the ground, but I knew it wouldn't be fair. Flopping to the ground, for a horse, is a bit of a process, which is why both of my horses slept standing up. I promised myself I would only flop Horse to the ground when I really needed it.

He nodded his head up and down in excitement and stamped one of his hooves in the dust. I knew if I held out any longer, he would let out a whinny and wake up half the town, so I snaked my hand into my back pocket and fished the apple out and he eagerly chomped into it. He went slightly cross-eyed and set to foaming at the mouth, and a green slime of horse drool emerged and started dripping off his face. He was in horse heaven.

"We're off to save Sheriff Langtry again," I told him. He nodded and kept on chewing. I pulled out a brush from another pocket and started working him over, sneaking looks behind me as I did to make sure Molly wasn't about to make a go at me. Then I put his blanket on, making sure there were no wrinkles in it, and saddled him up. I figured I'd let him walk around with the saddle on so he would understand he was getting ready to be put into work mode.

Once he was used to being saddled up, I opened the gate in the corral and walked him through. Then I walked him down the alley between my saloon and the falling-to-pieces courthouse and walked him to the front of the saloon and told him not to go anywhere. It was still cold enough to see my breath, so I walked around back and up the stairs into the house and set to making coffee.

Jeffers showed up at the back door just like he did most mornings.

"Morning Sheriff," he said.

"Call me Curly," I said, just like I always did.

"Whatever you say, Sheriff." No matter how much I tried, I could never get Jeffers to call me anything but sheriff. I let him in, and he sat down at the kitchen table and took off his hat. The only place he ever relaxed and took his hat off was around Sally and me.

It was Jeffers's morning routine to sip coffee with me and Sally and talk about food. Sally was a good cook, and I had a belly that welcomed just about anything, and we enjoyed our morning discussions.

"I always feel like stew when it's cold like this," Jeffers said, "but in a couple of hours it's gonna be hot enough to boil apples on the boardwalk."

"And that's the truth," I said, nodding. "You're going to have to keep an eye on Micah for me while I'm gone."

"If he gets to 'cleaning the bottles,' I'll stab him with a fork."

"You won't stab him at all. Not anymore. We've been over that."

"I reckon stabbing Micah was one of the highlights of my life," Jeffers said, sighing.

"It was only a one-time thing. If Spack Watson hadn't been semi-conscious, old Micah might have ended up having to get his leg hacked off."

"Fine!" Jeffers said. Despite his rough talk, I knew that he and Micah were secretly good friends.

Sally walked into the kitchen wearing the buffalo robe and sat down. It was her way of letting me know I would have to leave the robe with her.

"Morning Sally, I was just talking to the sheriff about what to make today."

"You can never go wrong with biscuits and gravy," Sally said. "It goes well with drinking. Sticks to a fella's ribs." She walked into the kitchen and grabbed a couple of coffee cups and came back and sat down.

"What's the extra coffee cup for?" Jeffers asked, looking around. He could be jumpy around strangers.

"I reckon it's for me," Wild Bill said. He was wearing his new get up, and his hair tumbled down in a feathery cascade around his head like a hair halo. Wild Bill walked over and leaned down over Jeffers, looking down at his scalp like it was some sort of treasure map.

"The fella that did this was a professional," Wild Bill said, nodding in appreciation. "One with a quality knife too."

"Wild Bill, this here is Jeffers. He works in the bar, but you might have overlooked him on account of I make him wear a big hat."

"In the back," Wild Bill said, nodding. "The cook."

Jeffers nodded, and even smiled, despite his clear discomfort.

"I don't think, Bill," Sally delicately said, "that he admires his scalping as such."

Wild Bill pulled a flask out of his new waistcoat and dumped a healthy amount of morning bourbon into his coffee cup. "No," he said, "I reckon not. I meant no offense Jeff..."

"Jeffers," Jeffers said.

"I meant no offense Jeffers. But I have seen my share of scalpings over the years, and sometimes I can't help but bring forth my experienced opinion on the matter."

"Well, you ain't the first. Hap Morgan, the ranger, or used to be ranger, whatever the hell he is, he inspects the top of my head every time he sees me. Says he can't help himself."

"I think biscuits and gravy is a good idea," I said, changing the subject before Sally could air out her insides right on the breakfast table.

There was a sudden booming noise coming from the back door, a knocking so loud it could only be Baxter and Merle. They weren't allowed inside the house anymore, as Sally had forbidden them after they'd destroyed their sixth breakfast table chair. Not on purpose, mind you. Destruction just came naturally to them. I got up and walked over and opened the door.

"Morning," Baxter said.

"Morning," Merle said.

"Good morning to you too Wild Bill," Baxter said, removing his hat and smiling like he'd just been given a new knife. I could see that he was smitten with Wild Bill and thought of him almost as some sort of toy.

"Baxter," Wild Bill said, tipping his coffee cup in his direction.

"Lordy. He knows my name..." Baxter said to himself out loud.

Sally stood up and walked into the kitchen and came back with two bundles of jerky. "For your saddlebags," Sally said. She doted on Baxter and Merle, and ignored their many flaws, turning the other way when they would get upset and whomp on somebody. Unlike myself, Sally was quite forgiving when it came to Baxter and Merle.

"Sun is starting to warm up the outside," Baxter said. "Reckon we should hit the trail soon."

"Baxter is right," Wild Bill said. "For this plan, we need everyone in place at the right time."

So, we all got up and Sally put a somewhat smaller bundle of jerky in my bag. The last time I'd gone off on the trail, I'd come back heavier than when I left, so now Sally managed my food intake, which I found embarrassing but impossible to stop.

"Bill, you keep a good eye on Curly," Sally said, giving me a hug and a smooch on the neck, something she knew would cause my whole neck to turn red. "Don't let him do anything stupid."

"I'll do my best," Wild Bill said.

———

It was mid-morning, and we were in the saloon doing some last-minute strategizing. We were also looking at our weapons supply and making sure everything worked. Wild Bill was practicing his quick draws and Baxter was sharpening one of his knives and I was looking at my Winchesters in appreciation of their shiny beauty. We all had our guns in our hands in one way or another.

So, it was certainly bad timing that a group of four men with bags over their heads should choose that precise time to come bursting through the saloon doors. They barged in to find themselves not catching anyone by surprise but themselves.

Sooner than they probably would have said was possible, they had eight different guns pointed at them.

"Oh," one of the men with a bag on his head said.

Another said, "Hey Mulvaney, I thought you said—"

"Quiet! Let me think!" the first man said.

"Hey Mulvaney!" I said. "That you under there?"

"No," Mulvaney said.

"Yes," one of the other men said.

"Could be," Mulvaney said, "we've made a mistake. I can see that you folks are busy."

"Did Milton send you?" I asked.

"No," Mulvaney said.

"Yes," someone else said. "He didn't say nothing about no Wild Bill Hickok or Curly Barnes though." The man put his guns away.

"Why are you here?" I asked. "The trial is in Amarillo."

"Not no more," Mulvaney said. "You ain't heard?"

"Heard what?" I asked.

"That Stephens boy escaped from the house they were keeping him in during the trial, and then up and came to Milton and made right off with Katie. So, um, that's why we're here. Have you seen them by chance?"

"Mulvaney," I said, "take that damned bag off of your head. I already know it's you."

Mulvaney looked around, came to a decision, and pulled the bag off his head.

"So you came in here, the four of you, with bags on your heads, because you wanted to ask and see if I've seen the Stephens boy and Katie Milton?" I asked.

"I can see how it might not look as innocent as it is," Mulvaney said.

The other three men pulled the bags off their heads.

"Milton has gone too far," one of the men said. His face was red and sweaty from being stuck inside a burlap sack. "And I would just like, on, I think, behalf of all of us, to apologize to you fine men for our behavior."

"This was a rude intrusion, I reckon," one of the other men said. "If you don't mind, let's just forget all this."

"Yes, please," a third man said. "Forgetting all this sounds like a good idea indeed."

"Put your guns and bags on the bar," I said. "That's as good a place as any to start."

All of the men immediately dumped their holster guns and waistband guns and shoulder guns and boot guns, as well as all their many varieties of knives, onto the bar. I put my Colts back in my holster and collected their weaponry. It was an impressive haul.

It was clear that none of the four men Mulvaney brought with him posed any threat at all. They were, to a man, adamant about not wanting to get in any sort of scrap, in any way at all, with the likes of me and Wild Bill. That's one of the upsides of being a famous lawman. Sometimes, all it took was my name for people to give up on any criminal behavior.

"Mulvaney, here's what's going to happen. We're all going to have a toot of bourbon to honor the fact that you didn't make us kill you. That would have been messy and pointless. After that toot of bourbon, you, Mulvaney, are going to walk down the Main Street boardwalk, knock on the jail door, and tell Deedee Yonder that you want her to lock you up."

"Aw, Sheriff, that ain't—"

"You came in here, Mulvaney, with guns out and bags over your heads. You're getting off easy."

"Too easy," one of his men said.

"In the morning, you will be let out of jail, and you will then ride on down to Milton and tell old Sam that you don't know where his Katie ran off to with Taylor Stephens, but they ain't in Silver Vein, and that if he knows what's good for him, he'll let the matter rest."

"I'm sure to catch a bunch of abuse if I do that," Mulvaney said. "I'd rather stay in jail, I expect."

"I'll tell you one thing, Sheriff," one of Mulvaney's men said. "I am retired as of right now. You can keep my guns. And I for one will never set foot in the town of Milton again!"

"Curly," Wild Bill said, reluctantly putting his guns away, "I believe I can see why people don't try to assassinate you. For a sheriff, you are very forgiving."

"I'll drink to that," one of Mulvaney's men said.

9

Later that morning, the three of us—myself, and Baxter and Merle—were mounted up outside the saloon. The serious heat of the day would soon arrive—and here came Wild Bill from the livery riding a tall prancing chestnut horse. I thought Horse, who was a Tennessee Walker, was a prancer, but he had nothing on Wild Bill's horse. His horse kicked its legs up so high that when it walked it almost looked like a cricket.

"I'm glad it don't have an umbrella in its teeth," Merle said.

"He bought the horse in New York City," I said. "I doubt it's ever been in the desert before."

"This here is Penn," Wild Bill said, "on account he was sired in Pennsylvania. He's five years old and full of piss and vinegar, something I can't say about your mount, Baxter."

Baxter's horse, Colonel, seemed so depressed by the prospect of hitting the trail that his head was already just about dragging in the dirt.

"Colonel may be long in the tooth, Wild Bill. But you watch, while his head might be droopy, he just keeps right on going."

Wild Bill grunted at that. He might hate Texas, and he

might hate Texans even more, but he had a lot of similarities with the Texas Ranger Frank Kilhoe. One of their similarities was the dismissive grunt. I had to admit there was one thing about Wild Bill all the dime novels got right. Nobody has ever looked better than Wild Bill Hickok when he was sitting on top of a horse.

The four of us turned our mounts north and headed out of town at an easy lope.

———

Bernie Waco owned the T Bar ranch, and while he was often grumpy and complaining, especially about the lack of rain, in the end he often did what was asked of him. As well he should, because we'd taken away his chief competition, the murderous rancher Torp Mayfair, whose scalp was at that very moment nailed to the wall in the jail as a reminder of what happened to those who crossed over into villainy.

We got to Bernie's ranch in the middle of the afternoon, and it's a miracle we got there at all. Wild Bill's horse might have been able to walk backwards and parade around with an umbrella in his mouth, but one of the things he didn't seem cut out for was walking. Not for very long anyway. The fact that Baxter's old nag had outperformed a horse that Wild Bill had clearly paid too much money for had put Wild Bill into a deeper mope than normal. Not one to give in to obvious defeat, he blamed a number of factors, including humidity, and a lack of quality oats, as factors. At one point, Penn thought he saw something to eat and leaned down and the bush he thought was food unleashed a bunch of thorns into his face. He almost bucked Wild Bill off in his agony. Which all meant that we didn't make very good time, as we were always having to wait for Wild Bill and his city horse to catch up.

"Camel," Wild Bill said, as he pulled up to the front of the T

Bar—and his horse, sure enough, squatted down on the ground like a camel to let Wild Bill dismount.

"That is some trick," Baxter said, trying to cheer Wild Bill up.

"An old Sioux trainer works for Bill Cody thought that one up. It goes over well with the audience."

I got off Horse like a normal person, as did everybody else, and we shook out our legs and I twisted around to get my back working again. I walked up and called to Bernie's house, and someone was sent to fetch him, so we set about drinking coffee and letting our horses lip up some water from a trough.

The T Bar was a big spread, and it was almost an hour before Bernie Waco finally dismounted from his sweaty horse and greeted us.

"The big cows get it, but the little ones are still ensnarling themselves in the barbed wire," Bernie said. I didn't know what he was talking about, because barbed wire at that time was a new phenomenon, and Bernie was ahead of the game compared to the other ranchers.

"Okay," I said. "Hello to you too, Bernie. We come in need of a small favor."

"What kind of favor?" Bernie asked, immediately on guard.

"It doesn't, just so you know," I assured him, before he could work himself into a panic, "involve anyone dying or getting dragged behind a horse or set upon by a gang of bandits. Do you know Sheriff Langtry over in Hendrix?"

"Aw," Bernie said, relaxing, "what's that old fool gotten himself involved in this time?"

"We don't know all the particulars, but it seems he's managed to get himself holed up as a prisoner inside his own jail. We don't know how many there are of them that's got him, but we do know how many of us we want them to believe we are—and to do that we need four volunteers. Now, before you start worrying, all we will ask them to do is make us look like a larger group than we are."

"Who's that fella you got with you?" Bernie asked, squinting at Wild Bill. "I have been made to understand from one of my hands that he sits his horse like one of us cow-boys."

I looked at Wild Bill, not knowing how he wanted to introduce himself. "I've spent many years looking at the world from atop a horse. The name's Bill Hickok."

I don't know why he left the 'Wild' off, because almost immediately Bernie said, "Wild Bill Hickok?"

"One and the same." The two men shook hands. Then Wild Bill leaned in and said, "I might have one more favor to ask you." Then the two of them walked off away from us, laughed a time or two, and then Bernie walked over to Wild Bill's horse, nodded a couple of times, and walked off.

"What was that all about?" I asked.

"Horse talk," Wild Bill said, kicking at the dirt with one of his tall leather boots.

Bernie Waco came back leading a tall Appaloosa gelding with long floppy brown hair that spilled down over his eyes. "This here horse was born and raised in the desert. Has plenty of wind. He's one of my personal mounts. We'll take that city horse off your hands until you get back. Do you want to take him for a test ride?" Wild Bill looked from his horse to the Appaloosa and back. Then he said, "I better explain things first," and he walked over and started whispering in Penn's ear as he unbuckled the saddle and removed his saddlebags and rifle scabbard.

"It's okay now," Wild Bill said, "Penn is upset, but he understands." He handed the reins over to Bernie and exchanged them for the reins of the Appaloosa. Then Wild Bill started whispering to the Appaloosa as he saddled him up. Then he hopped up on the horse without using the stirrups like I'd seen my Comanche friend Scout do a few times. Wild Bill put the horse through its paces, making sure it turned the way he wanted when he wanted and all sorts of other things his actual horse hadn't been up to the task to accomplish.

"I ain't gonna run across some Comanche wants his horse back, am I? I wouldn't want to have to get into some scrap because I'm sitting on a stolen horse."

"Aw hell, that horse was raised by us here at the T Bar," Bernie said. "The only thing that could happen is you might come across some stray, and he'll want to shepherd it back here. But, since there aren't any strays in these parts, that would be a highly unlikely event. I've got a supply of oats here, so don't you worry about your horse going hungry. This is a beautiful horse, but being raised back East, he ain't got the breeding for desert life. Ain't much oats in the desert. Not enough to keep this horse fed anyway."

"I will remember you fondly in my autobiography," Wild Bill said, "what do I call this fella?"

"His official name is Spotted Rump," Bernie said.

Wild Bill nodded. "Helluva name. I'll call him Spot. Spotted Rump sounds like something you eat and wish you hadn't."

Bernie handed Wild Bill's horse to some kid who didn't look to be but fifteen and was as pale as a white rabbit. Then Bernie walked over to me and said, "I can only spare two of my hands for this adventure of yours. Stringing up barbed wire requires a lot of labor."

We all looked at Wild Bill. This was his plan, after all. He nodded. "Two can work."

"Good. These two ain't always been cowhands, so they might be more useful to you than four of my regular hands. Then he turned to an older man that had a limp and suspicious eyes and whispered in his ear. The man stood up and rolled his eyes in disgust and limped off around the house and disappeared.

"Good thing you don't have them Texas Rangers with you,

Curly. Your friend Hap might recognize one of the two men I'm getting ready to lend you. You know how it is."

I nodded. The truth is the law outside of Silver Vein, in this part of Texas, which was about as far away from Austin as a person could get and still be in the state, was murky at best. Cow hands sometimes turned rustler, and rustlers sometimes went straight. More often, they went back and forth when it suited them. A fella good with a gun was in demand on both sides of the law. In truth, Baxter and Merle were basically paid by me to be my deputies so they wouldn't jump to the other side of the law. I was curious to see who Bernie had on the payroll. His old partner, Tack Randle, had up and started a ranch of his own with Wyatt Gilmore, and the two men made a game of swiping each other's cattle. They were still friendly, and still met from time to time in my saloon, but I'd noticed a growing seriousness between them, and wondered how long they would stay friendly. It wouldn't take but one misunder-standing to turn fun cattle swiping into a real range war.

The ranch foreman came back around the house with two men leading horses. Both of the men were lean. Both had mustaches and gun belts, and both of their jaws flew open when they saw Wild Bill Hickok and Curly Barnes waiting for them.

"This here," Bernie said, "is Montana Dan." Montana Dan tipped his hat. "Last name's McIntire. Dan McIntire."

"You know how to use that Sharps Carbine?" Wild Bill asked.

Montana Dan nodded. "Wouldn't be much good carrying around a rifle I don't know how to use."

"Now that might be factually true, but I wasn't asking you for any lip. I was asking a question."

"Yes, I'm good with it up to a couple hundred yards, I reckon, depending on the wind, and the target, of course."

"Of course. And you?"

The second man looked at the foreman, and they whispered back and forth, and then the foreman said, "We've been calling him Ned."

"What, you can't remember your own name?" Baxter asked. He was staring holes through Ned. Ned shrugged but didn't say anything. I could see there was something about Ned's demeanor that Baxter didn't cotton to.

"Okay Ned. How are you with a rifle?" Wild Bill asked.

"I can shoot," he said. He said it with a certainty that told me he could shoot, and that he couldn't remember what his name was because his real name was probably on a Wanted poster, maybe even in the jail back in Silver Vein. Wild Bill must have known it, too, because he asked no more questions.

"I appreciate it Bernie," I said. "We'll get your men back to you in one piece, probably two days from now."

"I wish you luck. You're going to need it if Sheriff Langtry is involved."

10

We were an hour northeast of the T Bar when Wild Bill said, "I missed all this," gesturing at all the nothing around us. We were, at that moment surrounded by nothing but patchy yellow grass and thorny shrubs that had been charred to death by the hateful ever vengeful sun. There was hardly any water, being a desert, and so there were only the rare clumps of trees dotted infrequently here and there on the horizon. To be a rancher in these parts, you needed a lot of land. And, even if you had a lot of land, like Bernie had with the T Bar, there wasn't enough to keep your cows from being skinny. There wasn't much in the way of landmarks out here other than the trail we were on in any direction. But at least it wasn't flat.

"What?" I said, looking for something, anything, but it was all just dust and brush and waves of heat, which was something you *could* see in every direction.

"There ain't no buildings as far as the eye can see, Curly. I've been to New York City. I've seen what can happen to a place when people get to messing with it, trying to make it better. You give people enough time, I reckon they could ruin anything.

Why Curly, they've got so many buildings in that city I felt all hemmed up. It's all hubbub and mayhem! Once you've been out here, to the frontier, there's no going back. When I look out at all the buildings that aren't here yet, it relaxes me."

"The tallest building I've ever seen is the courthouse in Silver Vein," I said.

"I saw a really tall flagpole in Fort Smith, Arkansas," Baxter said.

"It was really skinny though," Merle said. "Just go on and ignore Baxter. He just felt like he needed to say something."

"Merle thinks I'm starstruck," Baxter said, letting loose with a snort of a laugh. "Which is just silly."

"I agree with Merle," I said.

"So do I," Wild Bill said. "It's normal, Baxter, to act funny around people you respect. I'm used to people acting weird around me, like that fella in the restaurant asking me for some hair. I bet you he doesn't go around to just any regular old person, asking for a lock of their hair. As for myself, I acted funny around Bill Cody, always asking him questions about business and whatnot. He's the one who told me to grow my hair long, way back when we were scouting together. His hair is long, but unlike me, he hates it, and rolls it all up and shoves it under his hat when he can."

"Well," Baxter said, "it was Curly who went through a sash phase. Not me."

I didn't say anything. I just sat on my horse looking at the trail ahead, as if what Baxter said could just drift away with the dust and be forgotten. It was true that I had, for a very short spell mind you, taken to trying to wear a sash, and I even wore my guns for a cross-draw, like Wild Bill did. But the truth was, unless you're practiced at it, wearing a sash instead of a gunbelt is awkward. Also, the barrels of the guns tend to move about when you walk and prod the nether parts.

I understood Baxter's problem, because I shared it. I also

had a habit of saying things just to say things, on account of how I was worried that people might think I was being rude if I was to just listen. I've always been a restless listener. I blame it on my mother, who always had a story to tell, yet never did anything to make any part of the story interesting. Not to a little kid anyway. Mostly, the stories involved either sewing or pickling vegetables. She would get mad if you didn't look at her while she was talking, even though if you're *really* listening you might turn your head, so the ear is facing the talker. One time when I politely turned my head to better hear what she was saying, she up and hit me with a wooden spoon.

It was awkward and quiet—and I could tell my mind was coming up with all sorts of random thoughts in order to get some distance from Baxter's sash comment.

Thankfully, because Wild Bill was in his heart a gentleman, he let that little tidbit about my sash phase die.

"I could do this all day," Wild Bill said, happily being brutalized by the hateful and vindictive desert sun.

"Good," I said. "Because we *will* be doing this all day."

"Well, I suppose that's true," Wild Bill agreed, nodding his head. "This dry air ain't good for the hair though. When it comes to hair, what you need is moisture."

"Okay," I said.

"Where are we going?" Ned asked. I'd forgotten about Dan and Ned. They'd been completely quiet and riding in the back the whole time.

I looked at Ned, and said, "Hendrix."

Ned pulled his horse to a stop, and so did Dan. "Ain't no reason to go to that place. It's a dump!"

"And it smells bad!" Montana Dan said.

"If my horse knew where we were going, it would up and commit suicide," Ned said, which I thought was a bit much.

"It's Sheriff Langtry," I said.

"Oh," Ned said. "Him."

"He *is* the last one," Montana Dan said, letting out a world-weary sigh. "I suppose Wild Bill is right. Riding through the desert heat fighting off flies will be the highlight of the day."

"Beats being in New York City," Wild Bill said. Then he asked me if there were any Comanches about. I told him the few bands that were left mostly kept to themselves and camped out in the Llano to the south.

"Then maybe it's time we did some shooting."

———

"Dang," Baxter said, looking at Wild Bill's guns. And how fast they'd gone from his sash to his hands. Baxter would find himself staring, time and again, at Bill's hands, and never did see them move. They'd be hanging at his sides, and then, faster than Baxter could think, he'd have his pistols out and pointed at Baxter's face.

"Dang," Merle said, watching. "Baxter, I reckon he just plugged you full of holes."

"Look in my eyes," Wild Bill said. His guns were now back in the sash, looking like they'd never left.

Baxter put his guns away. "I reckon your guns is lighter," Baxter said, but it was clear he didn't believe it. In fact, I was pretty sure the opposite was true. Wild Bill's guns were heavier and longer.

"The key, Baxter, is to be the decider. If you let me decide when to pull my guns, I'll beat you every time. And the key to being the decider, is not letting the other fella know what you're deciding. If my eyes move or twitch, you will get the drop on me."

"Okay," Baxter said.

"Did you see anything?" Wild Bill asked.

"Dang," Merle said. Baxter had made no move for his guns at all, and somehow Wild Bill's were in his hands again.

"How did—"

"Let me give it a go," Ned said.

"Suit yourself," Baxter said, slumping away. I would need to find a way to get Baxter to cheer up again. Maybe I could let him stab someone in Hendrix. The sight of blood tended to kindle Baxter and Merle's spirits.

Ned said, "You don't mind Wild Bill, I'm not going to look at your eyes. I can see how helpful that was for Baxter." This made Merle laugh. I could see that Ned and Baxter were not going to be friends.

Wild Bill had his arms crossed, and an easy smile on his face. Pulling guns faster than anyone had ever pulled guns before put Wild Bill in a happy place, all moping forgotten.

The first time Ned stared at Wild Bill's hands, but that didn't help, because they moved too fast to be seen. The next time he looked at Wild Bill's big floppy hat, but that didn't work either. The third time, Ned broke down and looked in Wild Bill's eyes. Then he looked down and saw the guns pointed at him.

And then Wild Bill said, "What's your real name? It ain't Ned."

Ned looked back at us and said, "I've gone straight, I tell you!"

"Spit it," Wild Bill said. He was all business, and I was worried he might up and shoot Ned right then and there.

"Henry Ogden, out of Missouri."

"Stage robber," Wild Bill said, holstering his guns. "Ned! Why, you don't look nothing like a Ned! I reckon if we call you Henry it will be okay. Don't you?"

"Yes," Henry said, letting out a huge sigh. "For a moment there I thought you were going to actually shoot me." I could see that Ned, whose name was now Henry, was shook.

"For a moment there, Henry, I didn't either."

Well, nobody wanted to quick draw with Wild Bill after

that. We all saw that the Wild before his name was no accident. So instead, we started shooting things with our rifles. I was on much firmer ground with a Winchester than I was with my pistols. I was on the firmest ground when it came to whomping fellas, but we didn't know how many fellas were holding Sheriff Langtry hostage, and it was safer to plug a hole in someone from far away than it was to sneak up on them.

Montana Dan, as it turned out, could shoot just about anything with that Sharps of his, and Henry was no slouch shooting anything that moved from the top of his horse. I was better shooting standing up using Horse to steady my rifle. Wild Bill preferred to use his pistols, even though they weren't nearly as reliable as a rifle. Baxter and Merle were good with rifles and pistols, but preferred knives.

I hadn't known what to expect from Bernie Waco, but his two hands he'd lent out were a pleasant surprise, and I felt confident they would be good in a scrap if necessary.

After shooting all sorts of bushes and rocks, and a lightning-zapped charred up tree stump, we cleaned our guns and, as the heat of the day waned, made our reluctant way to the outskirts of Hendrix.

11

Hendrix wasn't much to look at. And it *did* smell bad, but that was due to a sulphur spring that farted incessantly just east of the town. At one point, people had moved to Hendrix for the healing properties of the spring. The town marketed its healing properties in the magazines and newspapers of Europe and even North Africa. You would have to be very desperate or sick to upend your life and move thousands of miles from home, and into the middle of some unknown town in the middle of nowhere in Texas. The people who did move to Hendrix had to learn the hard way that they would have been better off suffering poor health than putting up with the smell Hendrix emitted day in and day out.

People from Silver Vein hated Hendrix as a matter of principle because you couldn't live in Hendrix long before you started to smell like it. They could be very friendly, people from Hendrix, but it wasn't enough to overcome the smell. I could tell someone from Hendrix the minute they passed through the saloon doors. Even now, all these years later, I can't think of a single thing to recommend about it. It was dark all the time, even at noon, on account of a ridge that blocked out the sun. It was at the bottom of a steep hill on both sides, and every time it rained the town became a mud hole.

It was, as towns go, pointless.

As far as what was *in* the town goes, there was a saloon, of course—drinking was a logical daily activity for a town with nothing else going for it—and a bank, and a jail, and a general store that sold mostly buckets for bailing water out of people's houses. There were maybe a hundred woebegone sad fools who called Hendrix home, and what they did all day was anyone's guess. Most likely they killed time during the day lost in regret.

We made camp in a tangle of mesquite trees on the ridge outside of town and Baxter went to work on a fire. I had been practicing making fires, because on a previous trip I kept accidentally putting them out. But now that I knew my way when it came to making a fire, nobody wanted me anywhere near one. That was okay with me. Building up a fire is a lot of work. It takes a lot of walking for one thing. Where we were, outside of Hendrix, I would have had to range far and wide to gather up enough sticks and dead grass to start and feed a fire. Why do that when I could relax and jabber and sip on bourbon?

Unlike me, Baxter actually liked and took pride in playing with fire. Also, I could see that Baxter needed something to take his mind off the fact that Wild Bill could have killed him twelve times over. And then, making things even worse, he had to listen to Wild Bill complain about how slow he was, compared to his youth, and how his eyes were right next to useless. Baxter hadn't been himself since: his body language was as bad as his old horse.

Soon there was the welcome smell of beef steaks, which only sort of covered the wafting smell of the farting sulphur spring in town. My stomach was rumbling anyway, so much so that Wild Bill gave me a look while he was messing with his hair. Once he looked up at the blue sky and said, "Where's that thunder coming from?" Which should have made Baxter laugh but didn't. Instead, Baxter just looked up at the sky and walked off. Merle said something to him, and he came back and went back to his fire.

"I don't think this one's burnt," Baxter said, handing me a steak.

"Merle," I said, "can I talk to you a minute?"

Merle stood up from his bedroll and we walked off away from camp, and I said, "We've got to get Baxter right in the head."

"He's mopey," Merle said. "Wild Bill made him feel slow."

"He ain't slow," I said. "Wild Bill is fast is all. Maybe faster than anyone ever."

"It's calling into question everything Baxter knows about himself."

"Well," I said, "there's nothing wrong with this here steak. And Baxter thinks he burned it. And I can't have Baxter doubting himself the day before we have to clean up a town and rescue the only remaining Sheriff Langtry."

"He'll be okay tomorrow," Merle said. "He ain't one to mope for long."

We walked back to camp. I took the saddle off Horse, brushed him down, and gave him a carrot.

"You bring any more carrots?" Wild Bill asked, taking a big belt of bourbon out of his flask.

"I only brought two," I lied. I had six but didn't think it would be fair for Horse to have to share.

"Aw, that's okay. Spot ain't even my horse, though I do like him. Though not enough to keep him. No use wasting a carrot on a borrowed horse I suppose."

"We should get some sleep soon. Some of us have to get up early," I said.

"You fellas go ahead," Wild Bill said. "I don't sleep."

"Me neither," Baxter said. But then, not long after finishing his steak, he conked right out and set to snoring.

My stomach really enjoyed me eating that steak and let me know it by making all sorts of digestive noises.

"Curly," Wild Bill said, "you, by far, of all the people I've ever known, from all around the world, all the many people I've met in my long thirty-two years, have the most enthusiastic stomach."

"Thank you," I said taking a sip of bourbon. Wild Bill had already finished off his flask, and now he was eying my flask. "Your problem is you drink too fast. You polish off all that bourbon, what are you going to drink tomorrow?"

"Bourbon from the saloon in Hendrix."

"It might not have any. It's a dump, that saloon."

"I've never yet met a saloon I didn't enjoy," Wild Bill said.

I left that alone. I was biased when it came to saloons and didn't want to get riled up right when I needed to get some sleep. I left Wild Bill to his hand mirror and hair and flopped over onto my bedroll and considered the night sky.

———

I didn't sleep a wink, or so I thought, not with the ground being so pointy, but when Merle shook me awake, he said I had been snoring up a storm. Wild Bill and I and Baxter and Merle saddled up our horses, leaving Henry and Montana Dan in camp, and made our quiet way down into the unfortunate altogether useless town of Hendrix.

Three blocks from the saloon, and one block off the main road was where the saloonkeeper, Blove Thompo, lived. I knocked on his door. He answered it by shoving a scattergun in my face.

"Blove, it's me, Curly Barnes." The door opened slightly wider, and he took in the scene. "Get in here! And don't make any noise." Blove was hard of hearing, and all the noise was coming from him, but now was not the time for an argument.

The four of us walked in and sat down at a well-worn table in his kitchen.

"I guess you're here because of the sheriff," Blove said. He went into the kitchen and soon got a pot of coffee going. He handed out cups and now we were all sitting around sipping, waiting for the coffee to wake us up.

"All I know," I said, "is that he sent me a telegram asking for help."

"I sent you that telegram."

"You sent the telegram?"

"Who else is going to do it?"

I hadn't thought of that. I didn't know how to think like someone living in Hendrix.

"After he yelled at me from the jail window asking for help, I knew the guys who drink in the saloon were telling the truth. Not that I wouldn't have known anyway. Most days Sheriff Langtry does nothing but come to the saloon and drink. They've got him held prisoner in his own jail, all right," Blove said.

"Why?" I asked.

"It's the Butler gang," Blove said, shrugging.

Wild Bill leaned forward. "Jakob Butler? His outfit? Why, they're as long in the tooth as Baxter's horse."

Blove nodded, though he probably didn't fully understand the remark.

"Jakob's too old and addled to be leading much of a gang," Wild Bill said. "Could be this is the only town left he can still take over. Either way, that old scamp owes me a hundred dollars."

I didn't have any experience with the Butler Gang, though I'd noticed that the prices on their heads went down every time a new batch of Wanted posters came out. "How many are there?" I asked.

"Jakob and his brother Moe are watching over Sheriff Gantry in the jail, and then I reckon there are four others that sit in the saloon and play cards and get drunk all day."

"Six, all together," Wild Bill said.

"Are they gunmen?" I asked.

"Depends on the time of day," Blove said. "You know how it is."

"Any of them teetotalers?" Wild Bill asked. "Nothing worse than a teetotaler. They don't drink, and it makes them angry. Plus, being sober all the time can make a fella dangerous. It's also, in my opinion, bad for your blood."

"Of those four that hang out in the bar, ain't a one of them that don't drink," Blove said.

"Sounds pretty straight-forward," I said.

Which would not be the case at all.

12

When the sun came up, Montana Dan and Henry sat astride their horses looking down at the town. With the sun behind them, their shadows loomed large, making them look like giants. Their instructions were to just sit atop their horses unless they heard otherwise. Wild Bill's thinking was, the Butler Gang would drive themselves crazy trying to figure out why two horsemen would just sit and look down at a town all day. There were originally going to be four men on horse-back, which would seem like a more serious threat, but Bernie botched that part of the plan when he only gave us the two men.

"It was in Abilene that I saw it for myself," Wild Bill said, "how infuriating a man can be that just sits on top of a horse all day. It's a Pinkerton tactic. There was this fella I was playing cards with, Ohio Bradley, and he kept going in and out of the saloon driving himself crazy thinking about the two guys just sitting on horses on the road into town. The two men on horse-back didn't move at all. Not knowing why they were just sitting there, well old Bradley, he finally got so riled up he up and begged me to arrest him."

"Dang," Baxter said.

"What was he guilty of?" Merle asked.

"Paranoia," Wild Bill said.

After a depressing breakfast of some beef jerky and cold biscuits and coffee, somewhere around mid-morning, Wild Bill and I made our way down the grubby empty street to the saloon. The plan was for Baxter and Merle to show up a few minutes later and enter the saloon from the rear. We walked in and sat on a couple of old dumpy stools at the tilted poorly constructed bar, with our eyes on the cheap and unattractive back table, which, when we got there, was still empty. I ordered a cup of tepid coffee and Wild Bill ordered a cup of tepid coffee with cheap whisky in it. Wild Bill, I was learning, was almost never without some alcohol running through his blood. Knowing what he was capable of, and how fast he was, even if, as he told me, he was coming down with a disease he called prairie blindness—well, I wasn't about to say anything about him drinking whisky for breakfast. For all I knew, being sober might actually make him slower.

Blove was complaining about a skinny fella that liked to come in and sit with strangers and get them drunk, and then offer to help them get home. Then, once outside, he would whomp them over the head and take all their money. The fella was so unthreatening that sometimes he would pull the same trick on the same fella, sometimes as many as three nights straight.

"I don't know where he puts all the whisky," Blove said. "Because whoever his target is gets drunk, and he stays the same."

He sounded pretty familiar. "I wonder if he might hail from Wisconsin."

Blove nodded. "It's the first thing he tells a fella, is that he's from Wisconsin originally."

"Does he discuss his nether parts at all?"

"Frequently."

"That would be Wisconsin Slim. We ran him out of Silver Vein about eight months ago. He was harmless enough in the saloon, but once outside he turned feral, like a human raccoon. Tell him Curly Barnes was not happy to learn he has yet to leave the state. Let him know I'm on his trail. He'll absquatulate before the sun goes down."

"Will do, Curly."

"I wouldn't think this town would offer up enough drunks for Wisconsin Slim to survive on."

"Aw, it's mostly one old coot, Sorpo Gritz, that is the victim. Even though he's been whomped on nightly, he still up and invites that little fella to sit right next to him all over again."

I nodded. "He gets them drunk enough that they have no memory of getting whomped on."

I looked around the saloon. It had all the same stuff found in most saloons, most average saloons anyway, but it had clearly seen better days. Or maybe it didn't ever have better days and had always looked run-down. There was no piano or billiard table or food to be had. And, no offense to Blove, but he wasn't the best saloonkeeper in the world. Outside of a couple of bottles labeled Bourbon, there was not much in the way of variety.

"If Sherwood could see this place, I reckon he'd stop complaining about mine," I said. Wild Bill, if he heard me, didn't respond.

The saloon doors creaked open, as if in pain, and four men with long beards came walking in. They walked by us straight to a table in the back corner, not far from the rear entrance where Baxter and Merle were supposed to sneak in.

"A couple of bottles, barkeep," one of the bearded men said. He sat with his back to the wall, and I made him out to be the leader. Blove took a couple of bottles out from under the bar and some cloudy glasses and walked over to the table.

"Here you go, Mort," Blove said.

"If we need anything else we'll just toss one of these dirty glasses your way." If it had been my saloon, I would have already whomped the lot of them. They were an ugly sort, at least in the personality department, and I could tell, as an expert in such matters, that their behavior would only deteriorate with the addition of whisky. There are good drunks, and bad drunks, and drunks like Wild Bill, who didn't even get drunk, and drunks like me who never stopped talking. These were the rotten kind.

I looked at Wild Bill. This was his show, and I would move when he did.

"I reckon to let them get settled in," he said, looking down at his glass, looking not all that different from the drunk buffalo skinner I'd thought him to be only a few days earlier. "Your deputies ain't in place yet."

One of the bearded men got up from the table and walked up to the saloon doors and then walked out into the street and then came back through the tired grubby saloon doors and went and sat down again.

"They're just sitting up there on their horses!"

"They ain't moved any?" the leader asked.

"No. They're just sitting up there. You reckon them to be Pinkertons?"

This made the leader laugh. "You hold yourself too high, Mort. What Pinkerton is gonna come to this ass hair of a town and fool with a gang that should have already retired? We ain't worth a bowl of fresh piss to a Pinkerton."

"I reckon you're right. Maybe they're just lost. Or maybe the smell has stupefied them."

"Well, Mort," the leader said, "you're welcome to go on up there and ask them their business."

"It's too hot," Mort said. Then he turned around and looked right at us. "It ain't too hot for me to figure out these fella's business though." Mort stood up and walked towards us. Then Wild Bill did the dangedest thing and stood up and extended his hand and said, "Why, you must be Mort." Mort, before he knew what he was even about, stuck his hand out and the two men shook hands.

"Wild Bill Hickok, nice to meet you."

"Dang," Mort said, because Wild Bill was now aiming Mort's own gun at his belly.

"Hey, what's going on there?" the leader asked. But he was leaning back in his chair and was in no position to make any sort of move. Originally, this was supposed to be when Baxter and Merle covered the table from the rear. Mort had his own gun pointed at him by Wild Bill, so he couldn't do anything, and the other three men were still trying to figure out what was happening.

And then the gunshots started.

13

The shots came from out front of the saloon, out in the street. About ten shots from what sounded like at least four guns. I heard a grunt from out front, and the unmistakable sound of a fella falling off a horse into a pile of dirt.

"This never happens!" Blove cried out, and dove behind the bar. The leader of the group stood up and pulled out his gun and Wild Bill shot his elbow off with Mort's gun, then whomped Mort over the head with it, then dropped Mort's gun and pulled his own pistols out and aimed them at the table. I had my Winchester and aimed from the hip and shot the guy sitting to the right of the leader in the shoulder just as he was taking aim at Wild Bill. The leader was screaming to wake the moon and holding his arm as blood gushed out all over the place, and so Wild Bill took two quick steps and whomped him over the head to shut him up.

There was one guy at the table who never moved at all, and he threw his hands up over his head and surrendered, and I walked up and whomped the fella I'd shot in the shoulder. Three men were now on the floor, out of the fight, and one had his hands up to the heavens. We'd done our part, even without Baxter and Merle.

I walked outside and saw four men lying in the dirt, two of them were still squirming about.

"Sorry," Baxter said.

"Not really our fault though," Merle said.

"They started it," Baxter said.

"We were just minding our own business," Merle said.

"Couldn't be helped," Baxter said.

"No choice in the matter," Merle said.

"Who are these fellas?" I asked.

"They were coming out of the bank wearing bags over their heads and saw us and just up and started shooting at us," Baxter said.

"And we were just minding our own business," Merle said again.

"Henry shot one of them off his horse from all the way from up the hill," Baxter said, pointing. I looked up and Henry waved, and I couldn't help but wave back.

"This town ain't what it used to be," Blove said. He'd come out of the saloon and was now looking at the would-be bank robbers flopping around like fish in the dirt with bags over their heads. I kept my feelings on Hendrix to myself, though I doubted it ever used to be anything to speak of.

Montana Dan and Henry came down off the hill and joined the rest of us looking down at the failed bank robbers.

We listened to them flop around and moan and curse for a while, and then Wild Bill said, "This will make a nice chapter in the book," and winked at me. Then he said, "which way is the jail?"

I'd been so caught up in how the events went down, and how you can really never truly plan anything in this world, without some unknown bank robbery to screw it up, that I'd forgotten all about Sheriff Langtry.

"It's down yonder on the other side of the street where them two horses are," Blove said, pointing through all the gun smoke and dust.

Wild Bill looked down at the dirt. "Not sure this qualifies as a street," he said, spitting.

Wild Bill and I walked down the dusty street, with Baxter and Merle behind us. We left Henry and Montana Dan to look after all the bad guys lying about.

"Bill, I have to ask you something," I said.

Wild Bill looked at me and raised an eyebrow.

"Well, you see," I said, "back in Silver Vein you shot that fella in the kneecaps, and here you just shot a fella in the elbow. So, my question is, are you so sure of your shooting that you can practice even in the middle of a gunfight?"

"As it happens, Curly, in Silver Vein, because the fella was on the other side of the flappy doors, the knees were the first thing I could see when he was making his way into the saloon. I knew, with that fella, that if I missed, I could still shoot him once he got through the doors. He put himself at a huge strategic disadvantage coming through them doors like that. An experienced shootist would have never done such a thing. It's how I knew he was just a fan and not a serious threat. Now, with that fella here it was altogether different, as I was aiming for his chest and missed. It wasn't my gun, you see, as I was borrowing Mort's."

"I see," I said. "Because I was starting to think you had a thing against a fella's joints."

"This next part shouldn't be much of a problem. Me and Jakob have a history."

We were about thirty yards from the jail when a window shattered in the jail and a rifle emerged.

"That's close enough!" a voice yelled out. "We've got your sheriff locked up in here. The last Langtry! And we will shoot him if you come any closer!"

"Jakob Butler!" Wild Bill yelled, "I've come for the hundred dollars you owe me!"

"What the—"

Another window broke out of the jail and a head popped out and then, just as quickly, went back in again.

"It's Wild Bill all right! He's right outside!" a voice cried out.

"That's his brother, Moe," Wild Bill said, his eyes fixed on the jail. "He does whatever Jakob says. Which is too bad, because Jakob is always getting him mixed up in his criminal ways and is not at all a person worth listening to."

"Wild Bill wouldn't be in Texas! He hates Texas!" Jakob Butler told his brother.

"Well, I am here to tell you that he must have changed his mind. Because he's—"

That's when Wild Bill pulled out one of his pistols and shot the rifle Jakob had sticking out the window.

"These bullets go where I want them to," Wild Bill said, throwing me a wink.

"Shit!" Jakob Butler said. The rifle disappeared, and then another one replaced it.

"This jail is full of rifles, Wild Bill!" Jakob yelled. "I reckon we can hold you off for weeks!"

"Weeks?" Moe said. "We don't have enough food for—"

"Jakob," Wild Bill said, "I've got Deputy U.S. Marshal Curly Barnes with me. He's the law in these parts. You've got two ways this can go. One, you and Moe surrender yourselves, and go to jail and take your chances in front of a judge."

"What's number two?" Jakob asked.

"Yeah, what's the second one?" Moe asked.

"Number two is we shoot you full of holes and watch all the blood drain out, and I forgo the hundred dollars you owe me."

"Jakob!"

"I'm thinking, Moe!"

"Curly Barnes is a killer! And he's just standing right next to

Wild Bill, and they got two others with them that look like they've been in many a scrap! And who knows how many—"

"All right! Wild Bill!"

"Jakob!"

"I reckon we're coming out."

"Toss out all your rifles and guns first," I said.

"Okay. They ain't all ours though. Some of them came with the jail," Jakob said.

"One of the reasons Jakob Butler is so long in the tooth, he knows when a fight is over," Wild Bill said.

So, we watched as rifle after rifle after pistol after shotgun were thrown out of the jail into the dirt. When it was done, there was a hefty pile of them.

"Okay, that's the lot of them," Jakob said.

"Knives too!" Baxter called out. Good old Baxter was back to his old self again, craving new knives.

And so, knife after knife after knife came flying out the jail window.

"And so now, let's see the sheriff," I said.

We could hear some stumbling about in the jail, and then the door of the jail opened, and the last Sheriff Langtry walked blinking and stumbling out into the street. He had about a week's worth of snow-white chin whiskers on his face, which made him look like some old hermit from the Bible.

"Dang," Wild Bill said, "I thought *I* was old."

"Is that you, Curly?"

"I'm Baxter," Baxter said. "You walked right past Curly."

"I can't see nothing because of that blaring sun. It just lets you know," Sheriff Langtry said.

"Lets you know what?" Merle asked.

"Why, how important hats are! Being without a hat and a fella might as well be blind!" I guess a week stuffed inside your own jail can make even the paltry sun of Hendrix seem bright.

The door to the jail opened further, and Jakob and Moe Butler walked out with their hands thrown up into the air.

"Told you it was Wild Bill," Moe said. "Not that you ever listen."

"I thought Texas was the one place I was guaranteed to never run into you," Jakob Butler said, smiling. "Yet here you are."

"Here I am," Wild Bill agreed. "But I've been thinking on it, and I don't no longer consider this part of Texas to count as Texas. Ain't yet enough Texans out here to ruin it."

"Ain't enough of anything out here," Jakob sighed.

I walked into the jail and found the place a shambles. There were dirty plates of food and empty whisky bottles littering the floor, and someone had some fun drawing funny faces on all the Wanted posters. But I did find four sets of wrist irons, which we would need on account of the jail was no longer fit to hold any half-way creative criminal. And Ike Langtry had proven himself useless several times over where the law was concerned. If we put the Butler gang in his falling apart jail, they'd escape by morning.

Which meant we would have to take them all back to Silver Vein to a real jail where I could have Tiny keep an eye on them.

————

There were ten men all together. Seven if you count the ones still alive. Three of the bank robbers didn't make it. We herded them that were yet living into the saloon, where I broke down and ordered some cheap whisky from Blove. Wild Bill bought a bottle.

"I suppose I'll have to bury them fellas," Blove said, plopping some yellow liquid in front of me. I smelled it and took a cautious sip. It would do, whatever it was.

"What about the undertaker?" Baxter asked.

"An undertaker can't make a living here. We used to have one, but he left some months ago. Said we didn't have enough people dying. And now that Greater Hendrix has gone belly up…"

"Greater Hendrix?" I asked.

"It was a big bunch of houses we built for the people that would work the swamp," Blove said.

"The swamp?" Wild Bill asked, looking around. "Here?"

"That's what the people were for. To build the swamp."

"But—" I started.

"Why?" Wild Bill jumped in, swiping my question. "This ain't the right climate to support a swamp!" Wild Bill said, shaking his head in wonder. "But just for the sake of discussion, why would you even *want* to build a swamp?"

"You'd have to ask Greef Hanson," Blove said, shrugging. "It was his idea."

"And where would I find him?" Wild Bill asked. "I need to know."

"He died about a year ago," Blove said.

I shook my head free of the conversation—one that was no doubt typical for Hendrix—and focused on our new prisoners. With Jakob and Moe shackled up, the other four members of the gang were too mopey or were leaking too much blood to put up any sort of fight. Especially the guy who no longer had an elbow. He'd lost a lot of blood and could barely talk. The one remaining bank robber said he only went along with the robbery because he needed money. Which is why he was so mopey, on account of the fact that even if the robbery had been a success, the four of them would have fled town with only six dollars between them.

"You would think a bank with no money in it would be easier to rob," the remaining bank robber, who called himself Kid Barlow, said.

"It was just bad luck," Baxter explained. "If you'd robbed the bank an hour earlier, you would have gotten away clean."

"Or an hour later," Merle said.

"And nobody would have even chased after you," Blove said. "Hendrix couldn't raise a posse on a bet."

"And that's all supposed to make me feel better?"

"No. It's true though," Baxter said.

"What with the town having no sheriff, at least not one that wasn't locked up in his own jail, it seemed like a sure thing."

"If I weren't a deputy, I might have been tempted myself under such circumstances," Merle admitted.

Baxter and Merle had a bad habit of airing out their innate criminal tendencies and thoughts. I frequently had to remind them that they were technically lawmen and shouldn't say such things in public.

Sheriff Ike Langtry, the last of an ill-fated brood, was at the bar trying to stuff his face into a whisky bottle, looking to wash away a week of humiliating imprisonment. Wild Bill sat next to him, doing the same thing simply because he was awake. I couldn't help but wonder if something else might happen. Not that there was too much that *could* happen. Aside from the mostly empty bank, there were no other targets to speak of in Hendrix. None that would make having to *be* in Hendrix worth it. I'd had enough of the smell that Hendrix had hovering around it. Like an entire herd of cows all farting at once. I was ready to head back to Silver Vein.

"You need a deputy, Ike," I said.

"I do?" Ike said.

"Someone who would have your back the next time a gang of scoundrels decides they want to come and take the town over."

"Well now, I reckon that would make some sense. But I barely draw a salary as it is. Actually, now that I think on it, I *don't* actually get paid to do this. Unless'n you take into account the house they let me live in. So, I don't know that I could pay anyone."

"Dang," I said. I drew a salary and paid Baxter and Merle, and even paid Deedee when I was out of town, and she was looking after the jail. I paid Tiny in dessert pies—which was just about the only thing he ate.

"What do people *do* here?" Wild Bill asked.

This was greeted with a fair amount of silence.

"Can't say as I know," Blove finally admitted. "Most days nothing happens here at all. Sometimes I curl up and nap on that table yonder. Used to be you got people coming from all over the world to bathe in the sulphur springs. Then word got out that any healing the springs provided wasn't worth the effort to get here or put up with the smell either one. We used to have four restaurants, now we got but one, and it ain't open but two days a week..."

"Well Curly, Silver Vein has moved up a couple of notches in my estimation," Wild Bill said, taking a large swig of a sub-par and highly questionable bourbon. "Let's get on out of here."

14

Once the heat of the day was over with, the six of us, and our new collection of shot up criminals, headed south out of town back towards Silver Vein. We were almost to the top of the hill leading out of town when we heard a rumbling noise. I looked behind me to see what was going on—and saw a house just fall to pieces, tipping over into the street.

"Most of the houses are just empty," Kid Barlow said. "I reckon the termites done ate that one."

"Sheriff Langtry can keep that place," I said.

It was a quiet group heading back. I reckon now that it was all over, what was left of the Butler gang was lost in their heads regretting stuff. That's the way it is with criminals. I'm not talking about the occasional rustler or some desperate fella that ups and cheats at cards. And I'm definitely not talking about politicians, though they are all, each and every one of them, from the dawn of time right up to now, certainly criminals. I'm talking about the type that can't do nothing *but* the wrong thing. If it's against the law, then that's what they're going to do. Most of these types, who might start out bushwhacking people, then go on to rob stagecoaches and then banks, and then, later, railroads—well, when those folks get caught, you would be surprised how little thought they put into what it was they had done. So now that the Butler Gang was trussed up, leaking blood, and had some rifles jammed in their ribs, each of them was only just now considering what kind of trouble they were in.

As to me, I thought the whole thing had gone pretty well. None of us, and neither of Bernie Waco's men, had been shot or kilt. And we'd even foiled a bank robbery attempt we didn't even know about. And, perhaps best of all, we'd done all of it without having to spend a single night in Hendrix.

We made camp for the night about two hours from the T Bar ranch, but since we'd gotten up so early in the morning, with the exception of Wild Bill, who actually truly didn't seem to sleep, we were all pretty tuckered out, some of our prisoners could barely stay in the saddle—nobody felt like riding two hours through the desert dark.

I left Baxter and Merle to handle the prisoners, and get them off their horses, and truss them to things so they couldn't escape when it got dark. I could have let Montana Dan and Henry head back to the ranch, but I needed them to help keep lookout during the night. They weren't in any hurry to get back to the T Bar, as they were still excited about being part of a gunfight with Wild Bill Hickok and Curly Barnes and helping to foil a bank robbery, especially Henry, who had shot a fella off his horse from over a hundred yards—which was some achievement.

"The trick to that," —shooting a fella off his horse— "is it's like shooting birds. What you do is, you try to shoot them where they'll be when the bullet catches up to them," Henry said, looking around the fire at a group of famous experienced gunmen.

"I bet that's true," Wild Bill said, nodding his head, as if learning this for the first time.

"It's common sense!" Baxter said, not at all happy with Henry and his confidence, and especially not happy with the attention Henry was getting from Wild Bill. "Everybody knows what you just said."

"We couldn't have done what Henry did," Merle said, "on account of the fact that the fellas we shot were no more than six feet away."

"And shooting at us," Baxter put in.

"We were too close to think about where our bullets were going to be," Merle said.

"Our bullets were a lot closer than that one you got lucky with," Baxter said.

"It weren't luck," Henry growled.

"I reckon we all did a good job today," I said, as I could see that Baxter and Merle would soon start a brawl if they weren't distracted.

"Not me," Kid Barlow said. "I reckon I did a piss poor job."

"Well," I said, "you were just on the wrong side is all." I don't know why I was trying to make a bank robber feel better about himself. Maybe it's on account of how young he seemed. At the time, before I learned more about the justice system, I figured he still had a chance to choose a different life for himself.

"The wrong side ain't all that bad," Jakob Butler said, "once you get used to it."

"I expect you would be used to it by now," Wild Bill said, nodding, "as old as you are."

"Aw, Jakob ain't that old," Moe said. The two Butler brothers had their hands behind their backs and their wrist irons were looped around one another so they were essentially stuck together.

"How old are you, Jakob?" Wild Bill asked.

"Fifty?" Jakob asked.

"That's old, Moe." Wild Bill said. "You two had a good run, but that's all over now."

"Good run?" Mort bellowed. "You call being on the run every damn day a good run? Hell, I don't know what we were doing in Hendrix in the first place! Jakob saw that the town basically had a coot for a sheriff, a Langtry no less, and decided to take over a town that smelled like a diseased mule!"

"That's enough of that lip," Jakob said, "or I'm kicking you out of the gang."

"We ain't a gang no more!" Moe pointed out. "What we are is, is...just a collection of future jail birds."

"I'd kick you out, Moe, if you weren't my brother."

"Go ahead. Kick me out! I'm better off out here in the dirt breathing clean air than holed up eating stale food in some squalid jail!"

"Oh sure, easy to complain now," Jakob said. "You weren't complaining before we gave ourselves up!"

"The lot of you, shut your yapping," Montana Dan said. "I thought the bunkhouse was full of yappers, but you fellas sure do take the cake." Montana took his bedroll and walked out into the desert mumbling to himself.

As the sheriff, it was my job to tell everyone to shut up and keep some sort of order. But the saloonkeeper part of me enjoys a good jabber. Come tomorrow afternoon, they'd all be locked up in jail, so I was okay listening to them talk.

Wild Bill said: "I remember, Jakob, a time when there was a price of $1,000 for your head. Not the whole gang. Just you. And then, later, when you were cheating at cards in Abilene, it had gone down to $500. The last I saw it was only $100 for the entire gang. Which happens to also be how much you owe me."

"Aw, it'll go back up. I aim to shoot the judge if I can."

"That kind of talk will earn you a gag in your mouth you keep it up," I said.

"Let us know, Curly, if you want us to whomp him," Baxter said.

"Oh, I think Jakob can hold his tongue, can't you Jakob?" I asked.

"No," Jakob said.

So, Baxter whomped him. Then whomped Moe for good measure.

———

I stared into space listening to critters scurry about, and I listened to Baxter and Merle take turns snoring. I could hear Wild Bill brushing his hair, and various others sleep fart. I didn't have my buffalo robe, and my winter coat wasn't up to the task of warding off the chill of the desert night. Also, there was a rock poking into me. So, instead of getting any real sleep, I looked up at the heavens, and all the stars up there. Looking up at the stars is the one thing I could say I'd been doing my whole life. Whether back home in Illinois, sleeping on the roof of the house I grew up in, or looking up at them from the desert dirt while chasing after bushwhackers—the stars always comforted me. They reminded me that I was just one tiny little bitty speck in a giant world, and to me that meant that there wasn't anything I could do to screw it up. The world was way bigger than just me and would carry on just fine without me. I was but one tiny little flea on the world's largest dog. And knowing all that took the pressure off and made me feel better.

Slowly the sun woke up and shed light on us all. It was cold, and I was groggy from a rough night of flopping back and forth in the dirt. Wild Bill's hair looked great, and I caught him taking a nip of pre-dawn whisky. I got up to go pee, and I almost let loose on top of Montana Dan, who was sacked out under some rabbitbrush like a mummy. He seemed to have no problem sleeping in the dirt. I put my nether parts back in my pants and went looking for a place to take a piss that didn't have someone sleeping in it.

And then, dang if I didn't hear rifle shots.

BOOK II: THE LLANO

1

The shots came from the top of a small rise to the left of camp. I looked up there just in time to see what looked like a Comanche whomp some fella over the head. Then another figure with a rifle walked out from behind a Live Oak stump.

Everyone woke up and started reaching for their guns. The Butler Gang squirmed and tried to break free, but they were too trussed up to go anywhere.

"Come on now. Let us free! We're sitting ducks like this!" Jakob Butler said.

"Curly Barnes!" a familiar voice called out. "It's Frank Kilhoe! I've got Hap with me. We're coming to you! Don't shoot!"

I watched, incredulously, as Frank Kilhoe and Hap Morgan and a Comanche warrior that I knew by the name of Two Yellow Hairs (because he was married to a blonde woman who had a blonde daughter) walked down the rise. Not long after that, none other than Deedee and little Tommy Yonder walked up to our camp on horses.

Nothing good was going on. I knew that much. I'd left

Deedee Yonder back in Silver Vein, in charge of the jail. For Deedee to be out here could only mean something bad had happened. And for Two Yellow Hairs to be here was not good at all. He should have been with Scout and their band hunting further south in what was left of Comancheria.

"Frank. Hap. Deedee. This here is Wild Bill Hickok, and over here we've got the Butler Gang all trussed up."

"They're worthless," Hap said, dismissively looking them over. "Their scalp prices ain't worth the effort."

"Told you we was over the hill," Moe mumbled.

Frank pushed two men forward. "We found these two getting ready to ambush you fellas. Curly, you ought to have had a sentry up on that rise, to prevent just this situation from happening. Or you should have camped in a more protective place, not just off the trail like this. I reckon you're lucky we came along when we did." Frank was always criticizing me, and here he was, from out of nowhere, doing it again. His black and white beard was longer than ever, creeping halfway down his chest, but his gray wolf-like eyes still looked as deadly as ever.

"We thought we'd rounded up the whole gang," I said.

"Well, we found you two more," Frank said. He set about trussing up their hands behind their backs. One of the two men had a knot on his head you could actually see throb and grow and change colors. It was clear by the look in bis eyes that he didn't know where he was or what was which.

"This the last of them?" I asked Jakob.

"Never seen these fellas before," Jakob said.

"Want me to pluck out one of his eyeballs, get him to talking straight?" Deedee asked. She took a huge knife out of the scabbard on her hip and started swiping it back and forth. She was, if you can believe it, when she wasn't helping me in the jail, a schoolteacher.

"That's up to Jakob," I said.

Deedee dismounted her horse and gave the reins to Tommy.

Tommy and Scout were close, as close as a Dutch boy and a Comanche warrior could be anyway. I could understand, if something had happened to Scout, that he would want to help.

"Let's not be hasty," Mort said. "These are the last two members of the gang. They were in the privy when everything went down."

"I wouldn't trust a member of an outlaw gang to be able to count," Frank pointed out. "I think it best to consider the possibility that there might be more out there, waiting for an opportunity to free the gang."

"Never mind all that," I said. "What is Two Yellow Hairs doing here? And Deedee, why ain't you at the jail back in Silver Vein? And what is Tommy doing with you?"

It was too early in the morning to be this confused.

"It's about Scout," Tommy Yonder said. "They got him."

2

_____

"Who's got him?" I asked.

"I think it best to start at the beginning," Hap said, helping himself to a cup of coffee. "There's some language issues, of course, but here is what we've put together so far. A couple of days ago, Two Yellow Hairs walked into Silver Vein and—"

"Curly, you would have had to have been there to believe it," Deedee said, handing me a copy of *The Daily Silver Vein*. "He just walked down Main Street without an ounce of fear. I was sitting in the jail when Pap Kickins comes storming in telling me there's a wild savage covered in blood walking through town. So, I open up the door to the jail and poke my head out—and, sure enough, here comes this fella Two Yellow Hairs straight through town and right on into your saloon."

I could picture how Silver Vein would have reacted, seeing a Comanche warrior sauntering through town like he was out for an afternoon stroll. Many of the people in town had probably never even seen an Indian the whole time they'd lived in town. It probably gave people heart attacks.

"Tommy here," Hap said, "knows some Comanche words,

and he is the one who put it together. Scout and Two Yellow Hairs, and all the warriors in their band were off hunting, and when they came back, they found that all of the women and children and old warriors had been massacred. Though some might have escaped. I guess Two Yellow Hairs was told to come to you for help, so that's what he did."

"They slaughtered women and children?" I was thinking about how much effort went into bringing peace between Silver Vein and Rattles's band, and how that peace was probably no more. "Any idea who did it?" I asked. "It wasn't anyone from Silver Vein."

"We're getting to that," Frank said. "It was Federal troops. We don't know how many. But according to Two Yellow Hairs, they kidnapped his wife, Yellow Hair, and her daughter." I looked at Two Yellow Hairs, but he seemed to have no notion that we were talking about him, because he was carefully removing hair from the club he'd used to whomp one of our would-be ambushers.

"They have Scout and Rattles both," Deedee said. "And I knew I couldn't count on anyone in town to help, not with Indians involved. Silver Vein is filled up with nothing but cowards! So, I sent word to Amarillo and Frank and Hap came immediately."

"Rode through the night," Frank said.

"Who is watching the jail?" I asked.

"Tiny," Deedee said. "And if anything happens he can't handle—"

"The only thing Tiny can handle are dessert pies," I said. Tiny weighed probably four hundred pounds. His size and lazy left eye were usually enough to scare most people out of crossing him.

"If anything does happen," Deedee said, "I told him to go to my house and get China Jack." China Jack at one point had been an outlaw, but when Deedee found out how good he was at scrapping and throwing knives, she turned him into her personal bodyguard, and he taught Tommy the ways of knife throwing. He was exceedingly dangerous when called upon to be, and he would be more than capable of helping Tiny out. He wasn't much to look at, but if you were to have a go at him, you would somehow find yourself flying through the air and landing in the dirt in a heap.

"What do you want to do?" Hap asked.

"Only one thing *to* do," Wild Bill said, standing up and brushing himself off.

"And what's that?" Frank asked, spitting into the dirt. "And who might you be?"

This seemed to take Wild Bill back. Which made sense since I'd already introduced him. Clearly Frank hadn't been paying attention. Bill was so used to being recognized when he wasn't in disguise that he didn't know what to make of Frank Kilhoe not knowing who he was.

"It's me! Wild Bill Hickok!"

Frank looked him up and down and said, "so what would you have us do then?"

"I know Ranald MacKenzie. He's a brutal man, but he don't go in for the killing of women and children. Even Indian ones. We figure out how many troops have gone rogue, and we track them down, and convince them they've made a terrible mistake. All of which will make for a hell of a story."

"Wild Bill is writing his autobiography," I said, translating.

Frank nodded. "Two Yellow Hairs is gonna take us to where this massacre took place. Bill, if you're as good as they say, we could do with your help reading signs. Scout won't be able to help on account of him being held prisoner."

"Ah, so you *have* heard of me!" Wild Bill said. "I can track all right. Some of the stuff you read about me is actually true."

Frank nodded.

146

I looked at Baxter and Merle, thinking about what to do with them.

"Don't send us home," Merle said, reading my thoughts. "Scout saved my life, you know."

"He saved most of our lives, one time or another," I agreed. "Okay. Henry, you, and Dan escort the prisoners until you get to the T Bar, and let Bernie know Bill will need use of his horse for longer than anticipated and will return it eventually. Then I would appreciate it if you would escort Deedee and Tommy and our prisoners to the Silver Vein jail."

"Fine with me," Henry said.

"That shouldn't be a problem, Sheriff," Montana Dan said.

"I don't need no escort. I will have no problem escorting these fellas myself," Deedee said.

This was probably true, but I didn't trust Deedee. "Deedee, don't mess with them none. Just put them in jail and lock them in there. And have Doc Watson tend to their wounds, especially the guy with the shot-off elbow. He's not the best doctor in the world, but nobody's perfect. We can arrange transport to Amarillo later."

"Curly," Frank said. "Just so's none of these fellas say something that sets Deedee to carving on them with that knife of hers—something we all know she wants to do—"

I looked at Moe and his eyes looked like they might pop out of his head.

"—you might want to gag them."

"Tommy, toss one," Deedee said. And Tommy Yonder, in one smooth motion, let loose with a knife he had in a scabbard across his chest, and it flew through the air and stuck fast in the trunk of a tree less than six inches above Jakob Butler's head.

"I don't reckon they'll give me any lip," Deedee said.

———

"But that's New York City for you," Wild Bill said. "A whole bunch of buildings and a whole bunch of horse shit. And so, I made my way back to the frontier where I belong."

Two Yellow Hairs, not being able to understand English, had nothing to say to that, which didn't stop Wild Bill from talking. The seven of us were taking the trail at a lope, with Two Yellow Hairs and Wild Bill leading the way. I was riding next to Hap and Frank, and Baxter and Merle were a little ways back, as Colonel, while over-performing for a horse of his age, was a little beyond being able to handle sustained lopes.

"Deedee was lucky to catch us," Hap was saying. "We were in between bounties at the time, playing cards with Abe at the Oriental Saloon, when one of his deputies came in with her telegram."

"You mean Abe went back to playing cards? After he got shot playing cards?" I asked.

"Not much else to do in Amarillo, except spend time with a sporting lady and play cards," Frank pointed out. "And now he keeps his gun close at hand, on the table next to him." Even though I'd never seen Frank play cards at the saloon, I imagine he would be good at it, because his face didn't have changeable expressions. He could be happy or mopey and look the exact same way.

"Well, I'm glad Deedee tracked you down," I said. "Because she was right. We're probably the only people in all of Texas that would give an armadillo's ass about Scout and Rattles, or even Yellow Hair and her daughter."

"You should know that things will not go well for whoever is responsible," Frank said. "It is a great insult for a Comanche to have his wife stolen. If they raped her, things will be even worse. We will need to keep an eye on Two Yellow Hairs. If not, if he loses control of his rage, the Federal troops might invade even further into Comancheria and wipe out the rest of Rattles's band."

"There's no need to slaughter women and children and old folks," I said. "All they want at this point is to be left alone. It's been a good while since they've posed any serious threat." I was hopping mad, even sitting on top of a horse, and I could feel my skin turning red as a ripe tomato. Back when we were chasing after Torp Mayfair, we found ourselves in Comanche country, and ended up in Rattles' camp. While the warriors looked like they wanted to yank our heads off, most of the Comanches were cordial and curious about us. And now many of those people were dead.

"Well Curly," Hap said, "it could be we're gonna need to keep an eye on you as well."

"I ain't gonna blow my lid," I said. Though I wasn't sure if that was true. I thought about Sally, and how I would react if someone had raped or kidnapped her, and I could understand Two Yellow Hairs's rage. I was a pretty easy-going guy, especially for a sheriff out on the Texas frontier, but there are some lines a fella simply can't cross. And raping women is one of them. And, whoever these desperadoes were, they had Scout and Rattles, who I'd come to think of as friends. Sally thought of Scout like a son and introduced him to the importance of a good hug.

It seemed that Wild Bill was getting somewhere talking to Two Yellow Hairs, because he started speaking a language that sounded a lot more like Comanche, and a lot less like English, and Two Yellow Hairs was now the one doing most of the talking, as Wild Bill nodded along.

Then Wild Bill came back to join us.

"He says we've got about two days, give or take, which should put us at the scene of the massacre tomorrow just as the sun is setting. I suggest we camp early tomorrow. I don't know about you fellas, but I don't cotton to being too close to a lot of dead bodies in the night."

"I see you're making headway with the Comanche tongue," Frank said.

"It's got a lot of similar words to Cheyenne and Arapahoe. They've all been trading with one another for so long that their languages have a lot in common. I did stumble a couple of times early on there, and I believe I might have accidentally called Two Yellow Hairs a beef leg."

"You're doing better than I would," Frank said, "I only know a few words myself. You fought in the war, I take it?"

"I was a scout and a spy," Wild Bill said.

"Hap and I skipped the war and instead fought Indians and Mexican bandits on the Mexican border with the Rangers. Once the war started, it was up to us to fend for ourselves out here."

"Glad to hear you didn't fight for Texas in the war," Wild Bill said. "I don't have much patience with those who sought to protect human bondage. I was raised in Kansas, and I joined the war to free this land from slavery. And that goes for Indians too, now that I think about it. I am on the opposite side of any sort of bondage or repression. So, I reckon I'm on your side, Curly, because if the Federal troops have taken to slaughtering the innocent—well, I'm on the other side of that particular fight."

"When Jim Shepland got run out of Silver Vein, Torp Mayfair and his hired gun hands left him hanging from a tree to die. Instead of finishing the job, they went off to get drunk and celebrate. The sheriff somehow managed to climb the rope they used to hang him and untie himself. But he didn't have his horse or clothes or food or water. It was Rattles who found him and took him in and brought him back to health. And that was only the first time Rattles and his band came to our rescue."

I reached into my shirt and pulled out the eagle feathers Rattles had given me. "These here feathers, which Rattles gave me, have protected me ever since I first met him. I always knew there might come a time when we would be the ones having to save old Rattles skin, and it looks that time has come."

"Is he the one gave you that buffalo robe?" Wild Bill asked.

I nodded. Then I remembered it was actually Two Yellow Hairs who had given me the buffalo robe. Rattles had only let me borrow one. But that seemed hardly worth pointing out.

"That's one more reason to owe Rattles then," Wild Bill said, nodding. "He's keeping your bed warm while you're gone."

This made Hap laugh, even though it was obviously not funny.

"We didn't bring enough steaks," Merle said. I don't know where he came from. One minute nobody was behind us, and the next there was Merle. No sign of Baxter. Just hearing the word steak suddenly made me hungry, and I reached into my saddlebag and pulled out a piece of jerky and set to gnawing on it.

"Merle is right. Or is it Baxter?" Wild Bill asked.

"Merle," Merle said. "You can tell because I've been shot and Baxter ain't." Merle pulled up his shirt and showed off a small round scar on the right side of his ribs.

"Lucky," Wild Bill said. "A glancing shot. But I am not going to be in the business of lifting up shirts to see who is who. Where is Baxter, anyway?"

"He's back there plodding along on Colonel."

"I might just up and shoot that horse," Frank said, "just to force him to get better transport."

"Baxter is awfully sweet on that horse. He doesn't want to admit how old Colonel is getting," Merle said. "He's had that horse since we were kids."

"I can understand that," Wild Bill said. "I've fallen in love with just about every horse I've ever had—with the notable exception of Bluejay."

I didn't want to ask, didn't want to rise to the tease, but I didn't have to, because Merle did it for me and asked: "What was wrong with Bluejay?"

"Aw, he was a biter." Wild Bill reached over and pulled up his left trouser leg and showed what looked like a horse's mouth stuck into the side of his leg. You could see the teeth marks and everything.

"Dang," I said.

"I've seen worse," Frank said. "I knew a horse that turned into a meat eater and ate all of ranger Tom Dooley's shooting arm."

"That is most unusual," Wild Bill pointed out. "Horses are prey animals and are known by one and all to eat grass and alfalfa and oats and apples and carrots. I ain't ever heard of a carnivorous horse before. I reckon that horse was desperate."

"I didn't know Tom Dooley," Hap said. "But I've heard the story."

"I was there. I was the one that had to put the horse down," Frank said. "Otherwise, he might not have stopped with just the arm. I believe he was intent on finishing the job."

"If anyone's going to put a horse down," I said, "it might as well be you."

"Well, that's one thing we can both agree on," Frank said, spitting off the side of his horse.

"I didn't put old Bluejay down, but I never forgave him for the bite, and stopped riding him in the entirety."

"Horse would never bite me," I said. "Unless I told him to—which I don't plan on doing."

"Curly is the only one that horse will listen to," Frank said. "Whoever trained it knew what he was about."

"I can flop him to the ground now," I said. "If there comes a time we need to flop our horses, I will be the first to volunteer. Sally discovered a place on his right ear that triggers his flop response."

Frank looked at me like I was barking mad but didn't say anything.

"I can vouch for the truth of that statement," Wild Bill said. "I have personally seen the horse flop."

"I have no reason to doubt it," Frank said. "That horse is smarter than Curly."

"Better in a scrap too," Hap said.

"Of course, the important thing is being able to get up from the flop in the saddle. If I couldn't do that, I wouldn't even flop my horse to the ground."

"It's just like you to try and ruin my excitement. I've been working on getting Horse to flop on the ground for a long while now."

"I reckon we've done talked enough about horse flopping," Frank said. He didn't have much patience for jabber.

"Want to talk about New York City?" Wild Bill asked.

"No," Frank said. Followed by, "definitely not."

"Frank don't like cities," Hap said.

"Well, then that there is another thing we have in common," Wild Bill said. "If you had told me I had more than one thing in common with a Texan, I would have accused you of blasphemy, but it seems Curly is right, and you two are different enough from the typical Texan that I have decided not to categorize you as such, on account of the fact that I hate all Texans. Which is not to say that I hate Texas, mind you. Texas, without Texans of course, would be my definition of heaven on earth."

As Wild Bill said this, he gestured at all the rocks and shrubs and brutal desert sun as if he was pointing to the lushest landscape in the world.

"Talking," Frank said, "I am learning, is where we part in our similarities."

"Frank doesn't talk much," Hap said. "He's also not an eager listener."

"I'll listen to Scout or Two Yellow Hairs. I'll listen to things that are important. But I don't go in for jabber."

"If you want to jabber, Wild Bill, I'm happy to accommodate you. Sally says jabbering is what I'm best at," I said.

"Someone told me once that your name is actually James," Hap said, changing the subject.

"James is my actual given name, sure enough. Bill was my father's name. I started calling myself Bill because James was wanted at the time for assault. The guy I assaulted had no beef with me, as he was the one that started it—and besides, his reasoning on the matter was flawed. But the law didn't care and set to looking for me. So, I became Bill. Then, later, I gave myself my own nickname when I was telling some story to a journalist during a game of cards. I wanted him to think me a reckless card player, so I said my name was Wild Bill. The name stuck once it got printed in a newspaper."

Wild Bill could see that he had confused us all, because he then said, "It don't make sense when I say it out loud." Then he reached into his waistcoat and pulled out his flask and took a long slug of bourbon.

"You best keep your wits about you," Frank said.

"My wits does what I want them to most times," Wild Bill said, wiping his mustache on his sleeve. Seeing him take that slug of bourbon made me thirsty, but I didn't trust my wits to do my bidding, and also I knew Frank would admonish me, and so I stuck to water.

"How far are we away from any hostiles?" Wild Bill asked.

"Besides Two Yellow Hairs?" Merle asked.

"Of course!" Wild Bill said, shaking his head.

"Don't know," Frank said.

"I'll risk it," Wild Bill said, and took out one of his pistols and pointed it casually ahead of us and pulled the trigger. I saw some dust jump up, but as we got closer, I saw there was a dead rattlesnake on the trail that was leaking blood from where its head was supposed to be.

"Dang," I said. Because I had been looking in the same direction that Wild Bill was, and where I just saw dirt, he saw a six-foot-long rattlesnake. And he'd killed it with one shot! And he thought he was going blind!

"Rattlesnake is good eating," Merle said. "And we're out of steaks."

"That's a good point," Hap said. "Maybe a couple of us ought to range ahead and hunt up something for supper."

Because Baxter was taking up the extreme rear, it fell on Two Yellow Hairs and Merle and Hap to hunt up something for us to eat. One rattlesnake, tasty as it might be, wouldn't cut it. Frank, Wild Bill and I continued heading west, and slowly the land began to change, and canyons and gulches and mesas and arroyos and small dried-up washes sprouted up out of the ground, and the dust became redder, and there were now loose rocks under our horses' hooves, and strange rock formations cast long shadows, seemingly looking down on us. We were getting closer, headed deeper into the last strongholds of the Comanche nation. Rattles and his band were some of the last holdouts. The rest had either fled south into Mexico, fled north to join up with other Indian bands, or had given up and surrendered themselves to starve on a reservation in what is now called Oklahoma. Even though the Comanches offered little threat to American settlers anymore, the 4th Cavalry was raiding deeper and deeper into Comanche territory. A few years earlier no soldier would have ever thought to be out here. It would have meant certain and agonizing death.

"We knew this would probably happen," I said. "A Comanche warrior can't have a white wife and child. We knew if anyone saw Yellow Hair and her daughter, they would try to save them."

"You tried to save them too," Frank reminded me.

"I did, right up until Yellow Hair told me herself she was in love with Two Yellow Hairs and didn't want to leave him. Of course, I didn't know his name then. I saw them in Rattles' camp and assumed Yellow Hair and her daughter had been swiped and were being held hostage."

"I reckon you did the right thing," Frank said, "although at the time I thought different. The problem now is what these rogue soldiers might do to her. They won't think of her the same once she starts screaming at them in Comanche."

"I know it," I said.

3

That night we camped in a dried-up wash. Frank said if for some reason it rained—even somewhere a hundred miles in the distance—somewhere so far away we wouldn't know anything about it—we could all be washed away and drown. That sounded bad, but everyone else thought it was worth the chance—since it rained but rarely that time of year—to have the protection the wash offered. There were deep sandstone walls on both sides, which would make us hard to find, even though we didn't think anyone was looking for us. But you never knew. Just in the few years I'd lived in Silver Vein I'd noticed an increasing number of homesteaders out where they didn't belong, along with roving gangs of bushwhackers and desperate Indians fleeing the reservations.

Baxter was so laggardly he looked like a speck on the horizon.

"He ought to get himself a new horse," Frank said for the hundredth time.

"He loves that horse," Wild Bill said. "Just like I love my horse. I mean Bernie Waco's horse. My horse is—well, no matter. It's a city horse is all."

"What does one need with a city horse? That is a foolish-ness," Frank said.

"It is only a foolishness on account of I'm not in a city at the moment. Penn don't get scared of trolley cars or a bunch of hubbub."

"And yet here you are out in the middle of the opposite of hubbub with not a trolley car within a thousand miles."

"He didn't know he would be here," I said. "It is mostly acci-dental that he's even in Texas," I said.

"This ain't Texas," Wild Bill said. "Not in my book anyway."

"It might not be," Frank agreed. "We might be in New Mexico Territory."

"You know what I meant."

"Do I?"

"Curly said you were a burr of a conversationalist. And I can see it's true. You like to make talking as vexing as possible. I know the sort. Why, I'm better off talking to my new horse that ain't even mine than talk to some know-it-all ranger." Wild Bill was clearly mopey, probably because he didn't have enough bourbon in his blood. They'd gotten off on the wrong foot when Frank failed to recognize him, and now, instead of listening to his stories, he was correcting him.

"If you want to sally forth and talk to a four-legged mode of transport that cares only for grass and water, you won't see me stopping you," Frank said, spitting in the dirt.

And so Wild Bill tipped his hat at me and Baxter, who had finally caught up, and walked over and set to having a conversa-tion with Spot. I had conversations with Horse on many an occasion and actually understood where Wild Bill was coming from. Horses have big eyes, and their ears move this way and that, and they give you every indication that they are actually paying attention. Horses, like dogs, know how to listen. The same can't be said of most humans.

"Dang," Baxter said. "Colonel decided to take his time." The horse's head hung low and was almost dragging in the dirt, and he was foamy with sweat.

"Baxter, that horse is too long in the tooth to carry you on its back all day. I know you love the horse, but just look at him," I said.

Baxter dismounted and came around and lifted up Colonel's head. "He just needs some water is all."

"That horse will drop dead on you," Frank said. "I reckon you ought to let him retire. He's earned the right to spend his remaining days munching on grass. Besides, if we get into any sort of scrap, you're gonna need a fast horse. Also, and it pains me to say this, but if Colonel were to flop over dead, we would need to either eat him or hand him over to the Comanches to eat. Can't let a good dead horse go to waste. Not out here in the desert."

Frank was a blunt talker. But I could see Baxter knew he was right, because as soon as Baxter let go of Colonel's head, it drooped back down to about six inches off the ground.

"You're welcome to Molly," I said. "I stopped riding her once I got Horse, and she's done nothing but eat and grow lazy ever since. But if you can get her to lose some weight, she's a stout and fast horse."

"I reckon I'd be better off with a mule than ride Molly," Baxter said. "Where's Merle?"

"He and Two Yellow Hairs and Hap went hunting. I reckon they'll be along soon," I said.

But they weren't.

4

"Merle should be back by now," Baxter said.

"I second that opinion," Wild Bill said.

"Should we go look for them?" I asked.

"Can't," Frank said. "It's too dark. We'd need torches, and torches can be seen for miles, and we don't know who all is out here. Could be the entire 4th cavalry is making camp out there ahead of us somewhere we can't see. Hap ain't one to be snuck up on, so the chances are one of their horses come up lame and they've had to make their own camp somewhere."

"I also second that opinion," Wild Bill said, "much as I don't want to. I like Merle, even if he does nag me with too many questions. I guess we'll have to set out in the morning and see what's happened."

"If they've been ambushed, it ain't the Comanches," I said. "Not with Two Yellow Hairs with them."

"No, but there's plenty of other bad types roaming these parts," Frank said. "Could be Apaches or Kiowa—they don't like the Comanches one bit."

"Well," Baxter said, "might as well cook up that rattlesnake then, since it's all the food we're likely to get. I reckon it can feed the four of us. Unless anyone wants to chance the steaks we brought from Silver Vein, which has turned a funny color?" Not even Frank, who ate just about anything, thought that was a good idea.

It was now full dark, and, because of the high walls of the wash, it seemed even darker. Our fire would be unlikely to be seen by anyone in the area, as the fire was basically below the normal desert ground level, and smoke is hard to see in full dark. I was wishing Jeffers had come along, because I knew Frank to be terrible when it came to cooking. Next to Scout, who was captured, Hap was the best cook, followed by Baxter. Frank was dead last, and I wasn't much better. Wild Bill mostly drank his food, so probably didn't even bother with cooking.

"Baxter, I reckon you're the rattlesnake cook," I said.

"Aw, I can do it," Frank said.

"I wish you wouldn't," I said. "I'm too hungry to eat something all burned up and charred to death."

"The best way to eat a critter is to cook it until it breaks apart when you touch it," Frank said. "That way any diseases it might have are burned out of it."

I knew for a fact this was a flawed notion, but I let it go. Baxter took the dead rattlesnake and set to skinning it. I lay back on my bedroll, wishing like hell I'd had the ability to tell the future and had—despite what Sally wanted—brought the buffalo robe Two Yellow Hairs had given me; then I wouldn't be cursing Ely Turner for selling me a winter coat that was as warm as basically being naked. I used my saddle for a pillow and Horse's horse blanket, which smelled like years of horse sweat, to fight off the growing chill. I knew I wouldn't sleep well. I took a pull on a flask of bourbon I had in my saddlebag —and noticed Wild Bill looking at me. I decided I would sleep with the bourbon flask under my saddle in case Wild Bill decided to swipe it in the night. He drank too much bourbon and I reckon he was running low. Frank, I noticed, only drank coffee on the trail. Baxter was too busy skinning the snake to have noticed my flask, so I wasn't worried about him.

"Lots of stars out, not much sky to look at though," I said. Nobody said anything, probably because I'd said basically the same thing the night before. Frank had his pipe out, and I could smell the sweet tobacco smoke in the air. It reminded me of the saloon, and Micah, and how he'd probably sucked down most of my whisky already. Jeffers, in the beginning, when he'd first started cooking up chow at the saloon, had been good at keeping an eye on old Micah and keeping him in line. But now the two had become friends, and he was as likely to join Micah in plundering the whisky as anything else.

I thought about Sally and Bart, and pictured them sleeping under the buffalo robe, and that thought warmed me up some. But not for long, because it was just thoughts, and thoughts can only take you so far on a chilly night.

"Quiet out," Frank said. "I'd think this fire and smoke would attract curious coyotes and wolves and set them to howling."

I sat up and listened, and I could tell he was right.

"What do you reckon that means?" I asked. I was always more than ready to scare myself whenever I was sleeping in the dirt.

"Could mean there's a lion out there," Frank said. "Or it could be there's other people about we can't see."

"Could be it's *us* that's got them spooked," I said.

"Not with this smell," Frank said.

Baxter tended to the snake on the fire, and it sizzled and juices dripped out of it that made the fire crack and pop, and the smell was getting my stomach to rumbling.

"What did I tell you about that stomach of yours, Curly?" Frank asked.

"I can't help what noises come out of there," I said.

"A rumbling stomach can get a fella in trouble. Two Yellow Hairs can probably hear your stomach even now."

"Now *that* notion is a foolishness," Wild Bill said. "A strong stomach rumble is unlikely to travel such a great distance, even in all this quiet. Having said that, I do believe Curly has the loudest stomach rumble I've heard next to Nevada Bob. But in Nevada Bob's case, that's on account that an Arapahoe arrow went into his belly, and the hole it made never did heal up, and so there's no skin there to muffle the sound that comes out of that arrow hole when he gets hungry."

"Dang," Baxter said. "He just has an open hole in his belly?"

Wild Bill nodded. "He's got a patch on there, but it doesn't do anything for the noise. He's learned not to let himself get hungry because of the noise. Dang, but this dry desert air is rough on my hair."

Nobody said anything to that.

5

I slept briefly but spent most of the night looking up at the stars I could see waiting for morning to come. Just as I had the previous night and the night before that. As soon as the sun peeked up over the horizon, I was on my feet warming my hands with Horse's nose breaths. Then I hugged his neck, and nestled into it, because it was warm, and there was no part of my body that wasn't miserable with chill.

Frank was awake, smoking on his pipe and trying to get the fire going. Wild Bill was actually asleep, which was the first time I'd ever seen him in such a state. I looked at him and noticed that his mustache moved whenever he took in a breath, and then I noticed that he was now awake and looking back at me.

"Ought not to stare at a person when he's sleeping," he said.

"I just didn't know you ever did sleep," I said. "I'm glad to know it happens."

"I rarely do it on purpose. Sometimes it just up and happens anyway. I tend to have nightmares when I sleep, so I avoid it most times."

I didn't say anything to that. I hate to admit it, but I went off as soon as I could to join the war, and then ran away from the war almost immediately when one day I came across a pile of bloody hacked off legs. Once I saw how easy it was to get a leg blown off, and once I knew how keenly I didn't want either of my legs to end up in a bloody leg pile—well, that was it for me and war. So, I absquatulated and made for the frontier, which is how I ended up in Amarillo, which was so far away from Austin and the rest of Texas that you would hardly know there even was a war. But I didn't want to get into any of that. All I knew was I could understand how someone who *did* fight in the war might have a hard time sleeping at night.

For breakfast we had to settle for hard biscuits and coffee. And it would not be an exaggeration to say that the biscuits were still frozen solid and had the consistency of rocks. I put mine in a pocket to wait for the sun to warm it up into something that wouldn't yank my teeth out. Not Wild Bill though. In all things food-related, he ate his biscuit like a beast, in this case swallowing the whole thing in one go like a snake. I could see it make its slow way down his throat and watched as he poured some bourbon on top of it to help it make its way into his belly.

"Dang," Baxter said, speaking for all of us. I could tell that was one aspect of Wild Bill he had no interest in copying.

"You might try chewing," I said. "The only judge Silver Vein has ever died choking on a biscuit. His face was purple when they found him."

"Chewing is important," Frank agreed.

Wild Bill didn't answer because he was moving his neck in different ways, still trying to get the biscuit down.

Breakfast over with, we saddled up our horses and Wild Bill and Frank led the way, back in the direction we'd come the day before, to try and cut the sign of Merle, Hap, and Two Yellow

Hairs. We came across their sign around mid-morning, and so we headed north, following their tracks, which they'd made no effort to hide.

"Merle's tracks are these here," Frank pointed out. "You can tell by how heavy the tracks are on the left side because of the way Merle leans in the saddle."

"You can see here that he was looking back behind him," Wild Bill added.

I looked at the tracks, but they just looked like regular old horse tracks to me. I fully admit to not being good with tracking, whereas both Frank and Wild Bill had been tracking for years.

Then there were more tracks.

"Looks like it wasn't a horse going lame. They've got other fellas that followed them."

"That's probably why Merle was looking behind him," Wild Bill said.

Everyone but Wild Bill took out their rifles, and we kicked our horses into a lope.

Then we saw them in the distance. Or we saw some people anyway. We reined up our horses and I took a glass out of my saddlebag and took a quick look. It was them, sure enough. I could see Hap and Merle sitting in the dirt tied to a tree. Two Yellow Hairs had a rope around his neck and his hands tied above his head, and it looked like someone was poking something at his belly. There were about six unknown men surrounding them.

"Buffalo hunters, it looks like," I said, handing the glass to Frank. He put the glass to his eye. "I don't know what they mean to do to Two Yellow Hairs, but if they expect him to cry out in pain or show any sign of discomfort, they're going to be disappointed."

Frank handed the glass to Wild Bill, who put it to his eye and said, "Dirty looking group. Their horses have been well used. Buffalo hunters for sure. Lucky for us, I reckon those fellas are preoccupied with torturing Two Yellow Hairs. We should be able to get the drop on them."

"Again, we agree," Frank said.

———

The buffalo hunters were standing around gawking at Two Yellow Hairs while one of the men, he had a long bushy black and white beard, and an enormous buffalo coat that made him look like a buffalo standing on two legs, was holding a burning ember from the fire up to Two Yellow Hairs unblinking eye.

"I wouldn't do that if I were you," Hap said. "You would be making a big mistake."

"I reckon you already have," Merle said. He had a black eye and a cut on his lip.

"You two Indian lovers should shut your yaps you don't want to get the same treatment," the buffalo hunter said.

"Let's just hang all three of them," one of the men said. The rest laughed.

Then Two Yellow Hairs laughed. It was a loud laugh, and it infuriated the buffalo hunter.

"You think this is funny?"

Then Hap also started laughing, and Merle joined in. And the three of them carried on laughing as if they'd just heard the funniest joke in the world—laughing like demons they were.

"What the hell is so funny?"

Too late, the buffalo hunter turned around to find Frank Kilhoe, Wild Bill Hickok, and myself, Curly Barnes, pointing loaded weapons at him and his men.

"Oh..." the lead buffalo hunter said, then he made a play for his gun, and so Wild Bill pulled the trigger and shot a hole through the man's head, and he spun around and fell face first into the fire. The other buffalo hunters didn't fare any better.

They turned around and stood up, and ran this way and that, and tried to draw weapons. One buffalo hunter turned my way, and I shot him in the chest before he could raise his rifle. There was dust in the air, and smoke, and chaos—and then there was silence.

When the smoke cleared, six buffalo hunters lay in various stages of being dead.

Baxter dismounted and handed me the reins to his horse, and he set to cutting Hap and Merle free. Merle took one of Baxter's guns and walked up to one buffalo hunter crawling in the dirt.

"This is for my eye, you son of a bitch!" Merle shot the guy, who then stopped moving.

Two Yellow Hairs walked up to Baxter and took one of his knives he kept in his belt and walked up to the dead buffalo hunter in the fire and lifted his head up and took his scalp in one practiced motion. Then he did the same to the rest of the buffalo hunters. One of the men wasn't quite all the way dead, and his screams were terrible until he finally ran out of breath and stopped making any noise at all.

Hap walked over and picked up a deer hide that was wrapped around a bunch of meat. "We were butchering the deer we shot when these fellas called out to us," he said. "They were friendly at first, then they saw Two Yellow Hairs and turned on us. They had convinced themselves it was the Comanches fault the buffalo are almost gone, instead of themselves and the railroads. They planned on torturing Two Yellow Hairs to death and then hanging me and Merle."

"We was wondering what happened to you," Baxter said. "Didn't know buffalo hunters were even in these parts."

"I reckon they have to go further and further to find any buffalo to skin," Frank said. "At least the Comanches use the meat from the buffalo they kill. By the time they're done with a buffalo, there ain't nothing left for the buzzards to feed on. The same can't be said for buffalo hunters."

"Is Two Yellow Hairs okay?" I asked. "He looks pretty whomped up."

Wild Bill said something to Two Yellow Hairs, and made a bunch of hand gestures, and the two men went back and forth like that for what I felt was an exceptionally long time, before Wild Bill turned to us, shrugged his shoulders, and said, "He's fine."

He didn't look fine, but I let the matter go. Every day we didn't find and catch up with the troops was one day closer to Scout being made an example of.

"We need to go," I said. But then I thought of the man face first in the fire, and it occurred to me that in his current condition he no longer needed his buffalo coat. So, I hopped off Horse and walked over and took it for my own, trying not to look at the man's ruined head. The coat would swallow me whole, but it would be warm as an oven. Baxter and Merle dug through the pockets of the dead men and reclaimed all their knives and other weapons and got some new ones. Two Yellow Hairs claimed a Sharps carbine and a pistol.

"You ought to take one of their mounts, Baxter, as a back-up," Frank said. "That bay mare yonder looks like a good prospect." Baxter hung his head, then he walked over to the bay mare and untied her back legs where she'd been hobbled and walked her over to Colonel and looped her reins around the horn. "Just in case," he said. She was a damn sight better horse than Colonel, that was for sure.

"Just in case," Frank agreed, nodding.

"There's five more horses," Hap said. "Maybe we could all do with a spare mount."

And so, we collected up the buffalo hunters' horses, and we took their coffee—Wild Bill found a bottle of something he took to sipping on—and then we left the buffalo hunters to the lions and vultures and turned our horses west once again—ever deeper into the Llano.

Two Yellow Hairs led the way. He knew where their camp had been, and he told us—or told Wild Bill, who translated—it was now less than a day's ride. If we kept up a moderate pace, and skipped a noon feeding, and didn't run into more surprises, like more people we didn't know trying to kill us, we would get there by mid-afternoon.

The late morning sun beat down on us from above, and my sun-battered brain couldn't think of any reason why I'd ever thought it important to have a buffalo coat. It was hot enough to fry a dog. The desert, when it comes down to it, is dumb. At night, when the sun is gone, it's cold enough to freeze a fella to death; and, during the day, when the sun is out, it's hot enough to burn that same fella to death. There is no middle ground. Which is probably why only terrible things thrive in the desert. Every plant and clump of brush has needles on them. The lizards have horns on them and spit poison out of their mouths. The snakes slither sideways. And if you have the bad luck to find yourself out in the Llano, it is so monotonous and flat, a fella could easily get turned around and walk in hopeless circles until they finally up and died of thirst.

Luckily, we had Two Yellow Hairs, and the Llano was his hunting ground; he knew it the way I knew the saloon. Just after noon, when the sun was at its most belligerent, Two Yellow Hairs led us to a stream. You could have been twenty yards from the stream, and you would have never known it was there; but now there it was, snaking its way through the parched rocky shrubby ground, on its way to who knew where. We led the horses downstream and let them lip up water, and we went upstream and filled our own bellies. The water was cold, which surprised me because of how hot everything else was. I dumped my hat in the water and then dumped that water onto my head. Then I took my neck scarf and dumped it in the water and tied it back around my neck. Wild Bill took advantage of the water by washing his hair, which he said had gotten stringy from the heat. Frank had to look away to keep himself from admonishing him.

Full up with water, we mounted up and continued on.

6

"How long ago was it you think?" I asked Frank.

"About four days. Maybe five."

We had tied up our horses in a stand of cottonwoods and were walking through what had once been the Comanche camp. The scavengers had been at the bodies, but we could tell that there were seventeen dead: nine women, four old men, and four that weren't more than toddlers, two girls and two boys. Some had been trampled by horses. One baby had been slammed onto a rock, her skull cracked open like an egg. Three of the women had been raped before they were kilt, their clothes ripped open and their legs bloody. It was a horrible sight to see, and I couldn't understand how human beings could do such a thing.

Two Yellow Hairs was sitting alone, rocking back and forth, singing a song that set my neck hairs on end as tears freely streamed down his face. Frank and Wild Bill walked to each body in turn, pointing at things, and breaking down what all had happened. Me and Baxter and Merle stood together and let them do what they knew how to do. All I knew is that I wanted to murder each and every son of a bitch that took part in the butchery we were looking at.

"This ain't right," I said. "Not one bit of it."

"No, it ain't" Baxter said.

"Whoever did this just applied for a ticket to hell," Merle said.

———

"It went down like this, Curly," Frank said. "As you already know, the warriors, Scout, and Two Yellow Hairs and ten others, were all off hunting. There were, all told, about thirty here in camp. In addition to the seventeen dead, there were probably eleven others that got away, including Rattles."

"Rattles got away?" I asked. I'd seen an old man with white hair dead in the dirt, and I was so afraid it could be Rattles that I couldn't bring myself to look. I didn't want to see the man that brought Jim Shepland back from the dead, and saved my life, and trusted me with his son, all savaged and feasted on by coyotes and buzzards.

Frank shook his head. "He and Yellow Hair and her daughter took off on that white stallion you gave him, but they didn't get far. Scout and Two Yellow Hairs followed their tracks and gave chase—and that's when they saw the soldiers had caught Rattles. Scout, seeing his father held hostage, charged the group, and one of them shot his horse out from under him. We found the horse down yonder," Frank said, pointing.

"I know Ranald MacKenzie," Wild Bill said. "He's a tough soldier, and fearless, and as stubborn as the day is long—but he wouldn't go in for something like this. He graduated from West Point and has a sense of honor. I bet this here is something he knows nothing about."

"I've met the man," I said. "But I can't say what he is or isn't capable of."

"Some of the women and children got away," Frank said. "Most of them on foot and hid in a cave Two Yellow Hairs knew about, the entrance to which they covered in brush. It could be Rattles making his getaway distracted the soldiers, allowing the others to escape."

"We only found the tracks of six soldiers," Wild Bill said. "So, this could definitely be a rogue group. The soldiers that sign on for the frontier aren't as disciplined as they should be. A lot of them have grown blood thirsty."

Frank nodded in agreement. "Six soldiers came here. But only four left. One of them we found in a hole yonder with his throat cut. And we found another dead soldier at the bottom of a hill near where we found Scout's horse. His neck was broken. I reckon Scout kilt him before he got captured."

"Which won't help him any," I said. "What about the other warriors?"

"They rounded up some horses and went to the cave and then they all headed southwest into the canyons."

"What about the bodies?" I asked. "Once the soldiers left, why not come back and bury them? Why leave them to the elements and scavengers?"

"Because Two Yellow Hairs told them not to," Wild Bill said. "Curly, it took a lot of courage for him to walk into Silver Vein looking for you. He wanted to make sure if he could get you out here, you would believe him."

"Why wouldn't I believe him?" I asked.

"Because you're a white man," Baxter said. I could see the truth of what Baxter said, but it hurt my feelings anyway. When Jim Shepland died in my arms, he told me to "finish the job." At first, I thought he meant seeing that justice came for Torp Mayfair and his band of hired killers. But then I took it to mean following his philosophy of justice. Jim Shepland was color blind when it came to the law, and I aimed to be as well. The idea that after all that passed between us, after I'd spoken to Yellow Hair, and heard her express her love for Two Yellow Hairs, and let them be, that he still wouldn't trust me to believe what he told me made me sad.

But I understood it.

"So, I suppose we follow the soldiers' tracks," I finally said.

"Not quite yet," Hap said. "We have to help Two Yellow Hairs. We need to build some funeral pyres."

I nodded. "Hap, you and Baxter and Merle stay and help Two Yellow Hairs. Wild Bill and Frank--"

"Do you have to always call him Wild Bill?" Frank asked. "It sounds silly. I feel like Bill should suffice."

"I will answer to either one, and James," Wild Bill said.

"He's Wild Bill to me," I said. "That's just the way of it. We can't waste more time now that we've cut their sign. Otherwise, we might get there just in time to see Rattles and Scout swinging from a rope."

"It's closing in on dark," Frank pointed out. "These soldiers feel like they're home free. They don't know anyone's on their trail. They won't be traveling at night. Now, Curly, I know you're antsy, and I am too—I feel the same way about Scout that you do. And Rattles could have kilt us many times over. Hell, Two Yellow Hairs *would have* kilt us if Rattles hadn't stopped him when we first showed up in their camp chasing after Torp Mayfair—so I'm also keen to be on their trail. But there's no use trying to chase after them in the dark."

"Frank's right—goddamnit," Wild Bill said.

"Hurts to say that, I bet," Frank said, spitting into the dirt.

"It hurts me every time I agree with you. Yet I keep on doing it anyway, because you happen to keep saying what I'm about to say. And that just vexes me all the more, you damned pipe smoking codger."

Frank lifted an eyebrow. "Aw, I ain't as old as I look."

"You look like one of those fellas in the bible that lived to be nine hundred," Wild Bill said, throwing Frank a wink.

And I'll be danged, that made Frank throw back his head and laugh. In all the time I'd known Frank, I'd never heard him laugh. I'd gotten him to smile a few times—the kind of smile that looks like it hurts—but I'd yet to hear him laugh. But I guess Wild Bill had found a way to his funny bone.

We set up camp back on the top of a low rise where we'd tied up the horses. We didn't care to be down there in the camp with the smell of death, and the roaring of flies. We made sure to camp upwind. Hap and Merle and Two Yellow Hairs were off ranging far and wide, looking for and hacking up tree branches for the fires they would build the next day. Comanches didn't bury their dead in the Christian way. According to Scout, who would know, when a Comanche died someone would tie them on a horse and go out into the desert and find a cave or a narrow opening in a cliff and put the body in there and fill the place with rocks to ward off critters. That way none of their enemies could disturb the body and that person's spirit could go to the Spirit World in peace.

But we didn't have time for that. Two Yellow Hairs told us the next best thing was to burn them and send them to the afterlife with all their possessions. We'd already put each person's possessions in separate piles; even the children had their own small piles. Looking at all the piles got my eyes to leaking and I had to walk off by myself and sit down.

I remembered the copy of *The Daily Silver Vein* Deedee had given me, and I unfolded it. I figured a Pap Kickins editorial might distract me from all this unnecessary death.

Curly Barnes has been sheriff of Silver Vein for a little over a year, and now lawless Savages feel free to walk through the heart of town.

I changed my mind and put the newspaper away. It was coming on full dark—which meant it was starting to get cold—which meant it would soon be freezing. I took the buffalo coat I'd swiped and set to beating the ripeness out of it with a stick. Every time the stick hit the robe, a cloud of dust would jump out of it. But not the ripeness. The dead buffalo hunter who owned this robe, I figured, must have been born with some sort of disease that made him smellier than a normal person. Wild Bill had been ripe when he'd shown up in Silver Vein, and his buffalo skinner jacket made my eyes water, but this particular buffalo coat was another thing altogether. So, what I finally did was, I dumped some coffee on it. And danged if it didn't sort of work!

Hap was back to being our cook, and he was preparing a fire to cook the deer they'd kilt and hacked up the day before. There was also some spices that we'd taken from the buffalo hunters after they'd all been kilt, and Baxter had used the spices on the steaks, and it smelled delicious. I got an idea and took my buffalo coat and put it in the way of the fire's smoke in the hopes that the robe might end up smelling like deer steaks and coffee.

"You sure are putting a lot of work into that buffalo coat," Frank observed.

"I like to be warm, but I need to get the ripeness out," I said.

"I knew a ranger named Klok Montague, who had a smell so bad it one day kilt his horse," Frank said.

"He was only allowed to ride behind us," Hap said. "If he'd ridden anywhere else one of us would have had to shoot him."

I didn't believe this. "You can't kill a horse with ripeness."

"Sure you can," Wild Bill said. "Goddamnit! I did it again! But in this case, yet again, I find I am in agreement. You see, Curly, horses have a keen sense of smell. And if a fella smells rotten, a smart horse will either run that fella under a tree, buck him into the dirt and stomp on him, or, if none of that works, up and commit horse suicide."

"That's what happened to Klok's horse," Frank said, nodding. "He let his horse out to graze one morning, and that horse, he just let out a frustrated nicker and walked right off a cliff."

"His next horse was also smart," Hap said. "I believe his name was Clyde, and he did just what you said, Wild Bill, and went and broke Klok's neck by running him under a low tree branch."

"We buried old Klok somewhere near Goliad. He smelled better dead than alive," Frank said.

"That is some story," I said. "I wouldn't want Horse to commit horse suicide on account of this coat."

Frank sucked on his pipe and squinted his eyes up and said, "My God, Curly, you've up and turned my point on its head and have now gone and used it against me. I will no longer criticize your exertions as to that buffalo coat."

That was the time Frank apologized to me. He did it only the once—and it wasn't a straight apology—but I remember the moment to this day.

After our steaks, I was three days without sleep, and was in no mood to do any jabbering, and so I buttoned myself into my new buffalo coat and discovered it was the warmest buffalo coat I'd ever come across. But better than that, it softened up the dirt under me, allowing me to fall asleep almost as if I was back home under the buffalo robe with Sally and Bart. Cocooned inside my new coat, I couldn't see the stars, but that was okay. They weren't going anywhere.

———

We set out at first light—Frank and Wild Bill and myself. Hap and Baxter and Merle stayed behind to help Two Yellow Hairs.

I promised Baxter and Merle that we wouldn't make any moves until they caught up with us. But I didn't know if I would be able to keep that promise. There were only four of them, and if I saw them, I didn't think I would be able to keep my temper in check. I might do for all of them myself.

The soldiers' tracks were almost a week old, but the desert hadn't done anything with them, and they were easy enough to follow. They headed southeast. Four shod horses, and the three unshod horses containing Scout and Rattles and Yellow Hair and her daughter. Yellow hair's daughter obviously had a name, but I didn't know what it was.

"These rogue soldiers were just a scouting party," Wild Bill said. "I hate to say it, but I bet these tracks will take us straight to the 4th Cavalry."

"I reckon you could be right," Frank said.

"What do we do then?" I asked. "We can't take on an army."

"No, we can't," Wild Bill said. "I guess we'll have to figure something out when we get there."

"Curly, you need to be prepared for the fact that they will want to make an example of Scout. Rattles and his band have been giving the soldiers fits for years. At least that's how they see it. Swiping their horses, leading them in circles, trapping them in canyons and washes only they know about. Rattles might be the second most wanted Comanche in all of the Llano. Their most respected leader since Buffalo Hump himself. And Scout has also made quite a name for himself, since he spent time living in your home as a boy. And those soldiers will want their revenge. He kilt one of their own, after all."

"I know it," I said. I had been hearing about Scout's exploits from admiring but frustrated soldiers that came through town and stopped in the saloon for a couple of toots of whisky. It had always made me somewhat proud, hearing his exploits, but also worried. Sally and I still thought of Scout as the shy good-natured boy who loved nothing more than a hug and taught little Tommy Yonder to hunt and track and use a bow and arrow. The fact that the town couldn't accept him and bullied and harassed him to the point that we worried for his safety and sent him back to Rattles made us sad. It had been Rattles idea that he come to live with us, to learn our language and ways, as he understood that we weren't going anywhere, and that, year after year, more and more homesteaders would be crowding into the area—and that the Comanche would have to learn our culture so they could figure us out.

I think Scout's experience in Silver Vein convinced him that there was no way to be on good terms with people who didn't want him. I think it put a chip on his shoulder. And I couldn't help wondering if I'd never taken Scout to Silver Vein in the first place, if any of this would have ever happened at all. Scout spoke English pretty well, and I was sincerely hoping he wasn't using it to insult and rile up his captors. He was in enough trouble as it was.

"If it's as you say," Wild Bill said, "MacKenzie will probably hang him, but not without a trial first, even if it's just a show trial. And he won't do anything until he gets back to Fort Belknap."

Frank gave that some thought, and then said, "If that is so, and you know the man and I do not, we might be able to catch up to them before then. Fort Belknap is a fair bit southeast of here, and these tracks are heading southeast, heading straight for the flat part of the Llano. Could give us time to formulate a plan. The best thing we have going for us is they aren't expecting anyone to be following them."

"They seem pretty confident considering this is Comanche territory," I said.

"Not like it was even five years ago," Frank said. "Five years ago, we'd probably have been kilt ourselves being out here."

"Scout could probably escape if he wanted to. But not if they have Rattles," I said.

"Don't forget Yellow Hair and her daughter. He wouldn't escape without them."

"All this talk is fine and good. But all we can do right now is follow the tracks," Frank said, kicking his horse into a faster lope.

7

HASTINGS

Captain Shelby was taking up the rear. If he got too close to the prisoners, he was afraid he might kill them. Especially the young warrior that had foolishly charged them and kilt his buddy Horvath. That young warrior would have kilt Shelby too, if Hastings hadn't whomped him.

Except for the warrior, everything had worked out just as Major Hastings had drawn it up. The Indians were all asleep, caught by complete surprise. By the time most of the old warriors could get their weapons they were all either run through with cutlass or shot.

Sykes and Pulaski made quick work of the old women. Captain Shelby took care of the toddlers without even having to waste a bullet. Then, when it was just the younger Comanche women, they'd tied them up and had their way with them until they'd satisfied themselves.

The only thing that caught them up short was how much fight the white woman put up. She screamed and hurled curses at them as good as any Comanche.

"Looks like they don't need rescuing after all," Captain Shelby had said.

"They'll come around," Major Hastings said. The way he looked at the blonde woman, Shelby could tell the major was sweet on her. Which wasn't like the major. He usually was more practical about such matters. It was three out of four that wanted to do for the blonde woman and her daughter. They'd been enslaved by the Comanche long enough to learn the language—which, as Shelby saw it, meant there was nothing left to save.

Major Hastings was in the lead, with the old Indian trussed up to his white stallion, riding next to him. Any Comanche that could live long enough to have as many wrinkles as this one did and rode such a piece of horseflesh as that white stallion, was nobody to take lightly. He'd already proven himself a quick thinker, gathering up the blonde woman and the girl and fleeing while the others were still waking up. The old Indian never said a word, but there was a power about him that Major Hastings could feel. He had the sense that the man was someone important. Or had been at one time. But his time was past. Now he was just another rogue Indian that had an appointment with a rope.

The two women they had saved, despite their combativeness, were sullenly sharing Horvath's horse on the other side of the major. Sykes and Pulaski were riding right behind them, rifles at the ready.

Major Hastings couldn't help but keep stealing glances at the white woman. It had been a long time since the major'd had a woman that hadn't been rented or wasn't a spoil of war. He thought maybe this woman might be the one to change that. Despite her situation, Hastings knew that if she got cleaned up, she would be quite comely. Thankfully, it was early. She'd only just been saved. She just needed more time to adjust to her new circumstances, see that she was no longer enslaved, and then she would come to appreciate what the major had done for her. Once she came to grips with the fact that she was once again with her own people, she would soften up to him. One day she might even smile at him. Hopefully, that day would be soon.

Until then, he needed to get his soldiers and prisoners safely across the Llano and meet up with MacKenzie. He knew they were waiting for him to get back to camp and report. A scout would be roving the desert, waiting to lead them to the colonel and the 4th cavalry—who, for safety, never camped in one place for too long.

Major Hastings held up his canteen and turned to the old Indian and mimed taking a drink.

The Indian didn't say anything.

"The nicer you are, the nicer I can be," the major said.

The Indian didn't say anything.

He would though—one way or the other.

8

Hap and Baxter and Merle and Two Yellow Hairs caught up with us when we made camp that night. We were in a land of red sandstone buttes and mesas and cliffs and narrow trails between sheer walls that rose up to the heavens on either side. We'd seen bighorn sheep and the tracks of lizards and snakes in the crumbly red dust—but no sign of soldiers or any other humans. The tracks had turned away from the southeast and headed now almost due south, towards Mexico.

"We're a couple of days ride from the Pecos River. If I were the 4th Cavalry, that's where I might be camped out. Plenty of water, and it's not far from Fort Stockton," Hap said.

"Could be Hap's got the right of it. Could be it's not Fort Belknap they will head to, but Fort Stockton," Frank said.

"Could be these aren't even MacKenzie's men. Could be they belong to Major Bliss," Hap said.

"Only one way to find out," Wild Bill said, but it was hard to hear him because he was brushing his hair and it was flopped in front of his face, messing with the words coming out of his mouth.

"What's that?" Baxter asked. He was chomping into a piece

of fried ham from a wild hog they'd come across when catching up with us.

"Catch up with them and ask them, I reckon," Wild Bill said. "I don't know Major Bliss like I know MacKenzie."

"Could be they're just headed to the closest fort in these parts," Merle said.

"I'm with Bill on this," Frank said. "All this speculating ain't doing us a bit of good."

I didn't have much to add to the conversation. I just knew Rattles and Scout needed our help. I also knew I'd eaten too much ham and most of my attention was in my belly and not my head. Ham, like many other foods, is one of my weaknesses, and I didn't stop eating until sweat broke out on my forehead—and now I was miserable.

"I agree," I said, mostly because I didn't want to hear any more speculating. The truth was, we had no idea what was going on, and no amount of trying to figure it out was going to get us anywhere. Not knowing as little as we did.

Every once in a while, some critter out in the darkness would stumble and shale rocks would clatter down into the dust from above making me jump. If you had an active imagination, like I did when I was away from home, it sounded like something sneaking up on us. Like a lion or a pack of wolves or relatives of the hog we had all just been gnawing on.

"Probably just a mountain goat," Frank said, seeing me jump. "Lots of them in these parts."

"Well," I said, because it annoyed me to be seen to be jumpy, "they should go to sleep and stop walking about in the dark."

"Why don't you go up there and tell them?" Frank said.

"I don't speak goat," I pointed out.

This got a laugh out of Wild Bill, which made Baxter laugh, which made Frank frown. It seemed Frank and Wild Bill were more alike than not, and neither one of them liked it.

But Wild Bill had actually done the impossible and made Frank laugh.

Two Yellow Hairs and some of the other Comanches had given me the nickname Porcupine Pants, because one night, out in the middle of a winter storm, a porcupine took advantage of my sleeping warmth by sitting on me in the night. I remember it even now, the feeling of not knowing what manner of critter was using me for a pillow. My imagination ran wild that night, thinking it could be anything from a lion cub to a baby grizzly bear. The next day I found a bunch of holes in the back of my pants where the critter's claws had been. I had gotten off easy. I later learned it was a porcupine that had been sucking up my warmth. I was lucky I didn't startle it while it was sitting on me, or I might have woken up stuck full of needles.

None of that memory made me an easy sleeper out in the dark surrounded by strange noises. It was a cloudy night, and the moon wasn't much to speak of, being nothing more than a sliver, and so the dark was even darker than usual dark. I could barely make out Horse's rump as he nuzzled the dirt looking for grass to chew on. Once the fire went out, I knew my imagination would only get worse.

Out in the very far distance, I could see lightning. There was a storm out there somewhere. Lightning was no doubt coming out of the heavens, zapping at whatever trees might be out there. It was quite a show, the lightning. At least from this safe distance. I was glad we weren't sleeping in a dried out wash this time.

"Someone should stay up to feed the fire," I said.

"Curly, that's a great idea," Frank said, mumbling because of the pipe in his mouth. "I think that person should be you."

"Last time he fed the fire so well, it ate so much it died," Baxter said.

"I'll take the first shift," I said.

Frank nodded, and nobody else said anything. Not even

Wild Bill, who only slept by accident and would be up anyway. I felt he should have volunteered. It wasn't long before Baxter and Merle were snoring away, with Frank adding his own locomotive noises. Hap was a silent sleeper, and I couldn't tell what Wild Bill was doing. Two Yellow Hairs, much like Scout, preferred to sleep away from camp, out somewhere in the desert dark. He'd been quiet ever since they'd caught up with us, no doubt lost in his own thoughts, likely thinking up all manner of ways he would eventually get his revenge. I liked Two Yellow Hairs, and I'm glad he liked me back, because I wouldn't have wanted to be in his crosshairs.

I was glad for the lightning show, as it kept me company. After a few hours, my toasty buffalo coat decided it was time for bed. I don't even remember falling asleep.

9

HASTINGS

Major Hastings woke up to find that his prisoners were still trussed up. None of them had escaped in the middle of the night. You couldn't trust Indians not to try and escape. But they were still there, the old man and the warrior, and the two white women the Comanches had enslaved—the beautiful blonde woman and her daughter. It had been three days since their rescue, and the woman had yet to say a word, not even to say thank you. A couple of times the major made eye contact with the white woman, and she had hissed at him like a cornered raccoon. It was now clear that it was going to take longer for the woman to warm up to him than he originally thought. Which was too bad because he couldn't wait forever. He had wants and needs, and every day they got more insistent.

The four soldiers and the bound-up prisoners headed south out of the canyons and mesas and into the orange sandy flatness of the Llano. The day before, they'd found a skeleton of a man and a mule, with a wagon load of cotton. There was no sign of violence. It was probably just one more example of someone getting lost in the desert and wandering around until they died.

"I don't like the way the woman looks at me," Hastings told Shelby.

"She's gone Injun," Shelby said. "Ain't civilized no more. We ought to have put them two in the ground before we left that Indian camp."

"And the girl, she ain't said a word either," Hastings said, ignoring Shelby's comment. "I offered her a hard candy and she just looked at it in my hand like it was some sort of poison."

"She probably was born wild, major. She don't likely know about candy. She's more apt to be on firmer footing with a raccoon haunch."

"I will make sure she thanks me for saving her," Hastings said. He turned his attention to the two Comanches. "Look what you've done to her!" he shouted. The two Comanche, the old one with the white hair, and the younger one that attacked and kilt Horvath, just sat in the dirt, looking down and not saying anything. There were a couple of times where Shelby could have sworn it looked like the younger one could understand what he was saying. But the very idea, of a savage that could understand English, was silly in its impossibility. Shelby knew for a fact Indians had the same types of brains as animals, and animals couldn't speak English.

That night, Hastings asked Shelby to take the two Indians away from camp. He wanted the white woman to realize her predicament, and hopefully appreciate that he wanted to be her friend. He waited until it was just the three of them alone.

He smiled at the woman. "I mean you no harm," he said. He knew it seemed like a crazy thing to say. She'd seen him, in the heat of battle, kill a whole bunch of people. She'd seen him hack an old man to pieces. So he added, "I know we got started off on the wrong path, the two of us, but the truth of it is, I saved you and your daughter from savages. I am going to bring you back to your people. You will learn that I can be your friend. I want to be your friend." And the major gave the blonde woman his best smile.

She screamed a long string of curses at him in what must have been Comanche. None of it sounded good to Hastings. It sounded like she was most vexed by him. And she clearly didn't care for his smile. That was for sure. And then he remembered hearing that Indians weren't smilers. That smiling was a threatening thing.

But that was okay, he supposed. Because, in this case, it *was* a threat. Enough honey, Major Hastings thought, standing up. He would just have to take what he wanted.

"Suit yourself then," Hasting said. He walked over to the blonde girl and dragged her away from the fire and put a gag in her mouth to shut her up. Then he walked back to the blonde woman who looked up at him in terror.

"Once you get to know me, you'll think different."

The blonde woman screamed.

10

"Well, all I can say is, I am on record on many an occasion warning you that this might happen," Merle said, looking at the dead horse.

"He seemed fine," Baxter said.

"Like *hell* he did. We have, all of us, told you—no, warned you—that this precise very thing was more than likely, if not imminent," Frank said, looking at what would probably be his dinner.

"Good thing you have a spare horse," I said. "You have Frank to thank for that."

"I can't eat my own horse," Baxter said, looking down at his beloved Colonel. "*You* do it."

"You want me to eat Colonel?" Merle asked.

"Most horses you have to shoot in the head," Frank said. "I'd say you got off easy."

"Well, Frank," I said, "I reckon you're an old hand at this. What would you have us do?"

"Well, since Colonel was of an advanced age when he died, he's apt to be too gamey and tough to gnaw on. Old horses don't make good eating, despite Baxter's thoughtful suggestion. This desert ground is too hard to dig much of a hole in. Not one big enough for a horse anyway. So I say we—"

"Baxter might not want to hear this," Hap said. But it was too late.

"—cut open his old belly and let the critters have at him, and then shoot one of them critters and eat it."

"A horse, next to a dog, is the closest friend a person could ever have," Wild Bill said. "They trust you to keep them safe from predators. They transport you across deserts and prairies and cobblestone streets. Horse and rider form a bond thicker than mud. We will not be opening up Baxter's horse," Wild Bill said, clearly agitated.

"The kind of things I like to eat don't take to horse meat," I said. "Only things likely to be out here, and want old Colonel, are things like buzzards and crows and flies."

"All the same, if we don't cut open his belly, he will just explode. Better to poke a hole where the gases can escape from," Frank said. "It's only practical."

"Well," Baxter said, "I reckon old Colonel would want to explode, if'n he was given the choice."

"Baxter is quite fond of explosions," Merle said, with a knowing nod.

"It ain't really—" Frank said.

"It's not the kind of explosion the likes of which you might be thinking," Hap said delicately.

It really was a good thing we had the spare mounts. We decided to let Colonel be. In death he looked downright ancient. We would leave him be and move on. Such is life. Colonel, when it comes to horses anyway, lived a long life. By the time he died he was so long in the tooth, that's just about all that was in his head. On the other hand, when you compared him to Molly, and her spending the entirety of her days lazing about chomping on grass, no longer having to worry about anyone wanting to put a saddle on her and force her to leave home, Colonel didn't have it so good. I, for one, was relieved to see him finally move on to the great pasture in the sky.

You can't be a deputy and ride a slow horse.

―――――

"Dang. This horse steers funny," Baxter said. He'd been complaining nonstop about his new horse's manners and personality and behavior and smell and the way her head would suddenly pop up, as if she'd just come up with an idea, just when Baxter was least expecting it, once even bonking him in the nose.

"You'll get used to it," Wild Bill said, yet again. "Every horse is different. That horse had a different owner."

"And he was an asshole," Baxter said.

"Now Baxter," Wild Bill said, "you've only ever really had but one horse in your whole life. You can't expect to be used to a new one just yet."

"I don't care for her looks," Baxter said. "She's got too much fur."

"That's winter hair I expect," Frank said. "Them buffalo hunters came from up north. The horses still got their winter hair on. A couple of weeks and most of that fur will fall out."

"A horse can tell its hair what to do?" Baxter asked.

"Something like that," Hap said.

"And yet we have to go and get someone to cut ours off," Merle said. "Although, I don't go and get mine cut off. I do it myself. I don't like someone other than me waving anything sharp near my head."

"I agree," Wild Bill said, waving his hair around dramatically.

We were heading south, following the tracks, when they turned suddenly east. Wild Bill said it was on account of they had run into a scout that let them know where the main troops were. There was a new set of tracks that weren't there before. Said it must have been a pre-arranged rendezvous. Which I figured was probably true. Wild Bill had been a scout himself during the war, and no doubt knew what he was talking about. It was getting hotter, and the land, if you can believe it, was even flatter than the land west of Silver Vein. Sometimes you couldn't tell the land from the sky. I spent a bunch of time looking at the clouds, on account of there wasn't much else to look at. But, as flat is it looked, I knew there were small creeks and arroyos—but you had to either know where they were, like Two Yellow Hairs did, or stumble onto them.

"The sky is growing," I said. "I think I liked it better with the red rocks sticking out of the ground, even with the mountain goats kicking dirt and shale rocks down on us."

"Aw, this ain't nothing," Frank said. "You think this is flat, you should see the desert of Old Mexico."

"I'll take your word for it," I said.

"I once had to march through hundreds of miles of desert hotter and flatter than this here. Nothing but bleached bones for scenery. That's where I first learned the importance of a good pebble to suck on."

"There was also a salt lake all dried up," Hap said. "If it's the same desert I think you're talking about."

"It was way down there on the other side of the border," Frank said.

"I agree—goddamnit," Wild Bill said, and then he spit off the side of his horse. "About the pebble. Not the desert."

"How far up ahead do you think the rest of the soldiers are?" Baxter asked. "Are we gaining ground?"

"The way they're riding their mounts, I'd say not far. Less than forty miles if I had to guess. You don't lope along if nobody is behind you unless you're not going far. Unless you're eager to get somewhere. If they were expecting a long ride yet, they would be walking their mounts."

"I agree—goddamnit," Wild Bill said, and then he spit off the side of his horse.

"You don't have to spit and curse every time you agree with me," Frank said, spitting off the side of his horse. "Or you'll run out of spit and then where will you be?"

"I expect I'd be thirsty," Wild Bill admitted. "But I can't help it. I find agreeing with you so disagreeable, spitting and cursing just up and happens."

"If you die of thirst, I'll make sure the world knows you died in Texas," Frank said, smiling like a hungry wolf. When Frank smiled, it was almost worse than him not smiling.

"Aw, this isn't—"

"Oh it's Texas, all right. And, for all eternity, people would say that Wild Bill Hickok died in Texas."

"You trying to make me air out my insides?"

"Texas ain't so bad," Frank said.

"Well, it ain't worth dying in or for. I can tell you that much. In fact, the idea of dying in Texas is so disagreeable to me, I can guarantee it won't happen."

I wasn't so sure about that. There were plenty of ways Texas could kill someone—even without bringing Texans into it. There were snakes and wolves and lions, and poisonous lizards, and scorpions, and Indians and Comancheros and bandits—and that didn't even take into account the weather, which was often rude and intemperate, with freezing ice balls and twisters. Or you could just get lost and wander around in circles until the sun sucked all of your juices out and shriveled you up like a raisin.

Two Yellow Hairs pointed ahead, and said something, and shook his head, and then turned his horse around.

"What's he about?" Frank asked.

Wild Bill squinted, then he pointed. "Sandstorm."

I looked where he was pointing, and I could see that the sky looked dark with storm.

"Sounds like a thunderstorm out there," I said. "Thunder anyway."

Wild Bill squinted some more. "Oh my God! Look! There! Out in front of the sandstorm!"

"Shit!" Hap said.

We stopped our horses and stared. It wasn't thunder. It was a stampede of Buffalo, and they were all colored completely orange—and coming right at us.

"And here we are with no shelter to speak of," Frank said. "And no trees to climb."

"I say we follow Two Yellow Hairs," I said, turning Horse around. "He seems to know what he's doing."

Wild Bill caught up with Two Yellow Hairs, and they spoke some, and then he waved us on.

"It could be, Baxter, that Colonel saved your life by up and dying like he did. For this, you're going to need all the speed that horse has in her!" Frank kicked his horse into a run, and then all of us were following Two Yellow Hairs as fast as we could get our horses to carry us. We had no choice but to let our spare mounts fend for themselves. Yanking an extra horse along was slowing us down, and being too slow would get us all kilt. I looked behind me and I could see the sand was getting closer, and so were the thunderous hooves of a herd of stampeding crazed buffalo. If they overran us or if our horses got spooked, they would trample the lot of us into human pancakes.

Even though we were racing ahead of it, the thunder, and the howling of the wind, only grew louder.

11

HASTINGS

They were lucky they found the tree when they did. It wasn't much of a tree, and under normal circumstances would not have even caught their attention. But now, with the horizon blotted out by sand, it was their only hope. It was the old Indian that spotted it. And Hastings was no fool. At the moment, they were all on the same side. The side that wanted to stay alive. They had dismounted and let their horses go. The horses were so terrified they would have broken free of anything to which they might have tried to hitch them. And now the nine of them were all hovering around the trunk of the chunky mesquite tree, which they had lashed themselves to— and they listened to the wind howl and the thunder of the terrified buffalo. They could feel the orange sand sting any part of themselves they left unprotected.

Hastings had gallantly offered to use his body to protect the woman and her daughter—he figured now that they'd been intimate, she would feel grateful for the offer—but she had screamed and run off and would have been buried alive by sand or stampeded by buffalo, if he hadn't relented and let her be protected by the old Indian. Hastings had to admit, even though he looked a million years old, and was more wrinkled up than an elephant, the old Indian was surprisingly spry and strong.

They had met up with the scout the day before, a young corporal named Plowright, who'd immediately asked where the other scout was. Scouts, apparently, liked other scouts. Captain Shelby made up some story about Grimes getting stung by a scorpion and dying of fever in the night. It was such a detailed lie that Hastings was impressed. Plowright let them know Colonel MacKenzie had turned his troops east and would be waiting at a ravine near a trickle of a creek a couple days west of Fort Richardson. Hastings wasn't looking forward to having to explain to the colonel that he'd lost his scout. For all his experience and exploits, the colonel could be quite soft, and even paternal, about some of the younger soldiers under his command.

The nine of them closed their eyes and turned their heads to get away from the sand that whipped at them and took advantage of every nook and cranny on their bodies. Hastings had known a soldier who'd lost both his eyes in a sandstorm, making him permanently blind. The major knew not to open his eyes for any reason as he pulled his coat as far up over his head as he could.

The howling continued for some time. Even though his eyes were closed, the major could sense they were in the thick of things, because there was no light out there on the other side of his eyelids. The sand was so thick it had blotted out the sun.

And still the howling continued.

12

W e ran our horses at a dead run for a good ten minutes when Two Yellow Hairs suddenly disappeared. And then Frank and Hap also disappeared, and then Wild Bill, and then I felt the ground give way underneath me, and I was suddenly racing down a steep slope. Horse stopped running and pulled back and sat on his haunches as he lumbered down the slope.

"Okay Curly!" Frank yelled. "Now is the time to flop your horse!"

Even though we were in the middle of a sandstorm, and a stampede, the thought of being able to flop Horse to the ground filled me with excitement. I pulled up on Horse's reins and dismounted and grabbed at his right ear and yelled into his ear, "There now..." and Horse flopped right on over! A years-long goal finally realized! I lay down on his neck, and looked over, and saw that, dang it, everyone else's horses were also flopped over. Even Baxter's horse was flopped over, and he'd only been riding it less than a day!

"Keep your eyes shut!" Wild Bill yelled. Even though he was no more than ten feet away from me, I could barely hear him, as the wind was literally screaming at us now. I briefly peeked my head up and a pile of sand attacked my face, going up my nose and into my mouth, and all into my hair.

"Dang!" I yelled, but nobody could hear me. I couldn't tell whether Horse's eyes were open or not. The rest of him was calm and warm though, and his broad back made a great barrier from the wind. I wormed my way off his neck—he wasn't about to get up—and crawled in between his front legs and buried my face in his belly. He smelled like horse sweat, of course, but it was a far sight better than a mouthful of sand. From my new protected place, I chanced another peek—I'd never been in a sandstorm before—and I was surprised to see nothing but darkness.

"The sun's gone!" I yelled into Horse's belly. I listened to the fury of the wind as it whistled and whorled and tore at my clothes, and then the sand started to bury me and Horse both. Every minute or so I had to wipe the sand off me and Horse so the storm wouldn't bury us. Slowly but surely the wind got less howly, and the sun came back, and I was not getting buried in as much sand—and then, finally, I looked up, and the sand and buffalo had moved on, and all was silent—it was suddenly a perfectly sunny day, with a blue sky free of clouds.

I sat up and clapped the sand off me and looked over to see Frank and Hap and Wild Bill standing up and beating themselves clean. Frank somehow seemed to have avoided sand altogether.

Not Baxter.

"Baxter?"

An orange mound six feet away started vibrating, and then a hand shot up out of it and began frantically gesturing and pointing.

"You in there?" Merle asked.

A loud muffled roar emerged from the sand mound, and the hand turned into a fist.

"I guess so," Merle said. He walked over and started scooping up sand and tossing it over his shoulder. Slowly Baxter's arm and legs appeared, and the mound exploded as both Baxter and his new horse stood up, completely covered in orange. Baxter's entire face was the color of a pumpkin, everything except for his eyes.

I heard laughter, and I looked over and Two Yellow Hairs was laughing so hard he had tears shooting out of his eyes and had to sit down to catch his breath. Then he got back up and pantomimed Baxter and his big, bug eyes, and hopped around holding his belly.

"It ain't—" Baxter croaked, spitting sand out of his teeth, "—that funny."

"It's pretty funny, all right," Wild Bill said, shaking his hair out.

"Frank, how come you don't have any sand on you?" I asked. "You don't look any different than before the storm."

"Aw, I reckon Baxter took all the sand," Frank said.

"You and that horse are head to tail orange," Hap said.

"He don't exaggerate, Baxter. You should see yourself," Merle said.

"But now we've got ourselves a problem," Wild Bill said.

Frank nodded. "If the storm could bury Baxter, even here in this arroyo, I imagine it had no problem burying the soldiers' tracks."

"Dang," I said.

"Dang is right," Hap agreed.

"Fucked is more like it," Frank said, spitting into the orange sand.

We mounted our orange horses and continued on to the bottom of the arroyo where a small stream creeped along. The horses dipped their heads and nuzzled through the dust and lipped up some water into their bellies. I didn't care to drink dust water, but Frank insisted we do it anyway. Frank was mostly right about these things, but it didn't make it pleasant. I took my dusty hat and scooped up some water and slurped it down, dust and all.

——————

The flat prairie was still flat, but now it was also completely orange. There were no tracks of any kind. It was as if nobody, man or animal, had ever existed. After ten minutes of nothing at all, we finally saw a prairie dog stick its head out of a hole, but then he just put it right back in.

"And that is another problem," Hap said. "I bet this whole desert is full up with prairie dog holes and termite mounds, only now we can't see them on account they're covered up by all this orange dust."

"It seems almost rude to attack us with this kind of weather," I said. "In my whole life I never even heard tell of a thunderstorm made out of sand. Or a herd of stampeding orange buffalo. The sandstorm had chased after the buffalo and wiped out any sign of their existence too.

"I reckon we should continue east," Wild Bill said. "If we're lucky, maybe we could cut their sign. I suggest me and Two Yellow Hairs range on ahead."

"Just don't let that horse of yours up and break a leg in some unseen hole," Frank said.

"It ain't my horse, not technically, but I will take it slow. Maybe I'll let Two Yellow Hairs take the lead and follow in his tracks." Wild Bill pulled out the bottle of whisky he'd swiped from the buffalo hunters and took a slug. I realized I had the perfect excuse to take a swig of bourbon—to get the dust out of my mouth. Surely Frank would have no problem with that. Here I was a grown man, and yet, when it came to Frank, I was desperate not to give him an excuse to admonish me. If it was just me and Baxter and Merle, I was confident giving orders and ordering them about. But Frank made me feel like a stupid fool.

Wild Bill and Two Yellow Hairs went on ahead at a cautious lope, and we followed along behind at a walk, with Baxter complaining about his new horse. This time for being clumsy. Frank let Baxter know for about the hundredth time that his new furry orange horse had saved his life. And that, thanks to the sandstorm, Colonel had gotten a decent burial after all. This seemed to perk Baxter up, and he eventually stopped his complaining and started talking about knives.

Horse suddenly started bobbing his head up and down and nickering.

"He's got the smell of something," I said. Then we heard a couple of rifle shots out ahead of us. Then the other horses were all nickering and prancing about and we spurred our horses up into a lope.

We followed Wild Bill and Two Yellow Hairs tracks and came upon them standing over a dead orange buffalo.

"Well, I'll be," Hap said. "Dinner."

"Frank had the right of it," Wild Bill said. "Found this'n with a broken leg from a prairie dog hole."

"I thought all the buffalo were massacred off," I said. "Didn't think there were any herds left."

"They just about are," Hap said. "That was the first herd I've seen in two years. It's why those buffalo hunters were ranging so far south." Seeing the buffalo up close, what little I could make out while trying to get away from them, I was impressed by how large they were up close, all except for the calves, which were cute enough that I had a notion to take one home to Sally. She would like a little pet buffalo, so long as it didn't grow up to be two thousand pounds like its momma. But it would, and then Sally wouldn't like it anymore.

"Dang," Baxter said. I looked over and saw that he had a

couple of tears making a path down his orange face. "We might be the last fellas to ever see something like that."

I hadn't thought of it that way because I had thought I was about to die, but now that I wasn't about to die, I started thinking of it that way, and dang if I didn't soon have a couple of leaking eyes. A bunch of rough men turned soft at the very rare sight of a herd of still-yet-living buffalo.

"I'll say this, Bill, and it ain't saying all that much, but you ain't the worst Yankee I've ever met."

"Why Frank, you old softy," Wild Bill said. "I'll take that as quite the compliment, knowing your philosophy on talking."

"It's a rare event," Frank conceded.

"This is a lot of buffalo meat," Wild Bill said, "but there was no choice in the matter. He was done for."

"Buffalo's good eating," Frank said. "Better than horse."

"And I got more good news," Wild Bill said. "We're headed in the right direction. Up ahead are two more buffalo corpses that have been hacked up, and not by us either. We ain't the only ones come across this herd."

"I been thinking on it," Hap said. "MacKenzie has a supply outpost east of here, near Yellow Horse Canyon, which I believe he set up for his skirmish at Blanco Canyon. He's bringing the fight to the Comanche now. Yellow Horse Canyon has a stream in it that feeds into the Brazos. It's where I would bivouac were I getting ready to gather forces for another scrap."

"I don't know what any of that means," Wild Bill said, "but if it has water, and is in a canyon, it would make more sense than being out here on this prairie."

"Camp Richardson I think it's called," Frank said, nodding. "Let's head on east and see if we can cut their sign. I'd rather make a go at these fellas before they catch up with the rest of the 4th cavalry. We've done pretty good so far, to get this close. I reckon that Yellow Hair and her daughter are slowing them down."

I watched as Two Yellow Hairs went about butchering the buffalo. It was clear he'd done it before. Probably hundreds of times. And I heard him chanting and singing to himself as he went about it. I watched as he placed the buffalo's head—after he'd up and swiped out the tongue—on the barren orange prairie. I knew from Scout that he was doing that so the buffalo could fend for itself in the spirit world. We now had plenty of food, and some sort of vague plan on where the troops were headed.

I just hoped we were right.

13

HASTINGS

Major Hastings opened his eyes to see the entire prairie colored orange, with not a single sign of life. No tracks could be seen in any direction. The sand followed behind the stampeding buffalo and wiped them all out. But the scout, Plowright, knew the way to Camp Richardson, which he said was not really a camp, but more of a supply outpost made up of some rough traders clumped together on the outskirts of a ravine next to a small river.

It took a while to track down their horses, who, with nothing to graze on, and no way of knowing where they were, had clumped together out on the prairie about a half mile from the tree they'd all lashed themselves to. It was the old warrior that rattled when he walked, that knew where the horses would be, because he led them almost precisely to them. Which didn't mean anything. Comanches were known for their horseman-ship. It didn't make them any less savage. And it didn't mean they shouldn't hang. Hastings had no choice but to follow the Indians lead, especially during the sandstorm, and out here in the desert. But he wasn't fooling himself—he knew that old

Indian wasn't his friend and wouldn't hesitate to turn the tables on him if given a chance.

Hastings didn't care for the way the white woman looked at the two Indians. She was giving them the kinds of looks that he wished she would give him. It was like they were all family or something. The white woman had put up a fight at first when he'd taken her to bed, but then she finally gave in to her situation and the inevitable.

The blonde girl, even though she was gagged, nevertheless screamed like a wild bobcat trapped in a snare. That noise had distracted the major at first, and it definitely made things more difficult. He had no doubt that if she hadn't been tied up, she would have leapt on his back and clawed him the same way a wild cat would.

Once they got back to camp, Hastings knew he would have eyes on him, and wouldn't have the freedom he had on the prairie. He would no longer be the boss. Colonel MacKenzie would, and, knowing the colonel as he did, he would waste no time letting the major know it.

If he were in charge, the major thought, the Indians would all be on reservations or feeding the buzzards by now. The scout, Grimes, wasn't wrong when he'd suggested the colonel would be unhappy with the major's decision to attack the camp. He was soft when it came to women and children, even though the women were just as underhanded and sneaky as the men, and the boys would one day grow up to be men themselves. The way the major saw it, it was better to eradicate them and then claim the land for the homesteaders. People like his parents, who had come from Scotland to farm in peace. People back East, and people like MacKenzie, and all those West Point graduates, with all their notions of valor and morals and high-minded ways, were taught how to fight battles that didn't exist on the frontier and were just slowing things down.

"Not long now," Hastings said.

"We'll be there tomorrow at the latest," Shelby said. "That warrior, not the old man, but the one that kilt Horvath, we need to make sure that he hangs. And I say we do it sooner than later. No judge. No trial. Just a quick drop from a strong rope. I don't like the way he looks at me. And I don't care for his calmness. It's as if he isn't worried at all. He might not talk, but he's mocking us all the same—and I don't care for it."

"Want me to bash on him some? I don't care for the way he looks at me either," Sykes said.

"Me neither," Pulaski said. "Isn't bashing the Indians what we're supposed to be doing?"

Shelby walked over and squatted to look the Indian warrior in the eyes. He could see it there, even now: a complete and utter lack of fear. One time, back at home, he'd been walking, and he walked around a bend in the trail, and there was a huge black bear sitting there in the middle of the trail. He wasn't afraid of Shelby at all. He just sat in the trail, confident that it was Shelby who should be scared. And this young Comanche had the same calm look. And it infuriated him. Shelby thought back to when the Indian had jumped Horvath and wrestled him to the ground, and the sound of Horvath's neck when the Indian broke it, and he felt his hate and rage rise up in him, and it was all he could do not to run his knife across the Indian's neck.

"You gonna hang for what you did," Shelby said. "I'd like nothing more than to shoot you dead right now. Shoot you right in each of your eyes. Maybe I'll do it yet!"

Hastings said, "Good luck trying to scare him in a language he doesn't even know. It won't do you any good. You'd have to pull off one of his arms to get a peep out of him. The Comanches torture their own kids, you know."

"All the more reason to see the whole lot of them on reservations, if you ask me," Plowright said.

"Reservations, hell," Shelby said. "In the dirt. Buried and forgotten."

14

"I think my horse looks better this color," Baxter said. Slowly, but surely, he was coming around. "Orange suits her."

"It suits you as well," Wild Bill said. "In fact, it's quite the improvement. I can actually tell you and Merle apart now—and without having to take a peek up Merle's shirt."

"It's easy," Baxter said. "I'm the smart one."

"If being dumb is smart, then I agree," Merle said.

"What does that even mean?" Baxter asked. "You should pay more attention to the words that come out of your mouth, because most of it don't make no sense at all."

"You're as dumb as a pile of rocks is what I'm saying," Merle said. "Does that make sense?"

"You're just jealous," Baxter said.

"Of what?" Merle asked.

This seemed to stump Baxter, because he didn't say anything for a spell, until he said, "I can't remember."

We'd cut the soldiers' sign a couple of hours earlier—seven sets of tracks heading east. Two Yellow Hairs recognized one of the horses as being Rattles's white stallion, and one of the shod horses, he said, was carrying Yellow Hair and her daughter—

which made him happy that they were alive and itching to exact revenge.

The truth is, I was having my own thoughts of revenge. Me and Rattles had come together, and we negotiated peace between us. And that peace had held—until now. If the opposite had occurred, the peaceful violence-avoiding citizens of Silver Vein would have unleashed hell, and out of fear probably wiped out Rattles and his entire band. Pap Kickins would have gotten the whole town worked up into a righteous frenzy. Our accord had been so successful, that when the massacre happened, Two Yellow Hairs had come looking for me, walking right through town no less—not to kill me, but to ask for my help. And such was the strength of our agreement that no citizen had done anything more than watch as he walked right down the Main Street boardwalk to my saloon. Which is really saying something.

But now I feared the days of peace were over—and all that me and Rattles and Jim Shepland has worked toward would be wiped away. And that made me want to strangle somebody.

Even to this day, I find it amazing how Frank and Wild Bill and Two Yellow Hairs could look down at a bunch of dirt and know what it meant. I could tell the tracks of a lion from the tracks of a bear, but when I saw a bunch of horse tracks in the dirt, I didn't have any idea at all what to make of them. If I'd led the charge, I would have had to return to Silver Vein on account of being completely lost. But now that I think about it, I probably wouldn't have even been able to get back to Silver Vein. Right at this moment, as we walked our horses, Wild Bill and Two Yellow Hairs were pointing at this broken blade of grass and pointing at that dislodged rock—seeing things only they could see. All I saw was orange dust and some incomprehensible shapes.

Wild Bill slowed his horse up and worked his way up next to me and said, "We're getting closer. The horses can smell other horses and are pushing the pace. I would expect it could me a near thing, catching up to them before they reconnect with the rest of the 4th calvary."

"How far ahead of us, do you reckon?" I asked.

"I'd say they're a couple of hours ahead of us were we to go at them hard. But I can't say that for certain. At this pace, maybe three or four hours."

The horses weren't blown, but they were close.

"Let's go at them medium," I said.

It was mid-afternoon. Wild Bill was saying we could run into the rogue troops—or the 4th Cavalry—before the sun went down. I knew Colonel MacKenzie because he'd come through Silver Vein a couple of times. He'd stopped in the saloon, where he would take a table in the back and put his feet up and talk with another soldier who would write everything he said down on paper. Once you get high enough in the army, important people always have someone following them around, writing down whatever pops into their head.

The colonel did a lot of talking as I recall. And not much drinking, which I also recall. I think he sat in the saloon as a way of keeping his troops from getting drunk and causing trouble. A number of troops would walk into the saloon, after either being in some fort in the middle of nowhere or sleeping in the dirt, just ready to finally let loose; but then they'd see the colonel and realize they had to behave themselves. He always struck me as nice if a little on the serious side. Despite knowing him and him knowing me, I wasn't looking forward to meeting him in a situation where I would be against him. What I wanted, was to catch up with the savagers and put them in the dirt before they got anywhere near the 4th cavalry. But the sandstorm had made that unlikely. Which meant we needed to figure out what we—

"What are we going to do if we run into the whole 4th cavalry?" I asked.

"Turn around, probably," Frank said.

"And Rattles and Scout?" I asked. "We just let them hang?"

Frank spit off the side of his horse, indicating that he was disgusted with my question. "What do you want me to say, Curly? We can't, the six of us, take on the entire 4th Cavalry. If we do that, Scout and Rattles still hang, only we'll all be swinging right there next to them. And then Bill would not only die in Texas but be hanged in Texas. Maybe we can surprise them. But right now, we don't know what we're gonna be getting into."

"Could be we don't run into the 4th cavalry at all," Hap said.

"Let's hope on that," I said. I gave Horse a little of the spurs and we got into a faster lope, keeping our eyes out for sign.

15

HASTINGS

The good news was, thanks to that buffalo herd, they had plenty of meat. The bad news was they were lost. Not lost exactly, but definitely lacking in landmarks. The dust had coated everything they looked at in so much orange dust, they couldn't even see any trees. Even Plowright, who was supposed to lead them in, had to admit he couldn't do it without visible landmarks.

"There!" Shelby said, pointing. The major looked, and there, on the horizon, was a lone horseman with the blue coat of an Army scout. They waited, sitting on their mounts, for the newest scout to arrive.

"Major," the scout said. "The Colonel had a notion you and Plowright might have some trouble after the sandstorm. The name's Corporal Lansing."

"He was right, Corporal" Hastings said. "That sandstorm wiped away all sign."

"I've been coming out the last couple of mornings to take a look. The good thing about all this orange is, you fellas stood out. What's the story of these here?"

"We found a Comanche camp," Hastings said, "and saw

they had these two women held in bondage, so we rescued them. This warrior here ambushed us and kilt one of our men, Corporal Horvath. I aim to see him hanged for it."

The scout nodded. "The colonel is gearing up for something big. Good thing you got here when you did. We march north tomorrow. Surprised you found any Comanches at all where you were. They've been massing their forces in a canyon a few days from here in a place the Spanish called Palo Duro Canyon. Follow me. I'll take you to the colonel."

"Well lead the way, Corporal," Hastings said.

———

Once in camp, as expected, Hastings was no longer the man in charge. The first thing he had to do—because he'd been ordered to—was report to the colonel. The major went into the big tent and found Colonel MacKenzie behind his campaign desk, his big Irish Wolf Hound sitting by his side. The major knew it wouldn't take but a word from the colonel and the dog would leap up and rip out the major's throat.

"Major Hastings, we feared you and your men might have been lost to us forever, after that sandstorm made its way through here. In addition to the Comanches, we've got to deal with this crazy Texas weather. I can't tell you how happy I will be to see this campaign come to an end. Frankly, if it were up to me, I'd end it tomorrow and declare victory. But Washington wants to see this through, once and for all."

The major knew he was not to speak unless specifically told to.

"So, tell me about these captives of yours. I understand there is a white woman and little girl among them?" The major knew this was his chance to play to the colonel's sense of honor. And saving a white woman and her daughter was definitely honorable.

"Yes sir, Colonel. We were about four-or five-days ride west of here, on the other side of this desert, in a series of canyons, when we came across a Comanche camp."

"Excellent! We are heading north in the morning, as a number of Comanches are grouping in Palo Duro Canyon as we speak. After that business is done, we will take aim at this camp you've found."

"Well, colonel, there will be no need for that. We have already handled that camp."

The colonel had been looking out the flap of the tent, but hearing this, he turned and faced the major. "Major Hastings, you were under specific orders not to take any action, but to immediately come and report back. The reason I asked that you *specifically* take no action, is I don't want the Comanches getting riled up on my flank! Yet you tell me now that you have ignored these orders. I expect a quality explanation."

Hastings had been thinking about what he would tell the colonel at this very moment. He knew the colonel would sniff out anything that didn't sound convincing. "We came across the camp in the night, and we could hear screaming. The Comanches were actively raping the blonde woman, and torturing the little one for sport, and I didn't feel we could ignore it. The noises the woman was making were terrifying if I may say so. I am a veteran of these Indian Wars, and I have yet to hear such a horrible noise. I saw that we would have the tactical advantage when the Comanches went to sleep, and then we could rescue the woman and her daughter. So, I made a plan to attack the camp in the morning, and so we freed the white woman and her daughter from the savages."

"And?" the colonel asked. He had his reading glasses perched on the end of his nose and Hastings would have liked nothing more than to leap across the desk and strangle the man. His imperiousness, his West Point background, his upbringing, it was all there in that look he was now giving the major.

"We lost two men sir, but we killed an entire band of Comanches sleeping in their *tipis*. One of the Indians we caught, who is now our prisoner, was the one that kilt Corporal Horvath."

"And Grimes? I heard he didn't make it back to camp. I know his family, you know."

What had Shelby said? "Fever!" the major said, remembering the lie. "He was bitten in the night by some bug, could have been a scorpion, maybe some sort of spider. There was nothing we could do for him."

Colonel MacKenzie leaned back in his chair, removed his glasses, and let out a sigh. "Major, had you simply followed my orders, Corporal Grimes would yet be alive. And I wouldn't have to write a letter to his mother, which I will now have to do after you leave my tent. This is most unfortunate. But I do understand why you did it. When this campaign is over, you will of course lead us to this camp, and we will recover Grimes's body."

The colonel put his glasses back on the bridge of his nose and started sifting through some papers on his desk. Without looking up, he said, "You're dismissed, major."

Major Hastings stood up straight, saluted, turned on his heels and made to leave the tent. He was almost at the tent opening when the colonel called out to him.

"Oh, Major, one more thing. It is my understanding that the white woman and her daughter are not behaving like they've been rescued and have in fact behaved in quite a hostile manner to the soldiers assigned to look after them. Why do you think that might be? I would think, if it is as you say, they would be overjoyed to be rescued."

"They've been traumatized, colonel. I don't think they have yet to realize they have been saved." Major Hastings didn't dare make eye contact with the colonel. He was afraid he would see through the whole thing.

"Very well," the colonel finally said.

————

The major had the sense that the colonel didn't believe him. He needed to talk some sense into the blonde woman. If she continued to behave in a hostile manner, his story would fall apart. All it would take was a conversation with one of the scouts that spoke Comanche, and he'd be court-martialed and taken to Fort Leavenworth.

He found the tent where the woman and her daughter were being watched over. There was a guard sitting out front. It was the middle tent on the left side.

"I'll take it from here, Private," he said, approaching the tent. The private looked up and immediately stood up and saluted.

"Yes sir, Major Hastings, sir!"

"Go smoke your pipe. Be back in twenty minutes."

"Major Hastings, sir. I have orders not to leave the—"

"I just overruled those orders, Private. I'm only asking for twenty minutes."

"Yes sir! But Major? Be careful. That woman is as dangerous as a wolverine. She's already attacked two other soldiers."

"Thanks for the advice, Private. Now go have a smoke."

Hastings opened the flap and made his way into the tent.

He found the blonde woman lying on a cot. Seeing her lying down, the major almost couldn't breathe. She was so innocent and beautiful. But then the moment was gone, because she saw him and sat up and hissed something at him he couldn't understand.

"It's okay," he said, smiling, "you're okay now. You're safe."

She hissed some more things at him.

This was getting to be frustrating, Hastings thought. Tedious, really. How long does it take for someone to realize the predicament they are in? She was back with her own kind. She was where she belonged. It was time for her to realize this and come to terms with her new life—a new life which he would share with her. She was a strong woman. He admired that about her. She was tall and held her head high, despite all that she'd been through. And, in a new dress, and with some rouge on her cheeks, she'd be quite beautiful.

And yet, despite all the facts and circumstances, she still hissed and screamed at him.

"You need to learn your place," he said, in what he hoped was a reasonable voice.

"You are an ugly man," she said.

"Ah! So you remember how to speak English. It's clearly been a while, but—"

"I will kill you. Do not touch me. Never again will you—"

"We've been over this. Since you can understand me, understand this. You are mine now. Your life is with me. We will have a life together, you and me. That is the only way things can go."

He looked back at the blonde girl, but she wasn't paying attention. She looked to be asleep. And he couldn't blame her. She'd had a rough week. A rough life! It would wear out any little girl—even one who had grown up wild. She was curled up in a fetal position facing the wall of the tent, away from him.

He smiled at the white woman.

"We might as well start our new life together right now," Hastings said. He didn't have much time. How long had it been since he'd sent the private off to smoke? Maybe ten minutes?

He walked over and approached the woman, with his hands ready, in case she attacked him, which he knew was more than likely. Especially since they were just getting to know each other. New relationships were never easy.

He was just reaching for her when he heard a blood-curdling scream and felt a sharp pain in his back.

"Aiii!" he wailed, thrashing around, trying to throw the hellion little savage off of him.

"You stabbed me!"

"Major, are you okay?" the private called out from the flap of the tent.

"Get this little bitch off of me!"

There was a struggle, and then the girl was thrashing in the private's hands like a rabid tomcat.

"She's stabbed you major. You've got some sort of Indian knife sticking out of you. I'll get the medic." There was a commotion in front of the tent as several troops wrestled the girl to the ground and worked to tie her hands behind her back. The woman then lunged at Hastings and screamed and slashed at his face. He reached for his face in agony, and she raced by him, but there were many soldiers at the front of the tent now. One of them, thankfully, was Captain Shelby, and he calmly threw her to the ground and put a knee in her back and held her arms behind her while another soldier bound her hands.

"Major," Shelby said, "you might want to give up on romance with this one."

"Shut up!" the major screamed, sitting down on the cot and touching his face with his hands. He put his hand to his face, and it came back caked in blood.

This was going to be harder than he thought, the major realized.

16

"There's six of them now," Frank said.

"We should hang back," Hap said. "They don't seem to know we're on their trail, but with this dust, we'll stand out plain as day."

"I agree," Wild Bill said.

"Baxter won't," I said.

Everybody looked at me.

"Well, look at him. He's completely orange, and so is his horse."

Frank looked Baxter up and down. "Every once in a while, Curly..." Frank said. "All right Baxter, you range on ahead, and we'll come along behind." We waited and watched, and before long, Baxter blended in with the orange prairie, and if you didn't know where he was, you wouldn't have even seen him.

I got off Horse and started rolling around in the dust. Then I began rubbing the dust on Horse, turning him from black to orange. He didn't care for the change, but he was too polite to make any fuss. Frank and Hap and Merle and Two Yellow Hairs all followed my lead. Merle was so thorough he even put orange dust up his nose, setting off a sneezing fit.

Everyone was turning themselves orange but Wild Bill.

"I paid good money for these duds," Wild Bill said. "I reckon you boys will just have to go on without me."

"That won't be good for your book," I said.

"That is a foolishness," Frank said. "Bill, we're gonna need your shooting skills."

"It's not a foolishness to want to keep my duds from getting dusty. I paid good money for them."

We all just looked at him, trying to figure out what to do when Wild Bill suddenly perked up, smiled, dismounted and rummaged through his saddlebag.

"Aha!" he exclaimed. "My acting outfit!" And so, he changed out of the clothes Ely Turner had gouged him for and got into a buckskin shirt and pants. From a distance he would look like a deer or elk.

Now, thoroughly camouflaged, we mounted up and kicked our horses into a lope.

————

We caught up with Baxter just as the air was beginning to cool.

"They're camped out yonder, in a ravine. I got here in time to see them join the 4th cavalry. It was the six of them we're after."

"You see Scout?" I asked.

Baxter nodded. "They've got Yellow Hair and her daughter in a tent. Scout and Rattles are bound up and being looked over by a couple of soldiers. The guy who seemed to be their leader walked into the big tent."

"Reporting to MacKenzie, no doubt," Wild Bill said.

We walked along and then Baxter held up his hand and dismounted. Then he walked over to some prickly bushes and tied up his horse. We dismounted and did the same. Then Baxter squat-walked, and so we squat-walked behind him, and then, sure enough, a ravine came into view. We got down on the ground and wormed our way to the edge and looked down.

"Dang," I said. "There's a lot of them."

"About sixty I'd say," Hap said.

"Sixty-three, if you count the dog," Wild Bill said.

"What foolishness," Frank said. "Dogs don't count."

"That's MacKenzie's personal dog. He'd tear you to pieces if he was told to."

We backed away from the edge and crawled and crouched our way back to our horses to figure out what our plan was. Planning, I knew from hard experience, wasn't my strong suit. But that didn't always stop me from taking the lead on such things.

"I've got an idea," Wild Bill said. "Not a good one, mind you, but there aren't any. Not against that many troops." He told us his idea and we immediately agreed it definitely wasn't a good one. It was absurd and ridiculous. He claimed to have been inspired by playing cards with Tad Bowltree. We incorporated it into Two Yellow Hairs' plan, and my plan, and Frank's plan, to create one big group plan. Frank had a look on his face like he might need to visit the privy, but he kept his opinion of the overall plan, whatever it was, to himself. Hap just went about cleaning his Winchester and checking his bullets to make sure they weren't too infected with sandstorm dust. Seeing that, I did the same. Then we all did.

"So, which one of you wants to braid my hair?" Wild Bill asked.

Luckily, Two Yellow Hairs was willing. He knew his way when it came to braiding hair, where I would have been next to useless. We found a small creek, or Two Yellow Hairs did, and we cleaned up our orange faces and filled ourselves with as much water as possible. We said our goodbyes to Two Yellow Hairs and handed over all the remaining buffalo meat; he refused the steaks in favor of the organ meat, which we didn't want anyway. Watching him disappear, I found myself wondering if I'd ever see him again. I admired his part of the plan—and I hoped I could keep up my side of it. But all things considered, the overall plan was lousy. Sixty-three to six were not great odds, even with a good plan.

Our plan called for darkness, so we found a stand of stringy brush and tied our horses up and waited. The horses would need to be rested for what would come later.

"The moon is bright tonight," I said. It was about half full, but we had no problem seeing each other.

"We got some hours yet," Frank said. "Maybe some clouds will roll in. Hap, if you want to cook up those steaks, I reckon you could if you were to head off yonder a ways."

"Wild Bill doesn't look much like a Comanche in daylight," I complained. "His lip whiskers is but one of the many giveaways."

"It only has to work for a few minutes, Curly. Plus, the soldiers will be groggy with sleep. Why, I bet the ruse *will* work. You have to keep in mind: I'm an actor. If I can act like me and be believable, I reckon I can play a Comanche for a couple of chaotic minutes."

"It's a terrible idea," I said. "But since I can see that you're set on the matter, I will leave it alone."

"It'll work," Wild Bill said. "Let me borrow that buffalo coat of yours."

I looked over at the buffalo coat I'd swiped off the buffalo skinner, and I knew with sad and absolute certainty that Wild Bill was right: the buffalo coat would give his costume a better chance of surviving casual scrutiny. "Dang," I said to myself, and stood up and walked over to Horse and came back with the buffalo coat and handed it over.

"Borrow!" I said. "No gift!"

"What?"

"Never mind. Just take care of it."

"It smells like coffee," he said, sniffing it.

"Coffee," Hap said, longingly.

"Coffee would be a good idea. I reckon we can chance a fire yonder aways," Frank said again, "so long as the wind keeps on blowing the way it is."

"I think that's a good idea," Hap said. "We're gonna be up all night. And we're gonna need our strength."

"We can't chance Curly giving us away with that rumbly belly of his," Wild Bill said.

"I agree—dammit," Frank said, giving Wild Bill a wink.

————

The clouds didn't roll in, so we would have to hope the soldiers were all heavy sleepers. We had surprise on our side, and, of course, the incredible recklessness of our plan. Even if the soldiers were expecting us, I doubt they would be expecting such a plan as we were about to try.

When it was about three hours before dawn, we made our careful way to the ravine edge and looked down. We could see a couple of fires going and a few soldiers walking around, but not much else.

Wild Bill had gone off to scout a way down into the ravine. He came back in about twenty minutes.

"They're pretty relaxed down there. They've only got one sentry keeping watch on either side of the camp. I think we can get a drop on them and come up on em from behind. We need to do it before either one of them can raise an alarm."

I nodded. Now would come the riskiest part of the plan. This was the part where Baxter and Merle would have to split up. I knew from experience that they could barely function when they were away from one another.

"Give me ten minutes," Wild Bill said, rubbing his face with dust, and then he disappeared, silent as a cat. Not as quiet as

Scout, but pretty close. This next part of the plan meant that I had to go with either Baxter or Merle. I couldn't decide who to pick.

"I'll go with Curly," Baxter said. Which saved me from having to choose.

"Don't let him be noisy," Merle said. He smiled, pulled his pistol out of its holster, walked away in a crouch, and eventually the dark ate him up.

"Let's go, Curly. Follow me," Baxter said. I took out my pistol and followed Baxter away from the ridge. We skirted our way south, walking away from the soldiers' camp for about a quarter mile, and then followed a trail off the ridge down into the ravine. It was a longer walk than I had planned for. I tried to think of what I remembered of the layout of the camp. We were on the side of the camp where the horses were picketed. Some horses, you untie them, they just stand there and look at you. Other horses will take off immediately. Horse wouldn't go anywhere without my permission. He was a good horse. Molly, on the other hand, was the type that would immediately flee. I was hoping the soldiers' horses were all Mollys.

I tapped Baxter on the shoulder. "Remember, don't kill anybody. Just whomp." Baxter nodded, and he walked off into the darkness, on his way to take out the sentry. I made my way to the horses. I recognized Rattles's white stallion. I grabbed him and five other horses and walked off back the way we came, back to the top of the ravine, and tied them up with our horses. My legs were already sore. And I was just getting started. Then I walked back down and went to each horse I could find and un-hitched them from the picket line. I gave each horse a firm shove, hoping they would realize they could freely leave camp, and then made my way to catch up with Baxter.

I'm not very good at being quiet. I blame my feet. They're always knocking into rocks and bush roots and frequently cause things to clatter. But because there were sixty-three Federal troops including the dog sleeping about forty yards from me, I was very quiet. In fact, I'm not even sure I was breathing.

"Dang!"

That was Baxter. I found him struggling, sitting on the ground, putting on a pair of pants that were clearly too small for him. I looked over and found the sentry trussed up like a hog with one of his socks serving as a gag and wearing nothing but his underwear and remaining sock. He would be humiliated, and probably in a lot of trouble when he woke up, but right now he was snoring away as if taking a nap.

Baxter stood up and I heard a tearing sound.

"That's better," he said.

The bottom of the pants barely reached the tops of his boots, and the jacket sleeves made it only half-way down his forearms. From a distance, and in the dark, I hoped it didn't matter. We made our way, once again, up out of the ravine and made our way to the other side of the camp and then back down into the ravine to meet up with Merle. This plan, I could see, called for entirely too much walking. I didn't get much walking accomplished in a typical day. And it showed. My breath was coming out fast and furious. We found Merle in similar circumstances, struggling into his swiped uniform. I guess most soldiers were small compared to Baxter and Merle. Merle had taken the trouble of hiding his whomped sentry in a bush. We were closer to the camp and the tents on this side.

"Well," I said. "Only one way to find out if this is gonna work."

Baxter and Merle set off for the campfire as if they knew what they were about. A couple of minutes later, they came back with an angry looking man with an elaborate black mustache.

"This better be good," he said. I didn't know what he was

talking about, and it didn't matter because Baxter whomped him over the head, and he fell over into the dust like a fallen tree.

We dragged him over to the body-hiding bush and took his clothing.

"I think you outrank us," Baxter said, investigating my new uniform. It was true. We'd gone and whomped someone important.

"No wonder he was so rude. What did you say to him?" I asked.

"I told him you had some important information from Fort Belknap that couldn't wait. New orders," Baxter said.

"And that you'd sent us to come get him. He seemed pretty happy sitting by himself puffing on his pipe in front of the fire. He couldn't understand why you wouldn't come to him," Merle said.

"I said you insisted," Baxter said.

"And that you were an asshole," Merle said.

"As soon as Baxter said that, he jumped up like his butt was on fire. I think the higher your rank is, the worse your personality," Merle said.

Unlike Baxter and Merle, my uniform was a good fit. I couldn't help feeling powerful in it. I stood up straighter and had the urge to bark orders at someone.

I nodded stiffly at Baxter and Merle. "You men keep your eyes out," I said.

Then I walked into the camp.

17

The tents were laid out in two orderly rows. Each one was about fifteen feet long. There were three on each side. I walked between the rows and heard the reassuring sounds of snoring and farting. Beyond the six tents was the much larger tent, the one we'd seen the bearded soldier walk into, where we assumed Colonel MacKenzie slept.

On the other side of the big tent was another campfire, with someone sitting there.

"Quiet," I said. The man had a waxed goatee and a shaved head. He looked me over and nodded. I nodded back and whomped him over the head. My whomping expertise was well known and well deserved. I hit the man just hard enough to get him to slump over and set to snoring. I quickly tied his hands behind his back and put a gag in his mouth to chew on. Then I made my way to what I hoped would be a meeting with Scout.

This is where Wild Bill's plan kicked in. As he conceived it, he was going to trade places with Scout. And then, when they found out Scout was missing, and had escaped, they would be slowed down and bewildered by the presence of Wild Bill Hickok, the savior of Abilene, famous frontier scout and shootist, sensation of New York City—dressed up like an Indian in the middle of the Texas desert.

You can see why I thought this part of the plan was unrealistic. But it was too late to do anything about it. Even with my buffalo coat, there was no getting around the fact that Wild Bill and Scout looked nothing like one another. Wild Bill, for example, had eyebrows, whereas Scout picked his clean. There were many other differences.

When I walked back to our rendezvous point, once again walking up and out of the ravine, there was Scout waiting for me sitting on the ground.

"It worked!" I said.

"They will shoot him when they wake up," Scout said, standing up.

"We don't have much time," I said. "You and Rattles need to get Yellow Hair and her daughter and get on out of here. Two Yellow Hairs has gone on ahead. He will leave water waiting for you at places he said you would know how to find."

Scout nodded. "Yellow Hair and Little Yellow Hair are now tied up and being held in a tent with a guard." Little Yellow Hair! So *that* was her name!

I nodded my head, but it took me a moment to understand. "Dang," I finally said. "We hadn't thought of that. We figured you'd all be held in the same place."

"This man, Major Hastings, he has a black beard, and a fresh wound on his back. He won't let Yellow Hair out of his sight. He's fallen in love with her."

"What?" I said.

Scout nodded. "He thinks he can get her to love him back. He's raped her at least twice, and he tried again earlier but Little Yellow Hair stabbed him with a knife."

"How do you know all this?"

Scout shrugged. "Savages can't understand words. There's another one, Captain Shelby, and one day I will take his hair and his life. There are two more, and I will take their lives as well, but it's Hastings and Shelby that give the orders."

"We'll get your father," I said. "I have horses for you. Hurry before the soldiers wake up. When we free Rattles and Yellow Hair, we will send them up here."

"I want those men. Hastings will pay the biggest price. Two Yellow Hairs will want his revenge."

"Well, we'll just have to hope for the best. It all comes down to acting," I said.

Then, on that dramatic note, I went back down one more time into the camp. Baxter and Merle were now sitting by the campfires, supposedly on sentry duty. Yellow Hair and Little Yellow Hair were in one of the tents. Scout said they were being guarded. I needed to figure out which of the six tents she was in.

I walked up to Merle and told him the situation.

"It's the second tent on the left," Merle said. "It's the only one with a guard."

I nodded. "Apparently, this major Hastings has gone and fallen in love with Yellow Hair, and he has been trying to rape her into loving him back. I'm guessing it isn't working."

"Dang," Merle said. "So, what do we—"

"Lieutenant," a soldier walking by sleepily said, saluting me. He walked off a ways and I heard him empty his bladder. I looked down at my uniform.

"I have an idea," I said.

———

Before I knew what I was about, I was already walking over to the second tent on the left. Sure enough, there was a soldier sleeping in a chair, guarding the tent with his snores. I kicked him out of his chair.

"Wake your ass up, Private! Get out of here! Sleeping! After what happened earlier? You're lucky I don't put you in irons!" I was just making up stuff, but I must have gotten the tone of voice right, because the soldier picked himself off the dust, gave me a terrified salute, and said, "Sorry Lieutenant!" and ran off.

"Go get some sleep! We break camp in a few hours!"

"Yes sir, Lieutenant sir! And thank you sir!"

"Go!"

He ran off like his ass was on fire. It gave me a thrill to have such power, though not enough to actually want to be a soldier.

The private ran off without a backwards glance, and I walked into the tent.

18

HASTINGS

Maybe she'll like this soup, Hastings thought to himself. He felt bad about trying to rape the woman again. She'd been made a slave by a bunch of savages, and then she is finally saved, only to have the person that saved her lose his mind with lust over and over again. He probably deserved to be stabbed, he thought, especially since the stab wasn't deep, and was now bandaged up. His thinking on the situation might have been affected by the dose of laudanum the camp medic had given him, but he didn't think so. She would eventually see things his way.

He would prove to her that he was better than his previous actions. She would enjoy this soup, and later, in the morning, he would bring her coffee. He would even be nice to the girl that stabbed him. He would—

Hastings couldn't believe what he was seeing. Lieutenant Danforth just walked into her tent. Damned if he didn't. That horny no-good bastard! Major Hastings dumped the soup into the dirt in a rage.

This would have to be dealt with right away. He knew Lieutenant Danforth to be quite the ladies' man. The first thing he did whenever he got time off, was go and visit the whores. It's all the man ever talked about.

It was going to be hard enough to win over the blonde woman and her savage daughter as it was—the last thing Hastings needed was competition.

He made his way to the tent.

19

Yellow Hair was tied to her cot and curled up on herself like a punished dog. She peeked up at me with crazed terrified eyes.

I took my hat off.

"It's me," I said, perhaps a tad dramatically, "Sheriff Curly Barnes!" I had met Yellow Hair once before, when she told me she was in love with Two Yellow Hairs and wanted to stay with him.

"I'm here to rescue you!"

It took her a minute—but then she recognized me. She smiled, despite it all, she smiled. I smiled back.

"Both of you," I said. I looked over and saw Little Yellow Hair all trussed up in a chair with a gag in her mouth. I smiled at her, and she hissed at me. I didn't blame her. I'd never met her before, and I was dressed just like the troops that attacked their camp.

"You might need to explain things to her. I don't want her to have a go at me."

Yellow Hair sat up and said something in Comanche. Little Yellow Hair nodded.

I cut through the ropes tying Little Yellow Hair to the chair, and then the two of us went to work on untying Yellow Hair. Light was starting to peak through the tent flaps. The soldiers would wake up soon. The real ones.

We were running out of time.

20

HASTINGS

Major Hastings took the knife out of its scabbard. His anger was so great it almost blinded him. He was almost to the tent when the blonde lady and the girl ran out of the tent with Lieutenant Danforth right behind them. It would be just like Danforth to free the woman, so that she would think he was letting her go, so he could be the nice guy, so he could then have his way with her; and then, when he got what he wanted, he would just tie her back up again. It was a story as old as time itself. Hastings had done the very same thing over and over again all during the war.

But this was different. The blonde woman was his. He'd discovered her. He'd freed her from savages. He'd dragged her across the desert. He'd put up with her curses and had even been stabbed by her wild daughter. He deserved the blonde woman. He'd earned her!

But now that he thought about it, Danforth had a limp from a musket ball in his hip he got in the war. But now he wasn't limping. Maybe it wasn't Danforth? Or was it? Was the laudanum playing tricks on him?

What the hell was going on!

21

I didn't wait to find out if the bearded guy with the knife recognized me and just went up and whomped him. I didn't even think about it.

"Hey!" I heard someone shout.

And then everything seemed to happen all at once. The whole camp woke up all at the same time. And then soldiers were running this way and that, a bell was ringing from somewhere, and I was impressed to see that Yellow Hair and Little Yellow Hair could run as fast as a couple of gazelles. They soon scrambled up the side of the ravine and disappeared from view.

But where was Rattles?

"They're getting away!" someone yelled. The gig was up. Rattles had to be somewhere, but before I could find him, I heard a bugle blowing in alarm and I heard someone shout, "The horses are gone!"

Dust was everywhere and all was hubbub. And, for now, I was just another confused soldier. But it wouldn't take long before Baxter or Merle or myself got caught. My money was on Baxter getting found out first.

Then, sooner than I would have liked, the soldiers stopped

running around in confusion and came to attention and the dust started to settle and the whole camp was suddenly silent. I turned my head, following the eyes of the other soldiers, and there was Colonel MacKenzie himself, sitting astride a magnificent black stallion that would have given Horse a run for his money. His enormous pet dog was sitting in the dust next to him.

"You!" he said, pointing to a man with ratty blonde hair. "Captain Shelby! Just what the hell is going on?"

"The prisoners have escaped!" he said.

"I see. And the blonde woman and her daughter?"

"Yes sir. They have escaped as well."

"And why would they want to do that? Did we not rescue them?"

Captain Shelby grew quiet and looked down at the dirt.

"I expect an answer, Captain."

"I...don't know, Colonel."

"Because it just doesn't make sense, does it? If it is as you and Major Hastings say, and you have saved this woman and her daughter from the Comanches, they should be overjoyed to be safe here with us. Shouldn't they? And yet they seem to have escaped *with* our two Indian prisoners."

"Ack!" Major Hastings said.

I looked over, and, somehow, he was back on his feet. Clearly the man could take a whomp.

"You! You're not Lieutenant Danforth!"

I took my eyes off Major Hastings, who was still trying to get right in the head, and saw that Colonel MacKenzie was very clearly looking and pointing right at me.

"Me?" I asked, pointing at myself, "Why not?"

"What?"

"How do you know?"

"How do I—enough!" Colonel MacKenzie said.

I couldn't help it. I stood at attention. His voice had a surprising amount of authority to it.

"You are *not* Lieutenant Danforth. Tell me—"

That's when I lost my mind and took out my pistol and pointed it in the general vicinity of the most powerful man west of the Mississippi.

"Colonel," I said. "This is going to be a lot to chew on. It's me, Sheriff Curly Barnes." I removed my hat with a flourish, the way I'd seen Wild Bill do it.

"Curly Barnes? The saloonkeeper? From Silver Vein?"

"All of those things," I said.

"The Indians haven't escaped. They're still here, Colonel," one of the soldiers said, pushing Rattles and Wild Bill in front of the Colonel. I had to hand it to Wild Bill. He was giving it all he had. With his head hunched down in my buffalo coat and his braided hair, it was exactly as he'd said it would be. The soldiers were seeing what they expected to see. Some savage in an animal hide, same as all the other ones they'd seen.

"So, let me get this straight," Colonel MacKenzie said, "the Indians are still here, but the woman and daughter we *saved* from the Indians have escaped?" He put his head in his hands and rubbed his face, then shook himself.

"Curly, do you mind telling me why you're wearing Lieutenant Danforth's uniform?"

"Not particularly," I admitted.

"Unhand me!"

Colonel MacKenzie took renewed interest in the well-spoken Comanche.

"Turn those Indians to face me," the Colonel said. Suddenly Wild Bill lashed out with a fist, knocking the soldier who was holding Rattles to the ground. In the hubbub, Rattles made a run for it. By the time the soldier got back to his feet, Wild Bill had shrugged out of my buffalo coat and had his pearl-handled

Colts out, one pointing at the soldier in the dirt, and the other pointing at the soldier who had been pushing him.

"Don't anyone move," I said. "This won't take long."

"Don't let that Indian get away!" Captain Shelby cried.

"We're not here for gunplay!" I said. "But, Colonel, you should know if we wanted to, we could take out twenty of your soldiers in the blink of an eye."

"Ow!" someone said.

"Ow!" someone else said.

Baxter and Merle now had their guns out as well, each one stuck in the ribs of a soldier.

"I've got more men above," I said. Captain Shelby started running after Rattles, but he didn't get far because bullets started hitting the dirt at his feet bringing him up short and kicking up dust.

"Hold up there Shelby. Well Curly," MacKenzie said, sighing, "you've certainly got my full attention. Now can you *please* explain to me just what the hell is going on?"

"Not me," Wild Bill said. "All I know is I was minding my own business playing cards and drinking bourbon in a saloon. And then, when I woke up, I was out here!"

"Wild Bill Hickok?" MacKenzie asked, "is that you? What manner of madness is this?"

Wild Bill shrugged. "It's me, all right. Wild Bill Hickok! The fastest gun in the West! And so, it goes without saying that if anybody makes a play for their gun, they'll end up in the dirt. I'm hungover, angry, and very confused."

"I don't have time for any games!" the Colonel said, his face almost as red as mine sometimes gets.

This was the tricky part. For this part, I had to rely on what Scout had told me. "Before we travel down this road, I reckon you want your prisoners back."

"The woman and girl, as I understand it," MacKenzie said, though he didn't sound like even he believed what he was saying, "aren't prisoners. It is my understanding they were rescued."

"Well," I said, and then I paused because I didn't know what to say, and then I thought something up, and so then I said, "there's four that have escaped, and two of them are women, and, um, one of them is a little girl. So, I reckon it will only take four of your soldiers to get them back. I'd say that's fair."

"I'll decide how many soldiers to send!" Colonel MacKenzie bellowed. "I'm losing my patience here. I have been made to understand that the Indian that is now Wild Bill Hickok killed one of our troops. Which is a hanging offense. I don't know if you know it Curly, but I reckon you do, I am waging a war at the moment—and it is within my power to try you in a military court and hang you if I want!"

I nodded. "I'm not trying to mangle up any of your plans, Colonel. But I'll only allow four of your troops to get your rescued women and escaped Indians back. You've been told a pile of bull chips by your men."

The Colonel's horse's tail started twitching, and it started pawing at the dirt with one of its hooves.

Everything else was silent. Sixty-three soldiers and a dog—all seeming to be holding their breath. Things were very tense, and I felt like our plan was about to go one way or another. One way being the right way, and the other way meaning we were about all to get shot full of holes. None of us—well, I couldn't speak for Baxter and Merle—had any plans to actually shoot any soldiers. We weren't maniacs.

Finally, the Colonel said: "Very well. I need—"

"I'll go," Major Hastings immediately said.

"Me too," Captain Shelby said.

"Shocking," Colonel MacKenzie said.

Then another soldier said, "I reckon I have to go as well, Colonel." Then the guy with the beard slapped him on the back of the head, and he said, "I mean, I volunteer."

"I reckon I do too," a fourth soldier said.

"Why am I not surprised it would be you four? Fine! Major Hastings, you and your buddies can go bring back the women you claim you saved, and the two Indians. The rest of us won't waste any more time on this circus and will de-camp in two hours and head north to the Brazos. Now, Curly, if you'll kindly remove that uniform and lower your guns, I've got some horses that need rounding up. And If I ever see either one of you lunatics again, I'll shoot you myself."

I put my gun away. "I'll go," I said, "but there's some stuff you should know." And then I let him know everything that was on my mind.

BOOK III: RECKONING

1

———

"I can't believe that worked," Frank said, sucking on his pipe.

"Me neither," I said. Now that it was over, I felt like I might air out my insides. I'd basically threatened a decorated war veteran with my gun.

"My favorite part might be when Curly tried to convince MacKenzie that he really was Lieutenant Danforth," Wild Bill said, laughing, "and did you see the look on MacKenzie's face when I shrugged out of that buffalo coat?"

"Oh no!" But of course, it was too late. There was no way now to go back for my buffalo coat. I had no doubt that MacKenzie would make good on his promise to shoot me on sight. I had pushed my luck with the man as far as it would go. Besides, we didn't have time. We were once again out on the flat dumb shimmering prairie, the same prairie we had just crossed the day before, following the very same people back across it.

Rattles and Scout and Yellow Hair and Little Yellow Hair had a head start—it had taken Major Hastings and his men some time to round up their horses—but if they pushed their horses, the way we were hoping they would, they could catch up with them by dark. Our job was to chase down any of the four soldiers who might figure out what was planned for them and do the smart thing and try to make a run for it.

The winds in the night had pushed the orange dust into drifts and onto the sides of brush and cactuses, and so the grass was no longer orange the way it had been and was back to its normal yellow burned up color. It was still hot and dry—good for desert critters, but bad for Old Curly. I wanted a bath, a hug from Sally, several toots of bourbon, and a good night's sleep in something other than dirt. Yet, instead, I was in the middle of the desert, crossing it all over again, and I wondered how long we would have to do it. Then I decided to just be grateful for the fact that we were all still alive because we were incredibly lucky, and because of that we now had the luxury to think about dying in the desert.

"We went into a camp with sixty troops and came out without a scratch," I said. "It's absurd."

"I believe the plan was so far-fetched and incomprehensible, even the most disciplined cavalry would have been taken unprepared," Frank said. "I have been a part of many plans in my life, and this one was clearly the worst."

"That's why it worked," Wild Bill said. "It's just like playing cards with Tad Bowltree. You can't work your mind around something that makes no sense. You can't plan for someone that will fold with four kings in his hand, and you can't plan to wake up in the morning and find out your prisoner has gone missing and has been replaced with Wild Bill Hickok. All of this will make for a good chapter in my book."

"We were lucky Colonel MacKenzie was so eager to move on," Hap said.

"I didn't know soldiers were so short," Baxter said, changing the subject.

"I don't think it would have gone the way it went down if the Colonel didn't recognize me and Curly," Wild Bill said.

"It was clear he didn't trust Major Hastings," I said.

Wild Bill nodded. "I believe he's well aware of the nature of Major Hastings and his men. I highly doubt he expects to ever see them again."

"You think he knows what's coming for them?" I asked.

Wild Bill nodded. "The Colonel is a stickler for order. He is tough, and he has made his way deeper into Comanche territory than anyone ever has. But he doesn't go in for the mistreatment of women, and he wouldn't go in for the careless slaughter of women and children. I could see it in his face, Curly, when you told him about it."

After Major Hastings and Captain Shelby and those two other soldiers went off to prepare and go after their escaped captives, I'd given the Colonel an earful. I told him about the slaughter I'd seen, and I told him why Scout had kilt his man, and I told him about the other scout that had his throat slit and was left in some hole, probably by Major Hastings himself, and I told him about Hastings raping Yellow Hair, as well as the signs we'd seen of rape among the Comanche women who'd then had their skulls bashed in. And I told him about the peace Jim Shepland and I had worked so hard on, and how his men had ruined it. I let it all out. I needed him to know what actually went down and why we were in his camp in the middle of a dried-up ravine in the middle of the desert.

"I did make it plain how I felt on the matter."

"That you did. Your face was red as a beet," Wild Bill said.

"Do you think Two Yellow Hairs's part of the plan will work?" I asked.

"I do," Frank said. "The Comanches are quite good when it comes to using the arrogance of the white soldiers against them. The soldiers' horses will get blown. They'll get hungry and thirsty, and probably turn on one another. Remember how it was when we went after Torp?"

"How could I forget? I almost died of thirst."

"We all did. But the Comanches wouldn't let us. They led us to water. They wanted us weak, but they wouldn't let us die. I expect Major Hastings will play right into their hands."

The six of us followed the tracks in the dust at a brisk walk, curious to see how this would all play out.

2

"They're driving their horses too hard," Frank said. "In this heat, they will be blown by nightfall. And they don't have Rattles to lead them to water this time."

We were following the tracks at a relaxed pace. They headed southwest towards Mexico, and it was easy to follow them as there was a lot of bent over grass that Wild Bill said he could read like a book. He must have known what he was about because Frank never once thought to correct or admonish him. Which must have drove Frank crazy—he wouldn't be Frank if he couldn't find something to criticize. I was being very careful with my water, knowing that the sun wanted nothing more than to see our bodies have all of our liquids sucked out. I took tiny sips, and kept a pebble in my mouth, something I'd learned from Frank. Yep, I was becoming an old hand when it came to being miserable in the desert.

I was going to suggest we make camp for the night before it got too dark to see, but before I could, Hap said, "they've got torches. They're not stopping for the night."

"Aw, they'll have to. Otherwise, their horses will step in some hole," Frank said.

"Well, it doesn't look like they know that," Hap said.

"Scout and Rattles don't have torches. They could follow the tracks for—"

The torches went out.

"They figured it out," Frank said. "I say we make camp. I say we have a fire, so they know they're not alone out here. See if we can get them to thinking about us and wondering who we are and maybe tomorrow they'll push their horses even more."

"I'm hungry," I announced.

"All we've got are hard biscuits," Hap said. "The buffalo steaks have all been ate." We walked our horses another hundred yards or so, and then we could see the orange flicker of their campfire.

"This here is good," Frank said.

And so, we dismounted and hobbled our horses and made camp. It wasn't long, once the sun went down, for the desert chill to set in. That's another thing on the negative side when it comes to deserts. I make no bones about the fact that I am particularly sensitive to chill. I like to be warm and toasty when I sleep. Which is why, as each waking minute piled up on the other, and the air got ever cooler, I wanted to strangle Wild Bill. I let him borrow my buffalo coat on the one and only condition that he return it. But did he do that? He did not! He shrugged it off and left it lying in the dirt. And now I was going to freeze to death. It had only been dark for a short while, and it already felt like my hands had stopped working.

"Let's get some coffee going," I said, because I wanted to be able to feel my hands again. I'd reminded Bill a million times since I first realized he'd left my buffalo coat behind, how incredibly disappointed in him I was. He seemed to feel like it should have been my job to keep up with the coat, since it was mine.

"Let's save it for morning," Frank said. "We'll need our sleep tonight. And I'm a big believer in sleeping when you get the chance."

"Fine," I said, then I stomped over and pushed Baxter aside and warmed up my hands over the campfire. "This winter coat ain't cutting it."

"If you cared about that buffalo coat as much as you care about that jerky in your pocket, you'd have that coat yet," Wild Bill said, trying to unbraid his stupid hair.

"Dang, I miss that coat!" I cried.

"The key to staying warm, Curly, is a simple matter of telling yourself that the coldness is actually warm," Frank said. He was packing his pipe with tobacco, and he showed no sign of temperature distress at all. I knew once he got his pipe going, he would launch into some damn story or another about some experience he had that was extreme and horrible in order to make me feel ashamed for my warmth needs. But he was slaughtering the wrong hog if he thought I was going to—

"That makes no sense at all Frank! In fact, it is the very definition of foolishness!" I said, stealing his word.

Damn it! I couldn't help myself and let my emotions run away from me and had now gone and given Frank the opening he needed to—

"Curly, this right here ain't cold at all. This right here is downright *warm* compared to the cold you get in the middle of winter, especially if Buffalo Hump has made off with all your clothes and you have to navigate the frozen desert in your bare feet. Throw in all the desert needles poking out of everything, and the complete absence of cover, and no way to make a fire, and even if you could make a fire, it would only attract hostiles, and so you can see that this here is nothing to make notice of."

"I'm not cold," Wild Bill said.

I immediately vowed that I would not speak a word to any of them for the rest of the night. I reached into my waistcoat pocket for my flask of bourbon but stopped myself when I saw the look on Wild Bill's face. He was looking at me like a starving wolf.

"Well," I said, "I got to go out and take a piss." I needed to get away from Wild Bill and his bourbon lust. As a saloon-keeper I'd seen that hungry look hundreds of times. It was usually some miner, or some cow-boy that had just come off the trail after a long cattle drive, or someone Ely Turner had sucked all the money out of, someone who could no longer afford a toot of whisky. Not even the bad moonshine with the tobacco floating in it. Whenever I saw that look, instead of giving in to it, I would just go to the other end of the bar until someone other than myself broke down and bought them a drink. There were a lot of thirsty and broke miners in Silver Vein, and I couldn't afford to be giving away free toots to anyone other than the drunks that could afford it.

Lost to my thoughts, I realized I had wandered off far enough away from the campfire to realize how dark it was, and how, in reality, I had no idea who or what else was out there in that desert dark. I'd learned the hard way that you can be surrounded by Comanches and never even know it. Or you could know you were surrounded by Comanches because they made noises that kept you awake all night. I had my eagle feathers, but nobody could see feathers in the dark. Especially under a shirt.

I was about to work myself up into truly being scared when I remembered why I'd come out away from the campfire, and so I pulled my flask out and took a swallow and then I turned around to face the campfire—and Wild Bill was standing there.

He'd snuck up on me like a ghost.

"Thought I'd keep an eye on you, make sure you're safe," Wild Bill said, staring at the flask in my hand like it was his favorite hairbrush.

"Uh-huh," I said, feeling the bourbon warm up my insides.

"Just a swallow, Curly."

"Uh-huh," I said.

Wild Bill basically had bourbon coursing through him all day like blood. But, recklessly I thought, he'd gone and slurped up his entire supply. And then he stole the buffalo hunters supply and slurped all that down too. And now here he was horning in on mine, which I had been extremely disciplined in doling out to myself in very small sips.

"You were reckless," I said, letting my thoughts out.

"I'm sorry about the buffalo coat," he said. Which was the wrong thing to say, because it reminded me of how cold I was, and I got vexed all over again.

"You should be. But I was talking about your bourbon usage. You drank up your supply like water. And now here you are after mine."

"I didn't know we would be out here this long. I thought we were just going to Hendrix and back."

This was a good counterargument. Curly the former buffalo coat owner and Curly the saloonkeeper were now fighting each other in my head, until, finally, the saloonkeeper won out. I'd been where he was. You can't be a saloonkeeper and not have sympathy for drunks. Especially when they're your friends.

"Tell you what. I'm a saloonkeeper. I have seen that look before, and I know what it means. If I was to give you this flask, you'd just guzzle it all down without a second thought."

"No, I wouldn't," Wild Bill said, licking his lips.

"Tell you what. If you give me your coffee mug, I'll pour some in it," I said.

Wild Bill, defeated, nodded. "Very well, Curly." And he turned and walked back to the campfire.

I walked off a few more steps, and, knowing he couldn't see me, swallowed a couple of toots down. I put the flask back in my waistcoat and waited for Wild Bill to show back up.

I waited about ten minutes or so, and then I heard laughing. It was coming from somewhere out there in the darkness. I walked back to the campfire, but only Frank and Hap were there. Baxter and Merle and Wild Bill were nowhere to be found.

"You need to corral your deputies," Frank said. "They're out there giggling like a couple of schoolchildren."

This was embarrassing. Here I was the sheriff, and my deputies were acting like a couple of fools.

"Which way are they?" I asked. "Hard to tell in the dark."

Hap pointed. "Out yonder."

I followed his finger and set to walking and the voices got louder and then I bonked into Wild Bill's back.

"Curly, my problems have been solved!" He had a bottle of something clear in his hand.

I looked at Baxter and Merle, and both of them had big dumb grins on their faces.

"What is in that bottle?" I asked.

"Just moonshine," Baxter said, shrugging.

"Apple brandy," Merle said.

I grabbed the bottle out of Wild Bill's hand just as he was about to take a sip. "They're going to poison you to death!" I said.

"It's okay," Baxter said. "This stuff is the real thing. You think we would give Wild Bill bad moonshine? We took our time on this batch."

"He's telling the truth," Merle said.

I could see they meant it.

"I better make sure," I said. I suddenly knew the stuff was good. Baxter would never do anything to upset his hero, like make him air out his insides. And, knowing this to be the case, I suddenly found myself wanting to horn in.

I sniffed the bottle and made to take a swig when the bottle was ripped from my hand.

"You bring me your coffee mug, Curly, I'll pour you some," Wild Bill said.

"I'm a saloonkeeper," I said, immediately presenting him with a shot glass from inside my waistcoat.

His smile disappeared. "Dang," he said. I could see he was basically back to himself. Baxter's apple brandy had worked its way into Wild Bill's bloodstream. And so, he shook his head, laughed, and poured me a toot. I slurped it down.

"Curly," Wild Bill said, "we've got an idea."

"It was my idea," Baxter said.

"It was both of ours," Merle said.

"What is it?" I asked.

"Remember that night when we were going after Torp, and we couldn't sleep because we kept hearing animal screams and coyotes yipping all around us?"

"Of course I remember," I said. "But what's that got to—"

"*We're* going to be the Comanches," Wild Bill said.

"We're going to keep them up all night," Baxter said, and then lifted his head up and set to howling like a wolf.

Merle walked off and let out a scream that sounded like a crow with a broken wing.

"Frank is going to kill us all," I said. "He sent me out here to shut you up." But then I thought back to that long ago night, and how I never did get so much as a wink in, and how the next day I could barely focus, and a few times almost fell asleep on top of my horse.

So, I walked off about fifty feet or so and let out a hissing roar, trying to sound like something mysterious and terrifying, what I thought a rabid lion might sound like.

3

PLOWRIGHT

Corporal James Plowright didn't want to screw up. He'd been given his orders by Colonel MacKenzie personally. His mission was to follow Major Hastings and Captain Shelby and Sykes and Pulaski and the Indians, and, once they again had their prisoners, to lead them back to the 4th Cavalry. He was not, though, in any way, to interfere. If the Indians were to get the upper hand, he was to simply report that as well. He got the sense from the colonel that he no longer trusted Hastings and didn't really care one way or another what went down—he just wanted to know about it.

Plowright looked at the tracks in the dirt and saw that the men who had made all the ruckus that morning were following Hastings as well. He soon had the six men in sight. He could see the dust their horses were kicking up. Figuring the men were following Hastings, and knowing the major was following the Indians, he decided he could simply follow the men following Hastings.

He was curious about the men. One of them was the shootist, Hickok. He remembered reading about him in a newspaper but couldn't remember the exact details. And the other one,

Curly Barnes, well, he was famous. Earlier, when he'd been given the mission, it was by a very confused Colonel MacKenzie, who was, uncharacteristically for him, drinking at breakfast.

"Allow me, Corporal, to give you my account as to what I think happened this morning. Somehow, Wild Bill Hickok, in the middle of the night, changed places with an Indian, donning a buffalo coat and braiding his hair. Somehow, Curly Barnes, a saloonkeeper from Silver Vein, broke into camp, ran our horses off, and him and two other men got the drop on our sentries and Lieutenant Danforth, taking their uniforms and then mingling with our troops. Meanwhile, up on the ridge, who knows how many men were in position to pick us off."

The Corporal nodded his head. "Yes sir, that's what it seems like."

"It is, in all my years of soldiering, the weirdest situation I've had to suffer through. Wild Bill Hickok! You tell that back at Fort Belknap and nobody would credit it!"

"No sir, it does sound far-fetched."

"And yet, it happened! Out here!"

"Yes sir," Plowright said.

And then the Colonel gave him his orders.

―――――

That night, he decided he didn't want to make his own fire, because of how far the light traveled on the flat prairie. He decided he would skirt up closer to the other men's campfire and scope it out. He wanted to know more about the people who were riding with Hickok and Barnes.

Plowright found a bush and dismounted and tied the horse's reins to one of its scraggly branches and then he walked towards the campfire.

He was about fifty feet from the fire when he heard a blood

curdling scream. And then, extremely close, the howling of wolves. And then—something else—some sort of monster was out there in the dark. The noise didn't sound human, or like anything Plowright had ever heard in his life.

Plowright didn't care about who all was at the campfire anymore. He let out a scream of his own and turned around and ran through the dark mindlessly. Some sort of beast was—

Something grabbed his leg, and he went down in a pile of dust. He put his arms over his head, to ward off the claws or teeth that were going to tear into him at any moment.

It took some moments for him to realize that he'd snagged his foot on the root of a bush. He'd simply tripped. He took a few deep breaths and sat up.

There was a man with a beard pointing a rifle at him.

4

I was on my third or fourth monster scream, when I heard another scream. I looked at Wild Bill and he looked back at me, and we walked over to Baxter and Merle, and we quietly turned and made our slow way back to the campfire. That scream hadn't come from me, and it didn't come from any of us. Someone—or something—else was out there. It could have been Scout had swooped back around in the dark, with the same idea we'd had.

When we got back to the campfire, Hap was standing by the fire by himself.

"We have a visitor," he said.

———

"Coming in," Frank called in from the dark. "Found this'n here lying in the dirt. I think he—"

"Curly Barnes! It really is you!" the scout said.

"It's me, all right," I said, confused.

I looked over at Wild Bill, and I could see, even out here in the desert, that he expected to be recognized.

"I'm Baxter," Baxter said.

"And I'm Merle," Merle said.

"And the other two are Frank Kilhoe and Hap Morgan," I said. "Which leaves us wondering who you are."

And so Corporal Plowright, in excruciating detail, told us just about everything that had ever happened to him, more or less since birth. When he got to the part about the monster screaming and how he started running in terror, it got Wild Bill and me laughing. How we'd gone and scared someone we didn't even know was out there.

Once we'd cleared up who he was, it was soon obvious he posed us no threat, and so we all sat back down by the fire.

"I have a horse out there somewhere," Plowright said. "I'd hate to see it get swiped."

Hap looked up at the sky. "It's not too dark to find it if you know which way to look."

"I can find it," Plowright said, standing up.

"You're our guest," Hap said. "I'll go with you." Hap grabbed up one of his Winchesters and the two of them walked off.

"I think we've raised enough ruckus for one night," Frank said, yawning. "Sleep when you can."

The bourbon and moonshine had worn off and, despite the chill, I felt my eyes drooping, and soon I lay my head down and looked up at the sky. Looked up at all them stars. One of the things I always promised myself is that I would one day learn about the heavens. I did speak to an old coot in Amarillo once, when I was tending bar at The Oriental for old One Eye Ned. He was a former sailor from Maryland, and he seemed to know the name for each and every one of the stars. I remember they all had names that seemed designed to be immediately forgotten. Each one had a whole alphabet of letters in them. So, I never did get around to learning about the stars. But it didn't stop me from loving to look up at them. Sometimes, when I was looking up at the stars, one of them would suddenly race off somewhere, and it made me think of the stars as a slow-moving herd of space cattle. Every once in a while, it seemed to me, one of the herd would decide it'd had enough and was moving on. And I sometimes wondered if there was another Curly Barnes, out there on one of those stars, at that very moment, lying in a different desert, a space desert, looking back at me.

I wondered how long I would wonder on things before my brain stopped thinking up stuff to think about when suddenly warmth landed on me.

"Merry Christmas, Curly," Hap said.

My buffalo robe!

"Plowright, you're my new best friend! If you ever find yourself in Silver Vein, I'll stand you at least four toots!"

"The Colonel said if I ran across you to give Wild Bill back his coat. But Hap said the coat is actually yours. He was worried if he didn't get this coat back to you guys, you'd come back for it. And he made it very clear he very much doesn't want to see any of you ever again."

"Makes sense," Wild Bill said.

5

HASTINGS

"Looks like we're being followed, Major," Sergeant Sykes said. It was probably Colonel MacKenzie keeping tabs on them, the sergeant figured. He had noticed how little patience MacKenzie seemed to have for the major. He seemed to have fallen from the colonel's good graces. Sykes had been with the major for a number of attacks and battles, but ever since they came across the blonde woman and her daughter, the major hadn't been himself. Sykes'd had no intention of volunteering to go back out into the desert. He was getting tired of sleeping in the dirt and eating cold biscuits and worrying all through the night and during the day about getting kilt by Indians. But he especially hated the sandstorm, which was something the sergeant had never experienced before—had never even heard of—and he had no desire to go through one again.

Hastings walked away from the campfire to take a look where the sergeant was pointing. Sure enough, there was another fire. It was hard to tell how far away it was; it was just a flickering orange light in a sea of inky black darkness.

"You think it's more troops?"

The major shook his head and spit into the dirt. "I reckon it could be. More than likely it's those assholes that ran off our horses and snuck into camp, including the one who whomped me on the head and stole the blonde woman and the girl that stabbed me in the back."

And that there, Hastings thought, was the biggest problem with his plan. No longer in camp, he no longer had access to soup. So how could he convince the blonde woman to love him? Or at least live with him and pretend she did? Without that sneaky little girl always waiting for a chance to shove a knife into him? He was only interested in the blonde woman, but he didn't think—

"One of them is Wild Bill Hickok," Shelby said. "I saw his face and know it for sure. I seen him once in Abilene. He's fast with those pistols of his, and hits most everything he aims at."

"How in the hell is Wild Bill Hickok on our trail? I'm not sure I understood anything that went on back at the camp," the major said, shaking his head. Because of the healthy dose of laudanum he'd been given, most of his time back at the camp was a blur. He hardly even remembered getting stabbed.

"Well," Shelby said. "All I know is what I'm going to do when I catch up to that Comanche that kilt Horvath. I'm going to hang him myself."

Hastings nodded. "I expect I'm done with soldiering. Once we catch up and kill these Indians, I'm going to take the blonde woman for myself. I know what you're thinking, but you're wrong. She'll come around. You'll see."

"And that little girl that got the drop on you?" Shelby asked.

"I'll send her to some school back in Pennsylvania and then have her shipped off to Australia."

"Probably a good idea. But my sense is that woman is too far gone to ever come around. You wouldn't ever know if she was going to come after you in the night."

Captain Shelby, even though he was a capable and vicious fighter, with few if any scruples, clearly didn't know what he was talking about when it came to the thoughts of women. Hastings let the man talk—but he knew the truth, even if nobody else did.

"Well," the major said, "whoever they are is of no mind. It's the Indians and the woman we're after."

"We don't know how many there are, if they're after us," Shelby said. "If it's soldiers that's one thing. But if it's them others, and Wild Bill Hickok, we would be outgunned."

"We'll have to keep a sharp eye out tonight," the major said. "Them Indians might try to circle back. I ain't too worried about the fellas behind us, not tonight anyway, but let's hit the trail as soon as we can see the tracks in the morning. Pulaski, you've got the first watch."

"Yes, Major," Pulaski said. He hoped that nothing happened in the night. He hadn't gotten much sleep the night before, as he'd eaten too much stew—having not had a decent meal in a week, he'd overindulged—and so spent half the night in the privy. And then, just as he had finally got his belly somewhat settled down, morning came with all its confusing mayhem, and here he was, having spent all day on a horse listening to his belly gurgle—and now he was expected to stay up half the night? But he knew better to argue with the major. Not when he was in a mood like this. He knew enough about staying alive to know that much.

The major looked up at the sky and unrolled his bedroll and lay down looking up at the sky, and thought about the blonde woman, wondering if she was somewhere lying down, thinking about him.

Finally, at some point late in the night, the major fell asleep, lost in fantastical thought, and his pipe slipped from his sleeping lips into the dust.

———

"Where is my horse?" Sergeant Sykes asked. "I hobbled her up right next to all the other horses. Right here."

The four men, groggy from a long night of strange noises and the haunting yipping of coyotes and wolves, looked around in all directions—but the missing horse was nowhere to be found.

"No tracks...how can there be no tracks?" Captain Shelby asked.

"I reckon the horse has just wandered off," Hastings said.

The three others looked at him, to see if he was serious, but knowing better than to call him out on it, when Sykes said: "It's them Indians. One of them snuck in here while we were asleep," he said, giving Pulaski a hard look, "and covered up their tracks. I've heard of such a thing happening before. And now it looks like I don't have a horse no more."

"Well," the major said, mounting up, "I reckon you'll have to ride double with Pulaski. That or walk. But if you choose to walk, don't expect us to wait up for you."

"Well, dang," Pulaski said. He didn't know how well Maggie would put up with having to carry Sykes as well as himself. He *did* wonder why the Indians would take only one horse. If they'd taken one horse, with nobody hearing a thing, the sergeant figured they could have up and swiped all of them. That's what he would have done if he was a Comanche.

Pulaski mounted up on Maggie, apologized in her ear, and said, "Okay, Sykes, get on up here." Sykes smiled in relief, not wanting to walk, and, with Pulaski's help, swung up behind him in the saddle. Maggie stomped her hoof and made an exasperated whinny, but then seemed to take the extra weight in stride.

Captain Shelby kicked dirt into the fire, dousing it, and mounted up, and the four of them on three horses followed the tracks of the Indians.

6

"They're down to three horses. One of them is doubled up," Wild Bill said.

Corporal Plowright had left early in the morning to range on ahead. It was fine with us, letting Plowright do all the work. We could just follow him. Not that the soldiers' tracks were hard to follow. Even I could have done it. We took our time and had a breakfast of hard biscuits and enjoyed some coffee. A couple of days earlier I'd been sick of buffalo steaks. But now I would have killed for one. I'd had my fill of biscuits and jerky. I did enjoy the coffee though.

"That was probably Scout's doing," I said, slurping down my third cup. We were going along at a plodding walk, so I could drink my coffee without spilling it on myself. "I know for a fact they can swipe a horse from a fella as he's riding it, if they wanted to."

"What a foolish notion," Frank said. "Ain't a Comanche on earth can do that. Not while a fella is actually *on* the horse."

"I bet they could if they were on the horse, and it was dark," Baxter said.

"Scout could," Merle said. "Especially if it was in the dark and if the fella had nodded off. Or if he was an opium eater."

"There are no tracks for the fourth horse. It just disappeared. Whoever swiped the horse did a very good job hiding the tracks. Scout is playing with them all right. Making things just a little bit worse on them," Hap said.

I reached into my saddlebag for a piece of jerky, and pulled it out, and was about to set to gnawing on it, when I realized what I was about—being in the desert heat and all—and so put the jerky back in my saddlebag. Nobody saw me do it, but I was very proud of my restraint. But then my stomach began to rumble, even though I'd just gobbled down a biscuit, and I'd been told how loud it was, and so I decided to just have a little, just enough to keep my stomach from giving us away. Sound traveled a long way in the desert after all.

We kept Plowright from getting completely out of sight. He was pushing his horse faster than we were. We could see him kicking up dust, a small cloud of orange we could just barely make out on the horizon. If I were to stand up in the saddle and look in every direction, it would all be the same. Just nothing but flatness. And the thing was, I knew we weren't in the same flatness we had been in a couple of days earlier, even though it all looked the same. For all I knew we were miles away from where we'd been. If Wild Bill and Frank were to suddenly be struck dead—and Hap too, he would also have to suddenly be struck dead—and it was left to Baxter and Merle and me to figure out how to get back to Silver Vein, I knew for a fact we would wander in circles until we all dropped dead, and the buzzards got us.

At one point, I did see something. It looked like the biggest buzzard in the world, perching on something I couldn't see. It was only after we'd gone miles, and got closer, that I could see it was just a dead tree. All of the leaves were gone, and it was charred black by a lightning zap that had chopped it in half. Yet, because it was the only thing that wasn't brush or a bush, it occupied my thoughts for half the day.

"Dang," I said, "just a tree."

7

HASTINGS

"How come they aren't getting any closer?" Shelby asked. "They speed up when we speed up and slow down when we slow down. We aren't gaining ground or losing ground neither one."

"It just seems that way," Hastings said. "The desert can do some strange things."

No, it can't, Shelby thought. Not like this. Hastings was so obsessed with romancing some ruined white woman that wanted nothing to do with him that he wasn't thinking straight. The Indians were toying with them. It was almost as if they wanted to make sure the four of them didn't lose their trail. When you added in the fact that someone had swiped one—but just one—of their horses in the night, and you added in all the strange noises, including something that sounded straight out of hell, it couldn't help but make Shelby think that they should turn around and go back and join the rest of the 4th Cavalry. In another year, maybe two, these Indians would be either on a reservation or dead. But then, that Indian that escaped *had* kilt Horvath, Shelby's best friend in the army, right in front of him. Just broke his neck, damn near twisted it off, and left him lying in the dirt for the scavengers. Shelby himself had done the same thing to that scout Grimes, but that was different—to him, anyway. That was something the major wanted him to do. That was just him doing his job.

Even though the Indian *would* eventually die by Shelby's hands, this was not the way to do it. This was the opposite of the way to do it. Who knows? Shelby thought. In three days, they might be down to zero horses.

"This ain't right," Shelby said. "Something's off."

"You don't know what you're talking about," Hastings said. "I reckon they had to slow down because the woman and the girl want us to catch up. I think I was finally getting through to her. Think about it. What would you rather do? Live with a civilized man who could provide you a real roof to sleep under? A real kitchen to cook in? Real friends to laugh with? And all surrounded by your own kind? Or live out in the dirt with a bunch of savages, always on the run and never knowing the next time you were going to sleep in peace? Of *course* she's going to come to her senses. She *wants* us to catch up. And then, when the Indians figure this out, then they make her speed up. I bet you that's the way of it."

"Maybe," Shelby said. He knew he couldn't push the major too hard, or he would snap, and when he snapped, he was liable to do anything.

Pulaski and Sykes almost came to blows several times over the discomfort of having to share a horse. Maggie didn't seem to care for the arrangement either, and she tried to buck them off on at least three occasions.

"One of us should walk," Pulaski said.

"Yeah, you," Sykes said.

"It's my horse. If it weren't for me, you'd be back there in the desert by yourself!"

This was true, and Sykes knew it, so he lapsed into silence. It was also true that it had never been his idea to even be out here. He should be back with the 4th Cavalry. They all should be. Sykes had ridden with Major Hastings through many years and many battles, almost since he first joined up, and this was the first time he'd had reason to question the major. The major, as far as Sykes was concerned, was thinking with his nob. And that never did anybody any good.

———

All that day, the four men followed the Indians, never falling too far back to lose them, yet never gaining enough ground to catch up. Their faces, used to the sun, burned anyway, and their lips chapped, and their tongues swelled up in their mouths, and they were constantly thirsty. The horses needed water, yet there was nowhere to find it.

Major Hastings could feel his horse getting weaker, so he ordered everyone to dismount and walk. The sun was right in their faces now, and the fine orange dust reflected the sun back at the soldiers from below. But, thankfully, slowly but surely, the terrain was starting to change. The flatness was giving way to mesas and buttes, arroyos and washes and small box canyons, and the four men made their way ever further into Comanche territory.

Finally, thankfully, the sun set over the mountains that could now be seen in the far distance to the west, and the air grew cooler, and Major Hastings ordered the men to stop and look for a place to make camp.

"We'll find water tomorrow," he said. "And food."

"We better," Pulaski said, "or we'll be as good as dead. I only got a few swallows left."

Major Hastings gave him a look, and the sergeant busied himself unsaddling Maggie and brushing her down and, in a voice that Sykes could hear, apologizing to her.

Major Hastings had been in such a hurry to chase after the

escaped Indians, and the woman he would one day call his wife, that he had severely misjudged the amount of food they would need. He originally figured it would take no more than a day to catch up with the Indians and bring them back to camp. But the Indians got no closer, as one day became two, and two became three, and now, tomorrow, would be a fourth day. As a result, they had nothing but hard biscuits to eat.

Captain Shelby built a fire, and roasted some coffee, and the four men ate and drank in silence, exhausted and all but flayed by the sun.

That night, a little after midnight, the noises started up again, and the men tossed and turned, and slept little.

In the morning, even more exhausted than when they went to bed, they woke up.

The horses were gone.

But there were four skins of water in their place.

"They're toying with us all right," Captain Shelby said.

Major Hastings didn't say it, but he was beginning to think Shelby might be on to something.

8

_____

"Well," Frank said, "Looks like they're down to no horses at all."

"And no tracks," Hap said.

"It's like the horses disappeared," I said.

We'd been walking our horses, as the tracks had all gone in one direction, which was the direction Scout was leading them, when we saw the four soldiers in the distance, standing in the desert. We'd wondered what they were doing, why they weren't going anywhere. Now we knew. Without any tracks to follow— and no longer having any horses to ride—they hadn't known what to do with themselves.

"I reckon they're lost," Baxter said.

Hap nodded. "Once they finally set out," Hap said, kicking the charred wood where the soldiers had made their fire, "they walked off in the right direction."

If I stood up in my stirrups, I could just make the four men out. They looked like little, tiny ants. "They must be miserable by now," I said. I knew they were, because I was miserable, and I had horse and water both.

"They're thirsty, and I doubt they've slept any," Frank said.

"I haven't," I said. "Too many noises in the night."

"I reckon that was Two Yellow Hairs doing," Frank said.

"They should have gotten closer, and screamed not as loud so that I could get a good sleep in. I've barely slept the night through since I left Silver Vein."

"I hear screams in my dreams on a normal night. So, for me, nothing has changed," Wild Bill said.

"How long do you think they will toy with them?" Baxter asked.

"They will draw it out as long as they can," Hap said.

"Can you sense the Comanches?" I asked. "I can. I know they're out here—but they're like lions, you can never see them."

"They're out there, all right," Frank said. "Glad we're not the ones they're after."

"That's true," I said.

I hoped it stayed true.

9

PLOWRIGHT

Plowright looked at the four figures on the horizon. He saw they didn't have any horses, which meant, if they hadn't hobbled them somewhere, they must have been swiped. Since he wasn't allowed to interfere in any way—since MacKenzie didn't want to get the Comanches all riled up, because he couldn't afford attacks on the 4th cavalry's rear—there was nothing Plowright could do.

It was one thing to be told not to intervene, but it was another to see four fellow soldiers walking through the desert without horses. They would almost certainly die if Plowright did nothing. And he didn't want them to die because he had stood by and let it happen. He wouldn't be able to live with himself if he watched the desert kill them.

He decided he would take a closer look. And then he would report back. It would take five days, if he was lucky, to get back to camp and come back with fresh mounts, food, and water. So, the sooner he left, the better. But he needed to have a better idea of their situation. Maybe they'd hobbled their mounts and had them stashed somewhere. Maybe there was a shelter that Plowright couldn't see.

He would get close, then wait until dark and get a closer look.

10

HASTINGS

"Our horses are gone," Sykes said.

"I can see that," Major Hastings said. "I don't need you to point out the obvious."

"They left us water. Why would they leave us water?" Pulaski asked.

"They want to kill us," Shelby said. "But they don't want the desert to do it or see us do it to ourselves."

"We don't know what's going on," Hastings said. He knew—he couldn't tell them he knew because they wouldn't believe him—but he knew. Because it was so obvious.

It was the woman who left the water. She was looking out for him. She was obviously starting to finally reconsider her situation. Spending the night in the desert dirt certainly had helped things along. All the major now had to do was catch up to her—the rest would happen naturally.

"There aren't any tracks to follow," Sykes said.

"We don't need tracks," Major Hastings said, but then realized that they actually did. Without any tracks to follow, he didn't have any way of knowing which way to go. Even though there was only one way to go, and that was in whichever direction the blonde woman had gone.

For an almost humiliating amount of time, the major was at a loss. The four of them spent a lot of time standing around looking in various directions—all of which looked the same to them—making no move in any direction.

"There!" Shelby exclaimed. On the horizon, there was no mistaking it. It was the blonde woman and the girl. They sat astride their horses, the sun shining behind them, giving them enormous shadows.

"Told you!" Major Hastings crowed. "She's waiting for me!" he said, letting an inside thought out.

There was no other direction they could go. So, they plodded in the direction in which they'd seen the woman and girl. They walked and walked, from time-to-time catching glimpses of the woman and girl.

Shelby knew the major had lost it. The woman and girl were luring them ever deeper into a labyrinth of canyons and buttes and mesas and ravines, further and further into the heart of Comanche territory—further away from civilization and sanity.

They walked in near silence for the whole day, drinking the provided water and the last of their hard biscuits. The sun once again brutalized them on its way over the horizon. Major Hastings found a small box canyon that he claimed was the safest place they could make camp, as they couldn't be snuck up on from behind.

"I wouldn't mind getting snuck up on, if the one doing the sneaking were to bring more water," Sykes said. "It ain't like we got anything left for them to swipe."

"They might make off with your nether parts," Shelby said. That should shut him up, he thought.

They built a campfire out of some dead tree branches and the remains of a dead cactus. Pulaski, who'd had the extra burden of carrying what was left of the coffee, started roasting coffee beans.

"What's our plan?" Shelby asked when he had Major Hastings off to himself.

"Plan?" the major asked. "How would I know what the plan is?"

"Well, you're in charge," Shelby pointed out. "And we're out in the middle of a wilderness of—"

"You saw the plan with your own eyes. Which is to follow the blonde woman. Wherever she goes we go. It's the only way it can be."

"Let me ask you something. What if ain't the way you think? What if the woman is leading us into a trap? That girl stabbed you in the back with a knife she had hidden in her clothing. The woman screamed and cursed at you and slashed your face. She never gave you any reason to think that she cared for you in any way." Shelby hated talking to the major in this way, but someone had to tell him. And it couldn't be Sykes or Pulaski. The major would think nothing of killing either one of them were they to be honest.

"Shelby...don't you see? She was a slave of the Comanches. And we came along, and we freed her and the girl. We saved their lives!"

"Just out of curiosity, I'm going to suggest that perhaps we could entertain the plan we should have if we *do* have this wrong. As a back-up in case the woman *isn't* trying to rescue us."

"No need," Hastings said. "We've got the right of it. And Shelby, we're done talking about this. You understand what I'm telling you? Because I won't say it again."

"I understand," Shelby said.

I understand that we're all going to die out here, Shelby thought.

———

It was a dark night, but the fire reflected off the canyon walls, dancing back and forth and providing a reassuring glow that kept the dark at bay. Shelby reckoned he could see almost fifty yards, plenty enough to give them time to react if they saw a Comanche coming for them. He knew it was probably that Indian—not the old man but the young one that kilt Horvath—who had swiped their horses. And he knew it was probably the same Indian that left the water. And he also knew—with absolute certainty—that the blonde woman was luring them all into a trap. And, sadly, he knew there was nothing he could do about any of it because Hastings had gone around the bend crazy. Besides, they were too far gone to go back. There would be no going back. Not without their horses. Not without more water.

The major was sitting up against a shale boulder that had broken off long ago and tumbled from the cliff above, staring off into the night, lost in thought.

Sykes and Pulaski were lying on the ground trying to sleep.

Shelby lay down, and when he did, he realized he needed to piss. So, he stood up and walked away from the fire.

"Don't go too far," the major said.

"Don't worry," Shelby said. He walked out to the limits of the campfire's glow. It was darker, and Shelby found something almost mesmerizing about how incredibly dark it was out beyond the fire's light. He was far enough. Shelby listened intently for anything out of the ordinary. He didn't want to be caught with his nether parts hanging out if there were Comanches about. Satisfied he didn't hear anything, he started pissing. There wasn't much there. Just a sad dribble, a few drips hitting the sand. He was actually surprised he needed to piss at all. He figured his body would want to hold onto it.

He was just wrapping things up, shaking himself free of

remaining pee drops, and tucking himself back in, when he heard, from somewhere out in the darkness, a horse nicker.

Then he heard someone say, "Hush!"

Shelby crouched down and walked out into the dark and waited for his eyes to adjust. He hunch-walked in the direction he'd heard the voice. Comanches didn't use words like "hush." This was someone else. He could hear footsteps now.

"Who's out there?" Shelby asked.

"Uh oh," a voice said. Then: "It's Corporal Plowright. I brought you some water."

"Where are you?" Shelby asked.

"You fellas okay?" Corporal Plowright walked towards Shelby leading his horse.

"I'm glad you're here," Shelby said, shooting Plowright in the chest. He grabbed the horse's reins from Plowright's desperate clasp, pulled himself up into the saddle, turned the horse's head and headed off into the dark night.

11

"Was that a gunshot?" I asked.

"I believe so," Frank said.

12

HASTINGS

A few years from now everything will be different, Hastings thought. He could see the blonde woman, re-civilized now, wearing a comely dress, with her hair in a bow on top of her head, showing off her graceful neck. He could see the three of them at church, and he could hear the admiring comments from jealous men and admiring women. He could even see the blonde girl, civilized now, grown up into a studious girl proud to call herself Hastings. He would need to give them new names, of course. None of this would work if they didn't have good Christian names...

The sudden sound of a gunshot brought Major Hastings out of his fantasies and back to the present moment.

"Who's shooting? Shelby?" Sykes asked.

"He's not here," Pulaski said.

"Maybe he came upon a Comanche," Sykes said. "Shelby!"

"Shut up you damn fool," Hastings hissed, standing up. "We don't know who all's out there. We don't even know if it was Shelby that shot that gun!"

Hastings drew his pistol, and Sykes and Pulaski followed his lead. They followed Hastings away from the fire and into the dark. "He came out here to relieve himself," Hastings said. "I told him not to go too far."

Hastings took two more steps and the dark swallowed him up and all Sykes and Pulaski could hear was the sound of his footsteps.

"I reckon this is far enough," Sykes said. "I don't want to disappear into the dark."

"Me neither."

"We'll have to wait for morning," Hastings said, appearing back from the darkness. They followed him back to the campfire. He sat there looking like he wanted to kill someone, so Sykes and Pulaski left him alone.

Then, from somewhere out in the darkness, the screaming started.

"Is that Shelby?" Sykes asked.

"One of you make me a torch," Hastings said. "I'm going back out there."

Sykes found a branch that would do, and Pulaski put it into the fire and waited for it to catch fire. Hastings grabbed the torch from Pulaski and said, "Don't you two go nowhere," and walked out into the night once again.

Hastings followed the screaming and found Plowright leaking blood into the desert dust.

"Plowright?" Hastings asked. "What are you doing out here? Did MacKenzie send you?" He wasn't going back to the 4th Cavalry. No matter what the colonel wanted.

But Plowright was in too much agony to talk. Then, carefully, through clenched teeth he said, "He took my horse."

"Who did?"

"Why would he shoot me? I was here to help you."

So, Hastings now knew, Shelby shot Corporal Plowright and took his horse. He'd abandoned Hastings right when he needed him most. Now it would just be the three of them—and

Sykes and Pulaski, while hardened fighters, weren't close to being as good as Shelby in a scrap.

"The Colonel send you?"

The scout nodded.

Hastings looked around, then he came to a decision. "I'm afraid we can't do anything for you. We can't spare any water, and not even a bullet. So, I guess you'll have to let time kill you, which it will soon enough."

Major Hastings leaned over and took the bullets out of Plowright's gun and the knife from his belt.

Then he turned around and headed back to camp.

13

We saw the circling buzzards in the sky ahead of us and followed them to the scout, Plowright. He was fighting off the buzzards, beating them away with his fists and screaming. Blood covered the entire left side of his shirt and the top part of his uniform pants. It looked like the Comanches had left him a skin of water.

"Scat!" Frank Kilhoe yelled, and the buzzards did. They hopped off out of reach, waiting.

"What happened?" Wild Bill asked.

"Captain Shelby shot me and stole my horse," Plowright said. The effort made him cough up blood.

"That's enough now," Hap said. "You don't need to try and talk."

Plowright nodded. He wiped the blood from his lips with his shirt sleeve. "It don't matter. I'm dying. It doesn't really hurt all that much. Looking at all this blood, you'd think it would hurt more."

"Plowright, you deserved much better than getting shot by a fellow soldier. If I ever run across this Shelby, me and him will have words," Wild Bill said.

"He'll go back to the Colonel and make up some story," Plowright said, then doubled over on himself and had a coughing fit.

Then he stopped coughing and pushed himself up. "The major took the bullets from my gun,"

I didn't know what that meant, but Frank did. He dismounted and took a bullet from his gun-belt and offered it over. Plowright nodded and put the bullet in his pistol.

"Not yet," he said. "I want to just sit here for a spell."

"Come on," Wild Bill said. I hated to leave Plowright sitting there. I waited until we were out of earshot and said, "We can't leave him to the critters."

"We got no way to bury him," Frank said.

"We could at least find a place to put him where he won't get picked to pieces," Wild Bill said. "Not his fault he's out here. He was just following orders."

"That would work," Frank admitted. "In fact, that's what a lot of Indians do. They find some place hidden, where nobody can find and disturb the body, and cover it up with sticks and rocks."

"Anything is better than leaving him like he is," I said.

It wasn't long before we heard the shot.

————

Wild Bill scouted ahead and found a place where a cliff face had split in half, and we put Plowright in there. It was not fun. But at least the birds wouldn't get to him. It was all we could do.

As the dust had given way to brush and cactuses and craggy rocks and cliffs and canyons, and the ground had grown rocky, it wasn't easy to follow the three men. Wild Bill and Frank took the lead, winding back and forth on their horses, looking down at the dirt for the occasional broken stick or dislodged rock. There were more signs than I would have thought, but Wild

Bill told me the men were tired and dragging their feet, kicking up all sorts of things if you knew how to look. I bet I would be an easy person to track, because I kick over rocks whether I'm tired or not.

We weren't far now. I could see mountains in the distance, and giant rock walls were now rising up on both sides of us and we were about to ride down deeper into the canyon. At the bottom of the canyon, I could see a bunch of actual trees, tall cottonwoods, the biggest I'd seen, with a small river running through them. The canyon was probably about five miles across as the crow flies. We stopped our horses to take in the view.

"We're close," Wild Bill said, pointing. "Two Yellow Hairs made mention of this canyon, said when the walls grew into the sky to look out for—there they are!" he said, pointing off to the left. There were about five Comanches on horseback off to the left of where Major Hastings and his two soldiers were walking.

"Wonder what they're up to," Hap said.

14

HASTINGS

The blonde woman and the girl were within range now. Hastings felt like one final brisk hike, and they would catch up to them in about an hour. They were that close.

"We're almost there, boys!"

Sykes didn't share the major's enthusiasm. He didn't give a shit about the blonde woman or the girl, and neither did Pulaski. But, unfortunately for them, they were too terrified of the major's temper to do anything other than follow each and every order the major gave—no matter how dumb they were.

Pulaski couldn't help but notice they were now following the blonde woman as she and the girl turned off onto what looked like a narrow rocky trail into an opening in the canyon wall.

"Um, Major?"

Hastings didn't reply. He just walked ever faster. It got so that he was taking two steps for every one of either of the other two men. Soon, he was far ahead of them.

He'd seen exactly what he was looking for. She was waiting for him to catch up! She wanted to talk to him! She even smiled. Bared her teeth, anyway. Then she kicked her horse and disappeared into an opening in the canyon wall. The major followed—Sykes and Pulaski completely forgotten about. At this moment, the major didn't even know who Sykes and Pulaski even were, so intent was he to be reunited with the woman who would one day be his wife.

The narrow path through the canyon wall opened up and Major Hastings found himself in a narrow sandstone canyon that widened at the mouth and then narrowed again. The blonde woman, so close now, was just at the other end of the small canyon. She looked back at him, wanting to make sure he was following, gave him a real smile this time—and then disappeared from view.

"No! Wait!" Hastings yelled. His voice echoed and bounced and ricocheted in every direction at once, boomeranging back into Hastings' own ears.

Ahead of him, Sykes could hear the major's voice and he looked up and saw the major, now at the far end of the canyon, come up short, then stop walking entirely, then turn back towards Sykes and Pulaski—at which point he broke into a run.

The major ran right by both Sykes and Pulaski.

"I was wrong!" The major yelled. "Very much wrong!"

Sykes watched the major run back the way they had come, but Sykes could see there was now a group of five Comanches in warpaint on horseback blocking the canyon opening they'd all just come through. And, instead of the woman they'd been following for the last two days, on the far side of the canyon there was the Indian, the one that escaped. And, next to him was another Comanche, and when Sykes looked at him, the Comanche let out a terrible scream, raising a hand in the air. Sykes and Pulaski turned around and started running as well. The Indian's scream bounced around the narrow canyon and scrambled the brains of the three fleeing soldiers.

Major Hastings, running on nothing but terror, made the mistake of looking up. At the top of the narrow canyon, completely encircling the top of the canyon, were maybe a hundred warriors, all in warpaint, all staring down at him. Looking back down, Hastings saw that the mouth of the canyon was now completely blocked. The three men were completely surrounded.

There was nowhere to go.

Hastings stopped running.

Sykes and Pulaski joined the major and they all pulled out their pistols.

Pulaski had a thought, pointed his gun at the major and said, "Fuck you Major, you've done kilt us all," and pulled the trigger.

"Oh," Pulaski said, looking at his gun in wonder.

Hastings pointed his gun at Pulaski and pulled the trigger.

"Oh," Hastings said, realizing he didn't have any bullets in his gun.

"Oh," Sergeant Sykes said.

"Oh boy," Sergeant Pulaski said. "Looks like they—"

"I know that it looks like, Pulaski!" Hastings yelled.

Hastings put the empty gun back in his holster and pulled out his knife. That Indian that had kilt Horvath was now coming towards them on a horse. Next to him was the other Indian, the one that screamed, and he had a club in his hand. The canyon was silent now. Hastings could feel their eyes bearing down on him from above, but there was not a single sound except the whistling wind.

The two Indians pulled up on their reins and the Indian with the club dismounted from his pony, which had white paint around its eyes and neck and red and black handprints on its rump. The Indian walked up, staring into the major's eyes, seemingly boring holes into them. Without breaking stride, he clubbed Sykes across the face, and immediately reversed his arm and struck Pulaski in a backhanded blow that echoed off the canyon's walls. The two men fell to the ground.

The Indian sitting on his horse, the one Shelby had sworn could speak English, said something sharply in Comanche, and the one with the club stopped his arm right before he could crush Hastings' skull. He swore something in Comanche, tossed the club into the dirt, slapped the knife out of Hastings hand, grabbed him by the hair and yanked him screaming back towards the Indian on the horse.

"I didn't do anything!" Hastings screamed wildly.

"I'm not going to hurt you," Scout said.

"You *do* speak English!" Shelby had been right! The treasonous bastard had been right all along! About everything!

"Some," Scout said, shrugging.

"Well then, maybe we can talk about this!"

The Indian yanking on his hair yelled something in Comanche, and the man on the horse said something back, and the two went back and forth and then the one who had Hastings by the hair smiled.

He pulled out a large knife. Hastings could see that it was sharp. In fact, he'd been the one who sharpened it. It was one of his knives! From his saddlebag!

"This fella stole my horse!" Hastings cried. And then, "That's my knife!"

The one on the horse raised his right arm into the air and looked back at the mouth of the canyon. Major Hastings followed his eyes and saw the blonde woman and the girl. Neither one of them was smiling.

"It's you," Major Hastings said. "I've been following you! It's not too late! Say the word and we can live our lives together!"

The Indian on the horse rolled his eyes.

15

We made our way down into the canyon, but we had to rein up our horses when we saw a group of Comanche warriors in warpaint cross silently in front of us. A few turned and looked our way, their faces terrifying to behold with their eyes blacked out—but none of them came our way. They passed in front of us and disappeared from view.

"I held my breath that entire time," I said.

"They weren't interested in us," Wild Bill said.

"They might change their mind," Merle said.

"I talked to Two Yellow Hairs before he left us. He told them to leave alone anyone riding with the man in the funny brown hat." Wild Bill pulled his hat off and studied it. "I rather like this hat, though I concede it ain't the usual for these parts."

"You mean the desert?" Frank asked.

"No, I do not mean the desert. I mean Silver Vein, Abilene, Dodge City—the frontier. I won this hat off a fella from Brazil." Wild Bill put his hat back on.

We continued down into the canyon and found the trail to the right and took it. We kicked our horses into a rope and then we came upon old Rattles. I recognized the white stallion, of course. But now the stallion had its war paint on. There was another pony with him without a rider. When he saw us, he dismounted his horse, and we did as well.

"Rattles!" I said.

"Sheriff," Rattles said, clasping my shoulder and looking into my eyes. It's hard to explain, but Rattles looking into my eyes always had a powerful effect on me. A great sort of power went through him, and you could feel it up close.

"I'm sorry about those soldiers," I said. "It never should have happened."

"They were not yours," Rattles said. Clearly Scout had been teaching him some English.

"No."

"My people are angry."

"I understand. They have a right to be."

"Many of my people were killed, including my brother. Including children."

"I am sorry about that. It's horrible."

"Yellow Hair was raped."

"I know it," I said.

"You are to go no further," Rattles said, drawing his hand across his chest in a way not all that different than what I do when I have to tell some fella he's been cut off from drinking.

"Why not?" Merle asked. "We only just got here."

"We're low on water," Hap said.

"And we're out of food that ain't biscuits," Baxter said.

Rattles nodded. He walked over and took the reins to the pony and walked over to Frank and said, "Food. Water." Frank took the reins and nodded. The two old men didn't communicate with each other with their mouths. As grumpy and rough as old Frank was, he would always soften around Rattles. I don't know if anyone else saw it—and he would whomp me to death were I to have mentioned it—but Frank had a tear leak out of his left eye and snake its way into his scraggly beard. Just the one, though. But that was a lot for Frank. Frank had spent most of his adult life chasing after and fighting Indians. Rattles had spent most of his life fighting back. I think all that fighting made the two of them appreciate their friendship on a deeper level than the rest of us.

Frank nodded, took the reins, and wrapped them around the horn of his saddle.

"This canyon is sacred to my people," Rattles said, mounting up on his horse with surprising ease. "No white man can be allowed to see it and stay alive."

"I don't want to see it," I said.

"Me neither," Baxter said. "Not when you put it that way."

"That's as good a reason as any not to go any further," Merle agreed.

"Unless you want to suffer nightmares the rest of your nights, what is going on in that canyon is best left unknown," Frank said.

So, the six of us just stood there looking up at Rattles, none of us wanting to move until Rattles rode off down the trail and ran his horse into an opening in the canyon wall and disappeared. I didn't know if I would ever see him again.

"Must be a trail that cuts through the cliff," Frank said.

We stood there looking at the canyon wall where Rattles had disappeared. We were all a little reluctant to get back on our horses. I was saddle sore, and ravine walking sore, and sleeping in the dirt sore, and every other kind of sore. My entire body seemed to be mad at me all at once. I loved Horse, but my body was sick of him. I was thinking about the ride home, a three-day trip if we took it at a relaxed pace, and how much I was not looking forward to it, when, carried on the wind, I could hear a scream.

"Two Yellow Hairs said the name of this place is The Canyon of Screams," Wild Bill said.

"Let's go," I said. I mounted up on Horse, turned his head

away from the screams, and gave him a nudge in the belly. He seemed as eager as I was to get away from those screams.

The screams were getting worse. It was hard to believe such a noise was coming from a human. In that moment, I was very glad I didn't have to witness it. I'd seen enough of what an angry Comanche could do to a fella when they wanted to cause pain. They were experts in torturing. I'd once seen some Comanche children calmly place scorpions inside the ear of a fella buried up to his neck in the dirt.

The horses were disturbed by the screaming, just like the rest of us, and set to nickering and blowing and stomping their hooves in the rocky dirt.

We made our way back up the canyon, and the screams followed us. It wasn't until we got into the trees by the river that we could no longer hear them. And that's where we decided to make camp. The sun had yet to set, but we were in no rush. We were relieved that our job was concluded, and we needed to let off some steam. Days of chasing Hastings across the desert, then back across the desert, and the strange haunting noises every night had made us all tense. But now, all of that was gone, and we were starting to realize it.

Baxter explored what all was on the pony Rattles had let us borrow—old Rattles never let anyone have anything; I knew, sooner or later, he'd swipe his pony back—and found four pounds of salted buffalo, two rabbits, some buffalo jerky, spices, and several skins of water.

Before long we had a fire going and Hap and Baxter were cooking up the buffalo steaks. My stomach and me were eager to gnaw on a steak again. The only real problem—and by problem, I mean a real serious problem—is we were all out of bourbon. I'd sipped up my last drop the night before, and Wild Bill had been out for days—which he claimed was bad for his blood. If we were lucky, we would have to get some nips of Baxter and Merle's moonshine.

Merle was looking for a place to set his bedroll when he looked up and saw me and Wild Bill staring at him. I walked over and said, "Merle, I'm going to have to confiscate your moonshine."

"Dang sheriff, what for?"

"Okay. You can keep your moonshine, but there's a moonshine fee. You have to give me a toot. I need it, and as your sheriff, you need to give it to me."

"Me as well," Wild Bill said.

Merle looked at Wild Bill and handed over his last bottle of moonshine without complaint, so complete and reckless was his hero worship. Wild Bill took a swig, and I took a swig.

"Got enough for everyone?" Frank asked.

Between Baxter and Merle, we would have just enough.

"There's one thing wrong with all of this." Wild Bill said, sipping on his share of moonshine. "One piece of the puzzle still missing."

Frank nodded. "The fourth man."

"The man that did for Plowright, and left him to die in the desert," Wild Bill said.

"Shelby," I said. "Scout told me it was him and Hastings that were the two leaders."

"I expect, somehow, we haven't yet seen the last of that one," Wild Bill said.

"Well, he ain't out here now," Hap said. "We can eat our steaks and rest up in peace, for this night anyway."

"I'll drink to that," Baxter said. "A little bit anyway."

"Me too," Merle said.

And so, we did.

BOOK IV: SHELBY

1

SHELBY

Captain Shelby ran Plowright's horse like he had the hounds of hell chasing after him. He wanted nothing at all to do with the Comanches or Major Hastings, either one. He still would kill the Indian of course, the one that did for Horvath—but there would be time for that later. Right now, it was all about survival. When he'd left Hastings, he didn't even have a horse. But such was his respect for the major and his rage, he didn't want to chance the possibility that Shelby's abandonment could have shaken the major free of his insanity. For all Shelby knew, Hastings had found a horse to steal and was at that very moment chasing Shelby down to get his revenge.

Shelby hoped the Comanches would be happy toying and torturing and savaging Major Hastings and would be too distracted by their lust for revenge to worry about little old Captain Shelby. He'd seen the six men that had been following them, Wild Bill Hickok and whoever else, but they didn't see him. They seemed intent on following the major as he aimlessly went after that stupid woman.

He didn't know what to make of the major and his sudden

plunge into reckless lust. And the more he thought about it, the more he knew there was no way the major was on his trail. Maybe being out away from civilization for weeks and months, which became years, had muddled the man's mind until he could convince himself of some impossible domestic life that was never going to be. Shelby didn't know what had happened to the major's mind; all he knew was that the man that he had happily followed into scrap after scrap and battle after battle was no more. That man was gone forever, never to come back. He wasn't abandoning the major, he was abandoning what the major had become.

Shelby was in a pickle. He couldn't go back to Colonel MacKenzie and the 4th Cavalry, wherever they had made his way to, on account of someone was sure to recognize Plowright's horse and start asking questions. Questions he couldn't answer. He couldn't say that he'd shot Plowright in the chest and left him dead in the desert for the Comanches to find. He couldn't say that he'd abandoned Major Hastings and Sykes and Pulaski to fend for themselves on foot in hostile territory.

No, his time in the army was finished. All he had in the world was the stolen horse he was riding and the tattered uniform he was wearing. He had little water left and only a couple of hard biscuits. He would head east, and then north, back towards Amarillo and civilization. Away from the miserable sun and the vengeful Indians. And away from the ever-circling buzzards that followed him in the sky above—waiting for the desert to do him in.

Shelby stood up in the stirrups and looked around in every direction—and saw nothing at all. Nobody was coming for him. And he would know if they were. The desert was too flat and the horizon so very far away that he would have seen a cloud of dust even if it was miles away.

That night, Shelby tied the horse's reins to his right boot

and lay on the hard desert ground to sleep. Or try to. But it was too dark and there were too many scampering noises of unseen critters, along with the distant howling of wolves, and the closer than comfortable yips and yaps of the taunting coyotes. He realized for the first time that he was alone now. If anything came for him in the night, he would have to fight it off by himself. He'd once seen a coyote lead a dog away from camp so the pack could tear it to shreds. You see one coyote by itself, and it don't look all that scary. Kind of like a too-skinny dog. But you find yourself surrounded by a bunch of starved coyotes, and they could probably do for a man and a horse both.

Shelby (he was just Shelby now. Nobody would ever call him Captain again.) slept poorly and got up at first light. The horse must be hungry, Shelby thought. And thirsty. He hadn't been allowed to graze on what little grass there was, not tied as he was all night to Shelby's foot. He eased up on the horse's reins, and set out east, letting the horse tell him where to go. It was a good decision, because the horse eventually led the two of them to a small murky stream that trickled miserably and lazily towards Mexico. Shelby let the horse bend its head and lip up some water. He bent down himself, and, desperate, scooped some of the bitter and dusty water into his parched mouth. His body immediately let him know he should drink as much as he could. He drank until his belly jutted out and made sloshing noises. He made some sudden moves back and forth with his belly just to hear that sloshing noise. It made him happy, reminding him of his childhood, when he and his brother would—

Robert. Dead now. Blown to smithereens at Shiloh. He would have been twenty-seven if he'd lived. Thinking about his brother made his happiness dissolve, and he was brought back to his current reality. He was pretty much fucked, he figured. What were the odds that the horse would be able to find more water? What if the horse had just lucked into the water? What if the horse didn't know how to smell water at all?

What if he was giving the horse too much credit? How long before the both of them could walk no more, and settled, weak and dying, into the desert dust for all of eternity?

He needed to keep moving.

He mounted up and set off east at a walk, every once in a while, checking behind him to make sure he wasn't being followed.

It was weird to be by himself. And quiet. The only noises were the sound of his boots rubbing against the saddle, that rhythmic creaking noise, and the sound of the wind stirring up dust—and the horse's hooves when they struck the ground. He couldn't remember the last time he'd been by himself. Maybe never. Before he went to war, he'd been at home, and he was never alone there. So this, Shelby thought, must be the first time since birth he'd been alone like this. With nothing but himself to talk to. He could talk to the horse, but it wasn't his horse, it wasn't Jackson, and he didn't have much of a relationship with Plowright's horse. Didn't even know the horse's name. Besides, horses didn't count as people. If the horse could talk, Shelby figured, it would probably just complain. It would complain about the saddle and the bridle and the bit in its mouth and the lack of grass and water. There'd be no end to it. This thought made Shelby laugh out loud—and he started to think maybe he was going crazy. Being alone was making his thoughts louder, Shelby realized.

It was just after noon, when the sun was at its most punishing, that Shelby felt his first stomach cramp. Which was soon followed by another. And another. And then his entire stomach clenched up and he had to get off the horse.

He ripped his pants down just in time. For the next hour, his stomach seized, and his body worked to get rid of the dirty water Shelby now knew he shouldn't have drunk. At one point he got so mad he pulled out his gun and had a notion to shoot the horse, which seemed perfectly fine. But he couldn't, of course—so he dropped the gun to the ground, as it had grown too heavy to hold onto. Shelby grew even weaker, and his legs cramped up and he couldn't straighten them out. He felt a whoosh of wind and looked up and twenty feet away a vulture had landed and was now looking at him without fear—waiting.

Shelby wanted to shoo the enormous bird away, but he was too dehydrated and too cramped up to raise his head. He put his head against the scorching sand and regretted it as the sand immediately seared his already sun-scorched skin.

Shelby looked weakly at the horse, who seemed to be mocking him, calmly nosing in the sand for grass. Shelby didn't think it was fair. It had drunk more water than he had!

"Mister, you don't look too good."

Shelby painfully lifted his head up—and danged if there wasn't an old man on a mule with a long, bushy beard. He had a wide straw hat that reflected the glare of the sun into Shelby's sensitive eyes, burning a hole into whatever was left of Shelby's fevered brain.

"Sorry," the man said, taking his hat off. He dismounted from his mule and walked over with a canteen, which he offered to Shelby. "I heard you retching and then saw that you were squirting water out of your arse and figured you might be in a bad way. I ain't normally one that longs for company, so—"

Shelby couldn't reach the canteen because his arms were seized up in cramp.

"—Ah! Sorry! Here. I'll just tilt it into your mouth. Just take tiny sips or you'll puke it all up. I don't normally run into anybody out here. Used to be, you'd have your head going back and forth, looking out for Indians. Now I don't see anybody. You're the first fella I've seen out here in weeks. I come out here to find herbs, which I sell to a healer in Amarillo."

Shelby could slowly feel himself coming back to himself. It

had been stupid to drink that water. He should have known better. But his thirst had made him weak in the mind, and he'd been too delirious to question the water at all. Thank God for the old timer. Even in his weakened state, it occurred to him that the old hermit, or whatever he was, talked a lot. Shelby's arms loosened and his eyes watered and his tongue moistened back up and he found he was strong enough now to hold the canteen himself.

"Thanks, mister," he said, meaning it more than he'd ever meant anything in his life. Part of him wanted to cry.

"You can have that one," the old man said. "And I know where to find more. And I mean good water—the kind you can drink without airing out your insides."

"What's your name?" Shelby croaked.

The gray beard parted, and Shelby could see a couple of tobacco-stained teeth, and the man said, "Some call me Nebraska Bob. Others call me Hermit Bob. I don't really mind either one. Of course, I guess you could just call me Bob."

Shelby nodded. He pushed himself up and reached out and Bob helped him get to his feet. "Shelby. I'm awful glad you came along, Bob."

2

SHELBY

"It was right around here I had a lion jump me. Or rather jump on the back of my old mule Lumpy. Never heard a thing until it was already on us. This brush hides just about everything."

They were riding through a field of tall yellow grass. Shelby looked around and could see how easy it would be to get snuck up on, especially if it was a lion the same color as the surrounding grass. But he preferred the tall grass to the flatness of the desert. It might make it easier to get snuck up on, but it also made it harder to be seen in the first place. It wasn't just the grass that was changing, Shelby noticed. The ground was changing too. There was more vegetation, and less dust— and instead of having to look out for prairie dog holes, he now had to keep a watch out for rocks and loose shale, which could cause his horse to stumble or break a leg.

"How far away?" Shelby asked. He was stronger thanks to the water, but he didn't have enough strength to sit on a horse for much longer. He needed rest.

`"Oh, not long now. And don't you worry about that lion. I put this here long knife through the back of its head! Tell you what, I'll show her to ya when we get to my shelter. Now when you see where I live, you're not gonna think much of it. It's just temporary. It's only when I'm out here collecting. I got a real place just outside of town over in Amarillo. I only come out here a couple of times a year for a month or so. This year it's been six weeks as it's been dry, and the buds have been scarce. I reckon I got another week." Bob looked at Shelby. "Unless I had help, of course."

Shelby nodded his head. "I aim to get to Amarillo. The sooner I can get there, the better."

"Well," Bob said, "suit yourself. I can point out the way and give you something to eat and you can be on your way."

"No, I'll help you," Shelby said.

"I'll show you what to look for, and you can keep whatever that healer gives us for it. I reckon you could do with some money in your pocket."

"What you see right here is all I got in this world," Shelby said. He couldn't believe that in the throes of fever he threw his gun away. That had been a dumb thing to do. But Hermit Bob liked jabbering to Shelby too much to pose any threat.

"You're in the army, I see."

Shelby nodded. "I was scouting out with some others, and we got ambushed by Comanches a few days west from here. I was the only one that got away." Shelby figured he should keep things as close to the truth as possible. This old man was no threat, and if he went whole hog in on some whopper of a lie, in his state of mind he was like to forget what he said, and then he'd be caught out—and then, of course. he'd have to kill the old coot. Even though he liked to flap his gums, Shelby found that he liked the old man. It was nice to talk to someone you didn't think was going to slash your throat if you didn't do what they said. It had been a long time since Shelby had spent any time with people that weren't soldiers.

"You must have come from the southwest. Indians don't

cause much trouble in these parts, not anymore. We've done chased them all off. More likely to see buffalo hunters or cattle rustlers or bandits up from old Mexico. These parts is getting more civilized, sadly."

"Sadly? Why do you say that?" Shelby liked civilization. He craved it, in fact. He wanted nothing more than a bath, some new clothes, and a clean bed in a room by himself to sleep in. He'd spent too many nights sleeping in tents with other soldiers and was eager to do something fun like play cards for a change.

"Used to be I could find what I was looking for without leaving home. I could just walk a little ways from home and find fields of what I'm looking for. Then all these home-steaders showed up, with their goddamned goats, and them goats, well, they ate up damn near everything. Cows will eat grass, horses too, but not like goddamned goats. Plants don't grow anywhere goats have been. They turned grass to dust. And so, every year I have to go further and further from town."

"Dang," Shelby said.

"I don't mind being out here. It's quiet. I can hear myself think. But I've been out here long enough this time. See that rock yonder?"

Shelby could see a gray shale shelf of rock peeking up out of the yellow grass.

"I see it."

"That's the place. Home sweet home."

Shelby followed Bob as he skirted around the protruding shale outcropping for a ways, following a narrow trail, when, suddenly, there was a hitching post and a wooden trough full of water. Bob dismounted and hitched up his mule and unbuckled the saddle and pulled it off. Then he turned to Shelby and asked, "You think you can get off your horse?"

Shelby nodded, but he wasn't sure.

It turned out he couldn't, because his legs turned wobbly on him, and he fell to the ground into the dust.

"No," he said.

Bob put his saddle down and came over and hitched up Shelby's horse and helped him up.

"Take my shoulder. Let's get you inside. I'll take care of your horse." Shelby leaned into Bob and followed him as he led him right up to a bush growing out of the rock.

"Hold on," Bob said, and he moved the bush, revealing an entrance to a cave.

"Welcome home!" Bob said, leading Shelby inside.

3

SHELBY

There was a cot and a kettle and not much else. Bob lived light, that was for sure.

"Not much to it," Bob said, holding up his arms. "Truth to tell, I spend most of the day out hunting up herbs and plant buds. I only eat, smoke on my pipe, drink coffee or my moonshine—and sleep. Over on that wall yonder is the lion I was talking about."

Shelby looked over and, sure enough, there was a lion skin on the wall, with a hole right in the back of the head.

"Bigger than I would have thought." Shelby said, walking up and poking a finger in the hole.

"Even bigger when it was still alive," Bob said. "You want to sleep?"

"That's all I want to do," Shelby said. He was now eating from a can of peaches Bob had given him, and the sweet nectar revived him. He now was feeling good enough to realize how incredibly tired he was. It had, to say the least, been a long week.

"I won't keep you up. I can even lend you a blanket. But I'd take it wrong if you didn't share in a little of my moonshine. I make it myself. It's made with peaches. I've been drinking it for many a year and haven't poisoned myself yet. But it ain't for the faint of heart."

"You bet," Shelby said.

Bob walked off into the shadows and came back with a mason jar of clear liquid with a couple of peach slices floating in it.

"If you want to sweeten it, you can always add some peaches from that tin." Bob poured some of the clear liquid into a coffee mug, and Shelby took it with a grateful nod.

"You should probably just—"

But it was too late. Shelby took a big slug of the stuff, and his face turned red, his eyes bulged—and, after he swallowed it, and had a coughing fit.

"—sip it," Bob finished. Then, noticing Shelby's distress, he couldn't help but laugh, so much so that tears rolled down his cheeks and he had to sit down and catch his breath.

"Jesus!" Shelby finally squeaked.

"Told you it was strong. You ought not take such mighty swigs of stuff you ain't never had before," Bob said. "Your face is as red as a ripe tomato."

Knowing what to expect now, Shelby set to slowly and cautiously sipping. It felt good and warmed him up as it went down.

"I'm not trying to make you do anything you don't want to do," Bob said, lighting up a small cigar and taking a grateful puff. "If you want one of these, you have to ask for it."

"I do want," Shelby said. "Very much so. I lost my pipe somewhere and haven't had any tobacco since." Shelby didn't elaborate and Bob didn't pry.

"Now that we've got our moonshine and cigars going, fetch up your blanket yonder and I'll show you my favorite thing to do."

Bob stood up with a groan and fetched the blanket from his cot and walked out the front of the cave. It was almost dark, but compared to the cave, it seemed almost bright. He found Bob placing firewood inside a charred circle of rocks, which had obviously seen many previous fires over the years.

He took an apple crate, turned it upside down, and offered it to Shelby to sit on. Then he went to work on the fire, using his cigar to light some dried grass, which soon sparked. Then Bob found a pickle barrel and sat on it.

"Now, you just wait until it gets full on dark."

"Won't someone smell the smoke?" Shelby asked, thinking about the Comanches, or Wild Bill Hickok, and whoever the hell else might be looking for him.

Bob seemed to give that some thought. "Ain't no Indians in these parts anymore, as I mentioned earlier, so you can let that worry go. And, in all this thick grass, and in the pitch dark, even if you *could* smell the smoke, you wouldn't be able to figure out where it was coming from. I think we're safe, sure enough. When I first found this cave, I was worried, and I'll show you why later. In short, I ain't the only person to ever call this cave home. But I haven't felt in the slightest danger in years."

Shelby couldn't believe how lucky it was the old man had found him, in all those many miles of flat empty desert, even if he had found him with his pants down. He wondered what it was like to spend weeks living in a cave alone. He didn't know if he could do it. Unlike Bob, Shelby didn't really care to hear himself think.

"Just look at all them stars," Bob said. "Must be a million of them."

The stars didn't impress Shelby. They looked the same to him as they did every night. The two men puffed on their cigars and sipped on their moonshine—and Shelby listened as Bob talked. And talked. And kept right on talking. And then, at some point, Bob's soothing voice—which was now singing—

receded into the background, and Shelby's head nodded forward, and his empty mug of moonshine fell into the dirt.

4

SHELBY

The next morning, Bob shared some biscuits and coffee, and then the two men set off so that Bob could show him the ropes.

Shelby was much stronger now—the peaceful night of sleep had done wonders—and proved a good student. He was soon foraging far and wide, his trained soldier eyes acute at finding the plants he was looking for. That first night, Bob had been impressed with Shelby's first haul. If Shelby was going to get to keep half the haul, he figured he wanted as big a haul as possible. The Indian could wait. He was enjoying Bob's companionship, and liked how he didn't ask questions, and how he told stories and set to singing once he was drunk enough.

Besides, Amarillo wasn't going anywhere.

So, they stayed two weeks more, at which point Shelby was the better of the two men, probably because Bob's eyes weren't what they used to be. The only reason they left was Bob hadn't counted on having to feed two people, and the both of them were sick of rabbit and out of moonshine.

———

That last day, Shelby took in the cave for what he figured would be the last time. He would miss the place. It was safe and quiet, and Shelby could sleep without worry. Not for one second did he worry that Bob was a threat to him. The old man just liked to jabber and smoke his pipe and sip moonshine, sing and snore, just as he'd said.

"Before we go, there's something I want to show you. Bob lighted up a cigar and used it to light a paraffin lamp and he led Shelby into the dark recesses of the cave.

"Watch your step," Bob cautioned. Not knowing where he was going, Shelby was extra cautious. It got cooler the further in they went, as they walked ever further down. "I don't never come down here except to make sure there's no bear or lion or rattlesnakes when I get here first thing in the spring." Soon, Bob stopped walking and Shelby walked into his back.

"Sorry," Shelby said.

"Look at that," Bob said.

Shelby looked at the wall and there were all sorts of figures painted on the wall. Indians with bow and arrows and crude animals that Bob said were buffalo. "I don't know what that there is, but I reckon I don't want to know. It looks to be bigger than any elephant." Bob squatted down, making his knees pop, and said, "This here is some sort of lion. But just look at the size of those teeth. I've seen a skull back in Amarillo, so this here cat sure enough lived in these parts at some point."

All Shelby could think about when he looked at the crude drawings was the look on that taunting Indian's face. The one that kilt Horvath while looking right at Shelby...

It was time to go. He had unfinished business. His time with Bob had been nice, but he had an Indian to kill.

———

Taking advantage of the cool morning air, Shelby helped Bob hitch his mule to a small wagon, which was now stuffed with several burlap sacks full of aloe and ocotillo and agave and yucca and hemp and prickly pear. Bob put the bush in front of the mouth of the cave, and said, "See you next year," as if the cave was a person that could understand such things. Then he clambered up onto the small wooden wagon seat, and Shelby mounted his horse, which he now considered his—and the two men made their way to Amarillo.

5

Silver Vein was a mess. Maybe it was just my opinion, being that I was the sheriff and supposed to keep things more or less humming along and keep ruffians in their place. Or maybe it was because everything really did fall apart whenever I was gone. The first thing that happened when we got back to town was, I learned the Butler gang had escaped.

Well, that might not be exactly the right term for what happened.

Before I'd even stopped to say hello to Sally and Bart, I stopped by the jail to let Deedee know we were back. And when I got in there, I found all the cells empty.

"Deedee!" I said, waking her from what I could only assume was a daily nap.

"Why Curly! You're back! Did you save Scout and Rattles?"

"Yes," I said. "We got Scout and Rattles and Yellow Hair and Little Yellow Hair safely out of the clutches of the soldiers."

"I hope you smote them to smithereens and their ashes are feeding the fires of hell!"

"I reckon they might have suffered a worse fate than that.

Where is the Butler gang? Did the prisoner transport pick them up and take them to Amarillo already?"

"Oh sheriff, you ain't gonna want to hear this. Maybe you ought to sit down," Deedee said, standing up and offering me my chair.

Thinking she might be right, more or less knowing she would be right, I sat down.

"Tell me," I said.

"It was Tiny," she said. "It was what you could call a miscommunication."

Tiny, I knew, was frequently confused. But he was enormous and scary looking, and when you added a scattergun to the mix, well, the worst of men would loose their bowels if he was to come at them.

"What happened?"

"Well, that Jacob Butler, he's a wily one. I reckon he took Tiny in and determined that he was a simpleton. And, well, one morning before I came in, Jacob told Tiny they were supposed to be let out that day. Well, Tiny, he doesn't consider such things the way you and me might, and he looks at Jacob Butler and can't understand why he would say something if it wasn't true. And so, he just unlocks the cell, opens it, and lets the entire gang just walk on out the door."

"I see," I said, glad I was sitting down. How embarrassing. Here we had gone to all this trouble to save the last sheriff Gantry from being held hostage in his own jail, and foiled a bank robbery while we were at it, and the perpetrators hadn't broken out of jail, but had the door opened for them so they could just walk out!

"Frank Kilhoe must never know about this," I said. "I'd never hear the end of it."

"It gets worse," Deedee said. The way she said it sounded like she might have been enjoying herself.

"I can't wait," I said. If there was such a thing as sitting down while already sitting down, I would have done it.

"That Jacob Butler, he might be long in the tooth, but he ain't dumb. I'll give him that. Him and his gang walked right down the boardwalk to the livery and let Flody know that they needed their horses. Well, Flody, he should have known they should be locked up. But, seeing them simply walk in and ask for their horses in such a calm manner, he up and believes them when they tell him they were let out of jail. Flody doesn't know whose horse is what, of course. Montana Dan and that Henry fella were the ones that brought the horses to Flody. So, he tells them to get their horses themselves. Well, old Jacob must have a keen eye for horseflesh, because he picks the best horses in the livery. So, they saddle up, Jacob gives Flody a big tip, and then they just up and ride on out of Silver Vein."

"They took someone else's horses?"

"Indeed! Sherwood Floop had a black stallion he said cost him more than three thousand dollars—Wyatt Gilmore and Jimsom Pip also had their horses swiped."

"So, not only did we *let* them out of jail, they then walked down Main Street and committed *another* crime almost immediately."

"That's all true," Deedee said. "I yelled at Tiny and twisted his ear and threatened to take out one of his eyeballs, but he doesn't even know what he did wrong. I made him cry like a little boy, Sheriff. When I saw those tears in his innocent lazy eyes, I didn't have the heart to stay mad at him."

I nodded. "Aw, it ain't your fault Deedee. I suppose the price on their heads will go up now." I looked at the REWARD poster on the wall. Jacob Butler's capture was currently worth a hundred dollars. After this, it would probably be three hundred. More if the horses could be reclaimed.

"Anything else?" I asked.

"I got good news! You will be happy to know the saloon is doing big business. The miners have sucked up so much money from that Floop fella—he gives them all more cash money than they know what to do with—and it's all going straight from his fat wallet into your saloon. The miners are all giddy as can be, and they're all drinking themselves silly."

"I sort of feel bad for Sherwood, buying up nothing but dirt."

"Don't feel bad for him. He's an ass! All he does is insult people and look down his nose at us and brag about how smart he is."

I knew Deedee was right. He was full of wind, old Sherwood, and proud of it. The smartest person in any room. Still. There would come a day when he realized what a great idiot he was, and I didn't want to be there when he learned he was bankrupt.

I stood up and put my hat on.

"Well, Deedee, I reckon that's all the news?"

"Oh! The news!" Deedee walked over.

"You best get up. I don't want to reach into that drawer with your nether parts so close." I jumped out of my chair and gave her a wide berth. She reached into the drawer and came out with a copy of *The Daily Silver Vein*.

"You might not want to read this until you have some whisky in your belly."

It was too late. The headline was enormous:

**Sheriff Curly Barnes
Helps Butler Gang
Escape Justice.**

"I think I get the meaning," I said, folding the paper and putting it under my arm. "I'm going to head home and say hello to Sally, feed my horse, get this stink off me, and play with my dog."

"Sure thing, Sheriff. I'm sure you're gonna want Sally to tell you her news. And don't you pay no attention to that Pap Kickins. He's just a sad old man that likes to stir things up!"

"I know it." I walked out of the jail and took Horse by the reins and the two of us walked down Main Street and home. I was passing Doc Watson's office and saw the member of the Butler gang who'd had his elbow shot off sitting in a chair. I walked over and noticed his arm was gone.

"He took my arm!" the man said. He had a big happy grin on his face when he said it.

"I can see that. Sorry you ain't got an arm no more, but you were actually lucky. If Wild Bill hadn't been using Mort's gun, you might have been shot stone dead."

"You won't hear me complaining. I haven't been this happy in a long time."

"He's got you on drugs," I said.

"That ain't it. I'm finally out of the gang! As soon as Jacob saw me with this here missing arm, he up and kicked me out of the gang on the spot. Said I'd be no good to him since I couldn't shoot a gun no more."

"Dang," I said. "You shouldn't have to lose an arm to quit a gang."

"I'm okay with it. Never did care for Jacob Butler in the first place. Moe is the smart one, but his brother won't admit it. You be sure and give my best to Wild Bill if you see him. I reckon him shooting my arm off is just about the best thing that ever happened to me!"

"Okay," I said, shaking my head. "What's your name anyway?"

"Clete Evans. From Georgia originally."

"Okay Clete. Once you heal up, considering you can't shoot

a gun no more, I'll stand you to a toot of bourbon at my saloon."

"I'm okay with whatever that crazy doctor is giving me. But I'll take you up on it one of these days!"

I left Clete to his drugged-up reverie and set off for home. It felt like I'd been gone forever. I was looking forward to taking a hot bath and cleaning the trail off of me. Sally would be happy when she saw that I didn't gain any weight on this adventure. And that I was alive, of course. But once she got through with her relief, she would probably have a go at me for making her worry. Deedee had said a weird thing. She'd said Sally "had news." I was thinking about what that could mean and walking past the Mercantile when Ely Turner walked out, leaned against the door-frame, and actually smiled and waved at me—which was most unusual. What the hell? I thought. We both hated one another.

"Afternoon, Sheriff!" Ely said.

"Yes," I said. It was the hottest part of the day. And dusty. Something was wrong. Maybe old Ely had finally lost it. I would be happy to see him lose it, even though he did wave at me.

I made my way past the falling-to-pieces courthouse and took the alley to the back of the saloon where the corral was.

"Well, Horse," I said. "We made it home in one piece." I took off his saddle, and placed it on the top rail, then I took off the blanket underneath, which was drenched with Horse sweat, and I brushed him down, all the while keeping a sharp eye on Molly, who, even though she had a charmed life of doing nothing but eat all day, and had gained dozens of pounds due to her relentless sloth, nevertheless had a terrible and vengeful personality. She would have liked nothing more than to take a bite out of either me or Horse, for doing nothing more than being alive.

"Don't you pay attention to Molly," I said. "She's just an

asshole." Horse nodded his head up and down as if he agreed with me. And he probably did. He was smarter than most people.

"Well, there you are, at long last."

I turned around and saw Sally standing at the top of the steps with a huge smile on her face, her blue eyes bright and merry, her long hair waving in the wind—and wearing nothing more than a frilly undergarment. I looked around. If someone were to see her, they'd never forget the sight as long as they lived.

She must have been able to read my thoughts because she held her hand up in warning and said, "Nuh uh! You can't even think about having such naughty thoughts until you've cleaned the trail off of you. I can smell you from up here."

This was no doubt true. I smelled one of my armpits and had to hold on to the top rail to keep from fainting.

"Okay Horse, I'll be back with an apple later." I put the brush down and took the stairs two at a time and, knowing the rules, and what would happen if I broke them, gingerly leaned in so Sally could give me a welcome home kiss.

———

It felt good to be clean. Sally had been very thorough, so much so that she had no choice but to get in the water with me. We reunited, if you get my meaning, and I recounted to her all that had transpired since we'd parted. About Hendrix and the buffalo and the sandstorm and the dramatic and bizarre rescue. I left out the worst parts, of course. She told me about Two Yellow Hairs walking through town like he was simply out for a stroll—and how the whole town seemingly held its breath all at once. She told me about Bart coughing up a mouse on the floor. He'd apparently gone and grabbed up a mouse outside, but I guess its little feet and thrashing tail made him regret the whole affair, and so he coughed the mouse up on the kitchen floor. The mouse seemed dead at first, but then it stood up and shook itself off and ran behind the wardrobe. She'd had to recruit Jeffers to help wrangle the mouse up.

"But Curly," she said, nuzzling into my neck—letting me know she was about to tell me something I didn't want to hear —"the mouse escaped."

I sat up in the tub and looked around.

"It's in the house?" Here I'd just spend a week sleeping in the dirt surrounded by every sort of deadly critter one could imagine, yet the idea of one little mouse in the house made my skin crawl.

"No," Sally said. "Not in the house."

I turned and looked at her. And then I knew.

"The saloon."

"He ran out through the open door and took off down the stairs at a speed you could hardly believe."

"There's already one mouse down there."

"Jeffers said the new mouse has joined the old mouse."

"Inside the billiard table?"

Sally nodded meekly.

As if knowing he was the topic of discussion, Bart scampered over and sat down and looked at us. He looked like the most innocent dog that ever lived. It was impossible to be mad at him.

"Not your fault, buddy," I said. He had no idea what I was talking about.

"Deedee said you had some news. I'm guessing there's something else. Are you—"

"There *is* something else. But it's the kind of thing I have to show you. But we can do that tomorrow. I'm not pregnant—if that's what you're thinking." She grew quiet. I'd given her countless opportunities to get pregnant, but it didn't, and never would, take. I could tell I was going to get no more information from her.

"Tomorrow, then," I said.

"Yes, tomorrow."

———

After I'd cleaned myself up, I got dressed in dust-free clothes, and told Sally she needed to wear something more than some frilly thing, because Wild Bill was desperate for a bath, and as soon as I got into the saloon, he would want his turn in the basin. He'd talked my ear off about taking a bath and getting his hair clean for the last two hours on the ride back to town. So much so that Frank and Hap couldn't take it and decided to veer off and make their way straight to Amarillo. Frank had specifically given "Wild Bill's bath obsession" as the reason they were splitting off. Silver Vein was on the way to Amarillo. Most everybody went through Silver Vein to get there. So basically, they were going to sleep in the dirt and take the long way home —all because of Wild Bill's incessant jabbering about his hair and the importance of smelling good and being clean.

When I told Sally this, she started laughing. Sally has a great laugh. "Frank is such a grump!"

"Wild Bill did go on a bit," I said. "I expect he'll be up here quicker than a lightning strike."

I opened the door and made my way downstairs into the saloon.

"Curly," Jeffers yelled. "You're back!"

"Indeed," I said.

The saloon was packed and loud. I looked at the crowd— and I couldn't believe what I saw. All of the dirty and scruffy and broke miners were now finely dressed and all cleaned up. And I couldn't help but notice that they were drinking the good bourbon. Deedee hadn't been exaggerating. I made my way down the rest of the stairs. I could see that Wild Bill was singularly grimy. Well, he and Tad Bowltree. And I could see by the look on his face he wasn't happy about it. He was used to being the best dressed in any room.

"Curly, did you square it with Sally?"

I nodded. "She's—"

But Wild Bill wasn't waiting around. He threw back his chair and took the steps three at a time, opened the door to my house, and disappeared.

"Dang," Tad Bowltree said. "He's the only person I can beat at cards." He threw his cards down in disgust. I walked behind the bar and put a bar rag in my back pocket, transforming myself into a saloonkeeper.

"Thank God," Micah said. He looked thoroughly overwhelmed and all too sober. As busy as it was, he probably hadn't had time to sneak any bourbon into himself. He walked from behind the bar to the piano and laid his head down.

"Curly, my good man. It's been *days* since we last had a chat," Sherwood Floop said. In a room full of well dressed—and flush, thanks to Sherwood—miners, they were but nothing compared to the costume Sherwood wore. He was the very look of a London dandy. His black waxed mustache seemed to shoot off from his mouth further than ever. Which might have looked good in some city in Europe, or in New York City, but in the frontier town of Silver Vein it looked ridiculous.

"Sherwood, I see you've made the entire town rich." No wonder Ely Turner had been so happy!

"How they spend their money is their affair. But, yes, I have been very successful at investing in and preparing for the upcoming silver rush. I do say, I feel quite smart at the moment. You see, my fellow investors back in New York City are seeing their money dwindle away to nothing! What nabobs! What jobbernowls! What clodpates! What saucy coxcombs!" Then he let loose with his barking laugh that sounded almost exactly like a mule with something stuck in its throat. I had the sudden urge to grab his mustache and yank his head onto the bar. But I didn't. Because his belly would have softened the blow. Even if he was right about an upcoming silver rush, he was doomed to enjoy none of it, because there was simply no silver to be had in Silver Vein.

"How about a toot of the good stuff to celebrate?" I asked.

"Curly, my thinking exactly! I'll have a blue dynamo!"

"There's no such thing," I said.

"A lusty dragoon?"

I shook my head.

"Laos Gimlet?"

"No."

"Gin Binny?"

"Are these even real drinks?"

"Hornbill Betty?"

I turned around and walked to the other end of the bar.

"Fine! An American frontier bourbon! Curly, just you wait! When silver claims its throne as the new standard for currency, I am going to go back to New York City, that foul city of mutton heads, and buy the whole thing! I'll be the first king of New York!"

"Curly," Jeffers said, leaning over the bar. "Business has never been better. I'm already out of stew! Third night in a row!"

"That's great," I said. "How was Micah?"

"I got him a good one," Jeffers said, cackling and slapping his hand on the bar.

"Uh oh," I said.

"No, I didn't stab him or nothing. What I did was, I took some of the rotgut and dumped a little coffee in it for color, and switched out the good bourbon with it."

I looked over at Micah, and he smiled at me the way he did when he thought he'd gotten away with something.

"He drank the rotgut and thought it was the good stuff? He couldn't tell the difference?"

"He has no idea!"

"Jeffers! You're a genius!"

"I know!" Jeffers said, giving me a gap-toothed grin. Then his smile disappeared, and he said, "Curly, you should know that if things continue like this, we're gonna run out of just about everything."

I walked over and looked under the bar and, sure enough, there were only a few bottles left. I took one of them for myself and saved one for Wild Bill.

"Okay Jeffers, you're going to need to make a run to Amarillo tomorrow. I'll send Baxter with you."

Jeffers shook his head.

"I don't need to listen to his jabber. I'll take China Jack. At least he makes sense when he talks."

"Suit yourself," I said. I didn't know how long the bourbon rush would last, but it looked like I would need to double, or even triple, my normal order.

Jeffers was looking at me like there was something else he wanted to say.

"Anything else?"

"No!" Jeffers said, clearly lying, and then he turned around and walked off before I could extract whatever secret he was holding onto.

I looked to my right, and right there, at the poker table with Tad Bowltree, sipping on a mug of beer, was none other than Kid Barlow the attempted bank robber. Not only had he been allowed to escape from jail, he'd never even bothered to leave town! What a dumb criminal!

I walked over to him. He looked up and his eyes went wide.

"Sheriff!" Kid Barlow said. "I'll take two," he said to Tad, who dealt him two cards. Tad's clothing, I couldn't help but notice, had gotten ratty all over again. In less than a week he'd somehow managed to trash them.

"Barlow, why aren't you in jail?" I asked.

Kid Barlow shrugged. "That big guy said I was free to leave, so I left."

"And you thought that was okay? After robbing a bank?"

"He opened the door, Sheriff. What would you have done?"

That one stumped me. If I was in his place, and someone came along and opened the cell door, and told me I was free to go...

"Okay," I said. "Good point. Here's the deal. You're welcome to stay here if you keep on buying beer, and you can even upgrade to whisky. I don't have any particular reason to hold you, to be honest. You didn't technically steal any serious money. And your crime, such as it was, was in Hendrix. So, no real harm done. But I will tell you this. If you try anything in this town, that will be it for you. I'll put you back in jail, and nobody will let you out this time."

"Aw sheriff, I only joined them fellas to rob the bank because I needed money. And now I've got a good amount of it and I'm getting more."

I looked at Tad and could clearly see he was having a bad run.

I shook my head in wonder. Wild Bill really was the only person Tad could beat at poker.

"What?"

"Nothing," I said. "Barlow, I'll stand you to your first toot of Bourbon when you're ready, to seal our agreement," and I made my way back to the bar.

"Oh Curly," a voice I never liked to hear, called out. I looked over and—sure enough—there was Ely Turner, standing there looking like the happiest most satisfied man in the world. It was a horrible sight.

"You want your usual?" I asked. His usual was the cheapest

stuff I had, because he was the cheapest man west of the Atlantic Ocean.

"Not this time, Curly. I believe I'll have the good stuff!"

So, what did I do? I went and got one of the bottles Jeffers had doctored up, and poured Ely a toot of rotgut and charged him six bits.

I looked over and saw that Baxter and Merle were now playing cards with Tad Bowltree and Kid Barlow. I would have to keep an eye out. Baxter and Merle seemed friendly enough, but Kid Barlow had run out of the bank shooting at them. If they decided to take it personally, I would have a problem.

"All right, Ely. Let's go buy me some more expensive duds. This get-up got ruined in a sandstorm. I thought I was clever, and put my duds in my saddlebag, but that dust went right on in there and ruined everything."

Wild Bill, I learned, while I was up taking my bath and reuniting with Sally, had won a silver claim from Stooge McCaskill in a card game. Stooge wasn't much of a drinker, and was a hard worker, and so he rarely came to town and therefore knew nothing of Sherwood Floop and his buying up of silver claims. All he knew was that his silver claim was next to worthless. So, when he threw the silver claim into the poker pot, he told Wild Bill it was worth two hundred dollars, thinking he was putting one over on him. But Wild Bill, knowing all about Sherwood Floop, won the hand, and the silver claim—which he got up and immediately walked over to Sherwood and sold for six hundred dollars. Before Stooge could figure out what had happened, Wild Bill did the right thing and gave Stooge a hundred bucks out of pity. All of which is a long way to say that despite his flailing incompetence playing Tad Bowltree at cards, Wild Bill was flush.

"You sure you want to do that?" I asked. "You know he's going to rob you blind."

"Look at me, Curly. My hair and body might be clean, but

my clothes look like my saddlebag. I look like some sort of road tramp! Worse than I looked with that bloody old buffalo skinner coat. And look around you, at all these dooded-up miners. I can't be the drabbiest gentleman in the room! It simply will not do!"

I could see his point. Orange dust was plastered into his clothes, despite the time he spent trying to beat them clean. "I concede your point," I said. Though I hated any money—ever, at all—going into Ely Turner's greasy hands. And old Ely was in such good spirits that he didn't even notice I'd given him rotgut. He was sipping it and savoring it like the fool he was.

I could see it was going to be a good night. Maybe too good a night. The cigar smoke was thick, and the miners carried on, laughing and bragging about themselves to each other. All of their miseries were forgotten. Each and every one of them now saw themselves as geniuses. Baxter and Merle took advantage of their misplaced confidence to fleece anyone who sat down to play cards with them.

And Wild Bill, resplendent now in new duds, and sporting a startling yellow sash, held court at his own table, consistently winning against everyone but Tad. On one hand, Tad folded with four Queens and a ten. The next hand he won with a handful of nothing. Wild Bill was helpless in the face of such incompetence.

By the end of the night, the saloon was flush with coin, and I had made up for my week away from being behind the bar, making up for lost time by taking little toots of bourbon the whole night long. The only bad thing that happened was when I heard a high-pitched scream from the billiard table and looked over to see two white mice chasing each other across the felt, off the table, and into a small hole in the wall. A hole I promised myself I would plug up the next morning. Hopefully those two mice would grow to hate each other and do each other in.

At the end of the night, not too far away from dawn, Wild Bill and I drunkenly clomped up the stairs, and I passed out dead away in the comfort of my straw bed, the nuzzlings of my sleeping wife—who cared none at all for the way I smelled, but not enough to have a go at me—and my buffalo robe. The last thing I remember was Bart licking my forehead clean.

6

SHELBY

Shelby and Bob made their way into Amarillo, which was noisy with hubbub. Horses and carts and pedestrians walking this way and that. No soldiers. That was a relief. Nobody to notice a bearded guy in rags—Bob had loaned him some clothes—riding a horse with an army-supplied saddle. Three weeks ago, when he was still in the Army, if he'd seen someone looking like he did under such circumstances, he would have been most interested in learning the man's story.

"Loud," Shelby said.

"And busy," Bob said. He slapped his mule with the reins, and they made their way through the middle of town and then turned left onto a side street and pulled up in front of a wooden building with a sign that read: Doc Henry, Healer.

"This is the place," Bob said.

"I'll just wait out here," Shelby said. The fewer people he met, the better. Bob looked at Shelby, saw the determination there, and nodded.

"If you can help unload the wagon, I'll take it from there. I may look old, but these arms are as strong as ever."

The two men unloaded the back of the wagon—a dozen sacks in all—and Shelby waited while Bob went inside.

Twenty minutes later, he was back outside.

"We're in luck. The doctor was desperate for the stuff!"

"Why?" Shelby asked. "Who else would want it? Who else in this town would buy herbs and plants?"

Bob thought about that and narrowed his eyes. "He don't see it that way, and I ain't about to let him."

He tossed Shelby a small bag that clinked with the sound of coin.

"That'n is yours."

Shelby took a look inside and then poured seven dollars into his hand. "More than I thought," Shelby said.

"I gave you a little more. I would have only gathered up half as much if it weren't for you. Even throwing a couple of dollars your way, I still got more than I normally would. Besides, I enjoyed your company."

"I appreciate it," Shelby said. He enjoyed Bob too. But more than that, he enjoyed being someone he wasn't. Bob knew nothing of his past and didn't seem to care. While he was clearly curious about how he'd come to find Shelby shitting out his insides in the middle of the desert, he'd let Shelby tell him in his own time. After that, he'd never asked any other questions. Shelby liked being a regular normal person, even if he had to live in a cave with a hermit to do it. Sometimes he thought about how easy it would be to just let the Indian go and start a new life as the person Bob was willing to let him be. Maybe him and Bob could even go into business together.

But then inevitably his thoughts would turn to his old friend Horvath—and he knew there was nothing for it but to go and kill that Indian. It simply wasn't in him to do the reasonable thing. He was a killer in his heart, no matter how Bob treated him.

"I reckon I need to get some new duds," Shelby said.

"I reckon I do too. Then we'll hit the Oriental Saloon. I could use a quality cigar and some good whisky that wasn't made in a cave."

Shelby was also eager to play cards, and sip on some whisky that didn't taste like poison.

Bob cracked the reins, and the two men made their way back through town.

———

Shelby couldn't remember the last time he'd bought his own clothes. The army didn't give a fella much choice. Shelby was a Captain, and so he dressed like one every day. He bought a pair of used trousers and a rough cotton shirt and jacket, and a wide-brimmed straw hat—not much different from Bob's. He looked like a cow-boy, he thought, like someone who punched cattle all day.

Bob had been wearing the same thing every day since Shelby first met him, and so it was a shock to see him in a clean white shirt, and a jacket that didn't have a bunch of holes in it.

"I got one more thing to do," Bob said. "The Oriental is across the street yonder. Grab a spot at the bar for me if you can." Bob walked down Main Street and into the barber shop.

Shelby jumped off the wooden boardwalk and dodged and weaved his way across Main Street to the other side.

"Move it!" someone shouted, and it was all Shelby could do not to yank the man off his horse and poke a hole in his belly.

"My condolences," Shelby muttered, tipping his hat.

"My what?" the man shouted, but Shelby ignored him and pushed through the flappy doors into the Oriental Saloon.

Shelby was happy to see that he fit right in. The place was half-full. There were about ten or so people leaning up against the bar. There was a long mirror behind the bar and Shelby looked in it and didn't recognize himself. Like Bob, he was desperate for a haircut and a shave, but he figured the beard and shaggy hair was a good disguise. Nobody who knew the old Captain Shelby would look twice at the grungy cow-boy Shelby saw looking back at him.

To the right of the bar was a big round table full of people playing poker. One of them had a big black beard and a black hat and a gun sitting next to his hand. He looked at Shelby, and saw nothing of note, because he went back to his card game.

There was a staircase leading to the second floor, where there were a number of doors. Shelby knew that if he wanted to, and if he could afford it, he could take one of the saloon girls up there for a quick romp. The last time—

Shelby didn't want to think about that now. Taking a woman wasn't the same thing as legitimately renting one. Maybe he could win enough money at cards to let some woman pretend to be sweet on him for an hour or two.

He would need to win a lot of money to do that. Because, before he could pay a whore, he needed to buy himself a new pistol. He felt weird to have no weapon at all, aside from the rusty dull knife Bob gave him to chop plants with. He felt naked without a gun.

Shelby turned back to the bar and gave a signal to the bartender.

"You got whisky?"

"Of course. You might not know it, but this is a saloon. Selling whisky is what we do." The saloonkeeper had a stringy brown mustache that he waxed. It wasn't very convincing. He was too young to have real whiskers. Shelby could see enough of the saloonkeeper's face to know that he was having a playful go at him. Shelby had the sudden urge to hop on his horse and go back to the cave, where he wouldn't have to deal with regular people. Nobody joked with the old Captain Shelby. But they did this new version of himself. He would need to get used to that.

"I mean what kind of whisky you got? It's been a while, you see," Shelby said, trying not to come across as angry.

Someone put a cigar on the bar in front of him. Shelby turned and almost cried out. Bob had gone and chopped his beard off, revealing a set of teeth that would embarrass a horse. Shelby had seen the occasional brown tooth peeking out of Bob's bushy beard. But seeing all the teeth at once was a lot to ask a fella to do. The beard, in Bob's case, even as ragged as it was, made sound tactical sense. The cigar sticking out of his naked face was the same color as his teeth. His face, Shelby now noticed, was two different colors. Everything above the nose was brown; everything below was a pale and unsettling white.

Bob couldn't discern Shelby's thoughts, and turned to the mirror and said, "It's been a while since I've seen my own skin."

"Thanks for the cigar," Shelby said, changing the subject. "Can you tell this guy what kind of whisky I want?"

"Two top-shelf Irish," Bob said. "How's business Ned? Been a few weeks."

"Kind of slow this time of year," Ned said, shrugging. "No grass for the cow-boys to graze their herds."

"Fine with me," Bob said. Then he turned to Shelby and said, "Ned's father was old One Eye Ned. He started this place. Only had the one eye, you see."

Shelby didn't care.

Bob bit the end off his cigar and lighted up. Then the two men clinked glasses and took a swallow of silky Irish heaven.

"I'll say this," Bob said. "The Irish know their way when it comes to whisky."

The whisky did its job, and Shelby felt his nerves start to relax, and a contentment go through him. A month ago, he'd been on the run from vengeful Comanches, and maybe his own Army, and maybe even Wild Bill Hickok—on the run and sleeping in the dirt like an animal. And now he was puffing on an expensive cigar, sipping top-shelf Irish whisky, alive and well and not tortured and kilt. He could afford to be a little satisfied with his survival skills. He owed it all to Plowright, of course. If he hadn't run into him like he did, he would have suffered whatever fate Major Hastings had.

It was almost time to go and do for that Indian. And he had a clue where to start looking. Curly Barnes. It had been Curly Barnes that had helped the Indians and the white woman and her daughter escape, and he was convinced it had been Curly Barnes that came up with the plan that drove Major Hastings to drag them all far into Comanche territory in pursuit of some ruined white woman that hated him. He would find Curly Barnes, and he would make Curly Barnes lead him to the Indian—and then he would do for them both.

But now he would relax.

"I might go over there and try my hand at some cards," Shelby said.

Bob looked over at the poker table.

"The man with the beard, that's Abe Kilhoe. You watch out for him."

"He a good player?"

"Fair. But he was shot playing cards at that very same table not long back, and so he's quite jumpy. He's apt to shoot you if you try anything. The man next to him is Clem. He's an easy mark. On the other side of Clem is Sy Belmont. If you're going to take anyone for a lot of money it will be him. Abe is cautious. Clem is reckless but cheap."

"You sure know a lot about this place," Shelby said.

"When I'm not out on the prairie hunting up herbs, I'm in here drinking. Not much else to do in this town. You go play cards, and if you see me going up the stairs with some whore, don't judge me too harshly," Bob said, giving Shelby a wink. "Lorena is the only whore I spend time with. I reckon she's as close as I'll ever come to having a wife."

"I would never judge a fella for something like that," Shelby said. "Is Lorena pretty?"

"It's her personality I cotton to. She likes to dote on me. At my age I can't be too picky."

No, Shelby thought, not with those teeth. He could now understand why Bob had two nicknames. He'd just witnessed his transformation from Hermit Bob to Nebraska Bob. It could just as easily be Bearded Bob and Clean Face Bob.

Shelby walked over to the poker table, trying not to be intrusive in case it was a closed game. Abe looked up from his hand and Shelby caught his eye. Abe's eyes narrowed, probably trying to figure out if Shelby had any money.

"Pull up a chair," Abe said.

"Only if you let me win the first hand," Shelby said.

"That is one promise I can promise not to make," Abe said, laughing. "But this is a fair table. If you're up to it, you can win same as any of the rest of us."

Shelby sat down.

"What are the stakes?"

"We mostly pay for whisky money. Two bits to buy in, and we take it from there."

Shelby threw two bits onto the table, and the one called Clem doled out the cards. He won his first three hands, and then it was a long afternoon of ups and downs. Abe bought Shelby three shots of bourbon, hoping it would go to Shelby's head and make him reckless. But Shelby could hold his liquor with the best of them.

"That Nebraska Bob you come in with?" Abe asked. Shelby turned around and looked back at the bar and saw Bob talking and laughing with some skinny guy, who kept patting Bob on the shoulder.

"Yes," Shelby said, nodding, offering nothing more.

"You best keep an eye on him. The skinny guy is Wisconsin Slim. He's a crafty one when it comes to picking pockets and lifting another fella's money. He's been chased out of one town after another."

"He don't look like much of a threat. And Bob is stronger than he looks."

"Looking weak *is* his strength," Abe said.

"Are we playing cards?" Clem asked.

"I think we know who has the best hand," Abe said.

Clem tossed his cards onto the table in disgust. "Fold. Damn you, Abe!"

Abe let out a big laugh. "Relax Clem. I was just having a go at you."

Shelby was enjoying the game, even if Abe talked too much and liked to show off. Abe sort of reminded him of Major Hastings—the old Hastings, before he'd gone mad—the way he seemed to know everything. Other than that, it was nice to just be a regular old nobody, able to turn his back to the bar without having to worry about someone looking to lift his hair. Even though his time in the army had come to an end, there was a part of him that still worried some staff sergeant would tap him on the shoulder and dock his wages for illicit behavior. Colonel MacKenzie had been quite hard on gambling and drinking, though he'd been known to tip one back when he was of a mind to. Like most officers in the army, the colonel was a hypocrite.

Shelby tossed his two bits in and the other guy, Sy, on Abe's other side, dealt the cards.

The game kept going. For all Shelby knew, the game would continue on until the saloon closed on them. Shelby had a promising hand, but then some instinct made him turn his head to the bar.

Bob and the skinny fella were gone.

7

SHELBY

"Hold my spot," Shelby said. He stood up and made his way over to the bar. He caught Ned's eye and asked, "Where's Bob?"

Ned looked around and shrugged. "He didn't go out the front, or I would have noticed. Her night be upstairs with Lorena."

Shelby would have noticed that.

"There a back door?"

Ned nodded, pointing. "There's a door yonder that leads to the privy."

Shelby followed Ned's directions and walked out the door into a dark alley. Shelby ducked away from the door and waited for his eyes to adjust. All he had was the old knife Bob gave him. But Shelby knew from plenty of experience that even a dull knife could poke a hole in some fella's kidney.

He walked further into the dark alley—and then he saw him. Bob was on the ground and the little guy, who looked to Shelby like some sort of scavenger, like a turkey buzzard, was leaning over Bob like he was a dead elk.

"That's for me, you see? All for me, don't you see? You was

just holding it for me? Tomorrow, you'll wake up and not remember any of this and we'll do it all over again. Don't you worry."

The guy was nuts, Shelby thought, talking to himself like that.

"I wouldn't do that," Shelby said. He was six feet behind the skinny fella. Quick as lightning, and faster than Shelby could follow, Wisconsin Slim let out a loud hissing noise and whirled and lunged. Too late, Shelby saw the knife. He had no time to think. He could only lift his arm up to protect his belly.

A shot rang out just as the knife entered Shelby's left forearm.

Wisconsin Slim screamed.

"I've been shot!"

"That's right."

Shelby looked behind him and there was Abe in the doorway, smoke coming out of the pistol in his hand, and Abe started walking over, never taking his eyes off Wisconsin Slim. He seemed dead to Shelby. Just lying in the dirt.

"You okay?" Abe asked.

"That bullet took the strength out of his thrust. I've suffered worse." Shelby walked over to Bob and saw that he was alive and snoring. He went back to Abe, who was now going through Wisconsin Slim's pockets.

"Is he dead?"

"Seems like it," Abe said. "I reckon all of this belongs to Bob." He handed a bunch of coins and dollars to Shelby. It was more money than Shelby was expecting.

Shelby leaned down and picked up the knife that, if not for Abe, would have taken Shelby's arm off, and tucked it into his belt.

"Can you help me get Bob inside?" Shelby asked.

"Happy to. Curly wired me about this guy some months ago. I knew the skinny lunatic was no good, but I could never catch him doing anything. I'll need to get the undertaker—old Seth don't like to be awakened this time of night—but there's nothing for it."

"Curly? Curly Barnes the sheriff?" Shelby asked, hoping he didn't betray his excitement at hearing the name.

"The very one. He's the sheriff of Silver Vein."

"I've been meaning to head that way. I'll look him up and tell him about this business here."

"It will make him very happy. He'll probably give you free drinks. Curly is a good man, which is something you can't say for too many people these days. Most people these days is just out for themselves, if you ask me. People ain't civil like they used to be. You ask me, the more civilized a place is, the worse the people are. Curly and my brother are good friends. You'll find him at his saloon."

Abe and Shelby had almost gotten to Bob's snoring body when they heard a scurrying noise behind them. When they looked back, Wisconsin Slim was gone.

"Guess he wasn't dead after all," Shelby said.

Abe grunted. "On second thought, you might not want to mention this to Curly after all."

8

SHELBY

I t took two days to arrange everything. Shelby'd lucked into a much better horse. An old man Shelby found himself in conversation with at the Oriental Saloon, who called himself Jakob, must have been desperate—because he agreed to a straight up trade. Plowright's horse had been basically for the most part abused—and looked it. He'd lost weight, and his coat wasn't as shiny as it had been when Shelby had swiped it. Jakob assured him the horse he was trading, a black stallion far superior in every way, hadn't been stolen. That was the only question Shelby asked. He knew Jakob was lying, but he desperately wanted the tall black stallion. It was a horse fit for a general. He looked fast, and Shelby, considering his plans, might have need for a fast horse.

He'd given Bob only some of his money back. Bob took the money without even looking, which told Shelby that he hadn't been holding out. Which meant Bob probably wasn't Wisconsin Slim's only victim that night. The money he now had was just enough to buy an old Navy Colt and a box of bullets. The gun had some rust on it, and a stained wooden handle, but it worked well enough. His forearm still ached from where the knife grazed him, but luckily it wasn't his shooting arm. It would heal up soon enough.

He was ready.

He said his goodbye to Bob, who had some headaches from his whomping, but was otherwise in good spirits. As he should be. He was being looked after by Lorena—who clearly held the old coot in great fondness. She smelled like too much perfume, and she painted her face almost as much as a Comanche about to go to war, but Bob was an old man. His beard hid a lot of wrinkles, and without it, it seemed to Shelby like he'd aged thirty years.

"Maybe I'll be back next spring," Shelby heard himself saying. "We could spend a whole season collecting plant buds and herbs."

"I'd like that," Bob said. "But I don't think I'll see you again."

"Why not?" Shelby asked.

"You might not know it, but there's an anger about you. I don't know why or where it comes from. I'd suggest you tamp that stuff down, but I know it would do no good. There will come a point when someone says the wrong thing to you, and that's when the trouble will start."

Shelby thought about this. The old man was right. Trouble had been following Shelby around almost from the minute he'd been born. Trouble ran in his family, all the way back to the bible times probably.

Shelby smiled. "You could be right, old man. But then again, I might just surprise you yet!"

He kicked his new horse in the belly and set off for Silver Vein.

9

Sally's news, I learned the next morning, while eating at Kate's restaurant, was apparently waiting for me at Kate's house. I still thought of Kate's house as being the old sheriff Jim Shepland's house, because he'd built it himself and lived in it. I hadn't been to the house since the sheriff died. It was located further down Main Street than I ever ventured, as it was outside of my daily habitat. It was up a hill at the end of town.

Whatever news awaited me at Kate's house, I could see it was vexing Sally, because she was twisting her napkin like she wanted to tear it to pieces.

"This might make you mad," Sally said. "But when you see them, hopefully you'll understand."

"When I see them?"

"You'll see." I could have used all of my charm all at once and I knew I wouldn't be getting anything more out of her. It was something I needed to see for myself.

After breakfast, Kate came out of the restaurant and gave Sally a hug.

"Go easy on her, Curly," Kate said.

Oh boy. Whatever it was, it was something that both women thought would upset me in some way.

I followed Sally to the sheriff's old house, and she knocked on the door. Which wouldn't make sense under normal circumstances since Kate and little Jimmy were back at the restaurant.

The door opened, and I found myself looking at none other than Taylor Stephens and Katie Milton.

"Oh boy," I said.

"They didn't have anywhere else to go," Sally said. "Kate and I talked it over, and decided they could stay with her and little Jimmy until you got to town."

"Mulvaney came here looking for you," I said. "I thought he was crazy, thinking you might be here, but I guess he was right after all."

"We're in love," Taylor said. "And you were nice to me and know the truth of our situation, and I couldn't think of anywhere else to go."

"You've gone and gotten yourself in a whole lot of trouble," I said.

"My daddy made me say those mean things about Taylor. Ain't none of it true," Katie Milton said.

"I know it," I said. "But it won't matter now. Because now Taylor has gone and escaped from jail and kidnapped a pregnant woman whose father has a lot of money and an army of hired killers."

Sally brought her hand to her mouth.

"They didn't tell you?" I asked.

Sally shook her head.

"I don't know what to tell you two. I can see that you're in love. And I also know that Sam Milton is one of the world's great assholes, so you can't stay here. Sooner or later word will get out—this is a town full up with gossips—and then Milton will come to town gunning for you."

"What should we do?" Katie Milton asked.

"Let me think about it," I said.

Sally and I left the two lovebirds in Kate's house and made our way home.

10

It had been three weeks since we'd come back from the desert. Long enough for me to gain back all the weight I'd lost and then some. Sally and I didn't argue over her decision to hide and give shelter to Taylor Stephens and Katie Milton. I thought it was a stupid thing to do—but I understood why she did it.

Sally'd had a rough life before we ever met. At one point she was given to a pimp in Amarillo after the man who she'd come west with offered her up during a game of cards. The man she'd come west with had started out charming, and Sally was at the time wanting to make her way to Denver. And he'd said he would take her. He bought her clothes and treated her nice—but the longer the trip got, the meaner he got, until he finally got to the point where he wanted nothing to do with her. He would lock her up in their hotel room and go off into town to get drunk. Then he would come back and beat on her. Just writing these words down hurts to think about even now. One day, when the pimp in Amarillo was going to make her see a cow-boy he'd offered her up to, she climbed out the window of the whorehouse he put her up in and made her way to Silver Vein.

Being locked up was something she could relate to. And knowing Katie Milton was pregnant with child, it would have been impossible for her to do anything other than what she did.

Didn't mean it wasn't a stupid thing to do. And it didn't mean Sam Milton, were he to find out, wouldn't pose a threat to them and to us and probably the whole town of Silver. I was the sheriff, and sometimes a Deputy U.S. Marshal, I couldn't be in the business of harboring fugitives.

But I didn't know what to do. And until I could figure it out, there was nothing to do but let them stay at Kate's house and hope they kept their heads low.

Wild Bill was still in the spare bedroom. Each time we pressed him about his plans, he would say he was leaving "in a day or so." But then he never did. He claimed to like being in town and playing cards and drinking—and taking frequent baths accompanied by a singing voice that could melt paint. But I could see that he wasn't really enjoying himself. He only did all that carrying on because he was bored. He was a restless one, was Wild Bill. Me, I was happy to go basically nowhere and spend all of my day between the saloon, the jail, Kate's restaurant, and my own home. On most days, my activities covered about less than a quarter of what was a fairly small town. Wild Bill was different. He craved the open trail. He liked danger. He even courted it if he'd been drinking long enough.

Sally and Bart had become great fans of Wild Bill. For Sally, he would tell long and boring stories about New York City, and all the smelly soaps you could buy there. And he'd taken to taking Bart on walks. It made me a little jealous, seeing the dogs' loyalty be so easily corrupted. He claimed walking the dog helped his headaches.

But eventually, possibly out of guilt at taking so much

advantage of our hospitality, he announced that it was his last day in town. He was really moving on.

"Where you going to go?" I asked.

Wild Bill sat down at the kitchen table, and dang if Bart didn't up and jump into his lap. For Bill's part, he acted as if this was a common occurrence, and he took to absently stoking the dog's hair. "A friend of mine, Charlie Utter, is gonna be here today, and the two of us are going to lead a wagon train and head out for Deadwood, in Dakota Territory."

"I've never heard of it," Sally said.

"Never heard of Deadwood?"

"Never heard of Dakota Territory."

"Well, it's new," Wild Bill said. "And they actually got gold up there. Which means the card players will play for higher stakes. I ain't much interested in gold. But I do enjoy a lively town."

What he meant by lively town was he liked being in a place where he might have to get into a gunfight. He was, despite his denials, very much interested in remaining famous and not being forgotten. If I was to tell him that his fame would carry on long after his death, it would have probably shocked him to death. His deepest mopes were all about being forgotten when he died.

"Well," I said, "what are you going to do on your last day in town?"

"Oh, I reckon I'll grab a breakfast beefsteak at Kate's, slurp up about a gallon of coffee, and then do what I mostly always do, play cards in your saloon."

Kate would never have eyes for another man after Jim Shepland passed on, but she did grow to enjoy Wild Bill's polite company, and even let him sit at my table, which had always before been reserved for my exclusive use. He'd taken to having breakfast at her restaurant every day.

"Dang," I said. "Wish I'd known this was going to be your

last day or we would have gone to breakfast with you. We've done already ate."

"It's my fault. Curly, you'd be surprised to know I actually slept last night. It was a good sleep too. Made it all the way through the night and didn't get up until the sun started peeping through the windows. First time I've had a sleep like that in I don't know how long."

Sally smiled at this. "That means you feel at home here," she said.

"Why," Wild Bill said, smiling, "I reckon it does at that, Sally. Maybe you should call your spare room the Wild Bill room."

That was a foolish notion, but Sally and I laughed anyway.

"Baxter and Merle won't know what to do with themselves when you leave. You're their hero," I said. As much as he went on about that hair of his, I knew I would miss him too.

"I believe I will work on how to break it to them at break-fast. I've grown quite fond of them, too, even if they do set to gawking at me and peppering me with an endless cavalcade of questions."

"I bet when you leave, they both take up wearing sashes," I said, slurping on my fifth cup of coffee.

"Why Curly, if I have it right, it was you who took up wearing a sash."

"I don't—dang, I was hoping you wouldn't remember that."

"Aw, it don't bother me. But you can't have a go at someone for something you yourself have done."

"Sounds like something Frank would say."

Wild Bill turned his head, in the same way Bart does when a human does something they think is stupid. Then he said: "I think you're right—damnit. Excuse my course language, Sally."

"I wouldn't care to agree with Frank either," Sally said. "I don't mind Hap at all, but Frank I don't care for to be honest."

"Frank ain't domesticated," I said.

"He's a hard man to like," Wild Bill said, "but I did grow to respect him. Being an agreeable person, or being friendly in any way, any way at all...well, it just ain't in the man. Why, do you know, he and Hap just up and left us in the dark of night without even saying goodbye?"

There was a knocking at the door. Normally Bart would have started barking his head off and running around in circles, letting the entirety of the world know someone was at the door. But he didn't do any of that. He was too happy getting stroked on, sitting in Wild Bill's lap.

"Mangy varmint," I said, though not loud enough for him to hear. I stood up and went to the door, and there was old Jeffers, here for his morning chat with Sally.

"Come in," I said. "This is Wild Bill's last day in town. He's off to look for gold."

"Cards, Curly," Wild Bill growled.

"Well then," Jeffers said, "I shall wrestle up something good for this afternoon. Not the typical stew. Something more memorable."

And then Wild Bill shocked me by asking: "ribs?" Wild Bill, as long as I'd known him, had always been more interested in drinking. So, him expressing a food opinion was novel territory.

"I like the idea of ribs," I said.

"It'll have to be pork ribs," Jeffers said, scratching on his chin whiskers.

"I believe there's nothing finer than a smoked pork rib," Wild Bill said.

"You know, Jeffers, I've been thinking" —I hadn't really, but I was just then— "and, with all these miners flush, maybe we should up the food game and charge more. A plate of ribs with a cob of corn and some sugary beans, I bet we'd have a line out the door."

"We already have a line out the door. Speaking of which, ain't I supposed to go to Amarillo on a whisky run?"

I'd forgotten all about that.

"We'll figure something out," I said.

———

When I opened up the saloon that afternoon, sure enough, a line was already forming. Sherwood, as was his custom, was the first in line. With some help from Baxter and Merle, we ended up with a meal of pork ribs (3 per person) a cob of corn, sugary beans, and a glass of (hastily made) homemade apple brandy for two dollars. It was the most we'd ever charged for any meal since Jeffers had started cooking. It was more than Kate charged for everything but her biggest beefsteaks.

But it was Wild Bill's last day, which made it an occasion—it was the last day to make an ass of oneself in order to impress a drunken mopey shootist leaving what he considered to be a boring town. Even the guy who ran the livery, Flody, was there, dressed up in his Sunday finest, a brown wool suit pocked full of moth holes that strained itself trying to contain his hunch. He hacked and wheezed his way around the saloon, repelling one and all.

Wild Bill was holding court at the back table across from the billiard table. He sat with his back to the wall. It had been five weeks since he'd first walked into the saloon disguised as a buffalo skinner. So much had happened in that time. If Wild Bill had ever managed to write his memoirs as he'd planned, he could have filled up half the book with the goings on just since he'd gotten to Silver Vein. I didn't know it at the time, but at his final breakfast at Kate's, he'd finally given in and granted the ever-persistent Pap Kickins an interview.

Apparently, Pap Kickins presented Wild Bill with a concocted-out-of-thin-air interview he swore he would run if Wild Bill refused to talk to him. This made Wild Bill think it would be best to take the narrative away from the fantastical garbage that Pap had invented and replace it with an even yet more fantastical invention of his own creation. The interview, which would travel throughout the entire world over the next half century, bore zero resemblance to reality—but it would only add to his legend. In his telling, Wild Bill had caught the Butler Gang, freed Sheriff Langtry, and foiled a bank robbery—all by himself. The name Curly Barnes didn't come up in the entire interview! In his telling, the Butler gang grew in size to be a mob of forty hardened criminals.

But I didn't know any of that when I heard Wild Bill say, "Well, look what the cat dragged in."

I looked at the front of the saloon, through the cigar and pipe smoke, and saw a guy in dyed black buckskins, a belt with a big silver belt buckle, stuffed full of fancy pistols and knives, all covered up in trail dust. He had long black hair and a black mustache that looked like it needed attention. No wonder the two were friends, I thought. They both had the same hair philosophy. I would later learn Charlie Utter to be as keen and frequent a bather as Wild Bill.

"Bill!" Charlie Utter said, waving. I asked him for his guns and knives, and he handed them over with a smile, eager to greet his friend.

"I'm Curly Barnes," I said. "Welcome to—"

But he wandered off, not hearing any of my greeting. I noticed he sported a pair of beaded moccasins on his feet instead of boots.

"Charley Utter!" Wild Bill said, standing up. "I have missed your frequent admonishments. I want you to meet the boys. That there is Baxter..."

"Hey," Baxter said, barely looking up, no doubt lost in grief, knowing Wild Bill would soon be gone.

"...and this is therefore Merle..."

"Hey," Merle said.

"And the fellow behind you, who owns this joint, and who

has hosted me in his home these few weeks, is my great new friend Curly Barnes. He's also the sheriff, so mind your step, if you know what I mean."

Charlie Utter turned around and said, "I apologize for walking away from you. I lost my head in eagerness. I have, of course, heard all about you."

"Any friend of Wild Bill's is more than welcome," I said. "Most of them anyway."

"You ain't met Martha Jane," Wild Bill said, between cigar puffs.

"A hellion, she is," Charlie said.

I didn't know what to say to that, and never would. "You want anything to drink? We got, oh, we have apple brandy," I said, remembering we were all but out of whisky.

"Hmmm. Let me think on this. Show me the bar, why don't you?" I walked back to the bar. Charlie asked for bourbon. I told him we were very low. And then he saved my bacon by saying, "I happen to have several bottles of bourbon in my wagon. I was going to sell them in Laramie, but I reckon this place will do."

We haggled back and forth and agreed on a price. And then I walked with him to his wagon, which was larger than I was expecting.

"I do a fair amount of trading, ranging far and wide."

"It's a nice wagon," I said.

And then it hit me all at once. "I might have one more favor to ask you, and it's not small."

"I can only promise to listen."

And so, I told him about Taylor Stephens and Katie Milton. I asked if he could take them as far as Laramie—and I let him know that they wouldn't be a burden and could pay their way. I might have left out the part about Sam Milton.

"If it's okay with Wild Bill, it's okay with me. I'm quite the romantic myself, and I already admire the pluck of this Taylor Stephens boy."

That settled, we walked back inside, and Jeffers and Micah went about restocking the bar.

Charlie clasped my shoulder and leaned in and asked, "How's he doing?"

"Wild Bill?"

"Your new friend and my old friend. Is he staying out of trouble? How is his drinking? Is he gambling too much? Have there been any gunfights? He can be quite scrappy if he's allowed to."

I nodded. "He is staying upstairs with my wife and dog, which I believe has tamed him some. He's only shot one person here in the saloon, shot his kneecaps off to tell the whole truth, and he did threaten a couple of people, and one day during one of his mopes, he did take Frank Yonder by the ear and push him through the flapping doors into the street. They all deserved it if you ask me."

"Good! Good! I'm happy to hear that!"

"Then again, he considers this town boring. It could be he ain't better behaved so much as there is less opportunity to misbehave."

"I've had to bail him out of many a scrap," Charley said. "I've paid off sheriffs and saloonkeepers, apologized to women —the list is quite long indeed."

"Maybe the two of you should stay here," I said. "Maybe this town is good for him."

Well, old Charlie looked at me like I'd grown a second head.

"You think this is *my* idea? The only reason I'm doing this at all is to make sure he doesn't get himself kilt! I got no more use for Dakota Territory than Wild Bill does Texas."

"This *is* Texas," I said.

"Still?"

"It's a big state."

"He hates it, you know. I don't think he could stand to know he was living in Texas, no offense."

"I'm used to it," I said. "You hungry? There's ribs."

"I could eat. If this is his last night in town, I expect I'll need something to suck up all the whisky."

11

SHELBY

Shelby spent the night not far off the trail. The trail between Amarillo and Silver Vein was wide and got frequent use, and Shelby felt safe enough to build a fire. If anyone tried to bushwhack him, he was confident he could just shoot them. He hobbled his new black stallion under a mesquite tree and filled a tin bowl with water for the horse to lip up. He'd put the horse through its paces and found the horse an eager and exhilarating runner. No posse would be able to keep up with the horse. He named the horse Bargain.

Lorena had put together some food for him to have on the trail. Three pork chops, some bacon, and a loaf of bread. He built a fire and got out an old pan he'd bought in Amarillo and set about frying up a couple of pork chops, which soon started sizzling and sending up a smell that made Shelby's stomach rumble in anticipation. He sipped his bourbon and puffed on a cigar he'd bought in honor of Hermit Bob—which Shelby had decided was his favorite of the two Bobs—and thought about what the next day would bring.

If things went the way Shelby wanted them to, Curly would tell Shelby where he could find the Indian that kilt Horvath.

That Indian could now be just about anywhere, but he knew the Indian and Curly Barnes had some sort of connection. Why else help the Indian escape in the first place? He hoped he could keep a level head, because just thinking about that Indian was getting Shelby all worked up.

After that, when the Indian either had a hole in his head or was hanging dead from a tree, Shelby, well, he wasn't exactly sure what he would do. He would need money, so he might head to California to try his luck in some of the gold fields that weren't yet played out. Or he might just say the hell with America and join up as a merchant seaman and explore the world. He could even join a foreign army and fight for a different country. He knew he wasn't going to do it, but the other option is he really could make his way back to Amarillo and settle down there. Or give in, beg for forgiveness, and head back home—and see if his mom would take him back. But that would mean going to church four times a week and being a farmer, hunched over a pile of dirt all day. And that wasn't going to happen.

Maybe he would just join a gang. That was probably what he was best suited for. Even though he had been part of the 4th cavalry, Major Hastings had basically acted and behaved like the leader of a gang. The only thing missing was robbing people and banks. So, joining a gang was definitely a possible career path.

When he could no longer stand it, Shelby took the pork chops off the fire, waited just long enough not to sizzle his tongue off, and chowed down. After he was finished, he re-lighted his cigar, and lay back and looked up at the stars. After three weeks with Hermit Bob, he'd grown to have a greater appreciation for the stars. He was awed by the fact that he could travel a hundred miles, and look up, and all the stars were in the same place. Bob said the stars didn't move, but it was the planet that moved. Shelby didn't know whether this was true or not, but it probably was, because Bob had spent many years by himself contemplating such things, whereas Shelby hadn't put much thought in the stars at all until a few weeks ago.

Before he nodded off, Shelby sang one of Bob's favorite songs, which soothed him, and gave him vengeful dreams.

———

Shelby got up early in the morning, awakened by the bitter morning chill, rebuilt the fire back up, and fried up the bacon. Then he saddled up Bargain, which he noticed had an extremely luxurious saddle, all covered up with embroidery and expensive silver Conchos. *Of course* Jakob had been lying, Shelby thought. The horse was clearly stolen. Because how could someone looking like Jakob afford such a horse? Hell, he probably couldn't even afford a single Concho! Riding a stolen horse didn't bother Shelby, since his horse had also been stolen. He wondered if Jakob would come to grief and get in trouble when some soldier happened through town and recognized Plowright's horse. That would be funny! To trade an amazing horse for a skinny run-down horse, and still get in trouble!

Shelby walked Bargain a good bit further off the trail, dismounted, hitched the horse to a cottonwood branch, and set out practicing with the cheap Colt Navy he'd bought. After a few shots, he could see he would have to aim a few inches to the left of wherever he wanted the bullets to go. The barrel of the pistol must be warped, Shelby figured. Once he sent six straight bullets where he wanted them to go, he put the pistol away.

And then he mounted up, returned to the trail, kicked Bargain into a lope—and set off for Silver Vein and revenge.

12

The thing about these newly flush miners was, they couldn't control themselves. They eagerly ate up the ribs and slurped down too much bourbon too fast—and by mid-afternoon, many of them went home, back to their tent camps, to take naps. Some decided to save time and just up and take naps right on the bar. I could hear a few of them loudly snoring.

Wild Bill was in a sour mood because Tad Bowltree repeatedly found himself with superior hands, and Bill had seemingly misjudged each and every one of them.

"I thought you said he had his gambling under control," a panicked Charly Utter said. He was clearly traumatized by past Wild Bill behavior I'd never witnessed. It was clear now that during his stay in Silver Vein he'd been on his best behavior. I felt sorry for Charly, because he'd gone and signed up to babysit Bill all over again.

"He's not good with money," I said. "He has shopped at Ely Turner's Mercantile twice. *Nobody* does that. Usually once is enough before a fella finds out they've been fleeced. He also bought a horse back in—"

"Don't get me started about that silly horse. It's useless! It can open an umbrella, sure, but can it eat grass? Alfalfa? No, it cannot. Just knowing how much he paid for that dang horse makes me want to air out my insides! Give me another bourbon! My nerves are shot!"

Jeffers came over and asked if I wanted him to go and get another hog butchered. I looked around the room, and people were drifting out the door—all except the most star struck. Flody was still sitting at the bar, stealing glances at Wild Bill while fending off Sherwood Floop's frequent insults about him letting an outlaw gang make off with his black stallion. Sherwood was good with an insult, he had all sorts of English curses at his employ, but since Flody didn't know what any of them meant—it helped that he was desperately drunk, not being a frequent imbiber of bourbon—the insults missed their mark in the entirety.

"I don't think so," I said. "I think everyone has had their fill."

Frank and Deedee Yonder and China Jack sat at the small table in the middle of the saloon. Frank was a teetotaler, which didn't help his personality any, so it was up to China Jack to keep the conversation going. Deedee had eyes only for the billiard table, but because the saloon was so full up with miners, the billiard table was seeing constant use. Baxter and Merle had been driven from the card table by Wild Bill's growing vexation and were now sitting at the bar.

"My God Man!" Sherwood yelled, drawing my attention. "Curly, he's back. For the sake of cripes!"

I walked away from Charly and headed towards Sherwood.

"What's that, Sherwood?"

"My horse! He's at the hitching post! By God, he's come back to me! You're off the hook, Hunchie! What do you think the odds—"

A shot rang out, and Sherwood fell over, dead as Moses—

and there in the doorway was a bearded cow-boy holding a smoking gun.

"Why, Curly Barnes," the man said, "you're the very person I'm looking for."

13

In the blink of an eye, Wild Bill and Baxter and Merle all had their guns out, and every miner in the room shut up and stared at the ragged, bearded man standing just inside the saloon with the pistol in his hand.

"You're looking for me?" I asked.

"You are exactly the very man I am looking for," the cowboy said. The man looked familiar, but not enough for me to recognize him. It was Wild Bill who figured it out.

"The missing soldier," Wild Bill said. "The one that got away."

The man nodded.

"Captain Shelby, U.S. Army. Well, that's who I was before Curly here ruined my life."

"You ruined your own life by raping innocent women and slaughtering children," I said. For a second there, it looked like he was going to pull the trigger. So, I said, "You pull that trigger, Wild Bill Hickok and Baxter and Merle will shoot you full of holes and you'll bleed out right where you stand."

"I want that Indian. Your friend. He kilt my friend Horvath.

I want you to tell me where he is. You do that, and this don't have to go any further than this."

"You just kilt a man in my saloon. Murdered him in cold blood." Sherwood Floop was lying dead on the floor, his belly mounding up out of him like a small boulder.

"Well, that couldn't be helped. He got in the way of the bullet. I was aiming for that mirror behind you. The way I see it, that's on him. Let's just call it what it was, which is suicide."

I figured the best thing to do, in that moment, was not what my body wanted to do, which was loose my bowels, but instead do what I was good at, which was talking.

"I don't have any way to know where Scout is," I said.

"The savage has a name?"

"Everybody has a name," Baxter said, laughing at his own wit.

"You shut up!" Shelby said. "You're going to reach out to your Comanche buddy Scout, and you're going to do it right now! I know it was you. You're the one that let the woman and her daughter go. And that's what started this whole business! If it weren't for you those two Indians would be hanging in front of Fort Belknap by now. Instead, I had to follow Major Hastings into the heart of Comanche country. And it was all your doing! You ruined my life, I tell you! And I will have my revenge!"

"But I can't give you what you want," I said, quite calmly I have to say. Captain Shelby had clearly not fared well since he'd fled the desert. His eyes were jumpy, and his voice was ragged with rage. He wasn't in his right mind.

The saloon was quiet, and everyone was looking at us wondering what would happen next. We were in a standoff. Shelby was probably thinking what his next move should be. He seemed to finally realize that there was no good way out.

So, I offered him one.

"If you put that pistol down, the two of us can figure this out."

"You think I'm gonna fall for that?"

"That gun looks like it's been hibernating in a puddle of piss," Wild Bill said. "How do you know it won't blow up in your hand? I say pull the trigger. I doubt you'll even come close to hitting Curly. You do that and then I can just shoot you full of holes and then go take a piss. It's been a long day."

Shelby never took his eyes off me.

"You're lying! Why are you protecting that savage anyway? Colonel MacKenzie will have all the Comanches on a reservation in a year. Your pet Indian will be dead or in jail no matter what you do. So why not just give him up?"

There was more truth to that than I wanted to admit.

"Scout moves about from day to day, in those very canyons he lured you into, and all across the Llano. There is no way for me to reach out to him. So why not put the pistol down and we can discuss this. I'll even stand you a belt of bourbon."

"Abe said you were a good man," Shelby said.

That threw me for a loop. "Abe Kilhoe? In Amarillo?"

"I ran into another fella you know, little thin guy with the personality of a rabid mongoose. Something Slim."

"I see," I said, not really seeing. Shelby seemed to be stalling for time or looking for a way to lower the tension.

So, I played along. "I think I know who you mean. Wisconsin Slim. That fella gets around. I ran him out of Silver Vein months ago."

"Abe said you were a fair man, but I have every reason to doubt him. A fair man wouldn't protect a savage from getting what's coming to him. And if ever there was a Comanche that had it coming for him, it would be Scout. He killed a soldier in the U.S. Army. He also stole Jackson, my horse. And I aim to see that justice comes for him."

"Sorry, friend. It ain't gonna happen."

There was a sudden change in Shelby. Having a gun pointed at you tends to focus the attention, and slow everything down, and I could see the change in his eyes—some new calculation was going on in that enraged mind of his.

"It's not like I have a whole lot of promise in this here life. The army won't have me back. Not after you forced me to kill Plowright and take his horse."

"You didn't kill him," I said. "You left him to die. He was living yet when we found him, dying of thirst, surrounded by a dried-up puddle of his own blood."

"He wasn't dead?"

"Not when we found him."

"Well, no matter. Let's get this over with. Curly Barnes, I'm calling you out."

"I don't think so," Wild Bill said. "If it's a gunfight you want, I'm happy to give it to you. You call Curly out, it's me you're gonna get."

"I don't know, Wild Bill," Baxter said. "I'm Curly's deputy. I should be allowed to kill Captain Shelby."

"No, it should be me," Merle said. "Scout saved my bacon when I got shot. I owe him one."

"Enough!" Captain Shelby yelled. Then he looked at me, and I knew we'd pushed him too far. "Curly Barnes. You know what? Fuck it."

And he started to squeeze the trigger.

14

I closed my eyes. Captain Shelby was going to kill me and then get shot full of about forty holes. But I would be dead so none of that would matter. I would be dead, and Sally would be a widow and Bart would be a widower. I would be buried over in boot hill and Frank Yonder would yell at everyone at my funeral, those that bothered showing up, and—

"Throw one!" Deedee suddenly shouted.

I heard Shelby cry out and I opened my eyes and saw Shelby drop his pistol. There was a knife sticking out of his hand.

"Dang," he said, blood dripping onto the floor. He looked down at his pistol and bent over to retrieve it. He had no chance now, but he was too far gone to know it. Before he could reach the pistol, Wild Bill shot it repeatedly, until it bounced and clattered and finally fled out of the saloon.

I bounded over the bar and whomped Captain Shelby just as he was standing back up. He did what they all do and fell to the floor of the saloon in a heap.

I turned around, and looked into the shadows, knowing what I would find.

Little Tommy Yonder.

"I'd say China Jack's tutoring has paid off!" The little hellion that had once sat on top of the courthouse chucking rocks at innocent citizens walking up and down the Main Street boardwalk had just saved my bacon.

Tommy Yonder (I would never again think of him Little.) walked over to the conked-out Shelby and yanked his knife out of the man's mangled hand. "Scout is my friend," he said.

"The final piece of the puzzle," Wild Bill said, putting his pistols back in his sash. "The one that got away has been apprehended. I can now leave town in peace knowing he isn't out there as a lurking threat."

"What do we do with him?" Baxter asked.

"I have an idea," I said.

15

SHELBY

When Shelby came to, he was in a jail cell and there was a maniac standing over him. He moved to scramble away from the blinking drooling presence in front of him (that would be Doc Watson at his drugged out worst) but found his feet and hands were in irons.

"'lax," the man said. Shelby watched as a waterfall of drool stretched itself from the man's lower lip. It stretched and stretched and stretched—and then finally broke and landed on Shelby's leg.

"Sorry 'bout that," the man said. "I'm a just gone fix you up. I'm doctor."

This man was a doctor? Shelby looked down and saw that his hand had been bandaged up. And now that he'd come fully awake, he noticed that the back of his head hurt like hell.

"My head hurts," Shelby said.

"I've got sumtin' for it," the doctor said, pawing through a leather bag full of who knew what.

"Dis here is it?"

"Are you asking me?"

"No, I mean, but it is. Okay. Yeah. I reckon it is. I was lost there for a minute, but this is it. It's perfect for you."

Shelby watched as the doctor poured a liquid onto a rag. Shelby didn't know what the liquid was, but he figured the doctor was going to place it on the back of his head, where he'd been whomped. He hoped it would soothe the throbbing pain back there.

Instead, the doctor did an unexpected thing and opened the jail cell door. "Tiny," he said, and out of the shadows came the largest man Shelby had ever laid eyes on. He was twice the size of Major Hastings and then some. He had a huge bald head, with eyes that didn't quite focus and were too close together.

"Hold him down."

"I can hold myself down," Shelby said in a panic. "Really. You don't—"

Tiny came in and pushed Shelby down, and he couldn't budge at all. He might as well have been paralyzed. Shelby watched, terrified, as the doctor placed the rag over his face. Shelby didn't want to breathe, and so he didn't, but then he had to, and so he did, and...

———

When Shelby came to, he was no longer in the jail cell. He didn't know where he was. All he knew was he was completely naked, his arms and legs were staked to the ground, and he was surrounded by Comanche warriors. In front of him, sitting on a blanket, as still as a statue, was the old man with the gray hair. His face was covered in war paint. When Shelby looked into his eyes, he got nothing back. The man looked right through him. The man's arms rattled whenever he moved them, and he started to sing and chant.

Then, behind the old man, was the other one. The one Curly had called Scout. The one he was looking for, only, not under these precise circumstances. It was the one who'd kilt Horvath.

"You!" Shelby said.

Scout nodded. "Me," he said.

"You *do* speak English! I knew it!"

"I know some words," Scout said.

As Shelby watched, Scout pulled a long knife out of a scabbard on his hip, squatted in front of him, and started to sharpen it. The knife glinted and gleamed in the sun. Scout didn't say anything, just kept sharpening the knife.

"What happened to Major Hastings?" Shelby asked.

"When you rape a Comanche woman, what happens to the man who does it is up to her. Her name is Yellow Hair. She is the wife of Two Yellow Hairs. At her hands, your major suffered for a long time. He was strong. He didn't die until the tubes from his belly were pulled out and given to the dogs."

"Oh my God!"

"Look. These men? They were with me on a hunt. They were with me when you and your men killed their mothers and fathers, their wives and children. They are all entitled to something."

"You've got it all wrong!" Shelby exclaimed. "It was Major Hastings! All of it! We were just following his orders!"

"These men. They also follow orders."

Shelby was desperate for a way out of his predicament. "Curly said he had no way to communicate with you!"

"He lied," Scout said. Then he stood up, walked over to Shelby, and leaned over him.

Soon enough, Shelby screamed.

SOME LAST AND FINAL WORDS

Wild Bill and Charly Utter set out three days after they planned to, and headed for Wyoming, where they would meet up with Martha Jane Cannary, known in myth and lore as Calamity Jane. It was also where Taylor Stephens and Katie Milton disappeared into their new lives. Whatever happened to them is unknown. Wild Bill and Charly Utter and Calamity Jane eventually made their way to Deadwood, in what is now South Dakota. There, in Deadwood, Wild Bill would finally meet the end Charly Tuttle had tried so hard to prevent. He was shot in the back of the head by the coward Jack McCall. The date was less than two years after he and Charly left town—August 2, 1876.

I would never see my friend again. But at least he died doing something he loved—drinking, making up exploits about himself, and playing cards. He would be shocked to hear it, but his legend looms larger every day, and it's been close to fifty years since he took his last breath.

Scout and his band would soon enough flee to Mexico, but he didn't, and wouldn't, hang. One day, a couple of years after the episodes described here, Colonel MacKenzie, with a small company of troops, stopped in Silver Vein. The old Colonel walked into the saloon, ordered himself and his men a bottle of bourbon, spent hours at a couple of tables soaking in what civilization the saloon offered—and made not a single mention of what had transpired in the desert. He'd once threatened to kill me on sight, but then he must've forgotten all about it. I didn't bring it up.

Sheriff Langtry would go on being a terrible sheriff in Hendrix right up until the day he fell over dead one day while patrolling the empty dirty street. He would be the only Sheriff Langtry that didn't meet a tragic end.

Sherwood Floop's funeral was a subdued and somber affair, as most funerals are. But, in this case, it was subdued because only a handful of people attended. The reason for that is that Shelby's bullet took Sherwood's life before he could actually make good on buying up any of the miner's silver claims. Other than standing the miners to drinks, and offering good terms on their silver claims, fronting them some cash, no actual money would ever make its way into the bank accounts of the miners. Once Sherwood died, his father froze the funds and refused to transfer them from Sherwood's bank in New York City.

Overnight, the miners learned not only that they were broke all over again, but that even if they *did* find silver, it was no longer worth much of anything. But even worse, each and every one of them owed money at both Ely Turner's Mercantile, and the Ely Turner Bank. Ely Turner, in true Ely Turner fashion, had charged the miners enormous interest rates to loan them the money to buy the overpriced clothes they bought at the Mercantile.

In short, everything went back to normal.

— Curly Barnes,
Spring, 1928
Amarillo, Texas

ACKNOWLEDGMENTS

I'd like to thank all my early readers and those of you who have encouraged me to continue with the adventures of Curly Barnes. It wasn't easy. There were about three months where Curly and the gang were stuck in the middle of the desert waiting for me to tell them where to go—and they were running out of bourbon, and I could sense them starting to turn on me.

This book, like the two before it, couldn't have been written without a lot of help.

I'd like to thank Bart the dog, who will live in these books forever, but has unfortunately moved on to dog heaven, which Is no doubt full of beef jerky, squirrels to chase, and old socks.

I'd like to thank Larry Habeggar for once again finding typos and other things that needed fixing.

I'd like to thank David Bryzozowski of Bluespark Studios for what might be the best book jacket design yet.

I'd like to thank my brother, Will Shivers, for voicing and editing the book trailers for all three Silver Vein books.

I'd like to thank Janet and Erik and Sandy, for the peace and quiet.

And I'd like to thank my publicist, David Ivester, for the help and support.

ABOUT THE AUTHOR

Clay Houston Shivers grew up spending every summer at his grandparents' ranch near Georgetown, Texas, where he first became fascinated by the American frontier and discovered his love for Westerns. For the last twenty years he has worked as a freelance advertising copywriter, travel writer and photographer. *The Desperadoes of Gallows Gulch* is his third novel.

———

To learn more about Clay Houston Shivers and discover more Next Chapter authors, visit our website at www.nextchapter.pub.

The Desperadoes of Gallows Gulch
ISBN: 978-4-82418-900-4

Published by
Next Chapter
2-5-6 SANNO
SANNO BRIDGE
143-0023 Ota-Ku, Tokyo
+818035793528

7th January 2024

Milton Keynes UK
Ingram Content Group UK Ltd.
UKHW041004040324
438885UK00006B/467